THIEF

MARK SULLIVAN

Quercus

First published in Great Britain in 2015 by

Quercus Editions Ltd
55 Baker Street
7th Floor, South Block
London
W1U 8EW

A CIP catalogue record for this book is available
from the British Library

ISBN 978 1 84866 591 0
EBOOK ISBN 978 1 84866 593 4

10 9 8 7 6 5 4 3 2 1

Printed and bound in Great Britain by Clays Ltd, St Ives plc

Praise for the Robin Monarch series

'If you see Mark Sullivan, sock him in the eye for me since he owes me a night's sleep. *Rogue* is an explosive, brilliantly researched, masterfully paced, deftly plotted debut to a series I'm hopping onto for the long haul. Jason Bourne meets Robin Hood with a dash of Bond thrown in, this thriller will leave you shaken, stirred, and yes – exhausted. I had a blast' Gregg Hurwitz

'Fast moving and well written! *Rogue* reminded me of the Bourne books and movies, only it's much, much better' James Patterson

'A true juggernaut of a thriller, pure adrenaline in print. With the creation of Robin Monarch, Sullivan has crafted a Jason Bourne for the new millennium' James Rollins

'Filled with twists, turns, crosses, and double-crosses, Sullivan delivers a harrowing international thriller, while introducing one of the most compelling heroes since Jason Bourne' Lisa Gardner

'A compelling, page-turning blend of spy and caper fiction: it's Robin Hood for the twenty-first century. Loaded with intrigue, laced with detail, and full of bone-shaking action, *Rogue* is the fantastic start to an exciting new series' Jeff Abbott

'This lightning-fast read brings to mind Robert Ludlum and *Mission: Impossible* – and will definitely appeal to adrenaline junkies' Booklist

'A loud, brawny festival of action' *Publishers Weekly*

'Robin Monarch is a great character that readers will embrace. His attitude and gruffness make him neither all good nor all evil, just human' *Associated Press*

C333669595

Also by Mark Sullivan

Triple Cross
The Serpent's Kiss
Labyrinth
The Ghost Dance
The Purification Ceremony
Hard News
The Fall Line

The Robin Monarch Novels

Rogue
Outlaw

With James Patterson

Private L.A.
Private Games
Private Berlin

Forever, Betsy

In January 2007, Brazil's National Indian Foundation used satellite imaging to confirm the presence of sixty-seven primitive, uncontacted societies in the upper Amazon rain forest, thereby surpassing the island of Papua New Guinea as the region with the largest number of so-called lost tribes left on Earth.

1

THE THUNDERSTORMS BEGAN LATE that afternoon and continued on into the night, lashing the Argentine capital with six inches of rain that backed up the drains in the rich neighborhoods, and turned the streets to oozing mud in the slums.

Around nine thirty that evening, the fourth wave swept over Villa Miserie, the worst slum in the city, and drummed down on the steel roof of a small medical clinic. Inside, a missionary and physician named Sister Rachel Diego del Mar worked feverishly to save the life of a woman bleeding out after childbirth.

"Maria," she called to the woman, who was moaning. "You need to stay with me now. Your beautiful baby boy needs you."

The second Maria Vasquez walked into the clinic, the sixty-two-year-old physician had noticed the swelling around the pregnant woman's eyes, cheeks, wrists, and ankles, and suspected she'd developed a life-threatening clotting disorder. The doctor's suspicions were well founded. Tests revealed mom and baby were in mortal danger.

Sister Rachel had done a spinal block and performed a Cesarean section almost immediately, saving the baby. But ever since the baby's birth, Maria had been hemorrhaging. It took all of Sister Rachel's skills to stem the tide, but at a quarter to eleven she believed she'd done it. The young mother had lost a lot of blood, but her vital signs had stabilized. God willing she'd live to care for her baby boy.

The missionary hung her head, and thanked her lord and savior for guiding her. She'd been up for nearly nineteen hours, and felt woozy. Inez, the night nurse, sat in a rocker by Maria's bed, the baby in her arms. Sister Rachel told the nurse that she was going to clean up and get some sleep, but to wake her if Maria's condition changed for the worse.

"Yes, Sister," Inez said. "You sleep all night. I'll be right here."

The idea of an entire night's sleep was almost too much to hope for, the missionary thought. When she worked at the slum clinic, she rarely had more than four hours straight rest before some poor soul would turn up on her doorstep, sick or broken, and desperately needing her skills.

Sister Rachel was in no way bitter or self-pitying about her lot in life. Even after nearly thirty-two years as a member of the Sisters of Hope, the doctor believed she was doing God's work, and she prayed she would do that work until the day she died.

After showering and changing into a fresh set of scrubs, she let down her long silver hair and tied it in a loose ponytail. Then she headed to her office at the rear of the clinic, wondering how life was at the orphanage she ran outside the city.

The burden of the clinic and the orphanage sometimes felt too much. She looked forward to setting the weight aside for a few hours at least. Shutting the office door behind her, she turned on the light switch and pivoted to see her cot was made up already, which made her smile.

What would she do without Inez?

Then Sister Rachel heard a floorboard creak, and twisted left. A big man with a goatee was already upon her. He wore a black stocking wool cap pulled down over his ears. There was a small camera mounted on a harness strapped to the cap. Before she could scream, he clamped a hand across her mouth and jabbed her in the neck with a syringe.

In seconds the room swam toward darkness.

But before she passed out, she heard him say, "Let's see if you can save Robin Monarch this time around."

2

GREENWICH, CONNECTICUT
THIRTEEN WEEKS EARLIER . . .

IT WAS TIME TO steal the son of a bitch blind.

That pleasing thought coursed through the thief's mind as he huddled in a silver Range Rover parked at the Babcock Preserve, a three-hundred-acre park in Greenwich, Connecticut. It was December the eighteenth, the Friday before Christmas, and snowflakes were beginning to fall. The all-news station was calling for fifteen inches of snow by morning.

This suited the thief's purposes. Falling snow hid tracks. Falling snow erased your passing.

The last of the dog walkers and hikers reached their cars and left just after dark. The thief sat there, letting the snow build on the windshield without triggering the wipers until the Range Rover felt more like a cocoon than a car.

Finally, at 6:25 P.M. he reached over the backseat and retrieved a clothes bag that protected a two-thousand-dollar tuxedo he'd purchased three days before. He got out of the car, left it running, and locked it. He went over to the park's lavatories, new tux in hand.

Stripping out of clothes, the thief barely glanced at the tattoo

4

on his inner right forearm: the letters *FDL* laid out in scrollwork with a pickpocket's hand rising off the center of the *D*. He used white athletic tape to fix slender CO_2 cartridges to both inner forearms. To these he attached tiny high-pressure hoses that coupled into the rear of stubby stainless-steel tubes the diameter of a pencil. The open end of the tubes sat roughly where someone might take your pulse. Over these devices the thief put on a starched tuxedo shirt, and then trousers cut with an elegant drape. Looking in the mirror, tying a maroon bow tie that complemented a festive paisley vest, he appraised the mysterious Robin Monarch as if he were a different person all together.

Late thirties, well over six feet, and two hundred and ten pounds, Monarch was lanky and yet powerfully built. His face, however, was harder to pin down. With slightly dusky skin and gentle features, it was handsome, but also vague and malleable if the need arose. With the right makeup or prop, he could fit in almost anywhere.

To that end, Monarch slid rolls of cotton high inside his cheeks, and then put in contact lenses that turned his eyes sea green. They complemented the henna highlights he'd washed into his normally dark curly hair. To complete his disguise, he put on black-framed glasses with clear lenses, a small hearing aide, and an antique Patek Philippe watch that fit carefully over the stubby tube taped to his left wrist. High on his lapel he pinned a boutonniere that featured a sprig of holly and red seeds. Completing the transformation was a beautiful mouse-gray Chesterfield overcoat and bone-colored cashmere scarf.

Not bad, Monarch thought. Not bad at all. Now I look like any other pompous ass in the party pages of *Vanity Fair* or *New York Magazine*.

The thief exited the restroom to discover a Greenwich police patrol car idling next to the Range Rover. An officer was out and shining her light inside the vehicle.

Without missing a beat, Monarch walked over to the car, calling, "I'm right here, officer!"

Brunette, late twenties with a suspicious twist to her lips, the officer shone the light his way, said, "Always leave your car running and unattended, sir?"

"I'm sorry, can you repeat that?" Monarch said, turning his head so she could see the hearing aid. "I'm a bit hard of hearing."

She said it again, louder this time.

"Only when it's snowing and colder than a witch's tit," Monarch replied agreeably. "I was just getting changed for the Arsenault's Christmas bash."

"Driver's license?" she asked.

While she inspected an impeccably forged New Jersey driver's license that identified the thief as Asa Johanson, thirty-three, he wove his cover story in an easy manner. Johanson was an interior designer and friend of Louisa Arsenault. In fact, he'd just driven down from Vermont, where he'd been working on a complete redo of the Arsenault family ski house at Stowe. He'd needed a place to change, and the toilets seemed to do the trick.

After several long moments, the officer handed Monarch back the license and told him not to drink too much; the weather was going to get a lot worse.

Assuring her that he rarely drank, and that he had a bed waiting in Greenwich, the thief cheerily thanked her for her concern, and climbed back into the Range Rover. Glancing at the dashboard, he saw that he was far ahead of schedule. His plan had been to arrive at the gates of stately Arsenault manor at a stylish seven fifteen, during the height of the crush of the several hundred people lucky enough to have been invited to the mogul's legendary Christmas party.

But now, with the officer watching, he put the Range Rover in gear, waved, and drove off. The officer fell in behind Monarch and trailed him all the way to the Arsenault estate. It was barely seven when he rolled up behind a crème-colored Bentley and a jet-black Rolls.

The patrol car continued on. While he waited for the Rolls and the Bentley to clear security, Monarch fitted a tiny macro over the lens of his iPhone and slipped it into his pants pocket. Then he reached into the glove compartment, got an unopened pack of Rothman cigarettes, and tucked it inside the breast pocket of the tux.

The Bentley drove on through. A burly guard carrying a clipboard came to the window.

"Your name, sir?"

"Johanson," Monarch said, showing him a forged Christmas party invitation featuring an embossed golden tree. "Asa Johanson."

The guard glanced down his list, nodded, said, "Just you, Mr. Johanson?"

"My blind date stood me up. Can you believe the nerve of some guys?"

The guard coughed, said, "Pull up front. A valet will take your car."

"Where will it be parked?" Monarch asked.

He gestured back across the street. "By the stables. A valet will bring it when you're ready to leave."

"Perfect," Monarch said, and drove on through the gates.

3

THIS WAS THE KIND of job Robin Monarch loved. The stakes were admittedly high, but if he succeeded, the mark, in this case the tycoon, would be in no position to complain to anyone official.

The thief felt confident as he pulled the Rover up to the valet. He'd done his research. He knew his target, its location, and his method of entry. But he reminded himself that in this sort of setting, with several hundred people mingling inside a grand home, things would be fluid. He was going to have to adapt.

Climbing from the Rover, Monarch removed the Chesterfield coat and put it on a hanger in the back. He didn't want to stop at any coat check leaving the party. Tossing the valet the keys with his gloved hands, he strode easily up the heated walkway, heading toward massive carved oak doors that depicted a bull goring a fleeing bear.

The air was spiced and he spotted a pot of it brewing on a burner set discretely in some bushes to the left of the doors. From beyond the doors came Christmas music, a beautiful woman's voice was singing a soft jazzy rendition of "I Saw Three Ships (Come Sailing In)."

Before Monarch could knock, the door opened and caught him in a blaze of yuletide light and good cheer. The doorman stood aside, and the thief stepped inside a foyer that looked like a movie set, including an elevator with a burled walnut door, and a grand spiral staircase with a rail wrapped in fresh cedar ropes, flowing red bows, and pinpoint white lights that glinted like ice crystals falling on a bitter cold morning.

There were fifteen or so people in the foyer, all in evening wear and fine jewels, most of them moving toward a hallway and the ballroom, as Monarch remembered from the blueprints.

"Can I get your name tag?" asked a woman in a light Irish accent.

Two young, pretty women, the Irish redhead and the other an Asian with frosted hair tips, were throwing him winning smiles from where they sat behind a table covered in badges adorned with sprigs of mistletoe.

Monarch tapped the hearing aide, gave her a quick glance at the forged invitation, and said, "Asa Johanson."

That surprised her and she extended her hand, studying him. "I'm Grace Lawlor, Mrs. Arsenault's P.A. You're the late add then?"

"Is that a bad thing?" Monarch said, affecting chagrin. "The late add?"

"Not at all," Grace Lawlor said, playing with a string of pearls at her neck and smiling. "You are most welcome, Mr. Johanson. By the way, how do you know Mr. Arsenault? I didn't have time to ask."

"Oh," he said, taking the badge from her. "Beau and I go way back. We used to ski together at Stowe. We ran into each other at a gallery I run in SoHo and he insisted on having me out."

"Brilliant," she said. "He'll be thrilled to see you."

"Not as thrilled as I'll be to see him," Monarch replied, winked, and then moved aside as a new batch of the uber-rich arrived wearing enough mink, sable, and chinchilla to cause an emotional meltdown at PETA.

The ballroom ceiling was at least twenty-five feet high and made of embossed copper that picked up the soft light of several hundred electric candles and gas lamps that made the vast space glow as warmly as if the Ghost of Christmas Present was right there. Indeed, there was a strong Dickensian theme to the party. The ballroom had been decorated to resemble a snowy London Street, complete with trompe l'oeil paintings of storefronts including Old Fezziwig's and Scrooge & Marley's counting house. And the servers moving food and drink among the guests were dressed for the nineteenth century with top hats and hook skirts.

The irony of a guy like Arsenault using *A Christmas Carol,* the story of a skinflint redeemed, was not lost on Monarch. Worth northward of fourteen billion dollars, Arsenault was utterly ruthless, a polished, and yet callous man who had never sported a callus in his entire life. Though his wealthy parents had regularly engaged in philanthropy, the mogul rarely gave money to charity, braying often and publicly that fortitude and an enterprising spirit was all that anyone required to better their lot in life. No one, in Arsenault's opinion, required a handout or a hand up. The theme of the party suggested that the tycoon was spitting at the idea that someone like him could find his way to charity.

So much the better, Monarch thought when he spotted Arsenault across the room. Wearing a green and red cummerbund and a long-tail tux, the fifty-three-year-old was a six-foot-six, boyish-faced man with an egoist's posture and bearing. The mogul was sipping bourbon neat from a cut-glass tumbler and standing with a group of his cronies watching a stunning African American woman in an equally stunning evening dress sing a bluesy "Merry Christmas Baby" next to a black Steinway grand.

Monarch knew her.

Cassie Knox was the hottest female singer on the charts at the moment, a soul and blues singer with six Grammy nominations, and two top-ten singles in the past year. It had to have cost Arsenault a small fortune to get her to appear. Then again, everything about the party suggested that he'd spent several small fortunes on the evening.

Looking as if her face had recently been stretched, nipped, and tucked, Louisa Arsenault, the tycoon's wife, took the end of the song to rush up and embrace Knox. Then Louisa took the microphone and purred at the audience in a sweet Southern drawl, "Isn't she fantastic? Isn't she the best money can buy?"

Despite the singer's awkward reaction to that there were cheers all around.

"Beau?" Louisa said. "Would you like to come up and greet our guests?"

A hush fell over the room as her husband set down his bourbon glass on the lip of a marble planter and made his way up onto the raised platform, grabbing a flute of champagne from a passing waiter along the way. The mogul bowed to Cassie Knox, who looked embarrassed, and then kissed his wife and turned to the crowd, raising his glass and shouting, "A Merry Christmas and a profitable New Year to one and all!"

Monarch, who was already making a beeline for that empty bourbon glass, knew the tycoon was going to say that, word for word. As a matter of fact, he knew a whole lot about Beau Arsenault and his legendary Christmas party.

The mogul had come up on the thief's radar eleven months before, in the aftermath of the kidnapping of U.S. Secretary of State Agnes Lawton by the Sons of Prophecy terrorists. It turned out that the *Niamey,* the oil tanker the terrorists seized, had belonged to one of Arsenault's many far-flung companies.

Arsenault had also been a college classmate and client of Secretary Lawton's late husband, Bill, who was implicated in the kidnapping, and who took his own life before he could be arrested. According to reports Monarch had seen, the FBI looked at Arsenault but they'd found no connection to the Sons of Prophecy.

11

And to his credit, the mogul had supported Secretary Lawton in the wake of it all, even speaking at her husband's funeral when the rest of Washington had treated Bill Lawton as a pariah. Other than owning the tanker and knowing Bill Lawton, Arsenault looked like a stand-up guy.

Still, there had been something about the billionaire that bothered the thief. He'd gotten an old friend and colleague, Gloria Barnett, to look into the fat cat's background.

Barnett was brilliant at what she did—a hybridization of high-speed research, technical support, and crisis ops—and she was soon funneling Monarch everything that she could find on the mogul and his wife.

Arsenault was one of those guys born on third base. His father had been a successful oil wildcatter from Louisiana, and his mother came from an old-money Connecticut family. Their combined wealth had topped thirty million dollars, which meant their son had spent his childhood moving between a plantation outside New Orleans, the estate in Greenwich, and beachfront cottages on Galveston Island and Nantucket. Beau had been educated at Phillips Exeter, Yale, and Tulane Law School.

When Arsenault was twenty-four, his parents died in a plane his father, an expert aviator, was flying. The FAA believed he'd had a heart attack despite the fact he'd had an electrocardiogram the week before and passed with ease.

Arsenault had left Tulane Law to take control of the family fortune, and in twenty-nine years had expanded it exponentially to include companies and investments in everything from oil exploration and shipping to steel, pharmaceuticals, and government contracting. Along the way, he'd become a behind-the-scenes player in politics, spending lavishly in support of candidates who supported his causes in Washington.

In his daily life, the tycoon seemed to go out of his way to avoid the spotlight. His wife, however, was a different story. A former debutant from Shreveport, Louisa was a publicity hound. Barnett found articles in *Architectural Digest* that described Louisa's rebuilding of the plantation house, which was destroyed during Hurricane Katrina, and her renovation of the massive Georgian mansion in Greenwich. There was also a recent article in *Vanity Fair* that used the Arsenault's annual Christmas party to illustrate Louisa's ever-expanding social presence among the top one percent of the top one percent.

This was all stuff anyone with a bit of curiosity could have gleaned from the public record and the Internet, and hardly reason for someone like Monarch to target the Arsenaults. But Barnett had dug deeper than the public record and the Internet. She'd hired a guy Monarch knew only as Zullo, a computer security genius, to hack the mogul.

Zullo got into several of Arsenault's computers, put a tap on his mobile phone, and made similar inroads into Louisa's electronics. Zullo soon discovered that the mogul had made a ridiculous amount of money—roughly seven billion dollars—in and around the time the secretary of state was kidnapped.

Arsenault had divested and shorted the markets in the months before the incident, and then bought back into the markets shortly after Agnes Lawton's rescue. At the time, there had been speculation at high levels of the intelligence community that the kidnapping might have been less about religious extremism and more about political influence and profit.

But there was nothing Zullo found that said Arsenault's bold moves in the stock market had been anything more than the shrewd acts of a savvy investor. To the contrary, there was documentation—letters, e-mails, and the like—to prove that the mogul had been fearful of a stock market crash going back two years or more, and that he had been gradually reducing his exposure before going short. Arsenault's reasons for buying back into the market after the steep slide caused by the attacks had also been amply documented.

The Securities and Exchange Commission looked into Arsenault's big gains, but came up with nothing to connect the mogul to illegal activities. At least in that case.

Zullo and Barnett *did,* however, find ample evidence that Arsenault regularly engaged in questionable and illegal activities such as kickbacks, money laundering, and tax evasion. Despite his stupefying wealth, the mogul liked to hoard physical cash in various currencies, as well as gold coins, jewelry, and bearer bonds as a way of keeping significant sums of undeclared income close at hand.

That had gotten the thief thinking that the mogul's illicit stash might help Sister Rachel Diego del Mar, a physician and missionary who rescued orphans from the slums of Buenos Aires. Sister Rachel saved Monarch from that wretched life when he was a teenage gangbanger; he'd spent these last few years stealing money from crooks, rescuing people for cash, and giving it all to the missionary's cause.

So where did a mogul like Arsenault hide his loot?

Using construction plans as well as detailed digital blueprints, the thief was able to study the renovated mansion's layout, including an unlabeled space inside heavily reinforced concrete walls in the basement next to the wine cellar. Monarch believed that space held a vault, a likely storage place for Arsenault's stash. This is what had brought him to the Christmas party with a forged invitation, a place on the guest list courtesy of Zullo, and a need to grab that empty bourbon glass the mogul had been using.

"Merry Christmas, Beau and Louisa!" the party crowd roared around the thief, raising their champagne. "And a profitable New Year!"

Monarch snagged the cut-glass tumbler just as a waiter was

about to bus it. Cassie Knox and her band broke into "Have Yourself a Merry Little Christmas."

Arsenault took Louisa in his arms and they began to dance. Monarch glanced at his watch. It was seven thirty on the dot, exactly when the *Vanity Fair* article had said they would dance. You had to hand it to them: they had the Christmas party thing down to a science.

Monarch stood a moment watching the mogul and his wife work the floor as if they were trying out for *Dancing with the Stars*. He hated to admit it, but they were pretty good.

Then with all eyes on the host and hostess, the thief got down to work.

4

REACHING UP BEHIND HIS left ear, Monarch turned on the hearing aide. Fitting his fingernail beneath the stem of the Patek Phillip, he tugged it out about a sixteenth of an inch until he felt a click. Then he got hold of the pin that held the sprig of holly to his tux lapel and twisted it counterclockwise.

"Test," Monarch murmured, glancing over at the Arsenaults waltzing.

"Loud and clear," said Gloria Barnett. A tall, bookish, stoop-shouldered woman with wire-rimmed glasses and a shock of flame-red hair, she was staying about ten miles away at the Delamar Greenwich Harbor, a discreet five-star hotel.

The week before, Barnett had managed to pilfer a glass Arsenault had been using at a swank restaurant near his offices. But they'd found four different sets of fingerprints on the glass, which meant they had to be checked against the prints on the bourbon glass Monarch had just grabbed.

Monarch said, "Ready?

"Ready and waiting."

The room burst into applause as the mogul and his wife finished their dance and Monarch eased over by one of the Christmas trees set against the ballroom walls, pulled out the bourbon glass, checked it for prints other than his own, and found four sharp ones. Getting out the iPhone, he glanced around. Attention was still focused on the band, which had broken into "Jingle Bell

Rock." Monarch used the macro lens to snap several close-up photos of the prints before setting the glass aside.

Monarch sent the pictures, and said, "You should have them."

"Just in," she said. "Give me a few seconds."

"That's all we've got," he replied.

As more guests took to the dance floor and others lined up to dig into the sumptuous buffet, Monarch waited, wondering if the macro lens had picked up the fingerprints, wondered if his night was done, finished, right there, and right—

"We have a match," Barnett said. "It's number two. Repeat. Numeral two. Index, right hand."

"Got it. Make your call."

"Here we go then," she replied. "Watch him."

Monarch slid out from beside that Christmas tree, and located the Arsenaults still on the dance floor. The song came to a crescendo and then to an end. Arsenault had his hands overhead, cheering and clapping wildly along with his delighted guests before Monarch saw the posture of his head change by several sharp degrees. The mogul began to reach into his tux pocket, but his wife's bejeweled hand shot out and stopped him.

Monarch could almost hear Louisa scolding her husband for trying to take a business call during the party. The tycoon nodded, acted chastened, and then kissed his wife before heading off, looking as if he were going to mingle with his non-dancing guests.

But Monarch knew better. Once he was out of his wife's sight, Arsenault would check the caller ID on the phone, his private phone, a number known to only a select few, and then used only rarely and for the most delicate of situations. The mogul exited the ballroom into a broad hallway that ran back toward the foyer. He got out the cell phone while still strolling along. Monarch watched from afar, saw Arsenault listen to the phone, and then jerk to a stop.

Knew that would get your attention, Monarch thought, suppressing a grin as he pivoted and looked back toward the stage where Knox was crooning "Santa Baby" and looking very sexy. Arsenault rushed past the thief, heading on a diagonal across the ballroom.

Who you going to for help, Big Beau? Monarch thought, scanning the crowd in front of the mogul, and then spotting his likely target.

With a rectangular build, military posture, and a short, tight haircut, the man had a bull's neck that looked garroted by his tux collar and tie. His name was Billy Saunders. A former Boston cop, FBI agent, and counterterror specialist, Saunders was among the best security experts that money could buy.

Arsenault gestured Saunders aside and murmured something in his ear. Saunders went on high alert and asked several sharp questions that the mogul answered with equal sharpness. Saunders hesitated, but then nodded and moved off quickly.

Monarch could tell Arsenault wanted to either chase Saunders or flee the ballroom entirely. But before the mogul could do either, a gaggle of fifty-something women with stretched skin surrounded him and began congratulating him on his wife's latest high-society victory.

Saunders was soon back, however, with a woman in tow. Late forties, ash blond, handsome rather than beautiful, and wearing a navy blue business suit, Meg Pratt oozed Harvard Business School competence. Pratt was Arsenault's personal attorney, a woman who had to know the closets where the mogul kept his skeletons. She and Saunders nodded at Arsenault as they hurried past him, heading for the only other way out of the ballroom.

"Fish on the hook," Monarch murmured into the small microphone in the boutonniere pin. "Saunders and Pratt, too."

"I can be very convincing," Barnett said.

"Well done," Monarch replied, taking a glass of champagne off the tray from a waitress who was happening by.

Arsenault, meanwhile, watched his retreating attorney and security chief, and then pleasantly excused himself from the gaggle of stretched-skin women.

Monarch glanced at his watch. It was 7:55 P.M.

Trailing the tycoon and his aides out into a hallway lined with maple wainscoting and forest green and gold wallpaper, he saw the trio pause near the far end of the passage before disappearing through a doorway on the left.

"Looks like our instincts were spot on," Monarch murmured, heading for the nearest toilet, two doors down on the right. "They're going downstairs."

"Still the three?" Barnett asked as he entered the powder room, shut the door, and locked it.

"Unless there are guards down there," he said, turning and taking in the room at a glance, registering the fact that every inch of floor, wall, and ceiling was covered in beautiful Italian black-and-white glass tiles save a bank of mirrors, a tile vanity, and a black toilet.

Fishing in his left pocket, Monarch came up with and put on ultra-sheer latex gloves. Then he got that pack of Rothman cigarettes from his breast pocket, tore off the cellophane wrapper, and stuffed it in his pants pocket.

Carefully, he opened the box, revealing six cigarettes spaced neatly inside, two on each end, and two in the middle. Gaps between the cigarettes held four tiny darts, with slender shafts as sharp as acupuncture needles. Three were fitted with miniscule blue fins. The fins of the fourth were tan. A tube cut and painted to mimic a cigarette was nestled beside them.

Monarch slid one blue dart into that stubby tube taped to his right wrist. The lone tan dart went into the tube on his left wrist. A second blue dart dropped snuggly into the fake cigarette.

Setting it down, he pushed aside a small loaded syringe in the cigarette pack to remove a small container of breath strips.

Opening it, he spilled the contents on the counter. Four rectangular plastic strips came out, each carrying a numeral on its paper backing. Finding number two, which matched Arsenault's right index finger, he peeled back that paper layer, revealing a mild adhesive. As careful as a jeweler, Monarch laid the print replica across the latex-covered pad of his index finger. He swept the others up and pocketed them.

Someone knocked at the door.

"Be right out," he called in a slight slur.

Looking in the mirror, Monarch sagged the muscles of his face, and slid the glasses slightly down his nose while opening his eyes wide as if he were having trouble understanding his predicament. Then he put the Rothman pack in his breast pocket, turned his bow tie slightly askew, and snatched up the fake cigarette and the flute of champagne.

A bosomy blond woman spilling out of a tight, shimmering dress looked at Monarch with a New Yorker's sense of disgusted superiority, and said, "Thought you'd died in there."

"Sorry," the thief slurred, and staggered slightly, moving past her.

"Hope you're not driving," she called after him.

Without turning back to her, he waved his right hand, still palming the fake cigarette and proceeded not toward the ballroom, but to that door Arsenault and his handlers had gone through. He weaved down the hallway, acting like a man toying with the limits of alcohol consumption.

Abreast of the door, Monarch spotted the optical reading device set at handle height, slowed to a wobbly stop, and pivoted as if he'd realized he was heading in the wrong direction. The hallway behind him was empty except for two women waiting to use the powder room, and chatting about which sixty-grand-a-year kindergarten was necessary if their grandkids were to have any hope in life.

Taking a shaky step, Monarch reached out as if to catch his balance, and stabbed his index finger into the reader. Even though Barnett had made an exact copy of Arsenault's print, he had a moment's worry before hearing a click.

The door sagged.

"In," Monarch said, pushing it open.

"Godspeed, John Glenn," she whispered.

5

"FUNNY," MONARCH MUTTERED AS he stepped onto a landing atop a carpeted staircase, and eased shut the door behind him.

Muffled voices came to the thief, two males, one woman, obviously under pressure. He crept down the staircase to the edge of a game room filled with a dozen or more arcade games. Though the machines glowed, there was no one in the room. The door directly opposite the stairs was open into a dim hallway bisected by a shaft of light about halfway down.

Monarch went into the narrow passage, hearing the voices clearly now as he padded toward them, ready to shift personae in an instant.

"You should return to the party, Beau," the attorney, Pratt, was saying. "We'll take care of this."

"Two people cannot move all of this," Arsenault protested. "Certainly not in one night. My God, Meg, why would they come on a Saturday?"

"To make a statement," Saunders, the security chief, said. "Feds love doing that, especially Treasury agents and FBI."

"Has Estes called you back?" the mogul asked.

"Not yet," said Pratt. "But the woman you spoke with, she definitely used the word 'Exodus'?"

"Three times," Arsenault said. "Three."

"Then we don't take chances and we move," Saunders said. "Now."

By then the thief was almost to the light shining across the hallway. Taking a deep, calming breath he acted completely shit-faced as he stumbled around the corner into view, drunken bemusement spilling out every pore.

"*El bano, senors y senora*?" Monarch said in a slurred Spanish tone, waving the champagne flute at the trio.

They stood on the brick floor of the wine cellar, Arsenault, his attorney, and security chief, all looking at the thief in shock. A massive oaken wine rack behind them had been pulled out from the wall, revealing the face of a large closed safe with a green glowing digital mechanism.

"Sir," Saunders said, moving toward Monarch as he staggered into the wine cellar. "You're not supposed to be . . ."

The thief reached for the security chief as if he might collapse. As he did, he snapped his right hand back, super-arching his wrist. Monarch felt his forearm flex before hearing the dull thud of the air gun going off. The blue dart hit Saunders just above his cummerbund.

The security chief reacted as if he'd been stung by a wasp and slapped at it, shifting his attention just long enough for Monarch to veer off and shoot Arsenault at closer range, the tan-finned dart embedding dead center of his stomach.

"Damn it!" the tycoon shouted, slapping at his belly. "What was that? Are there bugs in here, Billy? And who are you . . ."

Saunders didn't answer, and neither did the thief as he went blowzily toward the confused attorney, the fake cigarette in his lips, and his hands patting his pockets as if for a lighter before expelling air hard and right at her from less than ten inches away. The second blue dart caught her in the right cheek. Pratt jumped back and howled.

"Stop right there," Saunders said behind Monarch in an unsure tone.

Still acting hammered Monarch looked over as if he were

23

seeing Saunders in triplicate. The security chief was carrying a Glock pistol and aiming it at the thief. Monarch could see the green laser beaming out of the aftermarket sight, and coursing all over his chest. He could also see Saunders's eyes, how they were wandering looser than they should have been.

"Hey, hey, no, senor," Monarch said in that slurred Spanish accent. "No need for guns. Carlos Munoz comes in peace man. Just need to pee. Too much champagne."

The security chief tried to get angry, but that emotion was quickly overwhelmed by puzzlement. He seemed to kiss the air before the pistol fell from his hand, clanked, and skittered on the bricks. Saunders reached out toward one of the wine bays along the near wall and missed it by a good six inches before crashing facedown on the floor.

"Billy, what's . . . ?" Arsenault said. "What's . . . ? Call . . . ?"

The mogul stood there, shaking his head like a man who'd forgotten his own name. His attorney looked dizzy before she sat down hard and fell over on her side, out cold.

Moving quickly to shut the wine cellar door, Monarch said, "Very effective stuff that diluted rhino tranquilizer."

"Told you carfentanil would do the trick," Barnett said in his ear.

"Anybody ever tell you you're the best?" Monarch said, turning back toward Arsenault who had gotten a different drug than his lawyer and security chief. The mogul was still upright, but acting like someone in an advanced stage of Alzheimer's.

"Whaaa?" the tycoon said.

"Senor Arsenault?" the thief said, affecting concern as he moved to the mogul, took his elbow, and led him to one of the chairs at the wine-tasting table. "Please. For you, the best seat in the house."

Arsenault blinked, nodded, but didn't seem to understand

why. Then he looked up at Monarch blearily, cocked his head as if in some recognition, and said, "I know . . . You are . . ."

"Your friend," Monarch said. "The safe, senor. You wish it open, yes?"

The tycoon started to shake his head, but then nodded. "IRS coming."

"Got to clear it out," the thief said.

"Got to bug out," Arsenault corrected.

That was the beauty of the cocktail the tan dart had delivered to the tycoon's system: ethanol mixed with midazolam created a hypnotic sense of well-being and total separation from reality. U.S. intelligence agencies had used a variety of the recipe for years. It was unlikely that Arsenault would remember much of the experience.

"Yes, we must to bug out, senor," Monarch said. "Give Carlos the combination and he opens the safe for you."

The mogul had trouble with that. He raised his finger, waved it uncertainly, and gave up. Finally, in a monotone, he said, "M-two-B-five-Z-twenty-six-P-eleven-C-eleven."

Walking straight to the digital pad Monarch entered the combination using his finger overlain with that replica of Arsenault's fingerprint. There was a whirring noise and the locks in the safe door relaxed and withdrew.

"We're in," Monarch said into the microphone.

"You've got forty-three minutes."

He understood. It was two minutes past eight. At eight forty-five, Arsenault was expected to raise another toast of holiday good cheer to his guests. The thief intended to be long gone by the time someone thought to come looking for the tycoon.

The safe was large enough to be called a vault, with room for a man of his size to duck down and step inside. Steel boxes and drawers were stacked floor to ceiling on both sides of the vault and along its rear wall.

25

Monarch went through them fast, finding eight or nine set aside for Louisa's extensive jewelry collection and an equal number that contained deeds, titles, and other documents. Every thirty seconds or so, he looked out to make sure that Arsenault was still sitting at his wine-tasting table with a look that said, "Was I just kicked upside the head?"

Ordinarily, given the quality of the jewelry, Monarch would have been stuffing it all into sacks along with the gold coins and bars that filled at least fifteen drawers. But there was no way he could carry even a fraction of what the Arsenaults had squirreled away in precious metals and stones.

Besides, Monarch believed there was something equally valuable and infinitely more transportable and negotiable in the vault. He found it, or them actually, stored in legal-size clasp envelopes in a wide drawer at the bottom of the rear wall.

Corporate and government "bearer bonds" are unregistered. There is no recording of ownership or the transaction that led to ownership. If you are in possession of such bonds, they are yours, hence the term "bearer." Prior to 1982, such financial instruments were commonplace. The United States used to issue them in denominations of up to a million dollars.

But in the late 1970s, due to their involvement in money laundering schemes, the issuance of such bonds in America was greatly curtailed. All bearer bonds issued by the United States prior to 1982 matured by 2007. But as of 2009, there were still about $100 million in bearer paper yet to be redeemed. A quick look in the first envelope and Monarch knew he was looking at approximately $4.5 million in negotiable U.S. instruments. The second envelope contained bearer bonds worth $7.2 million. The remaining three envelopes contained similar paper issued in 1977 by Ford and IBM, and worth $8.24 million.

Total haul: $19.94 million.

It was enough, more than enough, Monarch decided. He

tucked the five envelopes inside the jacket and under his left arm. Leaving the vault, he glanced at Saunders and Pratt, and saw they were laboring for breath. Animal tranquilizers can be tricky things when administered to humans. People under their influence have been known to suffer respiratory failure.

Arsenault, however, was still looking off into the distance with the stunned expression of an absinthe drinker on a binge, and in a singsong voice, kept saying, "I know . . . I know."

The thief retrieved the cigarette pack from his pocket once again. After reloading the fake cigarette with the last dart, he got out that small hypodermic syringe. By that time, the security chief was making asthmatic noises and the attorney was choking on every second breath.

Monarch checked his watch: 8:26 P.M. He now had nineteen minutes before someone might come looking for Arsenault and his aides. He found and retrieved the darts from Pratt and Saunders, and then used the syringe to shoot them each with diprenorphine, an opiate antagonist that would neutralize the effects of the tranquilizers. They'd come around within fifteen or twenty minutes, suffering headaches of biblical proportions but essentially okay.

Standing and turning to check Arsenault, Monarch figured it would be closer to an hour before the mogul would own his own thoughts. At the moment, he was pointing at the thief, jabbing the air as if he were on an invisible phone.

"Don't worry, senor," Monarch said. "You will feel better in the morning."

As he headed toward the door, he held the champagne flute in his left hand to camouflage the fact he had the envelopes clasped under his armpit, and had the fake cigarette between the index and middle fingers of his right hand.

"Exiting," he said.

Then Monarch opened the wine cellar door.

Louisa Arsenault seemed to have been reaching for that same door from the opposite side. The mogul's wife stumbled, surprised, looked right into the thief's face at close quarters, and then past him, seeing Saunders and Pratt on the floor, and her husband looking like he'd drunk the better part of the wine in the cellar.

"Who are . . . ?" she cried. "What is . . . ?"

Monarch smiled, raised the fake cigarette to his lips, and blew the last dart. It struck her dead center of her forehead. She squealed, stepped back, and raised her hands to swat at it. As she did, the thief grabbed her above her emerald and diamond necklace, plucked the dart from her skin, and threw her into the wine cellar. She crashed into the tasting table, and was going to the floor when he slammed shut the door.

"Fuck," Monarch said.

"What?" Barnett demanded.

"It's not good," he said as he began to jog back toward that arcade room and the stairs to the main floor. "Louisa got a good look at—"

Monarch heard the door to the wine cellar open behind him. He slowed for a step, looked over his shoulder, and saw Arsenault's wife holding Saunders's Glock. The socialite was squared off in a combat stance, arms rising, but unsteady on her feet, fighting the tranquilizer.

She won't shoot, Monarch thought an instant before the gun barked.

The bullet punched the thief in the gut, spun him around, and he crashed against the wall.

6

EARS RINGING, MONARCH THREW himself sideways toward the game room to avoid a second bullet. Glancing back, he saw Louisa succumbing to the drugs, dropping the gun, and pitching forward onto the hallway rug.

"I'm hit," he said, gritting his teeth, and struggling to his feet through the game room.

Barnett came back all business. "How bad?"

Looking down the thief saw that the cummerbund showed blood spreading. He set the champagne glass on a foosball table, and probed the wound in front and behind, finding no exit wound.

"Abdomen, lower right ventral side," Monarch replied, reaching the stairs. "It's still in there."

"Mayday?"

"Not yet," he said, though he felt like puking with every step.

"Can you bind it?"

"I'll let you know," the thief said, climbing the stairs.

At the top he could hear voices and realized he was sweating hard. Still holding the bonds inside his tux jacket and up under his left armpit, Monarch opened the door, finding several guests and staff members staring back at him.

"We heard a loud noise," one of the servers said.

"A shooting!" Monarch squealed in that Mexican accent. "Big Beau shot Louisa! I saw it!"

Gasps and screams went up, and he went on, "Call the police! Run for cover! The rich one, he goes insane!"

Whether it was fear of a pistol-packing mogul gone haywire, or fear of getting caught up in a scandal sure to be plastered all over the *New York Post,* everyone in the hallway broke into a blind sprint toward the ballroom and the front door. Monarch slammed the basement door shut, and went in the opposite direction, toward a pair of closed doors he knew led to Arsenault's library and private office.

The thief was suddenly and wildly thirsty. It's a common symptom of a gut shot. The body demands water to flush out the acidic digestive fluids seeping into the wound. There was a caterer's cart there in the hall. It carried coffee cups, saucers, and cloth napkins. Monarch stuffed a wad of napkins inside the cummerbund as he tried to run, provoking a true blast of pain, the first agonizing spasm to break through the early shock, so strong it forced him to wonder if he had the strength to get free of the estate before the police arrived.

Flashing on the interior of a prison cell—a common enough memory from Monarch's past—he swallowed the pain, opened the door to Arsenault's office, and stepped inside a room decorated like a British men's club. The revelers in the ballroom seemed not to have heard about the shooting because all he could make out was laughter and the strains of a cello as he shut the door behind him.

In front of the thief and to his left, a woman in an ankle-length black coat stood with her back turned, facing a credenza. She seemed to wince at the sound of the door closing, and then threw back her head, finishing a drink, and slamming down the glass before she said in a defiant tone, "I'm here as you demanded, Beau, but I won't do it. Not here. Not with your bitch of a wife and all those people in the house. In fact, I'm telling you we

30

won't do it ever again. And I don't care if your lack of support hurts my career. I really don't—"

Cassie Knox had turned enough by then to see Monarch. The singer's hand shot to her mouth, and she stammered, "I'm sorry. I thought you were . . ."

"The rich prick that somehow leveraged you into fucking him?" he said.

Her chin retreated a second, and then shot forward. "Who are you?"

"Someone else with a beef with Big Beau Arsenault," he replied, before being wracked with pain so bad he gasped and bent double.

"What's wrong with you?" Knox asked in alarm, taking a step toward him.

The thief looked up at her, realized the truth was the only way to get her on his side, and gasped, "Louisa shot me while I was stealing a chunk of Beau's secret, and highly illegal, cash stash so I could give it to orphans in South America."

The singer gazed at Monarch, head slightly tilted for several puzzled moments before saying, "What? Like fucking Robin Hood or something?"

"Close enough."

Knox smiled. "Serves the bastard right."

Realizing he had an unlikely ally, the thief said, "Can you help me get out of here? Just off the estate? To the stables? I've got a car there."

She hesitated, thought, and said, "You have the money?"

"Right here," Monarch said, growing weaker. "I'll give you a million untraceable dollars if you get me off this estate."

"Oh, no, you won't," the singer said in a scolding tone. "I'll help you, but Cassie Knox does not steal from orphans."

Monarch managed a smile. "Do you have a car?"

"Parked in their carriage house," she said, and put her arm under his shoulder. "C'mon, I know the way."

The pain pulsed through the thief's stomach with every step, but he drove himself to keep moving. Knox led him out the other door of the library and down a hallway off the kitchen, which was still bustling with caterers and cooks. He kept looking at the floor for blood, but so far the napkins seemed to be absorbing it all. Knox opened a door beside the pantry, revealing a staircase.

"Where's that go?" he gasped.

"The tunnel to the carriage house," she said. "You don't think folks like the Arsenaults go outside if they don't have to, do you?"

Monarch was light-headed, but managed to stay on his feet as she got him down the stairs to a narrow hallway about two hundred feet long, and decorated with the mogul's substantial collection of modern art. They exited into a carriage house, which was more like an auto museum with exotic cars stacked on lifts at the rear of the space.

"Leaving so soon, Ms. Knox?" a man's voice called.

The singer pivoted toward a security guard in his late twenties, smiled, said, "I have to be back in Manhattan so I can finish shopping in the morning, and my friend, Mr. Harris, isn't feeling well."

Wrapping his arms around his wounded gut, Monarch grunted, "Oysters, they do it to me every time."

"Snowing hard out there," he warned. "Nor'easter."

"Thankfully, I've got all-wheel drive, great tires, and fog lights," she said.

The guard hesitated before gesturing at a black Audi Q5 on the other side of the garage. "Your keys are in it. I'll get the door raised for you."

"Thank you," she said, and started to lead Monarch away.

"Ms. Knox?" the guard said.

She hesitated, glanced at the thief, and then looked back over her shoulder, saying, "Yes?"

"I just wanted to say what an honor it is to meet you. I'm a big fan."

Knox conjured up a thousand-watt smile, said, "Well, aren't you the sweetest thing for saying so?"

"Be safe on your drive," he said.

"I will," she replied, hurried Monarch toward the Audi, and got him in the passenger seat. Sitting down like that almost knocked him unconscious, and he could not help groaning as she climbed in the other side.

Concerned, Knox nevertheless started the car, and said, "I can't take you to a hospital like this. It would get out that I was involved."

"Just my car," the thief gasped. "It's across the street at the stables."

"I can do that," the singer said, and threw the Audi in reverse. They went out into the driving snow that had already blanketed the vehicles parked outside the carriage house. There was a line of cars ahead, driven by the valets for a nervous crowd of guests standing on the walkway, trying to look nonchalant but desperate to get off the estate.

Knox downshifted, went the wrong way around the circular driveway, taking them right to the gate and that burly guard who'd checked credentials earlier. He came around to her window, knocked on it.

"Nice driving," he said.

"I'm in a hurry," the singer replied.

"So what's going on up there?" he asked. "Usually people stay to all hours."

"Christmas shopping calls in the morning for me," Knox said.

The guard ducked down to look at Monarch. He smiled weakly, said, "Stomach bug. She's taking me to my car."

The guard stepped back, said, "That sucks. Merry Christmas."

The gate swung open and they drove onto the main road.

As a way of getting his mind off the pain, the thief asked, "So how did Beau get his claws into you?"

Knox hesitated, but then hardened and turned into the snowy stable road, saying, "He heard me sing in a club in Chicago, and he's the deep pockets behind several recording companies. He made it all happen for me."

"And threatened to make it un-happen if you weren't nice in return?"

"Sums it up," she said.

"Beauregard Arsenault, model citizen."

Knox snorted derisively, and then went quiet. It took them less than a minute to find where the valets had parked the Range Rover.

"You sure you can drive?" the singer asked.

"About to find out. Thanks for the lift."

He started to get out. She said, "Who *are* you really anyway?"

"Sometimes I don't know myself," Monarch said. "You leave first."

He could tell she wanted to ask more, but he shut the door and trudged in burning agony through the falling snow to the Rover. Knox waited until the thief was inside, had the engine going, and the headlights on before pulling away.

Following her taillights up the hill to the main road, he turned right when she went left toward Greenwich. Heading north, he passed the entrance to the estate. A stream of cars was exiting like rats from a sinking ship. Blue lights began to flash far behind him in the rearview mirror.

Throwing the Rover into four-wheel drive, Monarch pressed down on the accelerator, trying to put distance between him and stately Arsenault manor. For several minutes, he thought he was going to be able to make it the ten miles to the pickup point.

Then the pain turned excruciating. The thief tasted blood in the back of his throat. Sparkling dots began to dance in front of his eyes as he peered out into the blizzard, trying to stay on the road. But soon Monarch could barely tell the difference between the dots and the snow driven in the headlights.

He was done. He knew it.

Taking his foot off the gas, he triggered the microphone on his lapel.

"Mayday," he whispered, fighting to get the car over on the shoulder.

The thief never heard a response. The Rover's tires lost contact with the road, the shoulder, and the snow. It pitched forward and out into space. Seeing rocks and trees fly by in his peripheral vision, as if he'd driven off the side of a ravine, he was aware of plunging several seconds before smashing off something hard and then dropping again.

The thick tree trunk registered in Monarch's brain a split second before the head-on collision that banished him into darkness.

7

BEAU ARSENAULT HAD BEEN raised to believe that a man who drank before five had no real ambition in life, and a man who swore in public was destined to mediocrity. The mogul also had been taught that a man who failed to control his emotions was a fool easily played.

And yet, as his mansion echoed with the sounds of workmen moving tables and chairs in the foyer, and others in the ballroom painting over Dickens's London, Arsenault paced in his library, wanting to drink a fifth of bourbon, scream obscenities at the top of his lungs, and put his fist through a wall.

To make matters worse, he still had a colossal headache from whatever drug he'd been given. He hated that his mind felt foggy. He hated this sense of violation. He loathed being used. He despised the fact that he'd been played big time.

In my own fucking home, for Christ's sake!

And I can't say a fucking thing to the police!

For what seemed like the hundredth time, the billionaire thought about that drunk guy who'd wandered into the wine cellar, trying to see him in his memory. But the drugs had blurred

36

things. Was he Mexican or something? The only name he and Louisa had not recognized on the list was Asa Johanson.

Asa Johanson? That's not a Mexican name.

Who the fuck is Asa Johanson?

I don't care who he is! That weasel motherfucker is going to regret ever crossing Beauregard Arsenault. That weasel mother-fucker is going to suffer like he's never suffered before.

He knew he couldn't tell the police what had happened. But that didn't mean he wasn't going to get his money back, and wreak revenge.

Count on it.

Looking out the window at the snowy landscape, Arsenault calmed himself. In the greater scheme of things, the loss of the bearer bonds wasn't that hard a hit; they represented a small fraction of the stash he'd squirreled away. No, it wasn't the money. It was the principle of the thing.

That motherfucking lowlife ripped me off in my own home at my own Christmas party, for Christ's sake! That fucker worked me, worked all of us!

"Beau!" Louisa called, rapping at the library door. "Beau, are you in there?"

Arsenault cringed. His wife's voice sounded so high, reedy, and grating that it ratcheted his headache up a notch.

"Coming dear," he called, went to the door, unlocked and opened it.

Louisa entered and spun to face him as soon as he'd shut the door.

"I've been on the phone all morning with Evie doing damage control," she said in a low, conspiratorial voice. "We've told people exactly what we told the police, that you were not drunk last night, that you had some kind of allergic reaction to a new blood pressure medicine, and that the idea of turning a cham-pagne cork popping into a murder was someone's idea of a sick

37

joke. Evie's already talked to Page Six about it, and averted total disaster. They were on to it."

Evie Dickenson was his wife's publicist. She was supposed to guard their reputation from all press attacks, foreign and domestic.

"Evie ever hear of Asa Johanson?" he asked.

"Never," Louisa said. "And I've already fired the two idiots who let him get on the guest list. Where's Saunders and Pratt?"

"Still downstairs looking," Arsenault said.

His wife's voice lowered again. "I'm telling you again that I hit that man, Big Beau. Last thing I remember was a solid sight picture."

"I believe you, sweetness," Arsenault said.

"Then how did he get out of here without leaving any blood?"

"I have no idea," he said, feeling a blade of pain knife through his skull so sharply that he sat down in one of the leather wingback chairs, closed his eyes, and began rubbing at his temples.

"You sure you don't want to see someone?" Louisa asked. "I can call in the concierge doctor Evie recommended. She said he's completely discreet."

"No doctors," he said firmly. "We are limiting exposure. Are we clear?"

"Suit yourself," she sniffed. "Evie has no idea by the way."

His eyes flew open. "I should fucking hope not! She's the biggest fucking blabbermouth I know."

"Don't shout and don't be vulgar," Louisa shot back. "I am not the enemy here. We are in this together. And Evie is on our side."

"With what we pay her, I'm sure she is," Arsenault griped, and hung his head in his hands. He took a deep breath and moved his mind beyond the pain, rifling through what he knew and what he suspected.

The thief knew about the safe and its contents. How was that possible? Either he had an inside accomplice, or he'd hacked into the computers. Only five people knew about the safe: he and his wife, Saunders, Pratt, and the man who'd installed it. Since the installer would have no idea what they were going to put in the safe, and since Saunders and Pratt had proved their loyalty time and again, he was left believing that they'd been hacked by an expert.

That expert had also managed to get this Asa Johanson inserted into the guest list at the last moment, and used e-mails from Arsenault's personal secretary to do it. Once inside the party, the thief kept moving with his face always angled to avoid the security cameras, which meant he knew about them. And then that woman had called his private phone, and said, "Exodus. Air-conditioner repairmen coming tomorrow morning to check the wine cellar. Exodus. Exodus."

Air-conditioner repairmen.

Exodus.

How had they gotten those code words? Over the years he'd paid millions in bribes to top law enforcement officials in return for a promise to warn him if he was the subject of an investigation. Air-conditioner repairmen meant U.S. Treasury agents. Exodus warned of the highest possible threat, and Arsenault knew for a fact that no one had ever written these codes down. They had been agreed upon orally. Which meant that either someone deep in his back pocket had talked, an unlikely scenario, or someone had listened in.

He lifted his head, said, "What phone were you using to talk to Evie?"

"I'm not stupid, Beau," Louisa said. "It was a disposable."

"Don't use your regular cell or the house phone for anything until Saunders can sweep them."

"You think they bugged us?"

He nodded.

His wife turned grim and then suspicious, looking around the library saying, "You don't think . . ."

He understood, agreed with her thinking, but said, "I don't know."

Louisa's eyes flared and she hissed, "We're not having Christmas here then. I won't spend another day in this house until we know for certain."

"Grandkids will be disappointed, Big Mama," Arsenault said. "They wanted snow."

"Big Mama will make it up to them," Louisa said. "We're packing. I'll call Windham to get the jet ready. We're going back to Twelve Oaks."

Before the mogul could remind her that their plantation outside New Orleans could have been bugged as well, there was a sharp knock at the door.

"Yes?" Louisa demanded.

"It's Billy and Meg," said Saunders. "We've got something."

Arsenault got up fast and opened the door. His security chief and attorney entered, dressed casually, and holding paper bags. When he closed the door, Louisa whispered, "Is this room safe, Billy?"

"Swept three days ago," he replied.

"That doesn't answer the question, does it?"

The security chief reddened, and then shook his head.

Louisa let her displeasure show, and crossed to a cabinet and opened it, revealing the components of a stereo system. She plugged in her iPhone, and cranked the volume up on Miranda Lambert singing about the fastest girl in town.

They had to stand close to hear one another.

Saunders said to Louisa, "You hit him. We found a speck of blood on the carpet on the staircase."

"And he made a mistake," Pratt said. "There are prints on

the shards of a champagne glass that he threw against the wall in the game room."

Arsenault brightened at the idea of quick retaliation. No matter what the Sicilians said about revenge being a dish best served cold, he favored striking back as soon as possible. "How fast can you run the prints? The DNA?"

"Prints by tomorrow," Saunders said. "DNA minimum is four days."

"How did he get out of here?" Louisa asked.

The attorney and the security chief exchanged glances, before Saunders said, "He left the grounds with Cassie Knox, in her car."

Louisa was instantly irate. "Why that little ungrateful bitch!" She stared at her husband. "After everything you've done for that girl?"

Arsenault blanched, thought of Cassie Knox naked in a bed at the Four Seasons in San Francisco the week before, and said, "Let's not jump to conclusions. I would imagine he forced her to help him."

"Perhaps," Pratt allowed. "But it appears she dropped him at his car, a Range Rover that was parked down by the stable."

"And never called us," Saunders said.

"Maybe she didn't know he was wounded," the mogul said.

"Maybe," the security chief replied. "You want me to call her?"

The mogul thought about that, said, "I'll talk to Cassie. I'm supposed to meet with her Tuesday in Chicago."

Louisa looked at him sidelong. "For?"

"Her producers asked me to the meeting," he said quickly. "Her entire team will be there to discuss her coming year."

His wife hesitated, glanced at her husband again, and then said to Saunders, "It sounds to Beau like they bugged our phones and computers. How is that possible?"

Looking uncomfortable, Saunders said, "I don't know. With what we paid those IT security guys, the computers should have been bomb proof."

"A dud is more like it," Louisa said. "I want every computer we own checked and fixed. Am I clear?"

Chagrined, and knowing better than to cross her, the security chief said, "More than clear, Mrs. Arsenault."

She nodded sharply, said to her husband, "I'm packing."

Big Beau waited until his wife had closed the door behind her before leaning toward Saunders and Pratt.

He showed them passion, a rare thing, said, "I don't care if it costs me another twenty million, we're getting this motherfucker. Whatever it takes. He's going down, and he's going down hard."

8

MONARCH CREPT OUT OF the darkness, lying there with his eyes closed, becoming aware of things one by one. It was hot. He heard children laughing in the distance. There was a soft click, and a low beep every few seconds. He breathed in through his nose and smelled lavender and something more antiseptic. His right side ached. His face felt frozen. The last thing he recalled was snow, lots of snow, a storm, and cold and a tree coming at him.

Then he remembered. He'd been gut shot. He'd been bleeding. He'd called Mayday. He'd crashed.

Monarch forced his swollen eyes open and got them only to slits. But it was enough to see he was in a hospital bed. He was hitched up to IVs and monitors, and there were slat blinds open and fluttering in the hot breeze that carried the sound of those children laughing and playing.

His tongue felt thick.

Thirsty.

Water.

His head spun and he almost lost consciousness. He managed to turn away from the window, and saw an older woman with a long silver braid and a handsome, kindly face. She wore a lab coat, a stethoscope, and was scribbling on a clipboard. A small wooden crucifix hung on a chain around her neck.

"Sister?" he muttered weakly.

Sister Rachel looked up from her chart, and said in Spanish, "I was wondering when you'd come around, Robin."

"Water?" he croaked.

"You may have ice chips," she said in a no-nonsense voice, and left.

She soon returned with a paper cup and a spoon. She scooped out a few chips and put them to his lips.

After he'd had several scoopfuls, Monarch whispered, "Where am I? Clinic?"

Coming to his side, she said, "The new one at the refuge."

He nodded, let his eyes roam around the room and over the modern equipment. Though Monarch had paid for it, he'd not yet seen this new clinic at the Hogar d'Espera, the Refuge of Hope, the orphanage Sister Rachel ran in the foothills outside Buenos Aires.

"Day is it?" he asked.

"Monday, December twenty-third."

"How'd I get here?"

"Your friend Miss Barnett," she replied, taking his pulse. "She brought you on a private jet with a full medevac team that operated on you in flight. They got the bullet out of you. I've been treating you for sepsis."

He blinked, nodded, and licked his lips. "But I'm okay now?"

"Hardly," she replied in a diffident voice he knew all too well.

His eyes drifted shut and he saw an image of himself as an eighteen-year-old struggling up the side of a steep hill with a knapsack full of rocks on his back while she berated him for some shortcoming in his character.

"Do you want more ice chips?" she asked, breaking the memory.

More ice chips sounded like heaven and he opened his eyes to slits again, seeing her still standing there with a cup and a spoon. "Please."

After two more spoonfuls, he said, "Thank you."

Sister Rachel set the cup on the table beside the hospital bed, said, "Miss Barnett tells me you were shot in the course of some kind of government-sanctioned mission. Is that true?"

It wasn't true, but he said, "That's right."

She crossed her arms, clearly skeptical. "Then why didn't she take you to government-sanctioned doctors?"

Monarch smiled weakly and said, "Because she knew no one would take better care of me than you would."

"I don't like being lied to, Robin, especially by you."

"And I can't help it if Gloria wanted you to heal me. You've done it before, after all. Where is she? Gloria?"

"Out for a walk with Claudio."

Monarch smiled. Claudio was his oldest and dearest friend. He hadn't seen him in months.

"How long until I'm good to go?" he asked.

Sister Rachel stared at him through her wire-rimmed glasses for several long moments, and even as groggy as he was he could tell she was conflicted on many different levels.

"How long?" he asked again.

Finally, she snapped, "I don't know, Robin. How long did it take you to recover the last time I saved your life?"

"Six months?" he said, and groaned softly.

"It won't be anywhere near that long," she admitted. "But you're not out of danger from infection yet. Not by a long shot. That bullet perforated your small intestine in three places."

He suddenly felt tired, knew he'd fall asleep in seconds, said, "Thanks."

*

45

When Monarch awoke again, the air was cooler and filled with the voices of children singing. He listened, feeling the warmth of a dream realized.

He'd done terrible things as a U.S. Special Forces and CIA operative. Robbed men. Kidnapped them and held them for ransom. Killed them, too. But hearing the children's voices raised in song made him feel as if he were doing some good now, taking parentless children out of the slums and offering them a chance at a life he never had.

Doing that was worth being shot. Doing that was—

"Merry Christmas, my brother."

Monarch knew the voice. He weakly rolled his head left; saw Claudio Fortunato coming through the door. His oldest friend was in his late thirties with a wild mop of curly dark hair and a barrel chest. Claudio wore white linen pants, a black polo shirt, and sandals. On his inner right forearm, he had the same tattoo as Monarch, the letters *FDL* with the suggestion of a pickpocket's hand coming off the top of the *D*.

"Bring me a present?" Monarch whispered.

Claudio grinned and gestured with his chin toward the door where Gloria Barnett was entering. Built like a long-legged shore bird, Barnett had cut her flaming-red hair short, wore a pretty blue dress, and carried an attaché case.

She came over on the other side of Monarch's bed, kissed him on the forehead, said, "I knew you'd make it."

"Tell me," Monarch said.

"How we got you out of there?"

"Last thing I remember was going off the road."

"But not before you called Mayday," she reminded him, pulling out a bottle of Malbec and two glasses.

"I don't think Sister will like that," Monarch said.

"It's not for you," she said.

After pouring wine for her and for Claudio, Barnett explained that as soon as she heard the distress call she'd ordered in the extraction team from their layup positions around Greenwich. They staged accidents on the road north and south of the crash site. The rest of the team went immediately to the thief's position based on the GPS transponder in the Rover.

"You were lucky that Range Rover has excellent airbags or you would have broken your neck," Barnett said. "Tats and Chavez stabilized you, got you up the bank, and out of there in twenty-two minutes."

"Range Rover?"

"Still there, buried under the snow in a place no one would look, which means you had your senses about you right to the end," she replied. "We'll wait a month or so before sending a wrecker to get it."

Monarch nodded, almost drowsed, before saying, "The bonds?"

Barnett reached in her case, came up with a thick manila envelope, said, "Awaiting your instructions."

Monarch moved in bed, and groaned at the pain in his side before saying, "How much have you told Sister Rachel?"

"The minimum," Barnett replied.

Looking to Claudio, he said, "When can you move the bonds?"

Before he'd become a painter, Claudio had been a fence. As his art career had flourished, Claudio had abandoned the trade except when Monarch needed to convert stolen items into cash.

"They're all high quality, so they'll be noticed if we try to move the lot whole," Claudio said. "I say we wait two months before we start cashing them in, and then only in smaller amounts, say two hundred and fifty grand, slow, steady, and in different locations."

Monarch saw the wisdom in that, looked to Barnett. "You okay with that?"

"More than fine," she said. "The others, too."

On a job like the Arsenaults, Monarch gave each of his support staff five percent of the take, which in this case meant a million dollars apiece. He would also take five percent, and the rest, roughly fourteen million, would go to Sister Rachel and the children.

"It's good," he said softly. "If we gave her the lump sum, I think she'd balk."

Claudio agreed: "She'll be less likely to question it if it comes trickling—"

They all heard the slap of shoes coming and quieted. Sister Rachel came in, saw them all, and smiled. "Like old times," she said, then shooed them away from Monarch's bed while she worked.

After a few moments of silence, Barnett said, "Sister, now that you've got the clinic built, what's next?"

The question seemed to surprise her. "I don't know," she said.

"What do you dream of doing?" Monarch said.

"Yeah," Claudio said. "Wildest dreams."

Sister Rachel thought about that for a few seconds, and then replied, "I suppose I would try to buy the land north of us, so we could expand."

"What's it worth?" Barnett asked.

The missionary doctor said, "Millions I should imagine. It's a large piece."

Then she finished up with Monarch, said, "How is the pain?"

"No narcotics."

"Nonsense," she said. "If you're spending your energy fighting pain, you're putting even more stress on your body. Rate it on a scale of one to ten."

"Six," he said.

"Seven then," Sister Rachel said. "I'll be back after the evening service with some pills to help you sleep through the night."

Monarch gazed past her, saw Barnett and Claudio smiling behind their hands. Sister Rachel was the only person in the world who bossed him around this way, and they were highly amused.

She said, "Well, Gloria, Claudio, dinner is at seven, you'll join us?"

"It would be an honor, Sister," Barnett said.

"You know I never turn down a free meal," Claudio said.

Sister Rachel took one more glance at Monarch, said, "I have other patients to see. Two poor kiddos with the stomach flu on Christmas Eve."

After she left, Monarch looked at Claudio, said, "Are you going to make an honest woman out of Chavez tomorrow?"

For the last couple of years the artist had been in a torrid love affair with Chanel Chavez, another member of Monarch's team.

Claudio sobered at the question, said, "If she was here, I would, Robin. I swear to this on my soul, but Regina is not doing well. I talked to Chanel before I came over, and she was very down, said it might be Regina's last Christmas."

Monarch felt horrible. Chanel's sister had two young children and had been fighting breast cancer for more than a year.

"You talk to Chanel, tell her we're praying for her and Regina," he said.

Claudio nodded, looked at his watch, said, "Almost time for dinner."

Barnett stood, said, "We'll come back to see if you're up later."

Monarch tried to stay awake, but was asleep within minutes of their leaving.

When he awoke, the pain was terrible. He realized Sister Rachel was checking his bandages, and probing the wounded area.

"Infection?" he asked in a hoarse voice.

"Yes, but you're winning," she said, regarding him over the top of her glasses. "Here, I brought your medicine."

As a rule, Monarch tried to avoid narcotics or drugs of any kind. But he was in no position to argue with Sister Rachel. He opened his mouth and swallowed the pills.

Monarch watched her before saying, "Thank you for saving me that first time."

Sister Rachel tilted her head, looked at him quizzically, and then said, "You're welcome, Robin."

"You changed my life," he said. "I just wanted you to know that."

The missionary doctor smiled, said, "In your way you've changed mine."

He almost laughed to think how, but stopped himself, knowing the pain would be excruciating. Instead, he said, "What you said earlier, about the land?"

"Yes?"

"Merry Christmas, Sister," he said. "I think you should start making plans."

Her face fell, and she looked away.

"What's the matter?" he asked. "I thought you'd be happy."

Sister Rachel seemed to have an argument with herself before saying, "All the money, Robin. It . . . well, it makes me wonder sometimes."

"About?"

"Where it comes from," she said, her head bowed.

"Given my background, you mean?"

"I hate to bring it up."

Monarch felt his head grow fuzzy from the drugs, knew the less he revealed the better. But finally, he said, "This clinic? The money?"

She looked up at him, hands clasped, and he could see fear in her eyes, as if she did not want to know what was saving so many children from the streets and so many slum dwellers from disease and calamity. "Yes?"

"Remember last year when the U.S. Secretary of State and the foreign ministers of China and India were kidnapped by fanatics?" he asked.

A twitch of confusion passed through her face. "Yes, of course."

"I led the rescue," he said. "They paid me millions to save her."

A great weight seemed to fall from her shoulders. "You did? They did?"

"Yes," he said, feeling foggier as the drugs hit.

"Then why do you insist on anonymity with the donations?" she asked.

"Because anonymity is what I need to do my job well," Monarch said. "Whatever you may suspect of me, Sister, I promise you that everything I do, I do for you, and for the greater good."

The missionary doctor said nothing, just gazed at him. But the last thing Monarch saw before his eyes drifted shut and he fell deep into unconsciousness was a tear that rolled down her right cheek.

9

BEAU ARSENAULT LEFT THE limousine on Pearson Street on Chicago's near north side, and entered the Ritz-Carlton. His life could get complicated, and there was unavoidable stress in those complications, which his doctors had warned him was a real threat to someone who had a family history of heart disease.

The mogul exercised almost every day, but the only thing that truly relaxed him was gourmet chocolate. That thought made him move quickly into the hotel lobby where a concierge, a thin, taciturn man, waited with an electronic key.

"The usual suite, sir," the concierge said.

"Visitors?" Arsenault asked.

"Not as of yet."

"Excellent," the mogul replied. "You'll alert me if there are?"

"As always, sir."

Arsenault went to a special elevator and slid his key through a slot before punching the thirtieth floor. Exiting the lift, he hurried down the hallway, his mind conjuring up ways this all could go, and feeling slightly breathless. The key opened one of the hotel's ambassador suites with a commanding view of Lake Michigan. He was entering when his private cell rang. It was Saunders.

"You have something for me, Billy?" the mogul demanded.

"You're not going to like it."

Arsenault found this aspect of his security chief's makeup

annoying. He'd rather have the facts straight and then decide if they suited his purposes or not. There was no like or dislike about it.

"Do you have results or not?" he said as he walked down the hallway.

Saunders cleared his throat, said, "When my guys at the Bureau ran the prints on the champagne glass, one belonged to you, and the other one got my guys at the Bureau a visit from someone very high up in the judicial food chain."

Arsenault slowed. "Go on."

"My guys were told to forget they'd ever seen that fingerprint."

That made the mogul tighten up inside. "So you're saying what, he's with the government? FBI?"

"I don't know."

The hotel room phone rang. He crossed to it, said, "Well, find out."

"How?"

Lifting the ringing phone and setting it back down in its cradle, he said, "Throw some money around. That always works."

Snapping shut the cell phone the mogul wondered whether the robbery had been a cover, whether someone had targeted him, or was targeting him. He rubbed at his chest, sore from a morning workout, then went to the stocked bar and poured himself some bourbon.

Arsenault took a chair, sipped the sour mash, and let his imagination run to the hour ahead all the while considering what Saunders had told him. That's the mark of a first-rate mind, he thought, the ability to manage two or more trains of thought at the same time. Quite often, he had four or more going.

The lock mechanism whirred and the suite door opened and shut. Cassie Knox entered the room carrying several shopping bags. She spotted Arsenault and stopped dead in her tracks.

"Beau," the singer said.

"Cassie," he said.

Knox hung her head slightly. "I didn't know you were . . ."

"Coming?" he said good-naturedly. "You think I'd miss this treat? That would be like asking a great man not to eat chocolate, and you know how great men like to eat chocolate."

Her jaw stiffening, the singer set the bags down and took off her down coat and scarf. Arsenault drank the rest of his bourbon, got up, and started crossing to her.

When he was close, she said softly, "I can't do this anymore. I won't."

The mogul stopped, smiled, and said, "That right, Cassie? You're going to give up everything when you're so close to losing everything already?"

Knox frowned, looked up at him, puzzled.

The slap hit the singer hard across the left cheek and she staggered.

"You think there wouldn't be payment due after the way you betrayed me, girl?" Arsenault said in a low, vicious tone.

Knox held her hand to her face, crying, "What? I never betrayed you!"

The mogul grabbed her by the arm and dragged her toward the bedroom, saying, "Oh, my little dark orchid, yes, you did. You stabbed your benefactor, the hand that feeds you, right in the back."

"I don't know what you're talking about, Beau," she wept.

"You gave a man a ride off my estate on Friday night," he said coldly before hauling her inside the bedroom and kicking shut the door with his heel.

"What? I—"

Arsenault threw the singer on the bed, said, "Don't you lie to me, now. Only gonna get worse for you if you lie."

Bewildered, Knox looked around, said, "Okay, I . . . yes, I

remember now. He said he felt sick and asked me to drive him to his car over by the stable. I did. End of story. How did that betray you?"

The mogul studied her for several moments, and shook his head before slapping her again, this time on the other cheek. "There's more to it than that."

"You hit me again, I'm calling the police," she snarled through her tears.

"Darling, you have no idea about the things I own," he said. "Now you going to tell Big Beau? Or is your entire recording career, all the niceties of your life suddenly going to disappear, leaving you a bitter old girl?"

"There are other labels, Beau," she said.

"That's a fact," he allowed. "But a reputation is a terrible thing to shake, and I have the ability to change your reputation at the snap of my fingers. The critics would turn against you. So would the listeners. I'd make sure. Why? Because deep down, I am a vindictive man. A nasty affliction, but there it is."

The singer stared hatred at him, said nothing.

"What's it gonna be?" he said. "Fame or finished?"

Knox's jaw trembled before she said, "Okay, he said he stole something from you and Louisa shot him and he needed help."

"And you gave it to him?"

Knox looked at him, said, "He held a gun on me, said he'd kill me."

"Really?" Arsenault asked. "What kind of gun."

"A pistol, I don't know."

The mogul stared down at her. He'd never seen a gun, nor had Saunders or Louisa. Didn't mean the burglar had been unarmed, he supposed.

"He say anything to you?"

"About what?"

"Why he was stealing from me?"

She looked puzzled, but then nodded. "I'm paraphrasing, but he said you were an asshole and deserved it."

Arsenault swallowed at the anger rising in him. "That what made you want to help him?"

"He had a gun."

"That all?"

The singer glanced at his right hand, open again, stretched wide. "Okay, he said something about he robbed people like you to give money to orphans in South America."

The mogul squinted, said, "Like what, Robin Hood?"

Knox nodded. "Something like that."

That made Arsenault even angrier. He got ripped off so some son of a bitch could give money to poor kids? That was even worse.

I'm going to crucify this guy, the mogul thought, make him hang on the cross longer than Jesus did dying for my sins.

"That's it, Beau?" the singer said. "Can I go now?"

"You never called to tell me," the mogul said. "You helped a wounded thief escape my house and you never called."

"He had a gun. He said he'd find me if I talked."

He slapped her a third time, said, "I'd have protected you."

Knox rolled over and buried her face in the comforter of the king-size bed, sobbing and moaning, "What do you want from me?"

Arsenault enjoyed his moment of dominance before unbuckling his belt and letting his pants fall, saying softly, lovingly, "What great men have wanted from Thomas Jefferson on down, Cassie, gourmet chocolate to make the stress melt away."

10

SISTER RACHEL QUIETLY SHUT the door to the girl's dormitory at ten that night, knowing full well that the moment she shut the door at the bottom of the stairs, they would break curfew and start talking excitedly again among themselves. The same thing was going on in the boy's dormitory on the other side of the lawn.

It was as it should be, she thought. Children, especially orphans, love the Christmas season. The anticipation. The excitement it presents. The candy and food. The story of a child who grows up to change the world.

Sister Rachel went first to the chapel where other members of her order were decorating for a Christmas celebration. Seeing that they had things well under control, she moved on toward the clinic.

It was a warm, humid evening, and in the distance she could hear music playing and people laughing and singing. And that was as it should be, too. Was there a greater reason for celebration? Not in her world. The birth of Christ and the story of his life were real and tangible, a guide and a powerful motivation for her life's work.

Blessed be the poor, she thought as she reached the clinic. *For they shall inherit the Earth.*

Inside, the missionary doctor greeted the night nurse, who told her Robin Monarch was fast asleep, and his vitals were growing stronger.

"Go home, Luis," Sister Rachel said. "I'll stay with him."

"Are you sure, Sister?" Luisa asked, brightening.

"Completely," she said.

"*Felice Navidad,* Sister," Luisa said, bowed, and rushed out the door.

Sister Rachel walked to the doorway to Monarch's room. She walked in quietly, not wanting to wake him, and scanned the various machines monitoring and aiding his recovery. Luisa was right. His vitals were stronger.

The missionary doctor sat and studied Monarch, feeling conflicted. On the one hand, she loved Robin like a son. On the other, he was a constant source of worry, puzzlement, and uncertainty. It had been so right from the beginning.

Almost twenty years before, in the middle of the night, Claudio Fortunato had run into her clinic in the Villa Miserie, the worst slum in Buenos Aires. He brought her to *el ano*, a garbage dump where the poorest of the poor scavenged for survival. There she found young Robin Monarch sprawled in the mud.

He had been stabbed through the ribs and into his right lung, which had collapsed. She'd managed to save his life physically, but had found it much harder to reach him spiritually.

The process had taken months, but in Sister Rachel's memories that Christmas Eve, the arc of time shrank into moments. She saw herself by his bedside in the old slum clinic, gesturing to the gang tattoo on young Robin's inner right forearm after he'd grown strong enough to sit up.

"*Is* that what you plan to do when you're well?" Sister Rachel asked. "Go back to your life with La Fraternidad de Ladrones? The Brotherhood of Thieves?"

Angered, Robin said, "I've got no other life. My parents were murdered. I lived on the trash heaps in the *ano*, Sister. I ate garbage, Sister. The brotherhood rescued me, Sister."

"And the brotherhood almost killed you," she said.

Robin said nothing, looked away.

"Who stabbed you?" Sister Rachel asked.

Robin looked over at her and shrugged. "Just some random guy."

"You must think I'm stupid."

He blinked, but then shook his head. "I don't, Sister. You're a great doctor. You saved my life."

"Yes, I did, though I'm beginning to wonder why."

That seemed to upend him. "Why? Didn't you take like some kind of oath to help people or something?"

"You didn't think I'd be able to piece it together from your wounds? The slashes high on your right arm, the cut across your left wrist? You were in a knife fight."

"No," Robin began.

"You're lying to me," Sister Rachel said. "Your whole life has been spent lying, hasn't it? Lies, upon lies, one emptiness after the other. Lies are all you have to look forward to if you return to your old life, Robin. Sooner or later, the lies will disintegrate under the weight of truth—they always do—and you'll be in some other hospital or prison bed, or dead with an empty soul to show to God."

Sister Rachel fell silent for a long moment. "Or you can decide to end the lying and the deception and the thieving and the violence and become a better person, a stronger person, a person whose soul God would find worthy."

Robin gaped at her as she got up from his bedside, and made to leave.

"My soul has already been emptied," Robin called after her

retreating figure. "God will already find me unworthy, Sister. It's over for me."

The missionary doctor turned, her face softening. "God never finds the living unworthy, Robin. God always gives us a chance to redeem ourselves."

"What does that mean, redeem?"

Sister Rachel returned to his bedside. "It means that you take another path, a better one that helps make up for whatever it is you've done before."

"I don't understand."

She thought for a moment. "Have you ever seen a balance beam scale?"

"You mean like fence's have?"

Sister Rachel winced, but said, "Exactly. And now I want you to think of your life as a scale, and the weight of what you've done is far out there on that beam, pinning your life down."

For several moments he stared off into space and then hung his head, tears welling in his eyes.

"You see it?" she asked.

Robin nodded as tears dripped down his cheeks.

"Good," she said. "And now I want you to imagine yourself differently, acting differently, thinking differently, a young man with a purpose to his life, dedicated to the greater good. And I want you to believe that gradually, step by step, action by action, the weight on that beam will begin to shift and then come into balance, or better."

"I don't know what I'd do to deserve that," Robin choked. "Balance."

She took the boy's left hand in hers, saying, "It doesn't matter what you deserve at this moment. You just have to be willing to try to head down the right path. If you do, I promise you that God will show you the way."

*

At one point during that long night, Monarch roused and saw Sister Rachel there sleeping in the chair by his bed. The sight of her keeping watch over him was enough to eliminate any anxiety on his part, and he'd fallen back into a deep, dreamless sleep.

When he awoke again it was broad daylight, and he was surprised to see that Sister Rachel had left and Gloria Barnett had taken her place in the chair.

"You're an early bird," he said.

"I just wanted to say Merry Christmas before I left," Barnett said. "I promised my brother I'd make an appearance this year."

"Have fun," Monarch said, feeling the cobwebs clear. "That crazy aunt of yours going to be there?"

"I've been assured Aunt Lilly is banned from the time zone," Barnett said.

Monarch reached over and pressed the bed control to raise him more upright. He still felt weak, but also cleaner somehow, as if the poisons had drained during the night.

"What exotic locale will I be calling after you leave your brother's place?" he asked.

"I'm thinking Fiji," Barnett said.

Barnett had a condo in Boston, but was rarely there; she preferred to spend her time off at luxury spas in lush tropical settings.

"Enjoy," he said when she got up.

"As much as one can in Mobile, Alabama."

"Drink heavily."

Barnett laughed as she moved toward the door, said, "That's a thought."

When she'd gone, Monarch was left to the silence. He gingerly palpated the area around his wound, and was relieved to find that the pain had ebbed to a low throb. He *was* healing.

Sister Rachel came in then and fussed around him, checking his vitals.

"You're getting stronger," she said. "And no sign of infection now."

"That's good."

"It is good," she said, and then put her hand on his arm. "I have a present for you."

"Isn't that supposed to be tomorrow?"

"I tried to have them wait until then, but they insisted."

"They?"

The missionary doctor lifted her head, called out, "You can come in now."

Monarch was surprised when fifteen of the orphans came trooping into his room, and formed a semicircle around the foot of his bed. He recognized two of the kids right off, Juan and Antonio, boys he'd brought to Sister Rachel nearly two years before. Both of them had grown several inches and put on twenty pounds. They grinned at him.

"What is this?" he asked.

"Your Christmas concert, Senor Robin," Juan said.

The orphans broke into "Feliz Navidad" and made Monarch beam with delight. Their version of "Silent Night" nearly broke his heart. And when they finished with "Rudolph the Red-Nosed Reindeer" in Spanish he laughed so hard he thought he was going to bust a stitch.

"You like it, Robin?" Antonio asked as Monarch clapped.

He looked at Sister Rachel and then back at the children, said, "I think that may be the best Christmas present I've ever gotten."

11

CHRISTMAS EVE MORNING CAME cold and clear. A steady northerly breeze was blowing when seven mallard ducks set their wings and floated in through the canopy of the flooded oaks on the backside of Beau Arsenault's sprawling plantation. The mogul crouched in the water against the base of a big tree, his black Labrador, Malthus, beside him shivering with anticipation.

"Take 'em now," he growled.

Arsenault's son-in-law and his eleven-year-old grandson raised their shotguns and fired. His son-in-law missed twice. The boy dropped one mallard drake and missed the second.

The billionaire threw his Benelli autoloader to his shoulder, thought about the goddamned thief who ripped him off for twenty million to give to fucking poor orphans, and imagined the man was each and every one of the other ducks. He blew three out of the sky with three shots. The birds plummeted, splashed out in the decoys.

"Malthus, fetch," Arsenault said, satisfied. "Fetch 'em up."

The dog exploded off the stand and swam toward the fallen birds.

"Nice shooting, Beau," his son-in-law said.

"Nothing you couldn't do with a little more practice, Peter. I'm thinking your boy there is a better shot than you."

Peter was in his mid-thirties and shot his father-in-law a withering glance, muttered, "Always something."

"We limit out, Big Beau?" asked his grandson, who was shivering.

"You cold, Little Beau?"

"My toes some," the boy admitted.

"Yeah, you and I are done," he said. "Your daddy's still got three left."

"I'll wait," his grandson said.

"Nonsense," the mogul said. "I'll take you in, and your daddy can come back in with Cecil and Hank. Get you some of Big Mama's hot, spiced cider. That good with you, Peter?"

"I'm done," his son-in-law said.

"Nonsense," Arsenault said. "You finish up. Hear?"

Peter's jaw set, as if he were going to argue, but the mogul beat him to the punch, saying, "I'll leave you another box of fours in case you run out."

He turned to end the discussion, glanced at the two African American men in hunting gear sitting in one of two green johnboats floating back there behind them forty yards. "Cecil, you call for Mr. Peter, here? When he's limited out, you pull the set, make sure Malthus is dried and fed, and then you go looking for a place we can hunt day after tomorrow."

"Yes, sir, Mr. Beau," Cecil said.

"When you get back, you come up to the house, Miss Louisa's got something for you and your families for Christmas."

Both men smiled, and Cecil climbed out of the boat to help Arsenault and his grandson case their guns. Then the mogul hoisted Little Beau into the other johnboat, and climbed in after him. He pulled the anchor, started the outboard, and swung them away toward the slough bottom and the bayou. As he did, the bow crossed the image of his son-in-law glaring at him.

Arsenault nodded to him, thinking, *It'll do the little Jewish prick some good to understand he's still just a pussy.*

Peter Solomon was everything the billionaire didn't like in a man. He was liberal, an academic, and the outdoors made him uncomfortable. Worse, his income was a joke. He made a little over sixty grand a year as a history professor at Northwestern, far from enough to support his oldest daughter and his oldest grandson in the style an Arsenault should expect.

But Sophia loved Peter, so the mogul had set up a trust that kicked them an extra three hundred K a year. Funny how feeding a man, clothing a man, putting a roof over a man's head day after day, year after year makes him beholden, submissive, willing to stand in freezing cold water for hours on end if his benefactor says so.

Arsenault chuckled.

Then he thought about his interlude with Cassie Knox the afternoon before, how her cocoa buns had looked when he'd been behind her and—

"Big Beau?" his grandson yelled over the drone of the outboard. He was sitting up front, looking back. They'd reached the bayou's main channel.

"What's that?" Arsenault replied, turning them south.

"Santa coming tonight?"

"You know he is. Packing his sleigh right now."

Little Beau looked concerned. "I can't figure out how he lands that sleigh of his down south with no snow."

Understanding he was now navigating tricky waters, Arsenault hesitated before saying, "Teflon runners. They're nonskid. Land and slide on anything."

"Oh," his grandson said, before turning to face the front.

The mogul smiled as he rounded a bend in the bayou and

saw the plantation home he and Louisa had built after Katrina destroyed the old one. Though barely two years old, Twelve Oaks looked like it had been put together in the mid-eighteen hundreds, with a long low veranda facing the water and upper balconies with iron railings that wrapped the entire second floor of the mansion. In the windows, Christmas lights and candles glowed. Louisa loved the holidays and spared no expense decorating. Ever.

He pulled up to the dock, threw the lines to Little Beau, and made sure his knots were sound. Then he carried the guns and walked with the boy up the slight grade to a smaller structure known as the "shooting house."

"You keep practicing, Grandpa will take you down to Argentina next year," Arsenault said. "See ducks by the thousands."

"That true?" Little Beau said.

"Swear on my mama's grave," the mogul said.

"Dad come?"

Arsenault hesitated, but then thought of his son-in-law forced to be outside in a duck blind for six or seven days, and said, "Sure, he can come if he can get away from the classroom."

They went into the shooting house and sat before lockers just off the main room that featured trophies Arsenault had taken over a lifetime of hunting around the world. He and his grandson stripped out of the heavy jackets and muddy waders, set them out for Cecil and Hank to scrub and dry, and put the guns in the rack for Cecil and Hank to clean and oil. They took hot showers and got dressed in dry clothes, and walked together across the lawn to the main house.

There was a small army of cooks working in the kitchen under the watchful eye of his wife who was drinking coffee with their daughter, Sophia.

"Mom, I limited out!" Little Beau cried.

Arsenault's daughter smiled and threw her arms wide. Sophia

had his wife's dark, timeless beauty, the kind that could *easily* have attracted a man with much deeper pockets. But the mogul threw away that thought and said, "You'd a been proud of how the boy handled that gun, sight better than his daddy."

His daughter held Little Beau, asked, "Where is Dad?"

"Still out in the timber," her son said.

"Wanted to fill his limit," Arsenault said. "Be back with Cecil and Hank."

"You're cruel, you know that, Dad?" Sophia said.

"What are you talking about?" the mogul said, suppressing a smile. "Peter only gets out once or twice a year."

"Big Beau said I keep practicing he'll take me to Argentina next year," his grandson said. "Dad, too."

"Oh, Dad'll love that," Sophia said, rolling her eyes.

Wanting to change the subject, Arsenault looked to his wife, said, "I think Little Beau's got his heart set on some of your hot spiced cider, Big Mama."

His wife looked to one of the cooks, who nodded.

"When's everybody else getting in?" the mogul asked.

"Saunders called. He's on his way from the airport," Louisa said. "Everyone else is still flying, figuring to be here midafternoon or so."

"I've got a few things to finish up in my office before then."

His wife hardened. "It's Christmas Eve, Ebenezer."

"Just got to finish up a few things in the counting house," he replied.

Arsenault started out of the kitchen, but stopped close to Louisa, leaned over, and said quietly, "Cecil and Hank are coming up for their Christmas bonus. You put a thousand in a card for each of them? Throw in a spiral ham?"

"That too much?" she asked.

"Those boys work hard," he said. "Put us on a great hunt this morning."

She shrugged. "Your money."

"Yeah, it is," he said. "Tell Saunders to come straight up to see me soon as he gets in?"

His wife nodded, but she was watching the cook set a piping mug before her grandson.

"There," Louisa said. "Big Mama's spiced cider. Just like you like it."

Arsenault left the kitchen, wandered through the gorgeously decorated house, wondering how his wife had managed to pull it all off in such short order. Then again that woman was a force of nature.

He climbed the stairs to the second floor, went to his home office, and shut the door. Going to his computer, the mogul called up an e-mail account, and a file marked "Future Ideas."

Arsenault believed that the smart man never rested on his laurels, and therefore never got fat and lazy. To that end, he had a slew of sources, some paid in cash, others in favors, who pushed the billionaire the most up-to-date information possible about every conceivable investment opportunity. He read through the file nearly every day, evaluating the latest private intelligence reports, the most recent secret corporate developments, and other insider tips he could use to improve his bottom line. Sadly, there weren't many new e-mails in the file today, and all of them sounded like shitty deals to him.

He was closing down his computer when a knock came at the door. Billy Saunders, his security chief, came in, said, "Merry Christmas, Beau. You want your present now or in the morning?"

Arsenault grinned. "You got him?"

"That's why I flew down. I wanted to talk to you about this face-to-face."

Arsenault sobered, focused.

Saunders said, "I didn't get much, but I know who he is. Or

who he used to be anyway. Army Special Forces, then CIA for eight years, black ops, stealing state secrets, that kind of stuff. But he resigned and disappeared three years ago. His name is—"

"Robin Monarch," the billionaire said in shock.

Saunders's head retreated. "You know him?"

"I know *of* him," Arsenault said, becoming angry with himself.

"How?"

The mogul didn't tell his security man everything. That just wouldn't do. There were certain actions he kept to himself, and would continue to keep secret. He gave Saunders the heavily edited version.

"As I understand it, Monarch rescued Agnes Lawton last year."

Saunders was surprised to hear that. "I knew he stole the Iraqi battle plan before we invaded, but I didn't know that he . . . wait, I thought SEAL Team Six got Lawton."

"The SEALs were involved, but it was Monarch who tracked down the kidnappers and led the rescue," Arsenault insisted. "President Sands paid him millions to do it. Agnes told me so herself. That's not to leave this room by the way. It's evidently a national security secret."

"Of course not," Saunders said, sounding offended. "I wouldn't say a thing. But why would Monarch target you of all people? And how did he know about the vault, and the security, and the money?"

"You're my fucking head of security," Arsenault snapped. "You tell me."

Still, those were all good questions, all very good questions, but many of the answers that came to Arsenault were not very good at all. His anger flared again. He'd suspected thirteen months ago that Monarch might be a problem, a threat. Thirteen months ago, he'd even thought to have the man eliminated.

69

But life had simply gotten in the way, and Arsenault hadn't carried through on his instincts. Now he was paying for it. Monarch had targeted him, violated him, and ripped him off.

But why?

Twenty million dollars was a good enough reason, the mogul supposed.

But what if it was more than that? What if Monarch had been looking for evidence? That last thought stirred up Arsenault's stomach worse than a crawfish boil. Had there been anything in the vault that would doom him? Other than the undeclared valuables there was nothing. He was sure of it. Would they send someone like Monarch in to look around at his hidden assets? He couldn't see it.

But Robin Monarch *had* slipped into his house, drugged him, and stolen him blind. Not some other thief. *The thief.*

"Do you want me to find him, Beau?" Saunders asked.

"What do you think?"

"I don't have much to go on. I didn't actually see a file on him."

For a few moments, Arsenault debated how much he could or should reveal to Saunders. A part of him wanted to say nothing more, but he felt he had no choice now.

"I've seen an edited file on him," the mogul said at last.

Saunders looked surprised again. "How's that?"

"Agnes showed me a redacted dossier on him. After she told me the details of her rescue, I became fascinated by the idea that a thief could have pulled off something like that. I expressed my interest and the secretary, an old and dear family friend, showed me the file on him."

"What did it say?"

The billionaire rocked back in his chair, wanting to open a copy of the file on his computer to refresh his memory. But

Saunders would see the file and that was unacceptable. Instead, he told his security chief what he remembered clearly.

Monarch was the son of an Argentine con artist mother and an American cat burglar father. When he was twelve or thirteen, his parents were murdered outside a movie theater in Buenos Aires after they'd swindled relatives of the Peron family. The boy escaped into the slums. To survive he became a member of a street gang. Monarch still carried the gang's tattoo on his inner right forearm. FDL, La Fraternidad de Ladrones, the Brotherhood of Thieves.

Little was known about the years Monarch spent in the gang. But just before he turned nineteen he appeared out of nowhere in Miami, enlisted at an Army recruit station, excelled, went to Rangers, and onward and upward. Monarch ran a JSOC unit, an elite command of special forces operators from all branches of the U.S. military, before his criminal behavior during a classified mission got him a court-martial and put him in Leavenworth Penitentiary. It was supposed to be a fifteen-year sentence, but Monarch was offered his freedom less than a year later in return for stealing the Iraqi war plan.

The mogul knew very little about Monarch's activities during his subsequent stint with the CIA. That part of the file had been heavily redacted.

"I do know he became disillusioned with the agency about three years ago, and went out on his own," Arsenault said. "And he was the shadow man behind the Greenfields affair, which is what made President Sands look to him after Agnes was kidnapped."

Saunders thought about that, said, "A dangerous, resourceful man."

"Very much so," Arsenault agreed. "Which is why I want you to find out everything you can about him, especially his weaknesses, any leverage we might use to get my money back, and destroy him."

His security chief hesitated, said, "Or you could always just let it go."

The mogul snorted. "Why? Because he's accomplished? No, Billy, the way you deal with a man like Monarch is to learn him inside and out and then bring in people even more accomplished than he is."

Sounding unconvinced, Saunders said, "You have a budget in mind?"

"Money is no object. There's principle at stake."

"Okay. Where do you want me to start first? The CIA?"

Arsenault thought about that before he said, "You'd have to be Houdini to get records out of there. But something had to have happened to Monarch that made him want to leave the life of an Argentine gangbanger for the U.S. Army. And Monarch told Cassie Knox that he was stealing from me to give to orphans. My instinct says these things are all linked."

"I'll book a ticket to Buenos Aires for the day after tomorrow."

"Take the jet," the mogul said. "Tonight."

12

EVEN SISTER RACHEL WAS surprised by how far Monarch had come in the three weeks since his arrival at the Hogar d'Espera. He'd walked on Christmas Day, and stopped feeling crushed by the stroll down the hallway two days later. Though the stitch in his side continued as a nagging reminder of the bullet wound, he'd felt better each day, taking longer and longer walks in the foothills surrounding the Refuge of Hope.

Carrying a walking stick and a knapsack with water, Monarch left the orphanage's clinic around seven that morning, and went out into one of those glorious Argentina summer days. There was not a cloud in the sky. Within hours it would be blistering hot, but that early in the day there was still a cooling breeze blowing far inland off the ocean.

He intended to exit the rear of the compound, heading for a favorite trail. The voices of children stopped him. A dozen boys and girls were playing soccer on the new field. Monarch stood there awhile watching the kids stretching and doing drills, thinking once again how good it felt to give back to the place and to the person who'd saved him. All the difficult things he'd had to do in life, all the things for which he felt remorse, seemed neutralized, balanced out here.

"Are you looking at the good you've done, or waiting for me?" Sister Rachel asked.

The missionary doctor had come out wearing loose pants, running shoes, and a white long-sleeve jersey.

"Both," he said.

"What way are we going?" she asked as they headed for the rear gate.

"*El camino difícil,*" he said.

She paused, said, "The Difficult Way? Are you sure you're ready for that?"

"As sure as I was the first time I climbed it," he replied.

They went out the gate, and walked a trail that cut across the side of the steep hillside for a mile or so before coming to a junction. The main trail continued on across the face of the foothills, and the other took a precipitous route toward rock bands, outcroppings, and cliffs high above them.

"How are you feeling?" Sister Rachel asked as he paused.

"No rocks on my back," Monarch reminded her, and started his ascent.

The path was stony, friable, and climbed nearly straight up the face of the hill. Within fifty yards, he felt the stitch in his side grow, and sweat break out on his forehead. With every step he flashed on that first time up the Difficult Way.

"What good have you done today?" Sister Rachel had asked Robin as they started that first climb.

She'd brought Robin to the refuge from the slum clinic after he'd agreed to try to change his life. When he was physically able, she'd made him fill a knapsack full of rocks and forced him out on hikes, just the two of them, short at first, and then longer and more difficult.

Robin asked her repeatedly why it was necessary—the rocks, the weight—and she'd just given him the same answer: "Doctor's orders."

And now this question: "What good have you done today?"

Robin was not used to thinking in this manner. His parents had flaunted laws, and gone so far as to say that the rules did not apply to people who were crafty enough. He'd followed the eighteen rules of La Fraternidad de Ladrones up to a point. But he'd always been willing to bend the bylaws of the Brotherhood of Thieves to suit his purposes. He understood right and wrong, of course, but always managed to justify being on the wrong side of the law.

Sister Rachel's question, though, it wasn't a rule, and it wasn't a law. But it definitely annoyed him. *What good have you done today?*

"I fixed the kids' football," Robin said grunting with effort. This was the steepest climb she'd taken him on yet. "That's a good act, right? I patched the bladder and sewed the skin myself."

"Now we're heading in the right direction," the missionary doctor said, puffing behind him. "How did you feel doing it?"

Robin thought about that, shrugged, said, "I was just helping them, I dunno, just doing something that they couldn't."

"Right, but how did it make you feel inside?"

Over the years he'd spent inside the street gang, Robin had rarely talked about his emotions. Being a member of *la fraternidad* was all about skill, strength, and street smarts. Claudio had taught him to hide his feelings deep, especially if they suggested weakness. Now, however, Sister Rachel seemed determined to open up everything he'd been taught to close off.

"I don't know," he said, frustrated at all these questions she asked.

"Did you watch the children play with the ball?"

He stopped, gasping, staring up the hill and wondering if he could make it to the top.

"Robin?"

"Yes, I watched them play," he said, irritated.

"Close your eyes, then. See them playing, and tell me what you felt."

Robin realized he'd felt good, real good, and when he reexperienced the feeling in his mind there on the steep hillside he started to smile.

"There," Sister Rachel said. "That sensation. Do you know what it is?"

He opened his eyes and shook his head.

"It's selflessness," she replied. "It's putting others before yourself. It's time spent in service, not being served. Every time you do something like that you will feel that emotion, which is very close to the strongest emotion of all, which is love."

"Okay?" Robin said, climbing on and feeling confused all over again. No one had ever spoken to him like this.

"I want you to keep track of when you have that feeling and why," Sister Rachel said. "Every time it happens, I want you to write in your journal describing what you did to deserve it."

"Oh, c'mon, Sister," he groaned. "This isn't part of the deal. I mean, I left *la fraternidad,* isn't that enough? What's the point of all this?"

She did not reply, and stayed silent the rest of the brutal climb. An hour and twenty minutes after they'd started, the trail climbed a staircase of stone, crossed a shelf of rock and joined another trail in a T.

There was a wooden bench there. It was autumn and there was enough of a breeze blowing that Sister Rachel had to push back strands of unruly hair when she sat and took in the view. Buenos Aires stretched out below them. Dusk was fast approaching and the first lights were coming on. Robin shrugged off the knapsack, dropped it in the grass.

"Why am I carrying the rocks?" he asked.

Not looking at him, Sister Rachel said, "The rocks represent your sins, Robin. God's laws you have broken. The things you have stolen. All of it."

With that shocking news, she got up, walked to the knapsack and opened it. She reached in, rooted around, and came up with a stone about the size of an egg. She leaned back and whipped the rock off into the gathering darkness.

"You earned that by helping with the soccer ball," she said. "You will lighten your load with every good deed. Do you understand?"

Twenty years later, Monarch could still hear her voice ringing in his head when he finally reached that shelf of rock and sat on that very same bench, soaked to the skin, and feeling weaker than he'd anticipated. Sister Rachel sat beside him and he realized that she was getting older, less vigorous.

"What will happen to the refuge?" he asked. "I mean, when you're gone?"

The missionary pivoted her head, looked at him in annoyance, said, "I'll have you know I can climb the Difficult Way in half the time you just took."

"I know," Monarch said, feeling his heart rate finally slow. "I'm just thinking about the future. No matter what happens, your work needs to go on, right?"

She appraised him as if seeing him from a new perspective, said, "Yes. You're right. I don't like to think about it, but I should make my wishes known."

"What about that land to the north of here?" he asked.

Sister Rachel cocked her head, sighed. "I asked what it would cost to buy it. The landowner said six million."

"How big is it?"

"Nearly nineteen acres," she said.

"Counter at five million, and tell him there will be no financing involved," Monarch said. "Offer him a million dollars down payment. The remaining money will come in increments of two hundred and fifty thousand dollars four times a year for the next four years."

"But where am I getting that money?"

"From this last mission," Monarch said.

"And what did you do to earn the money?"

He lied, said, "It's classified, but I will say that the man at the center of the mission deserved everything he got."

Sister Rachel sat there several moments, her chin quivering before she hugged him and kissed him on the cheek, said, "You are a very good person, Robin Monarch."

Monarch bowed his head slightly, felt embarrassed, but hugged her back, and said, "I had an excellent teacher."

"Sister!" a boy called.

Monarch and the missionary doctor parted to see Juan running up the easier path.

"What's happened?" Sister Rachel called.

He stopped, hands on his thighs, breathing hard, said, "Someone smashed the windows and broke into the offices at the Refuge last night. They need you to come quick. The police are on the way."

13

CHICAGO
FIVE DAYS LATER . . .

BEAU ARSENAULT TIGHTENED HIS tie and gazed in the mirror at Cassie Knox, who lay on her side, back turned under the sheets in the Ritz-Carlton suite.

The color of her skin still amazed him, like nutmeg, cocoa, and a hint of cayenne. But ever since their brief "discussion" two days before Christmas, there'd been little to no enthusiasm for the mogul's chocolate fetish. Indeed, just now she'd lain there like a fallen soufflé while he pumped away, and grew angrier with her with each thrust.

This was the way he liked things, actually. In Arsenault's perfect world, the "protégée" came to him for mentoring and financial support, and he feasted on her dark flesh. When the protégée stopped knowing her place, the relationship in all its aspects ended. The billionaire very much enjoyed the cycle of finding a young woman of color in need of a rung up, providing it, and then pulling it away when he was bored. He'd been doing it for years, and it never failed to satisfy.

Cassie Knox, he thought, was about to feel the long drop.

"Good-bye," he said, and started toward the door.

"I'm on tour next week," Knox called after him.

"I'd heard that," he replied. "I'll let you know."

Arsenault did not wait for her response, left the suite, and strode toward the elevator with a renewed sense of anticipation. In the coming weeks, he'd witness the collapse of the once-promising young singer, and then grow excited as he cruised far and wide, looking for his next chocolate treat.

In the elevator, the billionaire checked his watch. It was just past five. He had time for a glass of bourbon before meeting Sophia, her dick of a husband, and Little Beau at the airport for a long weekend trip to the Telluride chalet. Though he looked forward to seeing his grandson, the thought of his son-in-law's prattling on the flight set Arsenault on edge.

The elevator opened. He stepped out, headed toward the bar.

"Beau?"

The mogul looked to his right and saw a tanned Billy Saunders hurrying across the lobby toward him, a big smile on his face.

"I hope good came of nearly three weeks in sunny Argentina," Arsenault said.

"A whole lot of good," Saunders replied.

The billionaire looked over at the entrance to the bar, and rejected it out of hand.

"Tell me on the drive to the airport," the billionaire said, and together they left the hotel, waited out front for the limousine to come around.

When they were rolling and the window between them and the chauffer had been raised, the security chief filled Arsenault in on everything he'd managed to discover.

"As you suspected," Saunders said, "there was a connection between Monarch's mysterious past and the orphans. Her name is Sister Rachel Diego del Mar. She's a missionary and doctor in the slums down there. She evidently saved his life when he was a gangbanger, turned him around."

The security chief explained about the clinic, and the orphanage in the foothills, both of which had become much larger in the past three years. He also described documents found in the orphanage office that detailed large anonymous gifts Sister Rachel had received in those same three years.

"You're saying Monarch paid for it all by ripping off guys like me?" Arsenault asked, already fuming at the idea.

"Or saving the secretary of state," Saunders said.

"Where is he?"

Handing the mogul an iPad, the security chief said, "At the orphanage recuperating from the bullet Louisa put in him. We got several pictures of him."

"We?"

"Let's just say Monarch has enemies."

Arsenault got irritated. He believed in situations like this the fewer people involved the better. On the other hand, a man's enemy was by nature his ally.

The mogul took the tablet, looked at some long-range shots of a big man climbing a steep hillside, with an older woman in tow. He swiped the screen with a finger, moving the pictures ahead, until there was a close-up of Monarch leaving the front gate of the orphanage with four or five kids, a soccer ball, and a broad smile on his face.

"That's him," the billionaire said. "That's the guy who darted us."

They were pulling into a private jet facility at Midway International on Chicago's south side. His grandson was standing outside, waving wildly. Arsenault's heart melted. God, he loved that boy.

"What do you want us to do?" Saunders asked. "From the looks of it, another couple of weeks or so and Monarch could be fully recovered. There's a strong argument to be made of taking him out right there, while he's in a weakened condition."

Little Beau was coming up to the car now.

The mogul said, "The bonds?"

Saunders's face fell. "Still don't know. This Sister Rachel hasn't gotten any of it yet, anyway."

The door opened and Arsenault's grandson cried, "Big Mama just called, said there's a storm heading for Telluride. There'll be fifteen inches by morning."

"Powder day!" the billionaire cried, climbing from the limo into a raw January wind and picking up the boy to hug him. "We better get moving then."

"Dad's not coming," Little Beau said when his grandfather had set him down. "His knee hurts."

"That's an awful shame," Arsenault said, hiding his relief.

After he greeted his daughter and they boarded the Gulfstream, strapped in, and took off, he went to the small cabin office at the rear of the jet while Sophia, Saunders, and Little Beau ate takeout ribs. It had been a long day already, with a meeting with his Treasury futures traders in the bond pits at the Chicago Board of Trade, and another with the executives of a major grain distributor he was thinking of buying. But he opened his laptop and the file that held the investment tips, reports, and proposals that had accumulated over the course of the prior day.

Arsenault's mind wandered briefly to the issue of Robin Monarch and the missing twenty million dollars, but then he summoned up his legendary discipline and forced himself to compartmentalize. Going through the file was not a trivial task. His father had taught him as a young man that it was easier to make money off other people's developed ideas than it was to imagine and refine your own. It had made him a billionaire many, many times over, and he never forgot it.

The mogul brought laserlike intensity to each and every item in the file, gauging the likelihood of potential future profits with only a few minutes of study. Like a nurse performing triage, he was filtering, looking for the most intriguing, the most promising, the most visionary. In the first half hour, he read and discarded a proposal to invest in a hemp gin in Saskatchewan that claimed to turn the fiber of the marijuana stalk into a fabric tougher and softer than cotton.

While some men might have jumped at the idea, Arsenault dismissed it. To the mogul's way of thinking you never wanted to extend the life of a product, not if you wanted to make any real money with it. Real money required products that were consumed, like oil, gas, food, and drugs; or products that had a limited lifetime, guaranteed obsolescence, like cell phones and computers. A shirt that wore like iron was nothing but a money loser in the long run.

The billionaire wanted investments where people's needs were being met, but not so fully as to keep the customer coming back for more and often. Sadly, however, there was nothing like that in the next six proposals he considered and discarded.

At first glance, the eighth concept didn't fit within his parameters either. But as Arsenault read, he found himself intrigued, and then curious.

The mogul checked the source twice. It was reputable enough. And the man who'd sent the tip along had been a moneymaker in the past. Arsenault reread the entire package again, realizing that there were aspects of it that were inconclusive. The raw data seemed intriguing, but the reasons behind the data were unknown. That was a problem in his opinion. Arsenault liked understanding the reason for innovation, whether it was the engineering or the discovery of— A light knock came at the cabin door.

"Grandpa's still working, Little Beau," the billionaire growled.

"It's Billy."

Arsenault hated getting interrupted almost as much as he hated multitasking. He'd run his life that way for more than thirty-five years, bringing intense focus to everything in his path, one at a time, making a decision about it, and then moving on.

But he took his eyes off the screen and said, "Come in."

Saunders entered, shut the door, and said, "Have you decided what you want done with Monarch?"

The mogul was about to tell him he had not, when an odd thought dawned on him. He glanced at the screen again, feeling the inkling of possibility unfold into a course of profitable action as effortlessly as one of Louisa's beloved honeysuckles budding and blooming on the vine.

"You know, Billy," Arsenault said, feeling a wickedly pleasant sensation build in his gut and at the back of his head, a good sign if there ever was one. "I just might have found a way to kill a bird with two stones, and make a shitload of money doing it."

14

EL CAZADOR, THE HUNTER, slipped from the car two full hours before first light. He padded down a familiar dirt road, and skirted a farmyard so as not to rouse the dogs that lived there. Beyond the farm, he took to the ditch and walked it to a culvert.

The hunter crawled through, and emerged on the other side of a ten-foot fence that surrounded a grove of almonds and olives higher up the hill. He moved steadily in the darkness and the shadows, thankful for the thin light of the waxing moon, and the rain that had fallen earlier, and now deadened his footsteps.

At the top of the rise, El Cazador looked to his right, downhill, and over a mud-brick wall into the compound. He moved diagonally until he found a spot in the roots of an ancient olive tree that suited his purposes. He dropped his knapsack, drank coffee from a thermos, and then settled in to wait for sunrise.

The hunter tried to be patient, tried to be calm. But after so many years, it was almost impossible to control his excitement and desire. He could feel them like energies swirling around him. At long last, he believed he was going to get his revenge.

*

85

Monarch woke up long before dawn, and couldn't go back to sleep.

It wasn't the pain in his right side. That all but disappeared a week before, shortly after he'd left Sister Rachel's care for the relative freedom of Claudio's apartment. No, it was the break-in at the offices of the Refuge of Hope that bothered him enough to keep him tossing and turning in Claudio's guest room.

The Buenos Aires police had decided that one of the older orphans had probably done the deed. Monarch remained unconvinced. After the uniformed officers had gone through the scene and left, he'd done the same, but with a criminal's eye for detail.

The window was broken with a piece of tree branch they'd found lying in the glass. Drawers had been opened. Files had been replaced haphazardly. But after the office staff had inspected them there seemed to be nothing amiss. Sister Rachel had checked the orphanage's safe where she kept the operating cash, and found nothing gone.

Monarch could not determine whether the refuge's computer security system had been breached, and again, the office staff said nothing seemed to be out of the ordinary as far as they could see.

So what had the intruder been after?

That question had nagged at him for the past two weeks. There was always a reason for a break-in. At Watergate, political operatives had been after political secrets. In most urban home invasions, drugs and drug addiction were behind the forced entry and theft. One of the older kids might have done it for a thrill, a statement of rebellion against the strict rules Sister Rachel enforced on the orphanage grounds. But this burglary didn't feel like that. Rebellious teens break things, and everything looked intact. Maybe things had been copied?

Knowing he wasn't going to get any rest, Monarch got up, put on clothes, and went out into the hall. He wasn't surprised to see bright lights glowing at the other end. Shielding his eyes, he went into Claudio's painting studio, which occupied the majority of the apartment's living space. His oldest and dearest friend had headphones on, a pair of shorts, and flip-flops.

Naked from the waist up, Claudio faced one canvas painted yellow and another blue. The artist made whipping motions with paintbrushes that stuck out between the fingers of both hands. The paint spattered over the yellow canvas: greens, and purples, oranges, whites, and reds, all of it creating a riot of color that suggested to Monarch the sky and the wildflowers that bloomed in the spring above the Hogar de Espera.

Seeing his genius friend caught up in the creation of his art, and not wanting to destroy it, Monarch backed out, got shoes, and gathered a few items before slipping out. He got Claudio's BMW motorcycle from the garage, and drove out into the night.

Though he saw no solid evidence he was being tailed, Monarch went on instinct and training. He performed several tight and quick changes of course, watching his back-trail, before heading back toward the refuge.

He pulled off the paved road a full mile beyond the orphanage, drove up a dirt two-track, and hid the bike behind some brush. Then he cut uphill and at an angle, pushing through scrub oak, operating by feel and the faint light the setting moon afforded.

Monarch wanted to be up high when the sun rose. He took the Difficult Way, ascending the steep, rocky face at a steady pace, still straining in the worst spots, but happy that his wind was definitely coming back. An hour after he left the motorcycle, the thief reached the bench. He eased down on it, happy for the sweat that made him shiver in the cool air and kept him wide awake.

The first light of dawn came soon enough.

The thief picked up the pack and kept a low profile as he scuttled forward to a position in the rocks where he'd soon be able to look down into the compound and the terrain and buildings all around it for a mile or more. Ever since the break-in, he'd been unable to shake the sense that the orphanage and the children were threatened, or being watched anyway.

He dug in the knapsack, and came up with a pair of Leica Geovid binoculars, his preferred long-range optic. Pressing the ten power glasses to his eyes, he started scanning the entire area, using a grid pattern to control the search.

In the gathering light, he picked up goats feeding on the land that Sister Rachel wanted to buy. Beyond the front gate, to the east, the road that came up from the city was sparsely traveled. A farm truck went by. A bus followed it. And then nothing.

Monarch swung the glasses toward a cluster of modest houses to the southwest, seeing a girl outside feeding chickens and a man chopping wood. Panning the glasses west, he peered into the few open spots in a grove of almond and olive trees that bordered the orphanage's south wall.

Slowly, methodically, as the dawn glow strengthened he dissected the shadows between the trees, looked for a silhouette against the dirt. He'd almost given up, when he caught something moving. It could have been an animal, the back end of a cow, but in Monarch's mind it registered as a man's torso and shoulders.

The thief again dug in the pack and this time extracted a 20-40-by-60 Leica spotting scope and a carbon fiber tripod. He trained the scope at twenty power into the gap in the trees where he thought he'd seen movement. For almost fifteen minutes, there was nothing but the fluttering of doves coming off their roost. Then the sun rose above the ocean's horizon and sent the first powerful beams of light across the city to the foothills.

The man moved a second time, showed his head.

There you are, Monarch thought. Now *who* are you?

Monarch dialed the knob, took the scope up to forty power.

It took him a few slight adjustments before the picture in the lens cleared, and from three quarters of a mile away he saw the man turn his head, revealing a deformed left ear.

"What the fuck?" the thief muttered.

It had been nearly twenty years, but he knew the man in an instant. Monarch had thought him long dead. But there was no mistaking that ear. Something acidic churned in his gut.

He put the binoculars and scope away, threw the knapsack on his back, and got up in a crouch. He scuttled off angle to where he'd been perched, moving around the side of the hill where he couldn't be seen or heard from the almond grove, and then made a scrambled descent that left him gulping wind in a brushy draw just above the orphanage.

He heard a car start, and drive away somewhere below him. He snuck forward, smelling wood smoke, and using the binoculars again to scan the almond grove, now less than two hundred yards away. Nothing moved. Nothing stood out.

Monarch risked being seen when he darted across a small meadow into the grove, but then slowed to a crawl when the terrain began to climb. He looked up at the cliff where he'd used the scope, performed rudimentary triangulations, and spotted the gnarled olive tree on the lip of the rise. But there was no one beneath it now.

Boot prints showed all around the tree. The thief circled the area until he cut the prints heading toward the road where he'd heard the car start. It had been more than twenty years since he'd seen the man. What the hell is he doing alive and here?

Before the thief could ponder this unexpected development further, he felt his cell buzz, alerting him to a text. It came from Gloria Barnett, said: "Call me. Possible work if you're up to it."

Monarch stood there in the grove, wondered whether he was in shape for work, then punched in the number. She answered on the third ring, said, "Switch to FaceTime."

Monarch made the switch on his iPhone, saw Barnett sitting in a chaise lounge with a tropical beach out beyond her.

"How are you?" Barnett said. "Sister Rachel says you're strong."

"Reasonably," Monarch said. "How's Fiji?"

"It was nice, but I've moved on. New Caledonia."

"You always were a trendsetter."

She laughed. "I like to think so."

"So what's this possible work?"

"Remember Sami Rafiq?"

"How could I forget?"

"He contacted me out of the blue by e-mail two hours ago. Wanting to find you."

"That's funny, because the last two times I've seen him he said he never wanted to see or talk to me again."

"Well, you did kind of fuck him over in Thailand last year," Barnett said. "And in Algeria a couple of years before that."

Sami Rafiq was a Lebanese expatriate who floated around the edges of the underworld, operating successful fabric stores while making a lucrative secret income as a first-class forger. Monarch flashed on his last memory of the man, standing in the pouring rain in southern Thailand, looking catatonic after surviving a firefight in a red-light district.

"Sami was well compensated for his troubles," Monarch replied.

"He did say that."

"You talked to him?"

"I did. He says to call him. Do it, and then call me back."

Monarch agreed, hung up, and then called the number she texted him.

"Rafiq."

"Sami? It's Monarch."

"Robin!" Rafiq cried. "So good to hear from you. I was hoping you'd call."

"What's the story? I was Rafiq enemy number one the last time I saw you."

He cleared his throat, said, "Yes, well, the money was much appreciated."

"You earned it," Monarch said. "Gloria said something about a job."

"A high-paying one, as I understand it."

"What's the target?"

"I don't know. The men who approached me wouldn't say."

The Lebanese forger said an old and trusted client reached out to him on behalf of an unnamed third party.

"They were looking for a thief," Sami said.

"To steal what?"

"I don't know, but my client said these people have deep, deep pockets, like money is no object."

Monarch thought about that, said, "Thanks, but no thanks, Sami. My targets have to be of a certain kind."

Rafiq sounded disappointed. "Don't you at least want to hear their story?"

"What's in it for you if I do?"

"A handsome finder's fee," the forger admitted.

"How much?"

"That's not your—"

"How much?"

Rafiq sighed. "One million five British pound sterling."

Monarch ran the numbers in his head. That was over two million dollars.

"Hell of a finder's fee," the thief said.

"It is," the forger agreed. "So the take's got to be big, right? Especially if you're executing a plan someone has already designed."

Rafiq was right, and despite his misgivings, Monarch was intrigued.

"Who's your client?"

"Please, I don't use names. I've never used yours."

"Fair enough," Monarch said. "How do I get in touch with him?"

"You don't," the forger said. "I was told if you were interested, the third party would ask you to meet them face-to-face."

"Where?"

"London."

Monarch thought about that, said, "And they don't know who I am?"

"They didn't want to know. All they wanted was a competent thief. I think you more than fit the bill."

"What did you tell them?"

"That you were ex–special forces, ex-CIA, and highly skilled. Did I lie?"

"Let me think about it."

"See that's the thing. There's a deadline. If you're interested, they need you to be in London tomorrow latest, and by the way, you'd be going there on their dime."

Monarch considered the proposal, ran the numbers again. Based on a five percent finder's fee, the take could be as high as thirty million dollars. Based on a fifty-fifty split, he could be looking at thirteen, fourteen million going Sister Rachel's way.

Am I ready? He supposed that depended on the challenges of the job.

And what about the man he'd seen studying the orphanage in the morning light?

"I'm not promising anything," Monarch said to the forger.

"Of course not," Rafiq said. "You look at the deal, take it, or leave it."

"I'll need a first-class round-trip ticket, and a five-star hotel in London. Coordinate it with Barnett."

"Pleasure doing business with you again," the forger said, and hung up.

A bell began to peal.

15

THE BELL HUNG FROM an ox yoke suspended on stone pillars by Sister Rachel's residence, a small cottage beneath the pines. She rang the bell three times, calling the orphans to breakfast, and was surprised when, before any of them exited the dorms, Robin Monarch came through the front gate, carrying a heavy knapsack.

As he crossed the lawn toward her, something about his troubled expression caused the missionary doctor's mind to fly back almost two decades. She saw her younger self in a heavy wool sweater, gloves, and hat following Robin up the Difficult Way on a winter day with a raw clipping wind in their faces.

By that point, six months had passed for Robin inside the Refuge of Hope, but she still was asking him that question, "What good have you done today?"

Robin told her about a chair he had repaired, and the wood he had chopped for the heat, and how he had worked with some of the younger kids on their reading.

"Very good," she said. "Your load will be that much lighter going down."

But when they reached the top, and he'd set down the pack, Robin didn't seem to feel any better when she reached into the knapsack, took a large stone and threw it away.

She said, "Something's troubling you."

He hesitated. "This knapsack isn't big enough for some rocks, Sister."

Sister Rachel considered him a long moment in the slanting winter light before saying, "Have you done big-rock things, Robin?"

Robin closed his eyes, nodded painfully, said, "The night you saved me, I killed the man who tried to kill me. His name was Julio. He was the *jefe* of *la fraternidad*."

She'd suspected as much, but had waited for him to confess.

"Was it in self-defense?" she asked finally.

"Yes, but it was a fight that I wanted to happen," he replied. "I just didn't realize he would try to kill me for real."

For several minutes she had not known how to respond, but then she did.

"Pick up your pack," she said.

"Are you going to turn me in, Sister? If you do, my parents' enemies will have me killed."

"You'll do no good rotting in a jail," the missionary doctor remembered saying. "But I think to even begin to atone for something like this, you are going to have to do something very, very good and to do it you are going to have to carry a very, very heavy load."

"You're getting me a bigger pack?" he'd asked, confused.

"No. This burden will ride on your shoulders and your shoulders alone."

"What is it?

As Sister Rachel told Robin what he had to do in atonement for murdering the leader of the Brotherhood of Thieves, she'd seen the crushing weight of the task almost buckle his knees.

"That's impossible," Robin said.

"Nothing is impossible," the missionary doctor insisted. "Not when you have the greater good on your—"

"Sister?" Monarch called out as a stream of sleepy kids stumbled from their dorms across the lawn, heading toward the dining wall. "Are you all right?"

Sister Rachel smiled, said, "Just thinking about old times, Robin. Why are you here so early? Are you feeling okay?"

"I climbed the Difficult Way this morning in record time, but I wanted to know if I'm good to fly."

Sister Rachel regarded him for a moment. "On a job?"

"Job interview."

"You're a grown, accomplished man, so I can't begin to tell you what to do with your life."

"Really?" Monarch said impishly. "You've done pretty well at it in the past."

She fought against a smile, and nodded, saying, "Okay, okay. I just . . ."

"What, Sister?"

"I worry about you, Robin. I never know when you're going to show up, and in what condition. The next time you might not be so lucky."

"I don't think this is that kind of a job," Monarch said to allay her fears.

"Really?"

"Some kind of consulting thing," he assured her.

The missionary doctor hesitated again, sure that there was something he wasn't telling her. But she said, "If you can climb with that pack, you can fly."

"Good," he said, then paused. "I'm going to have Claudio come up and stay with you while I'm gone. It shouldn't be more than a day or two."

"Claudio?" she replied. "Why?"

"It will just make me feel better," he said, and kissed her on the cheek. "In the meantime, I'd love to have breakfast with you and the kids."

96

Sister Rachel studied him as a loving mother might her grown son, and then slipped her arm through his, and said, "I think the children would love that."

Later that morning, Monarch returned to Claudio's apartment, found his old friend working on a painting of yellow flowers trembling in a breeze, and told him who he'd seen in the almond grove by the orphanage.

"Hector Vargas?" Claudio said, setting his brush down. "I thought he was dead."

"So did I," Monarch said. "But there was no mistaking that ear. Even now."

"What was Hector doing there?"

"I didn't get the chance to ask him."

"If he knew you had been staying at the Hogar, it is not a good thing."

"I'm aware of that. But why now? After all these years?"

"The man always bore a grudge," Claudio said.

"In any case, I need you to spend the next couple of nights there. Check out that almond grove at dawn."

"Where are you going to be?"

"London," Monarch said. "A job interview."

Claudio arched his brow. "You think you're ready for work?"

"Enough to entertain an offer," Monarch said.

"What's the job?"

"I don't know. But it's big money. Thirty-million-dollar take by my estimation."

Claudio whistled. "Source?"

"Unclear at the moment, but I'm going to get Barnett working on it," Monarch replied. "Take me to the airport in a couple of hours?"

Claudio glanced at his unfinished painting, said, "Sure. That will make two times this week I'll make that shitty drive."

"How's that?"

"Chanel is coming in tomorrow evening," he said.

"What about her sister?"

"She's rallied and wanted her to come."

"That will be good," Monarch said. "You going to finally ask her?"

"What are you, her older brother?"

"Sort of."

"Then the answer is . . . yes!"

"Yes?"

Claudio broke into a huge grin. "I already bought the ring."

Overjoyed, Monarch hugged his old friend and pounded him on the back, said, "I never thought I'd see the old dog on a leash."

"Don't tell anyone. I want it to be a surprise."

"Of course. How are you going to ask her?"

Claudio sobered, said, "I hadn't gotten that far yet."

"You'll figure it out," Monarch said, and hugged him again.

The thief went to his room to pack. Barnett called on FaceTime.

"You're all set," she said by way of greeting. "I'm forwarding your flight and hotel details to you now. These guys are deep pockets. They're sending a private jet and putting you up at One Aldwych."

"Who rented the plane?" he asked.

"I was about to look into that," she said.

"While you're at it, check into a guy named Hector Vargas. He's Argentine, mid-forties, has long rap sheet, and is supposed to be dead."

"Okay," she said slowly. "What makes you think he's alive?"

"I saw him this morning under unusual circumstances."

"And who's this Vargas to you?"

"One of the ten people most likely to try to kill me on any given day."

"Oh. In that case, I'll get right on it."

"Appreciate that," he said.

"I'm here to please," she said, and signed off.

At three that afternoon, Monarch and Claudio left the apartment and got in the artist's ancient white Toyota Land Cruiser.

"When are you going to join the twenty-first century and get something with a little fury under the hood," Monarch asked as they pulled out into traffic heading toward Avenue Bartolomé Mitre.

Claudio sniffed in his general direction after making the left-hand turn onto the wide avenue, heading north. "Who needs fury in a car? I just need it to go anywhere I need it to go. This fills the need, and will always—"

A black BMW came screaming up alongside the Land Cruiser, Monarch's side.

The thief glanced right, and saw the ventilated barrel and hooded front sight of an automatic weapon swing out the rear left passenger window

The man moving the gun had a shaved head and a deformed ear.

Hector Vargas in the flesh.

16

BEFORE VARGAS COULD PULL the trigger, Monarch reached over, grabbed the steering wheel of the Land Cruiser, and wrenched it hard toward him.

"What the—!" Claudio roared just before the front right bumper of the heavy Toyota slammed into the side of the BMW, hurling it off course.

The gunman opened fire.

A two-second burst raked the rear passenger window and blew out through the ceiling and roof before the BMW smacked sideways off a parked car. It caromed. Its rear end slung out into the road.

"Get us the hell out of here!" Monarch roared. "It's Hector!"

Claudio stomped on the gas, started to weave violently and expertly through traffic. "There's a forty-five under your seat," he grunted. "Use it."

Monarch reached under the seat just as Vargas opened fire again, blowing out the rear window and spraying the interior with glass. The thief got the pistol, an old Remington 1911, flipped the safety, and spun around and up onto his knees in the passenger seat. The moment the BMW's windshield came up in his sights, he touched off two shots. The bullets threw spiderwebs dead center of the windshield and caused the driver to swerve hard to his left.

Claudio dodged across traffic as the road passed under the

elevated highway. The BMW lurched back, got sideswiped, but managed to hold the road. Monarch saw Vargas trying to get his gun out the rear right passenger window. The thief fired another two shots, driving the gunman back inside.

Downshifting, Claudio blew through a red light and drifted them hard left through the intersection with Manuel Esteban. The BMW tried the same move and almost pulled it off before Monarch shot a fifth time, hitting the front right tire.

Vargas's car spun off the road, through a bank of newspaper boxes and across a sidewalk before striking the front of a cheese shop and shattering the front window.

Looking out the gaping hole where the rear window used to be, seeing Vargas and one of his men struggling from the vehicle, Monarch said, "Go back."

"Not a chance," Claudio snapped and hit the gas. "We want to be long gone when the cops come."

The thief wanted to argue, but then agreed when he saw two police cars skid to a halt and train guns on Vargas and his men.

"Cops got them," he said as his vision of the scene was lost.

"Good," Claudio said. "They'll fingerprint Hector, figure out he's not dead, and send him to prison. No longer a threat."

But Monarch's gut told him otherwise.

"Why the hell is he here?"

"Maybe he wants to kill us after all these years?" Claudio said. "Who knows? He was always a crazy mother."

The painter looked around at the damage to his Land Cruiser. "Goddamned Hector. He destroyed my baby."

They passed the rest of the way to the private jet terminal at Ministro Pistarini Airport in silence though every once in a while Claudio would look around at the wreck of his beloved truck and groan.

At the private jet terminal, Monarch got out, but then leaned back inside.

"Hector hated Sister as much as he did us," the thief said. "I want the refuge and the clinic in Villa Miserie under armed watch twenty-four seven until I return."

"Done," Claudio said, and drove off.

The thief found the pilot of the Gulfstream and customs and immigration officials waiting for him. He showed them a fake passport that identified him as Alexander Fischer, a German textile manufacturer bound for a meeting in London before returning home to Düsseldorf. His accent was perfect, and they waved him through in short order.

Crossing the tarmac, Monarch made note of the jet's ID and texted it to Barnett. He climbed aboard, accepted the stewardess's offer of a drink and ordered a double Moscow mule. Just before they took off, Barnett called, told him the jet was chartered out of São Paulo. The client was unknown at that point, but she was going to have Zullo try to hack his way in after hours.

"Anything on Vargas?"

"He's dead."

"Then his ghost just tried to kill me and Claudio before the police showed up."

"You're saying he's in custody?"

"I'm assuming so."

"I'll make sure."

"Smart," he said, thanked her, and hung up.

He downed the Moscow mule as they lifted off and banked northeast out over the Atlantic. The sun was low on the horizon, backlighting the steep hills and mountains west of Buenos Aires in a golden glow that soon faded into pastel smudges and then nothing but the sea.

Monarch finished the drink, ordered another. He drank it in short order, turned down the offer of food, and adjusted the chair, He asked the stewardess to lower the cabin lights so he might sleep.

Only then did he allow his thoughts to return to Hector Vargas. Why would he try to take us out now, after so many years? He could see the guy carrying a grudge. That was not hard to imagine. But why he would decide now, after more than twenty years, to exact his revenge?

Monarch had no easy answers. As he faded into unconsciousness, his mind sought out the last time he'd seen the man before today.

Almost staggering under the weight of what Sister Rachel had told him to do, Robin walked to the ramshackle building that served as the headquarters of the Brotherhood of Thieves deep inside the Village of Misery.

Nothing is impossible.

Repeating that over and over, Robin climbed the stoop and opened the door without knocking. He entered a narrow hallway amid the din of a party, having flashbacks to the celebration that preceded his knife fight with Julio.

But now there were girls inside the house, many of them, several dancing up the hallway from the kitchen, holding beers or drinks. Laughing at the top of his lungs, Claudio carried a pint bottle of rum and danced after the girls as if they were the only things in the world he would ever care about. Then his oldest friend spotted him, and gazed at Robin the way he often had when casing a possible burglary target, with calculating indifference.

"Claudio," Robin said.

"You remember my name?"

"We need to talk."

"No explanation about why you disappear for six months, and you just walk in here and want to talk, bro?"

"I was hurt bad and that doctor, Sister Rachel, said I needed to go away to fully recover. When she said I was up to it, I came."

"That's bullshit, Claudio," one of the girls yelled. "Everything he says is bullshit. You said so yourself."

That hurt, but Robin did not take his eyes off his friend. "I want to talk to you and the entire brotherhood. Now."

"Who do you think you are? *Jefe*? That boat's sailed," Claudio said.

"You?" Robin asked with a growing smile.

He shook his head. "Hector."

Robin almost said, Where's Hector? But then Vargas appeared behind Claudio. A tank of a man, mid-twenties, with a shaved head, that deformed ear, and a nose that had been broken too many times to count, Vargas had been one of Julio's top lieutenants.

"Robin," Hector said with a hard edge in his voice.

Robin dropped his chin, said, "*Jefe*."

Hector smiled. "You're not here to contest the vote, then?"

"Furthest thing from my mind," Robin replied, and meant it.

Claudio said, "He wants to talk to the brothers."

"About?" Hector said.

Robin glanced at the girls who were almost all glaring at him, and said, "Inked members only."

The new head of *la fraternidad* studied him several seconds, then said, "All you bitches and wannabes out of here. Party's over."

The girls grumbled and complained until Hector shouted, "I said out!"

They grabbed their purses and hurried by Robin, giving him hateful glances, while the gang's recruits sullenly avoided his gaze, and slammed the door behind them.

"Where you want to explain your proposal?" Hector asked.

"Where else?" Robin asked.

The new *jefe* turned and headed back down the hall toward a door and a set of steep stairs that led down into the basement.

In the glare of bare lightbulbs, wooden benches had been set up in rows with several chairs up front facing them. Robin was almost overwhelmed by memories of the night he fought Julio there, how they'd cleared the benches away and the basement floor had become a killing ground.

One by one the members of the brotherhood filed down the stairs. Some of the thieves were happy to see him. Others regarded him skeptically. But each and every one of them seemed curious to hear what he had to say.

"What are you up to?" Claudio whispered in Robin's ear.

"Just hear me out," he replied as the meeting was called to order.

"Robin wants to say something," Hector said, and left it at that.

But now that Robin was up in front of his brothers, he felt like an elephant had reared up on its hind legs and dropped its front feet on his back. For several beats, he honestly had no idea what to tell them, but then the pain where Julio's blade had punctured his chest suddenly came back, like some blowtorch licking at his ribs, eager for his lung.

He thought about that, decided it was as good a place as any to start, and said, "I almost died here in this room six months ago. You all saw it."

"Goddamn right I saw it," said one thief appreciatively. "Best knife fight ever. Sickest move for a win ever, Robin."

A murmur of emphatic agreement rippled through the brothers who seemed happy at his return, and even those who'd been skeptical were nodding.

Robin hung his head, said, "I wish it had never happened. I wish Julio was alive, and I was fucking dead."

There was some grumbling, but he held up his hands and they quieted.

"But it's done and I got to live with it," he went on, before

105

pausing, and letting pain ripple through his face. "I would not wish this feeling on any of you."

"What's the point of this, brother?" a voice complained.

Robin was confused, but saw that he had Claudio's rapt attention, and decided to speak directly to him and hope the rest would understand.

"Man, this, you, *la fraternidad,* saved me from the garbage piles," Robin said.

Many of his brothers nodded and grunted in approval.

"But it also dooms you."

Claudio's eyes hardened. So did Hector's.

"I'm telling you, this shit, this life, it only ends up in a prison cell, or crippled up, or dead. Shot or stabbed. Lights out."

"Or richer than sin," Hector said, calling out loudly. "Fucking mansion with them big-booty, titty girls lounging by the pool."

The brothers erupted in cheers and hoots, and Robin wondered why he'd bothered to come at all. Then he changed course.

"I'm all for the mansion and the girls lounging by the pool, don't get me wrong," Robin said. "That what flips your switch, have at it. But what if to flip that switch you had to do what you were really meant for."

"Like safecracking?" asked one of the younger brothers, setting off another round of snickers.

But Robin caught some uncertainty in Claudio's eyes and pounced on it. "What if you really were meant for something bigger than *la fraternidad*?" Robin asked. "An artist, say, or a painter."

"A painter?" Hector snorted.

Claudio looked puzzled, torn, but then nodded, and said, "Everyone has crazy dreams, Robin. So what?"

"So what if they were all possible?" Robin replied, and then looked to Hector. "Didn't you once tell me you wanted to build motorcycles someday?"

The new *jefe* scowled, said, "That was kid stuff. *La fraternidad* is real."

"But what if they were both equally real?" Robin said. "I mean, you have a choice, you could be a thief, or you could be a motorcycle builder, or a painter." He began to gesture around the room at the other thieves, remembering conversations he'd had with them over the years. "Or a guitarist. Or a nightclub owner. Or a chef. Or a clothes designer. Or a cook. Or a writer. Or anything other than being a thief."

Hector shouted. "But that ain't the way it is, brother. This is the life we've been given. It's been good to us. Saved me from the *ano*. You too."

"You're right, *jefe*," Robin replied.

"So there you go," Hector said. "Fucking end of story."

Instead of arguing, Robin paused, letting his attention roam the boys and young men in front of him, trying to figure out how to make them understand. And then he believed he did.

"Close your eyes," he said. "Go on."

One by one the members of the Brotherhood of Thieves closed their eyes and listened when he said, "I want you to imagine what you would be if you weren't a thief."

He paused. "How does it make you feel? Good?"

Robin watched many shoulders shrugging, but only a few chins nodding.

Robin talked to the nodders. "See? Sister Rachel says that good feeling is God telling you what you are supposed to do. It's showing you like your purpose in life."

"This is bullshit, and this is over," Hector said sharply. "You got God now? From that fucking Sister Rachel bitch?"

Robin hesitated, then firmed, letting his eyes roam over his friends. "She showed me a way to start over, and made me take the hardest road I've ever walked. But I feel better every day I keep going in that direction. I came here tonight because I want you to come walk that harder road with me."

"Say what?" Hector demanded caustically. "Leave *la fraternidad*? Go live with some church bitch and become some slave to rules? Fuck rules. We're not stupid, and we're not slaves, man. We're hunters. We're takers."

The other brothers broke into cheers, and threw their fists over their heads.

Hector laughed harshly, said, "Someone whack the fucking traitor. Screw that, I'll do it myself."

He tugged out a pistol from his waistband and started marching toward Robin, gun up, egged on by the brothers' cheering.

Before Hector could aim, Claudio stepped in front of him.

"That ain't right, *jefe*," Claudio said. "You can't just kill a brother for wanting a better life. I mean, he's delusional, but that's his problem."

"Can't just let him go," Hector said.

"Sure you can," Claudio said. "He was our best earner. Cut him some slack."

"What if he goes to the cops?"

"I'm no rat," Robin said.

Hector thought about that, and then lowered the gun. "Get the fuck out of here, man. Never come back."

17

FOUR UNIFORMED OFFICERS DRAGGED a handcuffed and manacled El Cazador into the cellblock. He'd been interrogated for hours. But he'd never talked. Never spoke a word. Just kept asking for a lawyer.

The cops decided a trip to the central jail in Buenos Aires might loosen his tongue. But seeing the hard and filthy men crammed into the foul cells, and listening to their catcalls and curses, the hunter went somewhere reptilian in his mind.

He had been in prisons and jails far worse than this in Chile and Bolivia. Uruguay too. And one thing he'd learned in all of them? When you spoke to authority, authority punished you. Better to shut up until you knew their game.

The police hated his strategy. They also hated the fact that they couldn't identify him because he had long ago removed his fingerprints and the tattoo on his inner right forearm with battery acid. Once, he had been just Hector Vargas. Then he'd started changing his name so often he began to think himself only as El Cazador, the hunter.

They were far down the cellblock when two of the officers threw him up against a wall, pinned him there. The others drew weapons and told the men in the near cell to back up. The door opened and they threw him on the floor inside.

The cell stank of piss and shit and men who hadn't washed in days if not weeks. It was all too familiar to him. He knew the men in the cell with him. He didn't know their names, or the crimes they were here for, but he knew them just the same.

Murderers. Rapists. Sadists. All slammed inside a confined space.

There was only one way this would go down.

El Cazador expected one of them to strike before he started up off the floor. But the first blow didn't come until he'd regained his knees. A mistake.

He caught the foot kicking at his jaw with both hands. He clamped on the toes and heel, and then bit viciously into the side, hearing the scream before twisting the foot so hard the ankle snapped spirally. He never gave his attacker a second glance, just lurched to his feet and backed toward the cell bars, hands up, ready for a fist or a *faca,* one of the plastic knives men like this always seemed to carry.

But none of them moved. He didn't either, not for a full five minutes, while the shithead with the broken ankle and bleeding foot writhed and moaned on the floor.

Finally, one of them, the biggest of the bunch, said, "You might want to wash out your mouth, man. Chico's feet, you never know what you might catch."

Several men laughed.

The hunter stepped forward, and spit on Chico. More laughed.

One said, "Piss on his head, man, we don't fucking care."

It was tempting. It was always smart to mark territory in a pack of dogs.

Instead, he motioned for one of them to move aside on a bunk. The inmate did, and El Cazador took his spot. He pushed back against the wall, pulled his knees up, and went off into a thousand yard stare that kept the others from saying a word to him.

Only then did he let himself think about the shithole he'd

gotten himself thrown into, and why. No one had died, but they'd charged him and the two men he'd hired with possession and discharge of high-power weapons in the course of a motorized gunfight with an unknown third party. Worse, after all those years, he'd had his chance to watch Monarch's body dance with bullets and die by his hand. And he'd missed. For a split second, he hadn't been the hunter. He'd been just pissed-off Hector and it had cost him.

Vargas felt the rage roar up through him. He wanted to rant and put his fists down the throats of every man in the cell with him.

You fucking missed! Fucking missed!

Those words rang again and again in his head, and he wondered whether that moment would be his everlasting prison. Did you get a chance like that twice?

Never. Definitely not when you're in jail on weapons charges. Vargas had blown it, and now he was going down for a long stretch where the smell of piss, shit, and sweat would be his constant companion, where constant violence would be the price of his place in the pack. He began to steel himself to it, to once again adopt the canine model of surviving on the wrong side of the bars. He had to stay alert now. Attacks could and would come from any and all angles in the coming days. It was just the way things were.

But right now, while the memory of his counterattack and Chico's screams were fresh in their mind, the hunter needed to sleep. He couldn't afford deep sleep. That would come later, after he'd forged allegiances. Until then, he'd doze right on the edge of blackness, ready to surface at a moment's notice.

Vargas stayed in that buzzing state for almost an hour until his cellmates began to shout in alarm. The hunter opened his eyes to see the four guards were back. They all had shotguns and were aiming them directly at him.

"Out," one of them said. "You've got visitors."

It was unexpected, but El Cazador uncoiled and went to the door. He knew the drill and put his arms behind him, felt the metal bracelets snap around his wrists before the door opened. They paraded him down the hall. Word of what he'd done in the cell had evidently spread. The inmates were all watching him. One called him *el mordador,* the biter. He wasn't about to correct them.

As he walked, Vargas braced himself for pain. One thing about the Argentine police, they were never afraid to use the heavy stuff and trickery. Don't say a word, he told himself as they led him to an interrogation room and shackled him to a chair bolted into the floor. Whoever they are, whatever they say: give no reply.

The hunter clung to that tactic when they left him alone in the room. He closed his eyes, and imagined he was floating in dark water, deafened to the outside world. He kept his eyes closed even when the door opened and two people came inside. He tracked their footsteps around the table, but kept still, floating and . . .

"Mr. Vargas, I am Esteban Reynard, an attorney hired to represent you."

El Cazador kept his eyes closed, said nothing, thought: hired?

The silence went on for several moments before another male voice asked in what sounded like Mexican Spanish, "Why were you trying to kill Robin Monarch?"

Vargas hadn't expected the accent or the question, and he popped open his eyes to find two men across the table from him. The near one was younger, late thirties, Argentine, slick, a sharp suit, the lawyer, Vargas guessed. The other wasn't Mexican. He was clearly a gringo, a dork gringo at that, with short sandy hair, nasty sunburn, and rose-tinted glasses. He wore an ill-fitting, dark linen suit, and licked his lips before saying again in that Mexican accent, "Tell me why you wanted to kill Monarch?"

Every voice in the hunter's head told him to remain mute.

Instead, he said, "Who the fuck are you?"

Reynard, the lawyer, said, "He's the one paying for me to help you."

"Like I said, who the fuck is he?"

Across the table, Billy Saunders calculated, again questioning his instincts, before saying, "It doesn't matter who or what I am. It only matters what I can do for you."

Vargas shot the lawyer a hard look before returning his attention to Beau Arsenault's security man. "What can you do for me?"

Saunders liked to bass fish, something he had in common with his boss. He knew well that when trying to lure a lunker out of the weeds, you had to tease him a bit, make the bite irresistible.

"I hear they torture here," Saunders said. "Plastic bags over the head. Water boarding. Beatings. They'll kill you if they have half a mind."

El Cazador's eyes never left Saunders. "So what?"

"So I am in a position to spare you all of that," Saunders said.

The prisoner cocked his head in disbelief and then looked at Reynard, the lawyer. "He can get me out?"

"*We* can," the lawyer said.

"How?"

"Does it matter?" Saunders said.

"It does if you've got some fucking idea of a jail break. Like you said, they kill people if they have half a mind."

"Nothing like that," Reynard said. "You walk out the back door. They report you as killed in a jail fight."

"That kind of thing takes money," the hunter said suspiciously.

"It does," Saunders said. "But that's my business, not yours."

Vargas leaned back, still skeptical. "Why?"

Saunders calculated again before saying, "As we share a mutual dislike of Robin Monarch, I think you can be useful to me."

El Cazador stared at him, and then snorted in dark amusement before saying, "You're saying you're springing me because you want me to fuck with Monarch?"

"In a manner of speaking," the attorney said.

The hunter broke into a grin at his great good fortune, and nodded at Saunders. "Then I'm with you, whoever the fuck you are."

"Good," Saunders said, and got up while Reynard assured Vargas that he'd be freed within the hour.

Saunders and the lawyer exited the interrogation room. Arsenault's security man nodded to the police commandant as he passed his office, pleased to have bought his cooperation for a mere twenty-five thousand dollars, thinking it money very well spent, something his boss would no doubt approve.

Indeed, when Saunders was free of the police station, and inside the hired air-conditioned car, waiting for Reynard to complete Vargas's release, he punched in Beau Arsenault's private number.

The mogul answered on the second ring. "Talk to me, Billy."

"It's done," Saunders said. "Monarch's boxed and has no idea."

"Excellent," Arsenault replied. "Now throw the thief a line and set the hook hard."

18

MONARCH LEFT THE TAXI at Canary Wharf wearing a khaki trench coat, a blue suit, white shirt, and a rep tie. It always was a smart idea to adapt your camouflage to the surroundings.

The air was dank and cold, the kind that bores into the joints. The abdominal muscles around Monarch's wound began to ache for the first time in weeks as he sought out one of several high-rise office monstrosities that faced the Thames River, and used a burn phone to text "I'm here" to a number Sami Rafiq had sent through Barnett that morning.

Despite the cold he waited outside until he felt the phone buzz.

"Suite 1414."

He texted the name, "Alex Fischer."

Monarch entered the building, showed security the fake passport, and asked for Suite 1414.

The security guard looked it up, said, "They just put you in, Mr. Fischer. You'll find the elevator to the bank over there."

A bank? Monarch thought as he crossed the dark marble

floor of the lobby and entered an open elevator made of brass and mirrors. What kind of bank hires a thief?

A private one, he discovered when he got off the elevator and found Suite 1414 with a smoked glass door that said:

PYNCHON & HORMEL
PRIVATE BANKERS
LONDON, ZURICH, HONG KONG

Before Monarch could text or knock, the door swung open, revealing a statuesque blond woman in her early forties. She was dressed in a conservative gray suit, pearls, and black pumps.

"So good of you to come, Mr. Fischer," she said in a refined British accent while holding out a long and very soft hand. "I am Emma Chase, in-house counsel here at Pynchon. Please, do come in."

Chase stood aside, and Monarch entered one of those rooms that scream of old money. Burled walnut paneling, the finest Oriental rugs, leather club furniture, and several paintings depicting horses riding to hounds.

"Would you care for some tea?" Chase asked, leading him through the room toward a door in the corner. "Coffee?"

"Coffee would be fine," Monarch said.

"Brilliant," she said. "Again, so good of you to come on short notice. Have you eaten?"

"I have, yes," Monarch said.

"We've arranged a room for you at One Aldwych," she said. "I hope it meets your expectations."

"I haven't taken the job yet."

She looked back, smiled winningly, said, "Oh, I'm sure you will."

Monarch followed the lawyer into a large office with a bank of rain-spattered windows that faced the Thames. To his right there was a wooden desk with neat stacks of files, framed photographs he couldn't see, and little else. To his left there was a tufted leather couch, coffee table, and matching club chairs.

"If you'll sign these nondisclosure agreements, please," Chase said, gesturing to three thin documents on the table.

Monarch made a show of scanning the agreements, and then signed, "Alexander Fischer."

"Brilliant," the lawyer said. "Thank you, and if you'll excuse me I'll arrange for that coffee. And Mr. Pynchon will be along shortly to brief you."

Monarch gathered this was Mr. Pynchon's office, and decided Mr. Pynchon made a pretty decent living. He would have Gloria check as soon as he'd heard what they had in mind.

No more than a minute passed before a man in his mid-forties, long and lean in a five-thousand-dollar suit, entered with Chase in tow carrying a silver coffee service.

"Christopher Pynchon," the man said in a crisp English accent, offering Monarch his hand and studying him with great curiosity. "I've never met a thief before."

"Really?" Monarch said. "I thought they were a dime a dozen in the private banking business."

Pynchon's expression hardened and his hand slipped from Monarch. "Yes, well, please sit."

Chase poured Monarch a cup of steaming coffee and he declined cream and sugar, preferring to drink it black. To his surprise, it was very good coffee.

"Colombian?" he asked, after she'd shut the door.

"Jamaican," Pynchon said. "Blue Mountain. It's the best coffee in the world as far as I am concerned."

It was good, excellent really, so Monarch wasn't going to argue the point.

"So," he said after several sips. "What are you interested in stealing?"

Pynchon glanced at his attorney, who said, "He's signed the documents."

The banker nodded, got up, and retrieved a thin file from his desk. He handed it to Monarch, said, "Please read this and then we'll talk."

The thief opened the file and found a scientific paper that was stamped, "Out for Peer Review." He scanned the title, the three Ph.D. authors, and the synopsis of the findings. He read it, glanced at Chase and Pynchon, and then read it again.

"Is this right?" he asked.

"You've read that fast?" Pynchon asked.

"Just the synopsis, but—"

"Read the entire thing," Chase said.

Monarch took up the coffee cup again and spent the next fifteen minutes studying the paper closely, and alternating between skepticism and fascination at the evidence the researchers used to support their findings.

When the thief finished the paper, he looked up and said, "Well, if they're correct, it's simply . . ."

"Remarkable?" Chase said.

"Incredible?" Pynchon said.

"Both," Monarch said, closing the file and setting it on the table. "But will it pass peer review?"

"Our clients say it might," Pynchon said.

"Wait, *your* clients?"

The banker nodded, said, "Our clients who wish to remain anonymous."

"And wish me to do what?"

The attorney smiled, said, "Find that place, those people, figure out their secret, and then steal us that secret. If you are successful, we will pay you eighteen million pounds sterling."

Though he tried not to show it, Monarch was shocked, and he sat back in his chair knowing it would be the largest single haul

118

of his life. Thirty million dollars to him alone? He couldn't even imagine what Sister Rachel could do with that kind of money. Rather than get excited about the possibility, he thought instead about why they'd be willing to pay so much.

"So who am I working for?" he asked. "Some—?"

"For this kind of money, who you work for is irrelevant," Pynchon said.

Monarch thought about that, and couldn't decide if he agreed.

"You think these scientists know what's causing it?" Monarch asked.

"They must have suspicions," Chase said. "You can see from the paper that they intend to return to do further investigations."

"When?"

"Early next week," Pynchon said, "according to our sources."

"So, are you interested?" the attorney asked.

"I'm more than interested," Monarch said. "But I've got to think it over, and I'm still a bit jet-lagged. Will you give me the night to consider it?"

The lawyer and the banker exchanged looks, and then Pynchon said, "You have until nine o'clock tomorrow morning. After that we'll go to our second candidate."

"I didn't know there was one," Monarch said.

Pynchon smiled sourly, said, "In our world, Mr. Fischer, there is always a backup plan."

Monarch called Barnett the second he'd left the building, had her start digging on Pynchon & Hormel as well as the three scientists who authored the papers. Was it possible? He must have asked that question fifty times during the course of the afternoon and on into the evening.

The thief loved London, the pace, the people, and the history. On any other trip he would have walked for hours through the city just soaking it in. But this time he'd checked into his room at One Aldwych and ordered room service.

Something felt off about the deal. Could it be worth that much?

Exploited in the right way, he supposed it could be worth a hundred or a thousand times what they'd offer to pay him to steal it. Which meant what? That the fourth party had the wherewithal to turn the scientists' research into a global product? It made sense to Monarch that some giant corporate entity was behind this entire scheme. If a company could get a head start on all the others that would likely be interested in the unpublished research, they'd make billions.

But was that bad? When Monarch looked at it from the perspective of the greater good, all the people who might benefit from the discovery, including Sister Rachel and the children, he could make the argument that stealing the secret was absolutely for the greater good. Yet, when he factored in the fact that this was the three scientists' discovery, and theirs alone, the path to the greater good was murkier and less defined.

Around eight, while Monarch ate an outstanding club sandwich and contemplated going out for a pint, Barnett called back on Skype. The tropical sun was shining behind her, but she was looking exhausted.

"When did you sleep last?" he asked.

"I'm following your lead," Barnett said. "Cat naps every few hours."

"When we're done, you need to get at least six."

"Promise," she said, and then told him what she'd found.

Pynchon and Tristan Hormel, an old friend from Eaton, founded the bank nearly a decade before. Both men had spent years working in the Swiss private banking system and decided to set up their own shop. Pynchon worked in London, Hormel in Zurich.

"They're outstanding at the whole private client thing," Barnett said. "I've found no mention anywhere of clients' names."

"The bank successful?"

"Can't put a value on the assets yet," she replied. "But Pynchon owns a massive townhome in Chelsea and a shooting estate in Scotland. Hormel has a lakefront compound outside Zurich, and is evidently bidding to buy an island in the Caribbean."

"What about the attorney?"

"She took a first in history at Cambridge, and then repeated the performance reading law at Oxford," she replied. "She also attended Georgetown Law and can practice in both Britain and the United States. She's single, and has homes in London, and the south of France."

"Could Zullo penetrate the bank's security?"

"He can try," she said.

"Forget try. I need to know who wants this done."

"I'll ask," she said, hesitated. "You think it's real?"

Monarch paused, said, "You think it's a hoax?"

There was silence, and then she said, "No. Once you see the bios on the scientists, you think this could be solid."

"Tell me."

"I'll send the complete work-ups before I crash," she promised, yawning. "But their academic backgrounds are first rate, especially Santos, the leader. Berkeley. Stanford. The whole nine yards."

The thief was about to ask another question when a soft rap came at his door.

"I've got to go," he said. "Get some sleep."

Yawning, Barnett waved at him before cutting the connection.

Another soft knock. Monarch went cautiously toward the door. It was ingrained in the thief. He knew of assassins who liked to knock at a target's door, and then shoot the second the light in the peephole changed.

Easing his wallet out of his pocket, he stood to the side and slid it over the peephole. No shot. That was a plus.

Monarch looked through the peep and saw the attorney Emma Chase with her hair down, holding a bottle of champagne and looking a little tipsy already.

He opened the door, said, "Counselor?"

The attorney smiled, said, "Call me Emma. Might I come in?"

Monarch thought about that. Couldn't hurt, and maybe he could get some information out of her. "Your wish is my command," he said.

Chase laughed throatily, pressed by him and into the room, saying, "This is quite elegant for an international man of action."

"The folks who employ Pynchon and Hormel don't fool around," Monarch said. "Spare no expense."

The attorney laughed, and said, "You have no idea."

Monarch took the bottle from her, checked the vintage. "Nice. Expense account?"

She laughed again, "Does it matter?"

"I suppose not."

"Given any thought to our proposal?"

"Much," he said, and popped the cork.

"And?"

"Still thinking."

"Maybe I can help you come to a hard decision," she said, and smiled.

"Not a bad idea," Monarch said, reaching for two glass tumblers that he filled with champagne. He handed her a glass and she sipped it. Her face was slightly flushed and yet she seemed amused.

"So," Monarch said. "Is this part of the strategy?"

"No strategy," she said. "I just . . ."

"Yes?"

"A woman in my business rarely meets someone like you,

Mr. Fischer. Mysterious. Dangerous. And, might I say, ruggedly built and handsome?"

Monarch smiled as she came closer, and said, "You might."

But before she could wrap her arms around him, Monarch said, "Just for the record: you have a personal stake in my decision?"

Chase made a pouting face, shrugged. "Not in your decision, but if you succeed, I make a small fortune. So I'm rooting for you, yes. But enough talk. Let's enjoy."

Even though he thought it might be a bad idea, Monarch said, "Let's."

An hour later, Chase lay in a contented ball under the sheets.

"Did I convince you?" she purred to Monarch who was up pouring champagne.

"More important did I convince you?"

"Most assuredly," she said, taking the drink.

"So who's the client?" he asked.

The attorney took a sip, cocked her head, and said, "I honestly don't know. And I don't know if Pynchon knows either. The referral came through Tristan."

"Hormel?"

"That's right," she said. "So? What can I tell them?"

Chase was one of the sexiest women he'd ever met, smart, beautiful, a real tigress when it came to love. And yet, lying beside her, looking into her eyes, his instincts screamed that something about the deal wasn't right.

He said, "I think it's time for plan B."

The lawyer laughed. "Are you saying you require a second shot on goal?"

"I'm saying, I'm out," Monarch said, setting the champagne aside.

"But . . . but why?"

"My Spider-Man sense is all tingly, that's all," he replied. "So unless you give me the name of whoever or whatever is paying for this job, I'm heading back to Argentina in the morning."

Chase sat up, said, "You're serious?"

"Very."

"Hardened decision then?"

"Diamond cutter hard."

"Well," she sputtered, getting up from the bed, gathering her clothes, and heading for the bathroom. "Too bad we won't get to celebrate your victory."

Though icy cold, before Chase left, she kissed him hard, said, "Oh, the things we could have done, mate."

"It is a tragedy," Monarch said.

"By the way, you'll have to find your own way back to Buenos Aires."

"Ouch."

"Better to be a team player," she said, and left.

As the door shut, the thief still thought he was doing the right thing.

His gut told him so and his gut rarely lied.

19

NEW ORLEANS NINTH WARD
8:00 P.M.

THE SUPERSTRUCTURE OF THE float was up, welded in place the week before. The hydraulics and various cogs had been installed three days ago. The chicken wire was finished the day before, and workers were laying on the last of the papier-mâché skin. Though the float had not yet come to colorful life, the theme and the characters were emerging: a giant court jester in a chariot whipping not horses, but outrageous monsters suggesting the Seven Deadly Sins.

It had been Louisa Arsenault's idea of course. The mogul's wife had studied literature as an undergraduate and never lost a chance to rub her education in other people's noses. Even her husband's.

But you had to admire the woman for putting her vision out there, Beau Arsenault thought as he stood off to the side in the hangar, watching Louisa inspect the construction. Her willingness to lead was what he loved about her, actually, along with her classic beauty, and her loyalty.

In the candy and sweets department, however, at least in the past five or six years, she'd been less than satisfying. Not that

125

Louisa had ever been fully satisfying to the mogul. He'd gotten a taste of chocolate as a very young man, and that was simply something his lily-white wife could never provide. He kept his little addiction nourished by being discreet. Arsenault owed Louisa that.

Oblivious to the clatter and noise in the metal-roofed building, the tycoon's mind drifted to his latest conquest in progress. Lynette Chambers was pushing forty, tall, big boned, big breasted, and gloriously mulatto. She sang in a band down in the quarter. The mogul had almost convinced Lynette that her dreams weren't over, that her hard work and talent was about to pay off, that she could be the next big—

"Beau?" Louisa said, breaking her husband's thoughts.

Arsenault startled, said, "Yes, dear?"

"What do you think?" she asked, gesturing at the float.

Having anticipated the question coming at some point, the mogul said, "I think it's a testament to your organizational skills that the float is in this state of completion with three days to go."

Pleased, Louisa said, "They'll be blown dry and the final butcher paper applied by morning. Then the airbrush painters will do their magic."

"Another triumph, my dear," he said, and kissed her on the cheek.

"Can't believe what they're saying about your protégé," his wife sniffed. "Well, I guess I can. That type always gets caught up in drugs and something tawdry. There's talk of her contract being cancelled. Had you heard that?"

Arsenault acted pained, nodded, said, "Broke my heart."

Louisa was about to reply, but then saw something she didn't like and swept away from him yelling at the poor soul who had not lived up to her stratospheric expectations. The billionaire watched her go, wondered if it was too early to inform her that he had a late business meeting. She never checked that sort of thing.

Before he could decide, his private cell phone rang. It was Saunders again. "Monarch turned us down."

"Did he?" Arsenault said. "Thirty million and he says no? That's surprising. I thought the odds against it."

"Good thing I have plan B in place," his security chief said.

"It is. And you have my permission to execute."

"I already took the precaution."

"I appreciate the initiative, Billy. When will that happen?"

"In the next few minutes. Would you like to watch? They're carrying cameras."

Charmed by the idea, and bored with float building, Arsenault said, "Where can I see it? I'm out and about."

"The limo computer screen. I'll patch you in."

"Give me a moment to extricate myself," the mogul said, crossed to his wife. He told her he had to leave on business, ignored her wounded reaction, kissed her, and left.

He found the Lincoln Town Car outside, and the driver, Owen, waiting.

"Mr. Arsenault?" he said.

"Nowhere yet, Owen," he said. "I just need the engine started. We need to make a video conference call from the back."

"Yes, sir," he said, and got in the car, and started it.

Owen was in his sixties, a wiry, little redbone runt, who'd worked for Arsenault going on fifteen years. Arsenault liked Owen because by nature he rarely talked. Owen also seemed to understand his employer's particular needs, but never mentioned them. To anyone. He just asked for the next destination and drove there. For that Arsenault paid Owen twice the going rate, and called it a bargain.

Owen climbed out of the driver's seat and shut the door.

Even so, Arsenault hit the button that raised the soundproof screen. Then he attached his laptop to the built-in screen in the backseat with a USB cord, and quickly called up an anonymous, secure Web site. The screen split into four quadrants and was soon fed by four cameras. Each showed a storm scene at night: driving rain, thunder, narrow muddy roads, more shadows than light. But in the flashes of lightning Arsenault spotted people huddled in the doors of shacks, squalor, and want.

The billionaire punched in Saunders's number, unmoved by what he was seeing. The poverty those people endured was simply the spin of the cosmic roulette wheel, and what winner cared about the losers in a game of chance anyway?

"Where did you get them?" Arsenault asked when Saunders answered.

"The guy in the upper right feed? He's had a beef with the thief going way back, and almost killed him a few days ago. He's eager to help. The others he recruited."

"What's his name?"

"I dunno," Saunders said. "He calls himself El Cazador. The hunter."

The mogul craned forward, watching from the hunter's point of view as he slipped deep into the shadows and stopped. Ahead through the rain, the camera caught the movement of a man standing beneath the eve of a cinder-block building with a steel roof. Behind the man, down the wall of the building, a bright light burned above the door, showing a red cross.

"Monarch pay for this place?" the mogul asked.

"I'm certain he paid for the improvements," Saunders replied.

He'll probably pay for more with my twenty million, Arsenault thought angrily.

"You're positive this Sister Rachel's in there?"

"They had a visual of her entering."

"Nothing shady about this Sisters of Hope group?"

"Not that I could find."

That last grated on Arsenault's nerves. He operated from the perspective that all people and all organizations, no matter how pure their purpose or intent, had dirt under the rug. This missionary, this doctor, had to be the same.

Not that it mattered. Sister Rachel Diego del Mar was Monarch's weakness. The mogul intended to exploit it, expose the thief's bleeding heart, and then squeeze it hard enough that he would have no choice but to bend to Arsenault's invisible will.

El Cazador started moving again, went straight to the man beneath the dripping eave of Sister Rachel's clinic. He spoke in Spanish. The mogul did not understand. But the man reacted, patting his pocket.

The hunter swung up, hit the man on the point of his chin with a sap of some kind, a blow so hard the man's head snapped back and he crumpled. He left him and went around the corner and into an alley behind the clinic. The thunder had moved on enough that the pelting rain was not enough to smother the sound of a baby crying and a woman moaning.

"What's going on there?" Arsenault asked.

"It's a medical clinic," Saunders said. "Someone's hurt."

El Cazador stopped once more and seemed to be looking deeper into the blackness of the alley. The mogul could see nothing. Vargas began to sing softly and drunkenly in Spanish, weaving as he went down the alley along a whitewashed wall topped with barbed wire.

A man appeared, demanded something in Spanish. The hunter tilted one way, and the other, before smashing the sap against the side of the man's head. There was a sound like a bat hitting a ball and the second man went down hard. El Cazador stepped over him, pushed open a gate into a narrow, lit yard crisscrossed with dripping clotheslines.

He went quickly to a window, set to work with a knife, and

soon had it open. The feed went with him as he slid into darkness.

It stayed that way four, maybe five minutes, to the point where the mogul was checking his watch, wondering how long this was going to take, and whether he should tell the driver to take him to the French Quarter.

But then a door opened, throwing a shaft of hallway light into a jumbled office. A light went on in the office, and Sister Rachel entered the scene. Arsenault thought she looked like a worn-out old bag. She twisted as the camera moved toward her. Her eyes went wide. Her mouth opened to scream. One hand slammed across her mouth, a second stuck a needle in her neck. A voice spoke in Spanish as she drooped.

"What did he say to her there?" the mogul asked.

Saunders said, "He wanted to know if she could save Monarch this time."

Amused, Arsenault watched as the limp woman was carried to the window, and said, "A fucking saint couldn't save Monarch this time."

They watched Sister Rachel's body pass through the window, and then carried through the rear gate in the rain. When they loaded her in a car that rolled up in the alley, the link died.

"Good then," Arsenault said, checking his watch. "Let me know. I'm going for dessert in the Quarter."

20

LONDON

MONARCH'S BURN PHONE RANG at 3:00 A.M.

Groggy, he turned on the light picked it up, said, "Gloria?"

"It's me," Claudio said in a tight, hard voice, and the thief immediately knew something was wrong.

"Chanel said no?" he said, sitting up.

"Haven't asked."

"Then?"

"Sister Rachel was taken from the clinic in the Villa Miserie a half hour ago."

"What!" Monarch shouted. "I told you to put guards on her!"

"I had Gato and Fernandez there and they were both knocked out!" Claudio shouted back. "I would have had more men in place, but she never told me she was going to the clinic!"

Calm down, the thief thought. Shouting helps nothing.

"Who took her?"

"I'm betting Hector," Claudio said. "The police are saying he was knifed to death in the central jail this afternoon, but my sources say someone sprang him."

"Son of a bitch," Monarch said, feeling his stomach lurch, trying to think. "Son of a bitch. The police there?"

131

"We're not even there yet," Claudio said. "Inez the night nurse called me after she found Gato and Fernandez out cold, and Sister gone."

"So you haven't talked to Gato or Fernandez?" Monarch said, punching on the speakerphone and heading for the bathroom.

"Inez said they could hardly put a noun and a verb together."

"She call the police?"

"I told her not to until I got there. Should we bring the police in?"

Monarch twisted on the shower, said, "Let me think about it. Chanel's with you?"

"Yes."

"Call back when you're there."

The line went dead. The thief showered, shaved, and dressed while his mind ran wild at the thought of Hector Vargas kidnapping Sister Rachel. Why? What was the point of that? Use her as a lure? Or take his revenge on him by harming her?

These questions crafted anger and built resolve in Monarch until he thought of himself as a juggernaut, an invincible, unstoppable machine. He grabbed his bag, headed for the door. He'd go to Heathrow, get the first flight to Buenos Aires, and in the meantime call in a—

When he yanked open the door, Christopher Pynchon startled and took a step back.

"What are you doing here?" Monarch demanded. "I told your counsel I was out, and I've got places to be."

The banker swallowed, said, "I was instructed to show you something. It will only take a moment of—"

"Another time," the thief said, and made to move by him.

"It's about the old woman," Pynchon blurted.

Monarch froze in his tracks, saw fear in the man, and said, "What old woman?"

Pynchon lifted his briefcase, said, "I'll show you inside."

"What old woman?" Monarch demanded.

"I don't know who she is," the banker said. "I assume you will."

The thief shoved the banker into his room, said, "So show."

Shaking, Pynchon got a laptop computer from the briefcase, opened it, and the screen jumped to a video player.

"Mr. Fischer?" the banker said. "I want you to know that I am only the messenger here, and expect you to treat me as such."

The video started in darkness, with just the sound of a man breathing.

Then a door opened and a shaft of light cut across Sister Rachel's office at the clinic in the Village of Misery.

The light went on in the office and she was standing there. When the hand clamped across her terrified mouth, and the needle plunged into her neck, Monarch felt a rage like no other explode and throw fire through his veins.

He sprang like a leopard at Pynchon, seized the banker by the throat, and slammed him against the wall. "You," the thief seethed. "You are a fucking dead man."

Pynchon's terrified eyes bugged out of his head as he choked, "Only messenger."

"You think I give a shit?" Monarch said, pressing his forehead hard against the banker's brow. "I will cut your fucking head off and serve it to your wife on a platter."

"No! Please!"

Monarch wanted to close his hand tighter on Pynchon's throat, slowly cave in the banker's windpipe, watch him struggle and fight toward lights-out. But the thief and soldier in him said to counterattack.

"Who sent you? Who hired you?"

"I don't know. Really!"

"Who does know? Your partner? Hormel?"

"He . . . he's dealing with a middleman in South America somewhere," Pynchon choked. "We're all just messengers."

"Do you have any idea who that woman is?"

The banker shook his head.

"She's a fucking saint. Like Mother Teresa."

Pynchon looked ill, said meekly, "I had no idea. All I was told to say is you do the job and she goes free. If not, she dies. They expect you on a flight to Brazil tonight, or she dies."

Monarch couldn't stop himself. He hit the banker in the gut with his free hand, tried to drive the blow all the way to his spine. With a sickening *ugh* sound, Pynchon pitched forward, his mouth wide open and his lips pulsing like a guppy's. The thief straightened him up, and grabbed his testicles through his suit pants. He twisted, pulled, and crushed.

All the blood in Pynchon's body seemed to seek his neck and head. His face turned a mottled purple, and so pressurized and stretched it looked like his muscles were trying to break free of his skin. Monarch hurled him to the floor, and stomped his heel on the banker's rib cage until he heard a cracking noise.

Pynchon vomited and made soft, flat, wounded grunts and blatting cries like a sheep that has been set on by a mountain lion. Monarch stood over the banker, let the ungodly pain do its work, let it sear his brain, and jelly the fucker from head to toe.

A minute passed, and then two. While the thief waited, his mind caught gear, and spun out possible courses of action: go to Buenos Aires; or go to Switzerland, find Hormel, squeeze him to get the middleman in South America, follow the money trail wherever it goes; or simply do the job in Brazil. The last option, he knew, could take weeks, but he felt he had no choice. If he didn't go, they'd kill her.

His burn phone rang. He answered, said, "I'll call back in two minutes. I have something to finish here."

Monarch saw Pynchon's eyes focus on him in abject fear. In all his privileged existence, he could see the banker had never encountered or even imagined someone like him. It showed in the banker's trembling, and wet stain in his crotch.

The thief crouched, and in a calm voice, said, "Your life as a messenger is over."

Pynchon started to whimper and nod. Snot was running from his nose.

"But this? Between us? It is not over. Do you understand?"

Still terrified, the banker started to nod, but then shook his head.

"Tell your partner and your attorney that I do not turn the other cheek when dealing with scum, even if they're wealthy scum with degrees and money. I am a man who believes in vengeance. The three of you *will* suffer for your involvement in this abomination. If that good woman doesn't come out of this alive, the three of you are doomed. I don't care where you hide, I will hunt you, Hormel, and Chase to the ends of the Earth, and I *will* make your deaths the stuff of nightmares."

Pynchon was shivering uncontrollably, a man lost in an ice storm.

"Do you understand?" Monarch asked.

The banker nodded feebly.

"Good," the thief said, hauling him to his feet. "Now get on your phone, and tell your pilot I'm on my way. And I'll need operating cash. A million U.S. should do it."

21

INSIDE THE CLINIC IN the Villa Miserie, Claudio Fortunato turned to Chanel Chavez, and felt his cold heart melt.

The short, pretty, powerhouse of a woman he loved was rocking a newborn boy while his mother slept. He'd never really thought of Chavez, a sniper by training, as the maternal type. But she was making it look natural, and it made him love her all the more.

Will she say yes when the time comes?

He'd had the ring in his pocket since picking her up at the airport the night before, but everything that had happened since then had blocked him from popping the question.

He said, "We should go."

Chavez yawned and nodded.

"I'll take him," said Inez, the night nurse.

"No, I will," said Maria, the boy's mother, who'd opened her eyes.

Chavez handed her the infant, said, "He's so precious. What is his name?"

"Anthony."

"That's a wonderful name."

136

"Thank you."

Wringing her hands, the nurse went to Claudio, and said, "Are you sure we shouldn't call the police?"

"It's complicated, but yes, I'm sure," he replied, and glanced over at Gato and Fernandez, who were lying in beds with ugly, raised bumps on the side of their heads.

He and Chavez had questioned Gato and Fernandez as the men drifted in and out of consciousness. Fernandez, who'd been guarding the rear of the clinic, didn't remember who hit him. Gato, the guard in front, said a man in his forties, stocky, and wearing a knit cap down over his ears had asked for a light before hitting him expertly with a sap.

It had to be Hector. And because someone high up in the police department had to have been bribed to let Vargas walk on weapons charges, Claudio had decided not to report Sister Rachel missing.

Monarch had agreed with the move in their last phone call before he got on the jet to Rio. They had also agreed on a three-prong counterattack. While Claudio and Chavez handled Buenos Aires, and Monarch worked Brazil, Gloria Barnett would fly to Zurich and meet John Tatupu, who'd been with Monarch in the U.S. Special Forces, and Abbott Fowler, who'd been part of Monarch's unit at the CIA. Those three would target Pynchon's partner, Hormel.

Claudio followed Chavez outside the clinic. Dawn was just showing in the eastern sky, and the Village of Misery was starting to come alive.

"Jesus that smell is awful," Chavez said.

"The *ano*," Claudio said. "It always smells awful."

Chavez looked away from him, hands in her back pockets.

"You okay?" he asked.

"I'm dead tired," she said. "I feel guilty leaving my sister. I'm upset about Sister Rachel, and I still think not getting the police involved is a bad idea."

"No," Claudio said firmly. "Getting the police involved *is* a bad idea. It's not just the corruption. They will start looking into Sister Rachel's life, maybe the orphanage's finances."

"So?"

"So if they dig deep enough, they will find out about me, and perhaps Robin, and then their investigation will become about us, and not her," he said. "Like Robin said, it is better if we handle this ourselves for the time being."

He could tell she still wasn't happy, but he would have to live with it. He loved Chavez. She was a smart, sexy, tough woman, but she wasn't criminal by nature. Claudio *was* criminal by nature, a strength in this sort of situation.

"I can get you a taxi back to my place if you need to rest and call your sister," Claudio offered, without rancor.

Chavez looked uncertain. "What about you?"

"I'm going to go door to door," he said. "See if anyone saw anything last night. And then I'm going to track down every former member of *la fraternidad*."

"To see if they've heard from Vargas?" she asked.

"Or seen him," Claudio said.

"Then I'll stay," she said. "I'll sleep when I'm dead. That good with you?"

The artist grinned. He loved her take-no-shit spirit.

"Course it's good with me, chica."

For the next three hours, they worked the shacks and slum buildings that surrounded the clinic on the hill above the garbage dump. In the heat, the stench was stupefying, but they kept on, asking everyone they encountered about the missionary. Nearly all of them knew who Sister Rachel was. Nearly everyone in the Villa Miserie had been to see her for one malady or injury or another.

But no one remembered seeing the doctor or anyone

suspicious around the clinic because they were all inside, taking shelter from the brutal storms that had raked the city.

Around noon, Claudio and Chavez reentered the alley behind the clinic feeling like they'd gotten nowhere. The artist felt like a failure, and that sickened him. Sister Rachel had been the first one to tell him he really could become a painter. The first one. He owed her so much it hurt. But he couldn't let that emotion keep him from acting with a clear head.

"We'll go back to the apartment," Claudio said. "You get some sleep, and I'll start calling the brothers."

"Sounds like a plan," Chavez said, yawning.

"Senor? Senora?" a voice called from behind them.

Claudio looked over his shoulder at a middle-aged woman wearing ragged clothes, and carrying a shirtless baby in a cloth diaper. She was acting nervous.

"Can I help you, senora?"

"Maybe I help you? You help me?"

"Okay?"

The woman said, "I see the Sister last night."

That got Claudio and Chavez's full attention, and they went to her.

"Go on," Chavez said. "What did you see?"

The woman acted even more nervous, then said, "We are hungry. My children are hungry and I am afraid. . . ."

Claudio understood, fished in his pants, and came up with fifty dollars worth of Argentine pesos, put them in her hand. "And that much again, if we find her."

She brightened, stuffed the cash in her bra, and gestured at the rear gate to the clinic. "I was at my brother's there, and I just heard the truck and looked out the window. I see her there, the doctor, all limp. Two men, they carry her out and put her in the back of a truck. They put blankets over her, and they drive away."

"The men," Claudio said. "Did you recognize them?"

She shook her head.

"They see you?" Chavez asked.

"No."

"What about the truck?" Claudio asked.

"What do you mean?"

"What kind of truck was it?"

"Oh," she said, shifting her baby to her other hip. "A farm truck, yes?"

A farm truck? Claudio thought.

"How do you know it was a farm truck?" Chavez asked.

She hesitated before saying, "When they put her in the back, some things fall out of there. When they're gone, I go out and look and there is a big, big cabbage in the mud."

"Where is it?" he asked.

"In our stomachs. I cut it up and boiled it. But not all," she said. "There's some left in the pot."

Chavez asked her if she could get some and bring it to them.

"Why?" Claudio asked when the woman trotted off.

"How many different kinds of big, big cabbages are there, and where are they grown locally?"

"Oh," Claudio said. "We can find someone to figure this out?"

"I'm sure."

The woman returned with some boiled cabbage wrapped in old newspaper. Claudio gave her the rest of the money, and Chavez thanked her. They retrieved Chavez's luggage from the clinic, walked out to the nearest main road, and hailed a cab. Chavez laid her head on his shoulder and dozed as they drove through the city.

Claudio felt the engagement ring in his pocket as if it weighed ten pounds. Part of him wanted to rouse her, and ask her in the taxi. Another part of him wanted to go down on his knees when they reached his apartment. But the better part of him knew it was not the right time, not with Sister Rachel missing or worse.

He would have to put the ring back in its box and hide it until Sister was found or released. It sucked, but it was what he would do.

Claudio looked at the cabbage sample Chavez held, before closing his eyes. He saw Sister Rachel clearly in his mind, and thought, *A farm? Out in the country? Is that where he's got you?*

22

SISTER RACHEL CAME AROUND in a blur. She felt sick, nauseated. Her eyes drifted open. A single bare lightbulb lit the tiny room, which seemed to turn slowly as if she were lying on the blades of a fan.

She was on a bare mattress on the cement floor of what used to be a bathroom. There was a filthy sink with a pump handle, an equally filthy toilet with no seat, and a shower with no curtain and no head on the pipe sticking out of the wall. The door was steel and featureless. The one window had been covered with a piece of plywood screwed into the wall.

What is this place? How did I get here?

The missionary doctor remembered being in the clinic, working on that poor woman Maria, trying to save her. She'd said good night to Inez, and gone to her office, and . . .

My God . . .

Her wrists were bound with duct tape. So were her ankles and lips. Her heart beat wildly. She thought of the children back at the Hogar, and it beat even harder. Were they okay?

Well, of course they were. The other sisters and Robin—

What had the man she'd seen in her office said? Something about Robin Monarch? Something about her saving him? Or could he save her? This time?

What other time was he talking . . . ?

Sister Rachel heard something on the other side of the door:

142

footsteps and then men laughing drunkenly. She felt her stomach curl. And she groggily took an inventory of her clothes and body. She was still wearing the purple hospital scrubs she used at the clinic. And she felt no soreness beyond a general ache from head to toe along with a desperate need to pee.

The missionary doctor tried to get over on her knees and elbows, but couldn't. Her arms and legs still felt weak and uncertain with whatever sedative they'd used on her. She managed to tear the duct tape off her mouth. She lay back, closed her eyes, and focused on her breathing, sucking in air through her nose slowly, holding it, and then exhaling hard through her mouth. She did it over and over again, twenty times in all, using her body's natural detoxification system to flush more of the sedative's effect from her.

When Sister Rachel tried a second time, she was able to use the sink to get to her feet. She almost passed out, but held on until her brain could take the change in position.

More confident now, she relieved herself in the filthy toilet, and then hopped back to the mattress and sat with her back to the corner. Bowing her head to pray, the missionary did not ask God why this had happened to her.

Instead, she asked God for the strength and the faith to endure whatever trials and dark times lay ahead of her. And she prayed that she be allowed to return to the refuge to continue her work.

There are more children every day, Lord, abandoned to the slums, consumed by poverty and sickness. Please let me continue to be an instrument of your compassion. Please let me . . .

The men outside the door were laughing again; she thought for a moment one or more of them were going to come inside. She felt neither fear nor anger hearing those voices, but when they ebbed away she couldn't help thinking about Monarch asking her what would happen to her work after she was gone.

A wave of fear and anxiety pulsed up through her before it turned to anger.

She was here, in captivity, separated from the children, and the clinic, her purpose in life, because of Monarch. This had nothing to do with her and her work. This was about his shadow life, she was sure of it. A weak part of her wanted to rue the night she'd saved him from the knife wound.

But a stronger part of her asked: who pushed him into the shadows?

In her mind, Sister Rachel saw a younger version of herself wrapped in a blue wool shawl opening the orphanage gate, and finding young Robin defeated.

"They would not come, Sister," he said. "The entire brotherhood. They laughed and jeered at me."

She put her hand on his arm, and led him inside the compound, saying quietly, "And men taunted Jesus when he bore his cross through Jerusalem. Do you know how many people have laughed at me for wanting to help the poor? Do you know how many times I've been threatened *because* I help the poor?"

Robin looked at her morosely. "You told me I had to do something big to be redeemed for the knife fight."

"And you still do," Sister Rachel said, steering him up the gravel drive toward the farmhouse and the barn she'd recently converted into the first real dormitory. "But now I want you to sleep for a few hours. When you get up, we'll climb again, and we'll pray."

"I can't do this anymore!" he shouted. "I'm sorry, Sister. I can't stay here, and climb up and down, and pray that purpose comes to find me."

Sister Rachel stopped him, and gazed earnestly into his eyes.

"Perhaps you're right, Robin," she said. "But this is not the time for you to decide that."

"Sister, please—"

"Go to sleep, Robin," she insisted. "For me."

Nine hours later, as dusk crept toward night, Robin followed Sister Rachel up the hill with the heavy knapsack on his back once more. Though he'd slept long and deep, he still looked crushed. The fact that he'd lost his family for the second time was not lost on the missionary doctor, and she'd spent the entire day thinking how best to handle the situation.

When they reached the top of the Difficult Way, Sister Rachel sat down on the bench while Robin took off the knapsack and set it between them. The coming night would be cold and crystal clear. Lights burst on below them in the city. She imagined that Buenos Aires looked spectacular and foreign to Robin that night, a place where he might have known the roads, but didn't feel like he could speak the language anymore.

"I think . . ." Sister Rachel began, and then stopped.

She'd never been one to hesitate before, and that made Robin turn to look at her. "You think what, Sister?"

The missionary squinted, discomfort in her cheeks before she replied, "I believe you must be naturally good at something in order to find your life's purpose. I was good at science, medicine, for example, and I cared about people, especially children, and that's how I found my calling."

Sister Rachel hesitated, and then said, "When I think of the things you are good at, Robin, your unique skills, I could not come up with a purpose that would be in line with the common good right away."

"Gee, thanks, Sister," he said, irritated.

"I said 'right away,'" she replied sharply, getting up and starting down the hill with him following. "But the more I thought and prayed, it dawned on me that you would make a good soldier. The military offers an education, food, shelter, and discipline, which I believe you could use in heavy doses."

"Me, a soldier?" he said, sounding surprised. "In the Argentine Army?"

"No," she said. "The U.S. Army. Your father was an American, correct?"

"Yes, but . . ."

"You were born in the United States?"

"Miami," he said.

"You had a U.S. passport?"

"Once upon a time."

"We'll get you another," Sister Rachel said. "It will take time, but we'll contact someone in Miami to get your birth certificate and then we'll go to the U.S. Embassy, get your passport replaced. I'll scrape together the money for an airplane ticket, and you'll be on your way to a new life, one far from—

The missionary startled from her memories at the sound of keys sliding into the lock. The door opened and a squat man in his late thirties, wearing a black wool hat pulled down over his ears, walked in. She remembered his face and the cap from her office at the clinic. He wore a red shirt, black cargo pants, and black shoes. He regarded her with amusement, as if he'd been looking forward to this moment.

"Been a long time," he said. "Been a long time coming."

Sister Rachel's head retreated several degrees. "Do I know you?"

"We met once," he said, closing the door behind him. "Different time. Different name."

His eyes were bloodshot, shiny. She smelled alcohol and cigarettes on his breath.

"I don't remember you," she said.

"No?" he chuckled. "You'll figure it out eventually."

"Why am I here?" she demanded. "Are you holding me for ransom? If so, you'll get nothing. I am a—"

"Not after your money, Sister," he said with a sigh. "I do this right, I get all sorts of money, and some long-overdue sweet revenge on the side."

The missionary studied him, wracking her brain, trying to figure out who he was. She still had no idea.

"You're taking revenge on me?" she asked.

He winked at her. "Way I see it, you were involved whether you meant it or not, so yeah. You're part of the package deal."

"What was I involved in? What did I ever do to you?"

Smiling coldly, he looked at the ceiling as if it held secrets. "You helped take what was mine, Sister. You and that piece of shit, Robin Monarch."

The missionary shook her head, still not remembering him. Then he drew up his right sleeve, revealing the acid-burned arm, said, "There used to be a tattoo there."

"You were a member of his gang?"

"Still don't remember me?" he said, and made a *tsk* noise. "Maybe this will help."

He tugged off the cap, revealing a grossly deformed right ear, and she knew him in an instant.

"I remember you. I don't remember your name, but I remember you. You took over the brotherhood."

He winked at her again. "I knew you'd figure it out eventually. Back then I was known as Hector."

"Hector . . . Vargas."

He smiled. "That's right. Hector Vargas." He said the name as if it were an old object pulled from a drawer, and it hung there in the silence that followed.

"Look," she said. "Robin and those other boys, they—"

"Why don't you shut the fuck up?" Vargas said, the smile

fading. "This is my world. And in my world, lame excuses get you nowhere."

He reached into his pants pocket, and came up with an elastic harness of sorts attached to a small plastic housing. He put the cap back on, and fitted the harness over it.

"Ever seen one of these?" he asked.

She shook her head.

"Called a GoPro camera," Vargas said. "Amazing HD quality. Really shows everything like up close and personal."

"I don't understand what you're doing. What you hope to—"

"Accomplish?" he said, and then chuckled. "Short term, this will keep the pressure up on good old Robin. Long term? That's a secret even I don't know."

"What? You're not making—" she began.

But he cut her off again, said, "You talk too much."

Vargas went to another pocket, came up with a small roll of duct tape. He came at her fast then, and slapped her face hard. She was so shocked by the blow, she didn't cry out before he stripped some tape, put it across her mouth, and then strapped it around the back of her head and across her mouth again snuggly.

Tears welled in her eyes and dripped down her cheeks.

Vargas went to his pockets a third time. When she saw what he held this time, Sister Rachel lost every bit of her dignity and began to scream.

23

RIO DE JANEIRO
TWELVE HOURS LATER . . .

THE STREETS BLARED WITH the pounding of samba drums, the trilling of whistles, and the blaring of horns. Hoarse and lusty voices called to mostly naked dancers, who shimmied and shook for Monarch's attention as he wove through an increasingly drunken and musky crowd celebrating the Friday of Carnival, the first really big street party of the celebration. The thief ignored all of it.

If I do this right, he told himself, *she survives. If I do this right, her work goes on.*

Monarch had to have complete and utter faith in that assumption of hope. Without it, he might falter. Without it, she might die.

And that, he vowed, was not happening. Monarch steeled himself for that level of trial, and turned off the main drag away from the late-day parade, wearing loose black cotton pants, a matching tunic, and rock-climbing shoes. In the small waist pack he wore beneath the tunic, he could feel the subtle weight of the tools of his trade: thin gloves, black hood, pick set, and the like.

Heading into the blocks around the Federal University of Rio de Janeiro, and trying to fit in among the academics and students walking to and from the celebration, he slowed to a stroll past a four-story office building that had seen better days. If the security system were just as shabby, the next hour would go easy. Maybe he'd even find the answer inside.

The thief wove figure eights in the blocks around the shabby structure killing time until night had fallen and the air was filled with choirs of insects that joined with the distant samba bands to form a wall of discord behind him. When he passed the target for the fourth time, all lights in the building were off save a single bulb over the front stoop.

Monarch found the dark alley that ran behind the structure. He glanced about before slipping into the shadows, tugging out the black hood, and putting it on. The gloves came last.

The pick case was in his hands and unzipped by the time he reached the office building's rear door. Given the age and general appearance of the place, he was surprised to find that the doors were steel and the Baden Locks new.

Would there be an alarm?

The thief guessed not, but decided to make sure. This was a simple B&E, but as in any skill the little things count. He got out a small Maglight, cupped the lens, and flipped it on. He cast the narrow glow around the perimeter of the door, and in the upper right-hand corner saw a steel conduit about the diameter of a pencil running off it. The conduit looked new and ran around the side of the building.

They're taking precautions, he thought. *They know the value of what they're on to. Well, it only made sense, right?*

Rather than bemoan this glitch in his plan, Monarch adapted, following the conduit around the corner to a control box above the electrical supply. Like the conduit and the locks, the control was new and digital. The thief wished he had thought to have

Barnett ship him some of the high-tech gadgetry they normally used to swiftly bypass such security systems.

Instead, he had to do it the old-fashioned way. From his pocket, he retrieved a Leatherman tool, and used it to unscrew the cover. The conduit spilled three leads: red, green, and black. It could have been much worse.

Monarch considered just disconnecting the telephone line and snipping the alarm lead, but figured there had to be a redundant and immediate response either way. So he dug into his pocket again, came up with a small spool of light-gauge electrical wire.

With the Leatherman the thief stripped off the ends of a single nine-inch length. He used the plier tool to form the exposed ends into narrow hooks, and then turned the flame of a cigarette lighter on them. When they glowed hot, he tugged the hooks against the red and green wires, watched them melt through plastic, and then bond with the underlying wire to form a loose circuit.

Enough current was still flowing to keep the controller from signaling a system failure, and triggering an alarm when he opened the door. He'd tear it all out as he left.

Monarch checked his watch, and saw it was half past seven. Dealing with the alarm had taken almost fifteen minutes. He wanted to be out of the alley and into the building as quickly as possible. The longer he remained in the public right of way, the bigger the chance of being spotted.

Monarch picked the new lock in less than a minute. But before he opened the door, he cut another length of wire, stripped it completely, and threaded it between the upper right-hand corner of the jamb and the door. Holding the wire there with his right hand, Monarch reached down and opened the door inward with his left, ready to sprint out of there if the alarm sounded. But he only heard that background thrum of bugs and the distant music of Carnival. Pivoting inside, he kept pressure on the wire where it met the plate of the alarm, and eased the door shut, and locked it. Turning on the small flashlight again, he walked halls and climbed stairs until he was outside a smoked glass door, with a sign that read VOVO INSTITUTE.

After checking around the door and finding no evidence of a second alarm system, Monarch picked the lock with ease and was soon inside a warren of four cramped offices with aging computers and beat-up furniture. There were names on the doors that allowed him to link what he saw in a given room with the dossiers Barnett had put together on each of the scientists.

The first office belonged to Philippe Rousseau, a French-Canadian who had a Ph.D. in botany from McGill University. The scientist taught at Rice University before coming to the University of Rio and the Institute two years before. The office was neat with many plants growing on stands set about the room. Some looked like dormant orchids, while others were blooming. There were several different kinds of succulent plants as well, one small, barrel-shaped, and armed with thorns, and another with long dagger stems. Besides a small stack of files, a ceremonial pipe of some sort, a lamp, and the desktop screen, his desk was clear.

There was no server for the computer. The screen and keyboard were connected to a CAT6 line that disappeared into the wall. A photograph on the wall showed Rousseau, a tall, thin man with a scruffy beard, hiking in the jungle. Another caught him near a dramatic waterfall. There was little else that spoke to the man's character or personality.

Todd Carson's personality, however, was widely apparent in the office across the hall. Behind his desk there was a framed certificate naming Carson as a second-team all-American infielder at Louisiana State. Beside it was a framed diploma from Berkeley, awarding him his Ph.D. in chemistry. There were fifteen or twenty pictures of the scientist, a beefy, jocular blond dude in all manner of outdoor scenes, from desert to jungle to surf and snowfield. In most he was grinning like he was having the best time of his life. In the few where he wasn't, he was with a stunningly beautiful woman with dark features and eyes that looked into the lens with a casual defiance.

In addition to the pictures, there were artifacts, and souvenirs from Carson's travels displayed about the room, many of them affixed to the wall, or crowding the shelves. But like Rousseau, Carson had no server beneath his desk, and little on top except the computer screen, and another one of those ceremonial pipes.

Monarch picked the pipe up, sniffed at the bowl, smelled something like vinegar, and set it down, thinking that there were no big filing cabinets in either of the offices. The two doors at the far end of the hall were locked. The one on the right was also dead-bolted. It took the thief three minutes to open it and step inside a room that was double the size of the other two. It smelled like perfume. Blackout shades were drawn and the curtains closed so he felt comfortable turning on a table lamp.

Monarch scanned the office, noting a closed door in the near corner, before pausing on a gleaming black safe that was bigger than a coffin. It looked completely out of place. He peered under the desk, and found no server, just a cable that ran out from the screen and lay disconnected on the floor. There was another cable coming out of the wall about three feet away, also disconnected.

These facts came together in the thief's mind. The scientists were using a single server for their research. The server and files were being stored inside the safe when the researchers weren't around. Monarch had not anticipated a safe. He would have to return the following night with the right equipment.

His training took over and told him to complete a reconnaissance run. The desk was completely bare. No pipe. No computer screen. There were three bookcases behind the desk, however, the lower shelves of which were filled with books on anthropology, biology, and genetics. The upper shelves held various primitive knickknacks, including yet another one of those ceremonial pipes occupying a place of honor between two framed doctoral degrees from Stanford University, one in anthropology and another in biogenetics.

On the shelf below the diplomas and the pipe were photographs featuring the recipient of the diplomas, that same exotic woman Monarch had seen in several of Carson's pictures. Her name was Estella Santos.

Santos ran the institute and was also the lead author of the research paper that had gotten Sister Rachel kidnapped. In one of the photographs, Santos was in her late twenties, standing in a graduation gown and cap with a handsome older man with much darker skin than hers, and an attractive Asian woman. To the thief's eye, the scientist seemed the perfect melding of both her mother and her father.

Another picture, faded, was of Santos as a young girl. She sat at the feet of an older woman with silken black hair, and skin that was the color of cured tobacco leaf. He figured she was in her late sixties, but could tell at a glance that she must have been stunning as a young woman. And the way she beamed at the camera suggested to Monarch that she was much younger in her mind than she was in her body.

A third photograph showed the view off the stern of a boat: a wide expanse of water shimmering in the soft rosy glow before sunset. Monarch studied it a second, wondering what significance it had, what clues it might yield before turning to the last picture.

In it, Santos stood with her arm about the shoulder of a younger woman with skin the color of oxblood, jet-black hair, and Indian features. They were on the lush banks of a muddy river, and couldn't have been dressed more differently. The

Indian woman wore a simple white T-shirt, faded floral-print skirt, and sandals. The scientist wore khaki shorts, a long-sleeve blouse, cap, and stout hiking boots.

But it was the expression on the women's faces that really caught Monarch's eye. While the Indian looked uncertain, the scientist was beaming as if this woman was everything she'd been looking for in life, the thing that answered all questions, confirmed all—

Monarch heard footsteps and then someone jiggling at the door to the suite. He bounded softly across the room, shut the door, turned off the light, and went to the other door, hoping it was another way out. Instead, he found a walk-in closet filled with women's clothes on hangers, and office supplies in a wall of wooden cubbies. Monarch shut the door, and then tucked himself in behind Santos's clothes.

He heard muffled voices coming, and then the office door opening and he could hear them plainly, two men and one woman.

"You read the rejection letter," Philippe Rousseau complained in accented English. "It was mocking. They won't publish."

A man Monarch took to be Todd Carson said in a deeper voice, "It called our integrity into question. Your integrity, Estella."

"And someday soon, we'll make them chew on their own words," Santos said. "Isn't that what Pasteur had to endure, the insistence on conventional wisdom? Didn't Madame Curie face the same things?"

"They did," Carson agreed. "Everyone who's ever made breakthroughs that profoundly affect human life has gone through this kind of knee-jerk criticism. We just have to man up and take it."

"Are you suggesting I'm not a man, Todd?" Rousseau demanded hotly.

"Nah," Carson said. "Just French. I understand the complex."

"Fuck you," Rousseau said.

"Cool down, the both of you," Santos said wearily. "I've got no time for this. The Bola Preta Ball at Scala starts in an hour and I need to be there."

"One of us should go with you," Carson said.

There was a pause before Santos said, "Actually, I hunt better alone, Todd. So, if you please, gentlemen, I'd like some privacy to get changed."

"What are you going to wear?" Rousseau asked.

"C'mon, Philippe," Santos said. "It's Carnival. Nothing less than the sexiest dress I own will do."

"And you have that here?" Carson asked with a hopeful tone to his voice.

"Right in my closet, but I'm not putting it on until you're both gone."

24

FUCK, THE THIEF THOUGHT as he listened to Carson and Rousseau leave the office and shut the door behind them. Santos is coming in here.

Did the clothes hanging from the high and low racks fully cover him? What if that sexy dress was right here?

The thief considered just overpowering the scientist and leaving. With the hood on, she'd never be able to identify him. But she would have security on the institute's offices beefed up even more. Maybe put a guard on duty.

Monarch slipped from behind the clothes, climbed up the cubbies until he was up on top, tight to the wall above the door. As her shoes padded toward the closet, the thief leaned out, pressed his hands against the opposite wall and then walked his feet up the wall behind him until he was braced flush against the ceiling. It was a core move and almost immediately he felt his wound site start to throb.

The door opened. The closet light went on. Estella Santos walked in about eight feet below the thief, tugging a blue short-sleeve shirt off to reveal a black bra and a very deep cleavage. She went to study her clothes along the opposite wall. She pushed aside skirts and dresses right where Monarch had been hiding, and isolated a flesh-toned dress with gold sequins.

The thief prayed Santos would grab her clothes and change in the outer room. Instead the scientist reached behind her back,

157

flipped the hooks, and then shook herself out of the bra. Monarch was so dumbfounded he almost lost his position and fell.

He willed his eyes almost shut, so he saw her moving like a shadow below him, putting on a flesh-colored bra and opaque, thigh-high hose. The wound was screeching at him now, and Monarch felt the sweat boiling on his neck and the crown of his head.

He felt the sweat begin to run when Santos grabbed the dress, a pair of pale high heels, exited the closet, turned out the light, and shut the door.

Swallowing a groan of relief, Monarch walked his feet down the wall onto the upper shelf so his body was no longer horizontal, but diagonally rising. He held the position, panting softly and slowly. But then the muscles around the wound site seized up, and he had to bite his lower lip not to cry out in pain.

He was tasting his own blood when he at last heard the sound of her high heels clipping across the wood floor, and saw the light under the closet door extinguish. The office door opened and shut.

"Oh, that sucked," Monarch grunted as he twisted and climbed down the cubbies.

He had to stand there a full five minutes before the convulsions stopped. It left him weak, and he wanted to go to his hotel room, sleep, and return the following night with his safecracking gear. But he recognized an opportunity, and the desire to exploit it was greater than his need to rest.

Monarch left the building without incident. He removed the bare wire once he had the lower rear door shut, put it in his pocket. He decided to leave the loose circuit attached, just in case he did have to return. Only then did the thief remove the black hood and gloves.

He took a cab to his hotel, showered, and put on gray linen slacks, loafers, and a short-sleeve black button-down he'd bought earlier that day. Outside, he hailed a cab, told him he was going to the Bola Preta Ball at Scala, and climbed in the back. Twenty minutes later, the way was blocked by thousands of revelers dancing. Monarch got basic directions to the Scala club, and climbed out.

There was Samba music playing everywhere, and people dancing all around him. The thief stayed focused, made his way to a narrow, cobble-stoned street in Lapa.

He found the Scala Samba Club, the roll up doors of which were flung open. The place was packed and guarded by security guys checking invitations and I.D.s.

Monarch backed off, and then swooped when he saw a young couple heading toward the bouncers. The thief bumped them from behind.

"Sorry," Monarch said, palming the invitation he'd plucked from the man's back pocket.

"No worries," the man, an Australian said.

He slipped off, and watched from out in the crowd as the young man tried to find his invitation. In the end, his name was on a list because they let him and his date in. Monarch followed them inside five minutes later.

Despite the raucous crowd, Monarch soon spotted the scientist. In that dress, with her athletic figure, bronze skin, and dark mahogany hair tugged back tightly against her head, she might have been the most beautiful woman the thief had ever seen. For several long moments he couldn't take his eyes off her. When he did, he saw that all the men in her vicinity were taking furtive glances at her and the unlikely object of her attention.

He was a much older guy, bald with a hunch to his back, and dressed in a fine linen suit. He seemed unimpressed by her beauty, but was listening closely to her as she spoke into his ear. When she drew back, he stared off thoughtfully, took her in at a long glance, and then shook his head. Santos used pleading hand gestures, but the result was the same, a resolute shake of the head. The scientist tried one more time, and then shrugged, shook the older man's hand and moved off.

This dance of Santos isolating some man or well-dressed woman, or groups of men and women, was repeated five or six times throughout the following two hours as Monarch observed the scientist discreetly and from a distance, noting that with every shake of the head, her shoulders dropped a bit more.

When she left the club, Santos bore all the signs of defeat. Bent slightly forward, hugging herself, she walked, searching for a cab, but they were all full. There were still thousands of revelers in the streets, which made Monarch's job easy. He followed her at a distance as she wandered along, lost in thought. She crossed a square by the arches of a white aqueduct, and into narrow streets, which quickly took on a seedy tone.

Where's she going? Monarch thought.

A blue van shot by and skidded to a halt by the scientist.

A door flew back. Three men jumped out. The biggest one wore a hood. Santos saw them coming, and started to run. The three men chased her down the sidewalk. One caught her by her hair and wrenched her to a halt. The other two put her arms in joint locks, and turned to drag her screaming toward the van.

The one who'd grabbed her by the hair felt a tap on his shoulder, and turned around only to take Monarch's fist to his eye. It made a crunching sound. He dropped.

The thief was already past the first man, heading for the big one with the hood, who reacted by dropping low and kicking in a long horizontal arc, trying to sweep Monarch's feet. It was a classic move in capoeira, Brazil's traditional martial art, but the thief easily jumped the kick, and returned the favor. He drove a knee into the side of the man's head, saw him sandbag, and spin around.

The third guy released Santos, dropped into a fighting crouch, and came up with a knife that he held like an ice pick. Such a hold is used to chop and slash. This guy knew what he was doing with a blade. Monarch, however, had spent years perfecting his own knife-fighting abilities.

"Run," Monarch barked at Santos.

The man twisted slightly left, faked high, and then chopped backhand and low.

Monarch spun backward off his front foot, moving just a few degrees off the arcing line of the blade. The thief's left hand darted out and grabbed across the top of the hooded guy's right wrist, got his fingers around the meat of his thumb, and drove his own thumb below the man's ring finger knuckle.

Monarch spun again to the rear, hauling the knife wielder around, and yanking him off balance. Then he pivoted his hips and torso powerfully back the other way, and used that sudden reversal of forces to viciously twist his bad guy's knife hand inward, over, and diagonally down until there was a splintering noise as the wrist spiral fractured.

He fell howling in pain, dropped the knife.

Santos screamed, "Help!"

Monarch looked up to see the scientist well down the block with the van in hot pursuit. He snagged the knife, took off, and caught up to her as the driver, a big guy, was opening the door. He saw Monarch, thought better of it, and threw the vehicle in reverse toward his fallen comrades.

"Are you all right?" Monarch demanded.

The scientist looked terrified, but nodded.

He glanced back down the street, and saw the other hooded men stumbling toward the van, said, "Let's get you out of here."

When he reached out to her, she shrank, said, "Who are you?"

"A Good Samaritan," Monarch replied. "Now let's go."

Santos looked uncertain, but then fell in beside him, trembling and starting to tear up. "I'm sorry," she said. "I just feel so weak all of a sudden."

"It's the adrenaline," Monarch said. "Here, hold on to my arm."

The scientist hesitated, and then did, glancing back over her shoulder. "They're going the other way now."

"Good," Monarch said. "Who were they?"

"I don't know."

"Word of advice? Don't dress like that and walk around lonely streets."

"I know, I . . . I didn't even know where I was . . . I . . . Where'd you learn to fight like that?"

"Here and there," he said.

Skeptical, she slowed, said, "What did you say your name was?"

"I didn't," the thief said, paused, and for some reason decided not to stay with a cover. "I'm Robin, Robin Monarch."

"Estella Santos," she said.

"Pretty name for a pretty lady," Monarch said.

The scientist smiled, glanced away. "So what do you do, Robin Monarch, besides saving damsels in distress?"

"This and that," he said.

"C'mon."

"I'm in the private security business."

"Lucky me."

"Lucky you," Monarch agreed before he spotted a cab and hailed it.

He opened the back door, let her climb in, and acted like he was about to close it before leaning in. "Any idea why someone would want to kidnap you?"

Santos dropped her gaze, said, "Not for money, that's for sure."

"No bad blood between you and anyone?" he asked.

"No," she said. "Not that I'm aware of anyway."

"Where are you going now?"

"My offices. And then home."

Monarch acted hesitant, and then climbed in beside her. "It will make me feel better if I make sure you're safe."

The scientist frowned. "That's not—"

The thief cut her off, said, "Call it pro-bono work, and afterward I promise not to bother you again."

"Well," she said. "You weren't bothering me at all."

Monarch looked at her, smiled. "That's good to hear."

Santos smiled softly, looked at her lap. "Are you here on business, Mr. Monarch?"

"Call me Robin, and actually I came in for Carnival," he replied. "It's been on my bucket list, and I was between projects, so here I am."

"You're kind of young for a bucket list."

"Deep bucket. What do you do?"

"I'm a researcher. At the university."

"And what do you research?"

She hesitated, and then said, "This and that."

Monarch grinned. "I suppose I deserved that."

"You did," the scientist said.

The thief fought the urge to press her, and stayed silent.

"Where do you live?" she asked.

"Here and there," he said, and laughed. "No, really, I have a ranch in Patagonia, but I'm on the road much of the time."

"You have a ranch in Patagonia?"

"Doesn't everyone?"

She looked out the window, said, "I gather you're quite successful with your private security business then?"

"I'm lucky enough. Money is not an issue, and I have to turn away work."

Santos seemed conflicted. He let her be conflicted. If this was to work, she had to believe it was her idea in the first place.

"That's our offices on the right," the scientist said, gesturing to the cabbie.

"Should I have him wait?" Monarch asked.

"No," she said. "Taxis are fairly regular here."

They got out. Monarch paid. The scientist had already opened the front door to the office building and went to a keypad in the lobby. She punched a number, said, "That's weird."

"What's that?" Monarch asked.

"It's blinking, something about reset," she said.

He looked at it with interest, said, "Probably a loose circuit somewhere."

"You'd know," Santos said, and climbed the stairs.

Monarch followed her to the suite of offices. When she turned on the light in the outer room, she said, "Sorry about the squeeze. There are six of us working here, and we're busting at the seams."

Six? Monarch thought. Who were the other three? He thought of that door opposite Santos's office, the one that had been locked.

"So what do you study besides this and that?" he asked.

Santos was at the mouth of the hallway. She looked back and said, "I study the science and culture of longevity."

Monarch acted surprised. "Interesting field."

"I like to think so . . ." she began as she headed toward her office, but then said, "Now who's here? Edouard? Graciella? Lourdes, are you there?"

The scientist stopped in front of the door opposite her office, and Monarch saw that a light shone beneath. Santos knocked, said, "Hello?"

There was no answer. She twisted the handle, pushed the door open, gaped in horror, and then broke into sobs, "No, Lourdes! Oh, my God, no!"

25

LOURDES MARTINEZ, SANTOS'S RESEARCH assistant, was naked, and sprawled on her back on one of three desks crammed together at the center of the small space. An electrical extension cord fit snuggly in grooves it had dug around the perimeter of her neck. Her tongue showed a blue shade, and her eyes were wide and red as bleeding.

Santos went hysterical and tried to go to the young woman, but Monarch restrained her. He didn't want the police involved, especially because he was involved, but he had no choice, and kicked himself for revealing his real name to the scientist. He could easily have used the Fischer cover and pulled it off flawlessly. Why had it been so important she knew his name?

"We need to call the police," the scientist said at last.

She broke down again. Monarch held her, and said, "I'll call. Is there somewhere you can sit down?"

Santos nodded through her tears, fumbled for keys, and opened the door to her office. It looked exactly the way he remembered it. Nothing out of place, not even the position of the safe dial, which he checked after getting her seated on the couch.

Monarch used the office phone to report the murder. Done, he crossed back to the scientist, who was daubing at her mascara-streaked cheeks, said, "Tell me about her."

"Lourdes?" the scientist said. "Very bright, very driven. She came to me from Harvard and was easily the best graduate assistant I've ever had. Compassionate, loyal, and strong. She has . . . had integrity."

"Boyfriends?"

"A few," she allowed. "But she was like me. She never let relationships get in the way of her work."

Santos said the same thing to Luis Neves, the homicide detective who showed up twenty minutes later.

Neves was in his mid-forties, with big bags under his eyes, a pushed-in face and fleshy cheeks. With the deep tan, black pompadour, and mutton chop sideburns he put Monarch in mind of a bulldog doing an Elvis impersonation. But the detective's line of questioning was far from comical.

The thief thought it was thorough, and smart. Neves put together timelines for both the scientist and Monarch. Santos said she'd last seen her graduate student around noon when she and two other Ph.D. candidates who worked at the Institute left to join the Carnival celebration.

The scientist said that she, Philippe Rousseau, and Todd Santos had gone out for an early dinner, before returning briefly to the offices around half past seven, where she changed into her dress and headed to the Bola Preta Ball.

"No one else was here?" Neves asked. "Just you three?"

"Here? In the offices? Absolutely."

Then the detective turned to Monarch, who spun the story of the international security expert in Rio for some R & R.

"You two hook up at Scala?" Neves asked.

"No," Monarch said. "Some guys attacked her beyond the aqueduct in Lapa. They tried to force her in a van. I stopped it."

"You report it?"

"I was about to when we found the body."

"It's true," Santos said, when the detective looked unconvinced.

"You got a card, Mr. Expert Ninja?" Neves asked.

"I do," Monarch said, and handed him a business card Barnett had designed that identified him by name as the principal at RMA Security Consultants, with offices in Washington D.C., London, and Miami.

In actuality, they were all postal boxes and the phone numbers automatically forwarded to Barnett, but it worked.

"So," the detective said. "You offer to come back with Ms. Santos to make sure she's safe after she's attacked, and you find Ms. Martinez's body?"

"Correct," Monarch said.

"You think they're connected?"

"Two violent acts in one night."

"Yeah, what's with that?" Neves asked, patting the top of his pompadour, and looking at Santos.

"I don't know," the scientist said. "I've never had anything happen like this in my entire life."

"Anything new in your entire life? Anything that would attract murderers and would-be kidnappers?"

Santos seemed to struggle again, before replying: "Our on-going research is promising. But I don't see how that gets Lourdes naked and strangled like that."

Neves nodded, said, "First glance she looks like she was asphyxiated while having sex. Supposedly makes the orgasm stronger. You know anything about that, Ms. Santos? Like who she was fucking?"

"No," she snapped. "Lauren didn't discuss her sex life, and neither do I."

They'd had the entire discussion so far in the anteroom of the suite, and before the detective could continue his questioning, there was a knock at the door. A uniformed patrolman stuck his head in and said, "You have visitors, sir."

"Let them in," the detective said.

A man Monarch recognized as Todd Carson came in first, looking ashen. He went straight to Santos's side, and said, "My god, Estella. Are you all right?"

"No, not really," she said.

Philippe Rousseau entered after Carson, wringing his hands, and saying, "Is it true? Lourdes is dead?"

The lead scientist nodded, tears welling in her eyes as she looked from him to two younger people who were bringing up the rear. Edouard Les Cailles was in his late twenties, disheveled, lanky, and drunk. Graciella Scuippa was in her mid-twenties, Brazilian, and appeared intoxicated as well.

When Graciella saw Santos nod, she held herself, moaned, "No." She hid her head against Edouard's chest, and burst into tears.

Choking back his own emotion, Rousseau's research assistant rubbed Graciella's back. The academics and their assistants all agreed with Santos's timeline. The three graduate researchers left the offices around noon, They were all drinking and having a good time, dancing in the streets of Central Rio around 2 p.m. when Lourdes Martinez announced that she had to go meet someone and would catch up with them later.

"She was real evasive about who she was meeting, and we were kidding her about a new boyfriend," Graciella said, crying again.

An older man exited the crime scene, came down the hall to Neves, and muttered something in his ear. The detective nodded, said, "I need to know where you all were between 7:45 and 8:15."

Carson said he was eating at a local Boteca. Rousseau had been jogging in Ipanema. The assistants said they'd been partying along with millions of others in and around the Central district of Rio.

"I was on my way to the ball," Santos said. "I have a taxi receipt."

"People see you at Scala?" Neves asked.

"Many people," she said. "I was there trying to raise money for our research."

"I'll need a list of names," he said. "And you Mr. Monarch?"

Monarch said, "Around seven forty-five I was taking a shower at my hotel. Around eight fifteen I was also in a cab, and yes, I, too, have a receipt."

He handed it to the detective, who studied it a moment and then nodded. "That's enough for now. But I'll need your contact information. Any plans to leave the country soon, Mr. Monarch?"

"No," he replied. "I kind of like it here."

"But what about Lourdes?" Graciella asked. "Her body, I mean?"

"There'll be an autopsy and then it will be released to her next of kin."

Carson's research assistant began to weep, "This is going to crush her parents. They were like her best friends."

Out in the hallway, Rousseau's assistant said, "What do we do now?"

"We go home," Santos said. "We sleep. And then we meet in the morning, decide on a plan of action."

"Did you raise any money?" Rousseau asked.

The scientists raised her chin, said, "I developed some promising leads."

"We're screwed," the Frenchman grumbled. "Our reputation will be in ruins."

"And the sky might fall in the morning," Santos snapped at him, and then looked at Monarch. "Shall we?"

"Wait," Carson said. "*He's* going home with you?"

"I'm checking her apartment," Monarch said, gazing at him evenly. "After what's happened, wouldn't you say it's the commonsense thing to do?"

"I could do that," Carson said.

"Not like him you can't," Santos said.

It was past two in the morning when the taxi pulled up in front of the scientist's apartment building in Botofogo. Drunken revelers were stumbling toward home. Two men and three women were laughing hysterically in the lobby. And the muffled thump and grind of samba music still echoed in the hallway outside Santos's apartment.

The scientist unlocked the door. Monarch pushed it open and flipped on the light. It had been trashed.

Santos was shocked at first to see her home life upside down, but then slowly turned furious as the extent of the search became clear. Every drawer, every cabinet, every closet, every piece of furniture had been emptied or overturned.

Santos's eyes watered and her jaw chewed the air before she covered her mouth and nose with her hands in a prayer pose and said in a trembling voice, "What's happening, Robin? I feel so . . . so violated."

"It's understandable," Monarch said soothingly.

"I should call the police," she said.

"I don't know how much good that will do," he said. "This place looks like it was run through by pros. How about I help you clean up, and figure out if anything's missing. I don't think they'll be coming back, but I'll sleep on your couch until morning."

Santos looked ready to argue, but then said simply, "Thank you."

As the thief worked to return the apartment to some kind of order he asked, "What do you think they might have been after, Estella?"

Again the scientist hesitated.

"Does it have to do with your research?"

Santos sighed finally, said, "It could be. The ramification of

171

our work is . . . profound. I'm not a businessperson, but I can see where it might be profitable."

"Why don't you tell me about the research?" he said.

"I can't talk about it."

"Pay me something, and my lips are sealed. Client privilege."

"I didn't know that applied to security consultants."

"It applies to this security consultant."

The scientist chewed her lip, and then got her purse, handed him a ten Brazilian Real note, and said, "Feel like coffee?"

"Love some," he said.

Over back-to-back espressos, she laid the situation out for him. Monarch listened intently and without comment until, finally, she said, "That's it."

"And you believe this is real, not just something they're telling you?" he asked.

"It's real enough to warrant further study," she said.

"But this academic journal wouldn't publish on that basis?"

"We got shot down by the peer reviewers," Santos said. "They didn't think the method of inquiry met rigorous scientific review, and referred to the population sample as entirely too small."

"That all?"

She laughed. "That and the fact that we have refused to reveal the location of this miracle. One of our peer reviewers, a real prick from Tulane, implied that it was a hoax."

"So that's what you need money for?" Monarch asked. "To go back?"

"Yes," Santos said. "And with the right equipment to do a full study."

"Why did everyone turn you down tonight?"

"Because we can't say the research is pending publication. Without that, no one wants to put up a dime."

"How much are we talking?"

She looked at him, rubbed the back of her neck, said, "I didn't want to—"

"How much?"

Santos sighed. "Two hundred and fifty thousand."

"Done," Monarch said.

"What?" she cried.

"I'll give you the two hundred and fifty thousand," the thief said calmly. "But on two conditions."

"Anything."

"One, I go with you."

Santos's face fell. "Anything except that."

"Why?" he asked. "You obviously need protection, and I'll be in a position to monitor my generous investment in your work."

She seemed uncertain. "And the other?"

"If this turns out to be legitimate, you give me first option on the discovery."

Tears dripped down her face. Monarch was puzzled.

"Okay, forget the option. Just think of the money as a donation."

She wiped at her tears and waved at him, saying, "No, I'm sorry, I'm never like this. But it's like you're some angel God sent to watch over me."

Monarch felt the conflict ignite in him. He'd already conned her into believing him a trusted ally, but when it came down to it, the thief was going to steal her secrets. He liked Santos, but he loved Sister Rachel.

"I'm no angel," he said. "Just a guy who'd like to see you succeed, and besides, there's nothing better than a great adventure."

"Adventure," Santos said, with a soft, knowing smile. "You have no idea what you're in for, Robin Monarch. Absolutely no idea."

26

ON THE OTHER SIDE of Rio, Silvio Juan Barbosa ignored the dramatic views of Sugarloaf Mountain and Copacabana Beach out his window, and rolled the nugget of his future around and around with his thumb, middle, and index fingers.

Worrying the nugget had a calming effect on the fifty-nine-year-old. Indeed, at the moment, it was the only thing keeping Barbosa from throwing one of his monumental tirades at the two men standing in front of his carved ebony desk.

"You had her and you let her get away?" Barbosa asked.

"No, senor," replied a brute named Correa who'd worked for Barbosa for years. "The doctor, she has a bodyguard now. A mixed–martial arts machine."

The other man, Gomes, had a black eye. "It's true, senor. A total machine."

Barbosa took this news with some surprise. Correa's sheer size and devotion to capoeira, Brazil's martial art, made him a terror in a fight. And Gomes was an expert in jiu-jitsu and a former cage-wrestling champion.

Standing up from behind his desk, Barbosa slipped the nugget of his future into his pants pocket and wondered what kind of man you would have to be to single-handedly take on Correa and Gomes and get the better of both of them in a street brawl.

Setting that aside, trying to focus his thoughts, Barbosa crossed to a giant map of Brazil framed on the wall. There were large red pins stuck in the map, clusters of them in places, especially so in Amazonia. His eyes traveled to a large area of the map depicting Brazil's far northwest corner where there were no pins at all.

He studied that area as his hand drifted to his pocket and retrieved the nugget. He would not surrender. Even if Estella Santos had muscle now, it would not stop Barbosa from fulfilling his heart's desire.

"If we can't force it out of her, we'll let her lead us to it," he said at last. "Use my jet, fly to Manaus, and get whatever gear you'll need for the jungle. Wait for her, and follow her wherever she goes. Just stay out of her bodyguard's way."

Correa's face screwed up. "But if we're in the jungle following—"

"Be smart about it, man," Barbosa snapped. "Use GPS transmitters. Plant them in their gear. Use the company helicopters. They're at your disposal. Bring satellite phones, weapons, and all the money you might need to make bribes. I don't care what it takes, gentlemen. Find me that ridge, and I'll make you both richer than your wildest dreams."

Both Correa and Gomes straightened up at that last bit.

Barbosa saw it and said, "But if you plan on returning empty-handed again, I advise you not to return at all. The consequences will be . . . well."

When they'd gone, Barbosa retreated into old habits. He'd gotten what he'd wanted in life by always having redundant plans.

He'd discovered a long time ago that the best method of achieving a goal was to attack it from as many angles as possible.

Barbosa retrieved a disposable phone from a desk drawer and hit redial. A moment later a man answered. "Yes?"

"Are you still with me?"

"Haven't you seen this morning's *O Dia*?" the man whined. "Page three?"

Barbosa's attention shot to the folded newspaper on the corner of his desk. He grabbed it, opened it to page three, and scanned the headlines until he saw the story of the young expatriate American student murdered in Estella Santos's offices.

"Was this necessary?" Barbosa asked.

"Very."

"No evidence left at the scene?"

"Nothing that can't be explained."

Barbosa thought through this development. He decided that the act, though severe, was worthy of some reciprocal gesture of trust.

"I'm sending reinforcements to Manaus," he said. "I expect you to assist them if need be."

"That's not a problem. Obviously we're willing to do whatever it takes."

"Good," Barbosa said. "I'll be in touch."

He hung up, put the phone back in its drawer, and kicked back in his chair, feet up on his desk, and held his future up so the sun caught it. At first glance the nugget didn't look like much. Irregularly shaped, it weight eighteen grams, a little more that half a troy ounce. The surface was scorched black and pitted, almost like hardened lava.

But the charring only covered one side.

When Barbosa turned the nugget over, the shiny side gleamed more brilliantly than mercury and a thousand times more valuable. He'd looked at it every waking hour since it was first dropped into his hand. He never failed to marvel at its beauty.

More precious than silver, he thought, more precious than gold. This is my future. I can see it as bright as the sun.

27

BEAU ARSENAULT STOOD IN the crowd on the corner of Basin Street and Canal, watching the Krewe of Dionysus Parade. Louisa's float was approaching, and he had to admit it was a showstopper.

The mogul's wife rode on a tower at the back of the float with two of her friends in gowns that evoked the Renaissance. Below the women, the Jester stood in his chariot, his leer huge and garish as he snapped a whip over the backs of the seven deadly sins. Envy was a bent-back old witch with an empty purse. A drunken ogre warned of Sloth. And Gluttony was a prehistoric hog.

But it was Lust that held Arsenault's eye the longest.

Louisa had depicted mythical sexual passion not as a faun, but as a striped centaur, part man with goggle eyes and his tongue hanging out of his head, part zebra with a black penis that drooped and came erect every few seconds.

How in God's name had she gotten that by the Krewe? The city?

People all around the mogul were roaring and pointing at the centaur's arousal and decline. Arsenault looked up and saw his

178

wife blowing him a kiss. He caught it, and transformed it into a thumbs-up that he pumped over his head. Louisa had done it again! The thing that people were going to talk about for months was that zebra's dick, which meant that the person people were going to talk about was Louisa.

His wife had a knack for getting herself known, and always in an inventive, sometimes risqué manner. The mogul loved Louisa for it. She was the best thing that had ever happened to him. He'd tell her so later when he got to the after party.

Arsenault turned and started to weave through the crowd partying along Basin Street, aware of the shabby Iberville housing projects to his left, and what it once was. Before the demolition in the early 1930s, Storyville had been the Big Easy's red-light district, and by all accounts one of the greatest in history, especially for men who liked chocolate.

Louis Armstrong's mother worked in there awhile.

So did hundreds of other colored gals.

Not for the first time in his life, the mogul cursed fate for having him born too late to have ever known such a pleasure palace. *Could you imagine?*

Arsenault could, and that fired up the longing in his loins. His new conquest, Lynette Chambers, was waiting for him at her club. If he played his cards right, he could be that centaur on Louisa's float. *Wouldn't that be too perfect?*

Digging in his pocket, he came up with a Viagra and swallowed it whole. Imagining himself a stallion, he turned toward the river and the French Quarter.

There were throngs of people in the streets, but the real noise was ahead and behind him when the burn phone in his pocket began to vibrate. He took it out, saw that Saunders was calling him, answered, and said, "Can this wait?"

The security chief said, "I thought you'd want to know where we stand."

Arsenault said, "Hold on a second." He got out a cigarette, another habit he hid from his wife, and lit it. He took a deep drag, and then said, "Go ahead."

"Monarch's definitely in," Saunders said. "He withdrew a quarter of a million from the account yesterday. He and Santos and her team have been spending it."

The billionaire took another drag, said, "On?"

"Scientific equipment, supplies, and transport," Saunders said.

"Specifics?"

"They bought three Zodiac rafts, four outboard motors, three fifty-five-gallon gas tanks," Saunders said as if reading from notes. "Ten solar battery packs. A water filtration system. Pack frames. It's a big expedition."

"What about the science equipment?" Arsenault asked as he blew out smoke.

"Three hard-case laptop computers," Saunders said. "A portable autoclave, an automated portable DNA sequencer with capillary gel and slab-gel platforms, a manual DNA SQ3 sequencer, Gene/Quant RNA/DNA calculator, DNA Centrivap system, Centra-CL2 centrifuge, and a miniature thermo-cycler. You want more?"

"No," the mogul said.

"They also chartered a small turbo-prop cargo plane. Leaving in the morning."

"Destination?"

"They haven't filed a flight plan, but I've got men on it, old and not-so-dear friends of Monarch."

"They didn't get carried away and kill Santos's assistant the other night?"

"They say no," Saunders said.

"You trust them?"

"They're pros getting a two-for-one here," he said. "I believe them."

"How mobile are they?"

"They've got a jet on standby. It will get wherever they're going well ahead of a cargo plane."

"Remind them they're not there to disrupt the research," Arsenault said.

"They understand the assignment."

"Good. Keep me posted."

The mogul hung up, finished the cigarette, and crushed it. He popped a breath mint, and set off again. Before he turned into the madness of Bourbon Street, he tore the SIMM card out of the burn phone and broke it. Then he twisted the phone until it snapped at the hinge. He tossed the pieces in overflowing trashcans as he passed.

Arsenault hated being in crowds like this, with lesser, sweating people pressing up against him. But this was where Lynette Chambers sang for her living. He felt his lips going a little numb, the Viagra kicking in.

What an incredible drug. Think of all the lives it's changed.

That caused him to look closer at the crowd flowing all around him, and then to think about that paper Santos and her colleagues had written. They'd failed peer review, but mounting a return expedition of this size indicated they were determined to come back with the needed proof. He wondered what it would mean if it were real, if it could be isolated, and then mass-produced?

When it came to sales this could be Viagra on steroids!

In the next second, his enthusiasm tempered considerably because he felt some unformed thought, a warning somewhere deep in his subconscious. Try as he might, he could not bring the thought whole.

It wasn't until he was on his way into the club where Lynette Chambers was singing that Arsenault was finally able to shrug off that sense of foreboding and imagine himself the stallion once more.

28

IT WAS BITTERLY COLD, even for mid-February, and light snow had begun to fall in the first light of dawn. Shivering, Gloria Barnett pulled the hood of her white down coat up over the white wool knit hat she wore over her red hair, and pushed back into the branches of a pine tree.

She had become used to the spa life and tropical weather since joining up with Monarch. If someone had told her even a week ago she would volunteer to get up at three in the morning for the third morning in a row to take a surveillance shift outdoors on a Swiss mountainside during the winter, she would have called him a fool, insane even.

But because Sister Rachel's life was at stake, there Barnett was, huddled under a tree on a steep face three hundred feet above and six hundred yards back from the lakeside estate of Tristan Hormel, the partner of the London banker who'd put the squeeze play on Monarch. Whatever it took they were going to get her back safe and sound.

She stamped her felt-lined Pac boots, and shivered again, but then unzipped her coat with white wool mittens, and pulled out

183

a pair of Leica 15 by 56 binoculars. Screwing them into the metal pan head of a carbon-fiber tripod, Barnett settled in behind the glasses.

Even though snow was falling the optics were so sharp and clear she was able to peer across the railroad tracks and the frontage road. The compound boasted four structures: a boat house, a six-bay carriage house, a three-thousand-square-foot guest "cottage," and a twelve-thousand-square-foot chalet that faced west-southwest. A high wall surrounded the place. Access from the frontage road was through a massive wrought-iron gate. Because of her position, Barnett was able to see diagonally down and through the gate bars, spotting two guards carrying semi-automatic weapons.

Barnett moved her attention back around the compound, scanning the openings in a loose scattering of fir trees around the cottage. She almost shifted her attention to the mansion, but then caught movement in those trees.

A large red and black German shepherd trotted through an opening and disappeared. A few moments later, she spotted a black shepherd to the east of the first one. It took another five minutes before she found the third, also a shepherd, with a black head and tan body.

At three minutes to six a man exited a caretaker's cottage and walked over by the stable before blowing a dog whistle. The dogs came in on three different fast vectors, bounding through the snow to the stable and then sitting before their master. He bowed over the dogs, rubbed their heads, and gave them treats and praise.

Then he gave a heel command and the dogs trailed him into the stable where she assumed there was a heated kennel waiting for them. Only then did Barnett turn her full attention to Hormel's home.

Lights glowed in many of the chalet's windows as the banker

and his family began their day. Hormel was married to Karen, a British national, and they had two children. As far as Barnett could tell, the Hormels led a life of luxury even by Swiss standards. The children, eleven-year-old Ingrid and nine-year-old Klaus, attended an expensive bilingual school in Zurich, which was roughly a forty-minute drive. Karen oversaw an extensive social life for the banker, as well as the estate and two other properties—a lavish ski condo at Gstaad, and a town house in Geneva that was undergoing renovation.

Hormel grew up in Zurich, graduated from the University of Geneva, and got his Ph.D. at the London School of Economics. He'd worked for a series of publicly held banks in England and Switzerland until joining forces with Pynchon eight years before in their private venture.

As Monarch had requested, she'd gotten Zullo involved, but so far the computer hacker had not yet been able to break into the bank's information system to look at its list of clients. Meanwhile, Barnett had done quite a bit of digging on the Internet. She'd found Hormel quoted from time to time in the Swiss business press, and mentioned along with his wife in the society columns. But little else had been written about the banker, except for the fact that he adored sailing and raced competitively all around Europe.

An article described Hormel as a "gifted captain and tactician," and quoted him as saying that while his wife and children enjoyed skiing, his passions were wind and water, and wind and ice. The article also mentioned that he'd invented a protective cage for his custom iceboat similar to those used in race cars.

"I have a family to think of, so I don't take as many risks as I used to," Hormel said. "But as soon as the ice goes out I'm on the water every morning before work. And in the winter, if we are not in Gstaad for the skiing, I live for sailing my iceboat when the conditions are right. Those days I go to work a little late."

In the past three days, evidently, the conditions had not been right because like clockwork, a minute after the dogs disappeared, a black, bulletproof Mercedes-Benz exited one of the carriage house bays, and pulled up by a side door. It opened and another armed guard exited, looked over the scene, and then opened the rear car door.

Barnett barely caught a glimpse of Hormel as he stepped out wearing a dark green homburg, a green double-caped overcoat, and scarf. His ducked his head against the snow, and then he was inside. The guard climbed in after him.

The Mercedes pulled out, drove to the gate, waited for it to open, and then headed north toward Zurich, where the bank had its primary Swiss offices.

Barnett pulled a two-way radio from her coat pocket, and clicked it twice. She heard two clicks come back, and pocketed the radio. A mile or so to the north, near the village of Räbmatt, Abbott Fowler would be getting ready to slide in behind the Mercedes and trail it.

The snow lessened, but the breeze picked up and the wind chill forced her to turn her face from it. She thought about her bed in the suite at the Four Seasons, imagined herself submerged up to her chin in hot water, and hung in there, waiting out the forty minutes until a second car, a gray Audi Q6, came out of the car barn and parked at the same side door.

This time, Hormel's wife and children emerged. Though they had a driver, there was no armed guard as far as Barnett could tell. The Audi left the estate and headed north as well. Big John Tatupu would trail that car to the private school the children attended, and then stay on Hormel's wife during her day.

I think I'm good, Barnett thought, making one last look through the binoculars at the house, the grounds, and the gate. The only person moving was the dog trainer leaving the stable.

She was about to pack it in, head back to the car she'd parked on a forest road a little over a mile to the south, but she caught a flicker of movement downhill two hundred yards to her right. She pressed her eyes to the binoculars again.

For a few seconds Barnett saw nothing but the snow falling on leafless hardwood trees above the frontage road. Then she spotted a tree limb that became the barrel of a gun and a figure in snow camouflage holding it. He had his right shoulder ironed into a tree trunk, and was aiming uphill at her through a telescopic sight.

She threw herself to the ground an instant before a bullet sheared off one of the tripod legs and smacked the pine tree behind her. Knowing a second shot was likely, she snatched the fallen tripod and the binoculars, and started crawling fast through the snow. She hoped her white outfit and low profile would keep her out of his sights until she could reach denser cover.

When Barnett was just shy of the deeper woods, she heard a bullet whiz past her head. It sent her into high gear. Lurching to her feet, she lunged toward the thicker woods, making erratic cuts back and forth with every step. Barnett suffered from scoliosis, and moved awkwardly even when she was relaxed. That awkwardness probably saved her, kept the sniper from getting a solid sight picture on her until she'd stumbled into the wood line and out of his line of fire.

Barnett stopped for a few beats, gasping for air, and reassessed. That had to have been one of Hormel's men. They were onto the surveillance and ready to do anything to protect the banker. The gunman had been at least two hundred yards down a steep hill and she had a head start she needed to maintain. She tugged off the hood, held the busted tripod and binoculars across her chest, and started to head out across the steep side hill.

When she realized she was leaving tracks in the snow, she

began to run as hard as she could given her awkward gait. Barnett reached an opening in the forest, a hundred-yard-wide rock-strewn avalanche chute that she crossed as quickly as she dared. *Is the rifleman alone? Does he know the area? Was he calling allies to have them circle around to the forest road?*

She'd no sooner had that thought than she heard the thud of the rifle going off a third time. It must have been a snap shot from across the opening behind her because she never heard it hit.

Barnett knew that he was going to catch up to her, not far ahead, probably on the narrow bench she had to cross before reaching the road.

What would Monarch do?

She took off in a last frantic sprint.

What would Monarch do?

He'd go on offense using whatever weapon he had.

But Barnett had no gun, no weapon at all. And she was built like a rail, delicate, with very little power. For a few moments she was panic stricken.

What do I do? There's nothing I can do to—

She reached the near end of that long, narrow bench in the woods. There was a sheer granite cliff to her immediate left and downed trees choking the way forward. In that change in topography and barrier, she saw her weapon and her chance.

Trembling with nervousness, Gloria stepped into her tracks from the morning and walked ten yards. Then she stopped and walked backward five yards, putting her boots right in her tracks. She leaped sideways over the trunk of one tree, and into an almost natural blind formed by the exposed root system of another.

Peering through the roots, keeping an eye on her back trail, Barnett stripped the binoculars off the tripod and let them drop in the snow at her feet.

Then she shakily held the two remaining legs of the tripod like a long baseball bat, set her feet so her left shoulder faced her back trail, and waited. She could hear rocks clack against each other as her pursuer crossed the chute.

The snow picked up. She heard him curse in German. Ever so slowly, Barnett turned her head enough that she could see through the roots. He was right behind her and to her left now, no more than twenty yards away.

He had his rifle cradled in one arm, and was wiping the snow from his eyes with his free hand. Trying to breathe slowly, Barnett waited until the sniper stepped almost parallel to her before twisting and lashing the tripod at him.

He caught her movement, and stutter-stepped back, trying to swing the gun her way. But the metal pan head of the tripod struck him above the eye, stunned him, and opened a gash that gushed blood.

He dropped to one knee.

Barnett swung again, hitting the side of his head with a dull cracking sound. He flopped over in the snow, unmoving.

For a second or two, she was frozen in shock. It had worked!

Then she realized she might have killed the gunman and felt sick. She'd never killed anyone, not even close. She wasn't a field agent. She was a runner, for God's sake.

Stepping back across the log so she could see better, Barnett sighed with relief. He was bleeding from both head wounds, and his breathing was erratic, but he was definitely alive.

Barnett took up his gun, the binoculars, and the broken tripod. Figuring he'd come around at some point in the next hour, she left him there and stalked her way to the road. She waited in the trees off the road until she was sure the car wasn't being watched, and then ran like hell.

Five minutes later, she turned onto the highway away from Hormel's estate, the defroster on high, and the gun in the trunk.

Forty minutes after that, she was in the bathroom in the suite at the Four Seasons, lowering herself into fourteen inches of deliciously hot, steamy water.

Barnett lay back, feeling the cold cook out of her, and relived her counterattack in the woods. She smiled, thinking that even Monarch would approve.

Then she went back through everything that had happened before that first rifle shot. The dogs going to kennel at first light. Hormel and his bodyguard leaving a minute or two later. A break and then his wife and children leaving.

Three days in a row, they'd done virtually the same things at the same time. It was a strong pattern.

If the pattern breaks, we can exploit it even if Hormel's men know we're watching the estate.

29

MONARCH DOZED IN A window seat of a Saab 350 turbo prop cargo plane until they hit turbulence. His head jerked slightly. He startled awake, looked around groggily. The seat beside him was empty. Across the aisle, Todd Carson was sleeping next to Philippe Rousseau. In front of them the two graduate students were slumped over in their seats.

Monarch's head jerked slightly again when Estella Santos leaned over his seat from behind.

"Sorry to wake you, but look out the window," the scientist whispered. "There she is. The mother of us all."

Monarch came fully awake, turned his head, and saw that the sun was rising. The dawn light gave him his first look at the Amazon. It flowed in ribbons and loose braids through dense misty jungle toward a narrow lake that stretched north. As far as he could see there was only water and rain forest canopies glowing in a golden light that took his breath away. The thief had been born and raised in cities, but he was always moved by primitive places and untouched wilderness.

191

"What do you think of her? My river?" Estella Santos said, sliding into the seat beside him.

"I think she's beautiful."

"Upriver, where she is young, that's where you'll see her real beauty," Santos promised. "Coffee?"

"Perfect."

With a thermos of coffee, she filled a cup for him. Monarch glanced at his watch, and saw it was nearly five thirty. They'd left Rio at midnight, and landed once to refuel.

"How much longer?" he murmured after taking a sip of the strong coffee.

"To Manaus? Not long."

The thief drank again, and looked back out the window, seeing flocks of white birds circling above the jungle canopy. The scene unfolding below might have mesmerized him on another day, but he was on a mission to save Sister Rachel. That was all that really mattered.

The soldier in him started taking a mental inventory of the gear they'd amassed on short notice. Santos had a detailed equipment list since coming out of the jungle the last time, and it had merely been an issue of dividing up the task of buying it all. From the time Monarch had promised her the money, she'd been on the go, chartering the flight and arranging for the equipment to be moved to the airport even as she dealt with the death of her research assistant.

The scientist had insisted they delay their departure until Lourdes Martinez's father had her coffin put aboard a flight to the States. Homicide Detective Neves was there to see the body off as well. Neves had refused to answer any questions about the autopsy, and gotten angry when Santos told him they were all heading deep into the Amazon for an indefinite period of time. He'd demanded to know exactly where, and the scientist had refused to say. With no cause to arrest or retain anyone, however, he'd let them take off with demands that they report in immediately upon their return.

Who killed Lourdes Martinez? Why? Was her death related to that attempt to grab Santos?

The sun rose higher in the sky, revealing deeper parts of the jungle and throwing a glimmering sheen across the river. The thief pushed thoughts of the slain assistant and the equipment into a box in his mind, closed it, and opened another that held Sister Rachel.

He prayed Vargas or whoever had her was keeping her in good health, and that she was staying mentally strong. Monarch had been imprisoned several times in his life, once for nearly nine months, and he knew how debilitating the experience could—

Santos leaned across him, gestured to the northwest.

"That's the main channel of the river out there."

The vast river plain seemed to have quadrupled in size with lake after lake spilling into the wide muddy river. It was awe inspiring, and for several long moments he gave into the spectacle. They banked out over the main channel and followed it west, and the thief's gaze swam back and forth, catching sight of hundreds of tributaries feeding the mightiest of Earth's rivers like so many veins.

He glanced over at Santos, whose eyes were glistening with excitement that struck him as deep-rooted.

"You never did tell me how you got onto all of this in the first place," he said.

The scientist cocked her head thoughtfully, and said, "It's a long story."

"Pour me another cup, and give me the high points."

Santos hesitated, poured him more coffee. She told him that her father, who was Brazilian, got his master's degree in electrical engineering at the University of Southern California, where he'd met her mother, a second-generation Japanese who worked as a secretary at the school. When Estella was born, her father's grandmother came from Brazil to help with the baby's care.

"Vovo stayed," the scientist said.

"Wait, your institute is named for her?"

"That's right," she said. "Vovo cared for me throughout my childhood. She lived with us until she passed away my first year in college."

Monarch remembered that picture in Santos's office that showed her as a girl with that older woman with the tobacco-juice skin and the beaming smile.

"Vovo had this energy that was just remarkable," Santos recalled. "She was fun. She was strict. She was loving. She always worked hard, and demanded you did, too."

Vovo spoke Portuguese, some broken English, and an Indian dialect. From the time Santos was a baby, Vovo had spoken to her in that dialect. She picked it up quickly. Her father spoke some of the language, but Estella got better at it.

It was as if the great-grandmother and great-granddaughter shared a secret tongue. When the old woman put Santos to bed she often spun fantastic stories in the language. Many of the tales described Vovo growing up deep in the Amazon jungle.

"She said she lived in a hidden valley that was the most beautiful place on Earth," the scientist said. "They slept in caves and beneath underhung cliffs, and there was food growing everywhere. Life was easy. Every night they sat around fires and told stories of their people, and how they were the valley's protectors."

Monarch saw where her story might be going. But Santos surprised him. She said her great-grandmother told her there were tribal shaman in the valley who claimed to keep records of every birth and death, and because they studied the stars and the moon as the gods had taught them, they claimed to know the age of everyone in the tribe.

The scientist gazed off into a distant memory. "I must have been six or seven when she told me that some members of the tribe, boys and girls, died around the age of sixteen, but others passed away in their sixties and seventies. She also claimed that there were tribal members, often these shaman, who lived to more than one hundred and forty years old."

The thief's face screwed up skeptically. "How is that possible?"

"Exactly my reaction," Santos replied. "By the time I was ten or eleven I just thought it was Vovo making these crazy stories up. She had a way of embellishing everything. Truly fantastic."

For example, the scientist's great-grandmother said that during her childhood, when one of the sixteen-year-old children died, their bodies were burned, and out of their ashes came other adolescents given to them by the gods to become part of the tribe.

Vovo told her great-granddaughter that she had been frightened as her sixteenth birthday approached. But she awoke that day feeling fine and expecting to be married off by sunset to one of several young men in the tribe. Instead, her parents gave her a special drink. As she finished it, they wept.

"Vovo said the next thing she knew, she was lying out in the jungle wearing a ragged yellow dress," Santos said.

The pilot came on over the loudspeaker, said they were ten minutes from landing. The other members of the expedition began to rouse.

"To be continued once we get on the boat?" Santos said. "We have a long journey to Tefé and then beyond."

Monarch was fascinated, wanted to press her, get the rest of the story, but he could tell she was already thinking of other things.

"I look forward to it."

Out the plane window Monarch watched the jungle give way

to clearings, farms, and shantytowns before a surprisingly large city appeared on the horizon. Manaus sat on a lake formed by the confluence of two big tributaries of the Amazon, the Negro and the Solimões, and, according to Santos, the capital of Amazonia had long been the largest trade and industrial base in northern Brazil, with almost two million residents.

"This doesn't feel remote at all," he said, noting the soccer stadium, the spires of old churches, and minor skyscrapers.

"It's the major jumping off point into real jungle," Santos said. "The road system beyond here is virtually nonexistent. You can go deeper by plane, but with this much gear it would be insanely expensive. We'll take a high-speed ferry to Tefé, about a hundred and twenty-five miles upriver. Beyond that it's largely untouched wilderness to the Peruvian border, where the terrain starts to rise toward the Andes."

Monarch lived on a small *estancia* in Patagonia, near the southern end of the Andes, and he wondered what the great mountain range looked like this far north. Before he could ask Santos whether the mountains were visible from the river basin where they were going, the plane dropped altitude and landed.

It was all business for the next few hours. The plane took them to a private hangar where they transferred the supplies and equipment from the cargo hold to a flatbed delivery truck. The heat and humidity built with every minute and was brutal by the time they were finished.

"I need a shower," Monarch said. "I'm drenched."

"You could take twenty showers a day and it wouldn't make a difference," Santos said. "There'll be no getting away from the heat and humidity where we're going. You have to slow down and drink a lot of water or it will get you for sure."

Monarch was only half paying attention to her.

A private jet had landed and taxied to a stop on the tarmac two hundred yards away. Six or seven men wearing dark sunglasses, shorts, and colorful shirts poured out of it, heading into another hangar. He would have written them off as well-to-do tourists were it not for the way they carried themselves. They were alert, heads roving about, and their gait studied: balance forward, hips and shoulders square to the ground. To Monarch's eyes, their posture read combat, and their actions screamed military-trained.

"Robin?" Santos said.

Monarch startled and looked away from the jet and its passengers to find the scientist gazing at him with her arms crossed. "Didn't you hear me? We're ready to go. We've got a van waiting outside."

Beyond her the flatbed was already in gear, rolling toward the open back doors of the hangar. The other scientists and their assistants followed on foot.

"Sorry," Monarch said, picked up his knapsack, and glanced over his shoulder again seeing that the men were all inside the other hangar except a shaved-head black guy built like a linebacker, pulling a carry-on with wheels.

He saw the man for a beat or two and only from behind, but Monarch had the odd sense that he reminded him of someone.

30

MONARCH WANTED TO STROLL down there and try to get a better look at him and the others, but Santos was impatient. He turned and went with the scientist to the van. They left the airport, and drove into Manaus, a city literally hacked out of the jungle, and built up by pioneers, who'd erected municipal buildings, theaters, and churches.

It was overcast and misting that day, and the temperature at noon hovered at one hundred and two. Even so, he wouldn't use the air conditioner. Instead, Monarch hung out the window, taking it all in. He reveled in the smells of exotic places. Here he caught the scents of peppers and frying oil, bread and brewing coffee, oxen and goats.

Braying donkeys, sheep, and people crowded the narrower streets near the fish and meat markets, where a rank stench pervaded. Against it all pulsating funk music blared from shops and booths. Vendors yelled to him, offering their wares. A group of kids broke from the crowd, and came up alongside the taxi begging. Monarch threw coins and bills at them and caused a minor riot that made him genuinely happy in one sense and somber in another.

He loved helping poor kids, but they'd made him think of Sister Rachel.

It had been roughly four days since she was taken. Monarch had been held against his will and knew what day four felt like.

Unless she was blindfolded or deprived of light, the first two or three days would pass quickly. But ninety-six hours into her captivity, even if she were being treated well, Sister Rachel would begin to despair. It broke his heart, but knew from personal experience that doubt has a way of creeping up on you in your darkest hours.

They made a series of stops to fully stock their food supplies, and to buy spare plugs, wires, and hoses for the outboard engines. They had a late lunch of incredibly good pulled pork sandwiches before driving down to the lake around four that afternoon.

They parked near the old customhouse and the central pier where three multideck, surprisingly large and colorful ferries were docked. Hundreds of passengers and animals were leaving the ferries all at once, creating a pushing, yelling, crying mob on the wharf.

Santos went to the ferry office to negotiate and pay lading charges for the supplies and equipment. Monarch let Carson, Rousseau, and their graduate assistants oversee the loading of the gear into a hold on one of the high-speed river vessels.

With more than thirty minutes until they set sail, he walked to a small park between the wharf and the old customhouse, and dug out a satellite phone he'd bought in Rio.

He tried to call Claudio, but got his machine. Monarch said he'd try to call later. He next phoned Gloria Barnett, and found her defrosting in a steaming bath at a four-star in Zug, Switzerland.

"We've been on the Hormels for three days," she told him. "The estate's a fortress with armed guards and dogs patrolling at night. Hormel travels in a bulletproof limo."

"Someone feels threatened," Monarch said.

"Definitely. Zullo's having no luck getting into his computers, personal, and professional. He thinks Hormel has been down this road before."

"Hacked?"

"Affirmative. The firewall and security system is custom and state of the art. Zullo still doesn't quite understand it."

"So what's the plan?"

"Tats and Fowler aren't back yet, but I think there's a chink in the armor we might be able to exploit, grab Hormel, and squeeze him."

"They have any idea you're there?"

Barnett explained what had happened earlier that morning. Monarch listened in amazement to her account of being chased through the snow, and then setting up an ambush with a tripod for a weapon.

Gloria? She was the best black ops runner in the world, but flunked out of the CIA's field program. *To take out a guy with an improvised weapon was, well, incredible!*

"What are you laughing at? That was the scariest moment of my life!"

"No, no, I'm laughing at . . . I dunno . . . the fact that you are much more devious and resourceful than I give you credit for. Gloria Barnett you are a . . . a beast!"

She giggled, and replied, "I had a great teacher. The scientists have any idea what you're really up to?"

Monarch shifted uncomfortably, said, "No."

"Any angle we're missing?"

"Sami Rafiq," Monarch said. "He got me into this."

"He was pretty pissed at you after Thailand."

"I know," Monarch said. "If you get the chance, call him, tell him I'm not happy."

"He'll have a nervous breakdown."

"Treachery has repercussions."

He heard the ferry horn blow. "Gotta go. Leave me messages or e-mails."

He hung up before she replied, and then headed to the wharf. Monarch pushed aside thoughts of the Lebanese forger and wrestled with conflicting emotions over deceiving Dr. Santos. She was a good person, hard working, with high ideals, not the sort of scum he usually set out to fleece.

And the work Santos was doing . . .

Sister Rachel had always preached to him about the importance of the greater good. But where did the greater good put the missionary's life when balanced against the kind of scientific breakthrough Santos's research promised?

So what was really at stake here? Ownership? Christ, stealing ideas happened all the time in university labs. He'd heard of a guy who actually invented the computer mouse at MIT, and never got a cent from it.

The ferry horn sounded again. He trotted down the wharf knowing when it came right down to it, no matter how good a person Estella Santos was, he would take her secrets and he would trade them.

He owed Sister Rachel that much and more.

31

SISTER RACHEL KEPT TAKING deep breaths and letting them out slow as she prayed to God to save her from what was to come.

It was only a matter of time now. Vargas had fed her hours ago, so it would not be long before she heard the key in the lock again, and her trial would begin again. It had been that way yesterday, and the three days before that.

The missionary had always believed that her conviction in God would be enough to weather any storm, endure any challenge. Her devoutness had taken her to the Sisters of Hope and to the slums. When the odds were completely against her, belief had enabled her to build up a clinic, and then an orphanage.

But this was different. For the first time in her life, she truly understood the torture and hardship Jesus went through during his forty days and forty nights in the desert. For the first time, she understood what it was to face evil in a battle for her soul.

Pure evil. There was no other ways to describe Vargas, and still she sought to understand him. How had he gotten that way?

Her question led her, as it had several times in the past four days, to memories of she and Robin climbing down the steep hill behind the orphanage the afternoon after he'd failed to sway any of his brothers away from the gang.

*

"You'll think about going to America and joining the military?" Sister Rachel asked. Light was waning and Robin had become a silhouette on the trail in front of her.

He didn't say anything for several moments, and then replied, "I will."

Before she could take the conversation in another direction, both Sister Rachel and Robin alerted to the bell ringing at the front gate to the orphanage. It kept ringing every minute or so, seventeen times in all by the missionary's count.

When they entered the compound by the rear door, one of the Sisters of Hope, an older nurse named Evangeline, hurried to them, rubbing her hands together.

"Why doesn't someone answer the bell?" Sister Rachel asked.

"There are many unsavory men outside the gate, Sister," Sister Evangeline said with a worried tone. "We have spoken to them through the porthole, but they will not say what they want other than to talk to you."

"To me?"

"Yes, Sister," Sister Evangeline said.

"You can get cleaned up, and ready for dinner," Sister Rachel told Robin, and set off toward the front gate. Many of the orphans were standing in groups back from the gate, watching it with apprehension.

She paid close attention to their reaction. She'd found over the years that orphans had the uncanny ability to sense possible trouble. The missionary opened the porthole to the gate, and saw in the dim light from a streetlamp a large group of men. She frowned, took two steps to her right and flipped a switch, turning on the outside lights.

"Why did you keep them in the dark?" she asked Sister Evangeline.

Sister Evangeline had no answer, lowered her head, said, "I don't know, Sister. They troubled me."

Sister Rachel noticed that Robin was standing with several of the older children. Returning to the porthole, she saw the men, most of them in their early twenties, all of them hard and suspicious.

Except the handsome lanky kid with the wild curly brown hair, who said, "You remember me? Sister Rachel? I was the one who told you about the stabbing in the *ano*?"

She remembered him then. "Yes."

"My name is Claudio. We are all friends of Robin."

He showed her the tattoo on his inner right arm, said, "Do you really think I can become a painter?"

Her heart beat wildly, before she replied, "Claudio, you can become anything as long as you do it in the name of a greater good."

"What about being a motorcycle builder?" asked a second young man, who stepped up beside Claudio to peer into the porthole at her.

"I don't see why not."

"A cook?" another called to her.

"God loves good cooks, just as he loves all who serve a purpose."

"Well, then," Claudio said. "You have room for seventeen of us in there?"

"You'll have to earn your keep, but we'll make room," Sister Rachel replied, and, ignoring Sister Evangeline's doubtful stare, lifted the iron bar that locked the gate.

When Claudio and sixteen brothers trooped through the open gate, the missionary looked to Robin, who grinned and fought back tears.

"You've done a great and difficult thing," Sister Rachel told him hours later when Claudio and the others had bedded down in the barn, and the children had all gone to sleep in the dormitory.

"Does it help me?" he asked. "I mean, with that scale?"

"I should think it helps a great deal, Robin. I'm very proud of you."

Robin beamed, nodded, and headed off toward the barn and his brothers.

Sister Rachel watched him go, and wondered what else he might be capable of. Though his moral compass was hardly true, she believed he was all possibility and energy, a boy who—

The gate bell at the orphanage pealed once more.

This time the missionary went alone and turned on the outside light before opening the porthole door to see a muscled young man with a shaved head and a deformed ear glaring at her.

"I want my brothers, bitch," he said.

"Your brothers are sleeping," she said calmly. "They need a good night sleep if they are to go another way in their life. Would you like to join them?"

"Join them," he said, spitting the words back at her. "You tell those fucking traitors, Robin and Claudio and all the other cowards that the brotherhood lives on without them, and the brotherhood never forgets. You tell them one day they'll die for what they've done. You too, bitch."

Before she could say anything he spun on his heels, and walked off. Five or six other men appeared from the shadows and trailed him.

The key slid in the door lock, ripping Sister Rachel from those long-ago days.

The dead bolt threw. Panic surged through the missionary, and she had to fight to remain calm when the door opened, and Vargas entered.

Glassy-eyed, a lot drunk, he was holding a roll of duct tape, and that thing he used to attack her soul.

"Time for more payback, bitch," he said. "Like I told you, *la fraternidad* never forgets."

Refusing to show him fear, Sister Rachel said, "I forgive you."

"Aw, that's sweet, so Christian of you," Vargas replied. "But here's the thing: El Cazador does not believe in God, and he does not forgive. Never have. Never will."

32

THE FERRY WAS A madhouse.

All four decks above the hold were jammed with people and chickens, parrots, and geese in cages, and tied-up goats, and every other thing you could imagine. Families camped on their luggage or boxes up top, and lounged in hammocks they slung from the ceilings on the lower decks. The ship came about and headed west, upriver. The sun broke through and beat down with a shimmering intensity that made the humidity that much worse. The smell of humanity and the river was everywhere.

Ashore, the modern skyline of Manaus gave way over the next hour to riverbanks and low hillsides covered in ramshackle wooden hovels built on stilts and painted in pastel blues, pinks, and greens; and then to larger shacks and fishing villages and the confluence of the two rivers that formed the lake.

Santos pointed out where the Negro River came in clear from the north and the highlands of Colombia, and where the Solimões River flowed muddy from the vast jungle basin. The ferry passed over the seam of clear water giving way to the silted current, and chugged upstream into one of those braided deltas Monarch had seen from the plane.

The forest that lined the Solimões was dense, towering, and many hues of green. Mist hung from the treetops and licked at vines that bloomed with scarlet and crimson flowers. There were birds flying everywhere, big white ones soaring high above the canopy, brilliant blue ones flitting in the lower branches, and magenta ones darting over the river as insects hatched.

"What kind of trees are these?" Monarch asked. "They all look different."

"Because they are different," Santos said. "On a single hectare of jungle in this area, you could find a thousand different species of trees and plants. In the entire basin there are believed to be more than eighty thousand different plant species, but more are being discovered all the time. You're looking at the lungs of the world, Monarch. Without the diversity of trees and plants in this basin, life as we know it, would end."

"What about global warming?"

"That won't affect the rain forest much, as a matter of fact," she said. "These trees have been growing here since prehistoric times, much hotter eras than are predicted by climate scientists in our future. Unless they are cut down by farmers clearing land, or miners stripping them aside so they can get at the minerals underneath, the trees will be around long after humans are gone."

The researcher said this all with such passion that Monarch reappraised her, asked, "Do you do everything with such intensity?"

She smiled, cocked her head, and said, "Well, of course. If you're going to do something, don't be half-assed about it."

"Personal creed?" he asked, amused.

"That was actually my great-grandmother's advice," she said.

"Vovo," Monarch said.

"That's right."

"You kind of left me in the lurch on her story. You cut me off when she woke up in the jungle in a ratty old dress."

"A ratty old yellow dress," Santos said, smiling again.

As they sailed deeper into the Amazon rain forest, Santos told Monarch that her great-grandmother had screamed for help upon finding herself alone, but soon realized that she'd been abandoned. Walking in bigger and bigger circles, Vovo finally stumbled onto a game path, and started to follow it.

She walked for days along the game paths, eating fruit and drinking water from streams, before she found a wider trail that led her to a fishing village on the banks of the upper Amazon.

"She couldn't speak a word of Portuguese," Santos said. "And the people, especially the women there, treated her horribly, called her *mulhar da cavena*. The cave woman. Things like that. I think they were cruel because Vovo was so beautiful. Ultimately her beauty saved her."

Santos said an older couple gave her great-grandmother a place to sleep and food to eat in return for work. Through them she learned basic Portuguese. There were men after Vovo almost from the beginning. One in particular, a fisherman whom she found repulsive, was always trying to get her alone.

One day the ugly fisherman cornered her on the riverbank away from the village where she'd gone to do laundry. He knocked her down and was tearing her clothes off when a man yelled out. He was on a boat fifty yards out from the bank and had a rifle.

"My great-grandfather was the most handsome man she'd ever seen," Santos said. "He rescued her and fell in love with her at first sight. He was a mining engineer from São Paulo, and within six months she was married to him, and having his children."

"Is that true?"

"Absolutely," the scientist said. "My great-grandfather kept meticulous records, and journals. I've read every one of them, and actually it's because of his papers that I started to believe some of her old stories."

"How's that?"

"Vovo died in 1994," Dr. Santos recalled. "It shocked us all.

Honest to God, she was strong, healthy, and happy to the end. Just passed on in her sleep. I was really shaken up by it, though. We were very close, and I started going through her things."

Santos found a fireproof box of documents that included her great-grandfather's university diplomas, photographs, will, and journals. The birth certificate of the scientist's father's father was there as were those of her grandfather's siblings. She also found Vovo's marriage license. It read that on July 19, 1898, Vovo, whose legal name was Ulé Cavernas, married Tomas Fuego. He was twenty-five. She was seventeen.

Santos stopped talking, leaned on the ferry rail, and gazed at Monarch, said, "Do the math."

Monarch was good at figures, so he was surprised he hadn't seen it right away, even before she told him to run the numbers.

"She was one hundred and fourteen when she died?"

"Give or take a year," Santos said, nodding. "We can't be too sure of those original shaman calculations."

Monarch remembered the snapshot of Vovo and Santos as a girl, and was mightily impressed. He'd guessed Vovo had been in her sixties.

"So she was in her early nineties when she came to care for you?"

"Give or take another year."

"That's incredible."

"Exactly, my reaction. You would never, ever, have thought she was that old."

"Did she tell you she was that old?"

"Never." Santos laughed. "You'd ask, and she'd say she was as old as a Brazil nut tree or something like that. I figured she was in her eighties around the time she died."

"Did your dad think she was that old?"

She sobered. "He died the year before she did. I never had the chance to ask him."

"Your mom?"

Santos sobered further. "Early on-set dementia."

"God, I'm sorry," Monarch said.

"Me too," Santos said, chewing the inside of her cheek. "My mom's situation drove me here as much as Vovo's old—"

A miserable-looking, soaking-wet Graciella Scuippa appeared, and said, "We've got to rotate shifts. You can't believe how hot it is down there."

Todd Carson's research assistant had been below deck guarding the equipment since they'd left nearly two hours before.

"I'll go and relieve him," Santos said. "We'll do hour shifts."

Monarch said, "I'll go with you."

"*I'll* go with you, Stella," Carson said, fixing Monarch with a stare. "I need to talk to you about a few things anyway."

Figuring it was probably better to maintain civility, Monarch said, "I'll get the next shift."

Santos and Carson returned an hour later looking drained. When Monarch entered the hold, he almost immediately had trouble breathing. The air was so saturated and superheated it felt like a full-on steam bath. He took off his shirt, and sat down, resting his back against the cargo net that covered the big outboard motors and the deflated Zodiac rafts. His eyes adjusted and he could see other men in the hold, guarding their valuables as well, and watching him.

Monarch closed his eyes, and a few moments later heard Philippe Rousseau climb down the ladder and come to sit down beside him, gasping, "It's like being in the third circle of hell down here."

That opened Monarch's eyes to study the French Canadian botanist. "You've been to the third circle of hell?"

"Read about it," Rousseau said. "You?"

"I've actually been past the third circle quite a few times,"

Monarch said. "This is just a mind-over-matter deal, not even close to the third wheel."

That quieted Rousseau for a few beats, then he said, "What's with the tattoo?"

"Something left over from a few lifetimes ago," Monarch replied.

Two or three minutes went by, and Monarch was starting to drop into a heat-induced trancelike state when Rousseau said, "Estella won't fuck you, in case you were wondering."

Monarch squinted at the botanist, said, "I wasn't wondering."

"You must be the first man on Earth who upon meeting Estella Santos hasn't."

Monarch said nothing, but remembered doing the human fly in her closet at the institute. She was absolutely stunningly beautiful. And her breasts and hips were works of art. There was no doubt of that, but he'd been trying to avoid thinking about her in that respect. Allowing himself to fantasize about her could cloud his judgment. For Sister Rachel's sake he had so far refused to let that happen.

"Carson has been trying to get in her pants from day one," Rousseau remarked. "He follows her around like a puppy dog, hoping one day she'll drop her panties and bang him senseless."

"Uh, huh," Monarch said. "And you?"

"Me?" Rousseau said. "I wanted to fuck her the moment I saw her, but she'll have none of it with me, Carson, or you. She says it keeps things easier when she's the only woman around on an expedition."

"Smart lady, Dr. Santos," Monarch said.

"I wondered for a while if she was a lesbian," Rousseau said thoughtfully. "But Lourdes said she had male dates out of the office."

"You sound like you're obsessed," Monarch said.

"Just interested," he said. "And you're not?"

"Nope."

"You gay?"

"Nope."

"Insane?"

"That's debatable."

"What's in it for you then? If you're not here to fuck her, I mean, why are you *really* here?"

"I like adventures, and she needed protection."

"But you bankrolled this."

"That's right."

"What do you get in return?"

"First option to try to set up a deal once she's authenticated and patented the discovery."

The botanist stiffened, said, "I certainly didn't agree to that."

"If you've got some side deal with her on this research, I'm sure she's taking care of you," Monarch said reasonably.

"There was another funding option, you know," Rousseau said, obviously unhappy. "She turned it down without even consulting us, and then cut a deal with you. Estella does this kind of stuff all the time, and it frankly pisses me off."

"That's between the two of you," Monarch said.

The botanist stewed on that, before saying, "Well, in any case, we're a long way from patents and options. We don't have enough data yet to support the overall claim. And we have little clue as to what is responsible for the phenomenon."

"You must have suspicions," Monarch said.

The botanist studied him, nodded, said, "I believe it's a plant, though which one I have no idea. That would be like looking for the needle in the haystack. You'll see once we get in there."

"What are we talking? One, two days more travel?"

"Three if we're lucky," Rousseau said.

"Why aren't we just hiring a helicopter?"

"Try bringing that idea up to Estella and I guarantee you that you will never, ever fuck her," the botanist said. "She has it in her head that she can learn their secrets and let them be, leave them the way we found them forever."

"Kind of noble when you think about it."

With a dismissive flip of his hand, Rousseau replied, "Leaving them the way we found them is impossible. People said the same thing the last time one of these lost tribes was discovered in Papua New Guinea. In one generation they were done, the culture destroyed."

33

THE SUN WAS FINALLY slanting toward the horizon by the time Monarch came up out of the hold with Rousseau. Though the temperature on deck hovered in the mid-nineties, it seemed cool after the stultifying heat in the confined space below. The two graduate assistants weren't happy about it, but they went down the ladder to take their second watch.

Monarch went to the stern, and sat on a coil of rope where he could catch the breeze. He tried Claudio again, and this time his friend answered.

"Any luck finding Sister or Vargas, brother?" Monarch asked.

Claudio told him about Maria, the woman who'd seen Sister Rachel put into a pickup truck that had also been carrying produce.

"That could be one of thousands around," Monarch said. "No license plate?"

"She said they drove off with their lights off and it was dark and raining."

"And the brothers? No one has been contacted by Hector?"

"Not yet, but then again, I've been trying to talk with the ones who followed you to Sister Rachel. Maybe I should be looking for the four or five who stayed with him after we were gone."

"Alonzo? Tito?"

"They're around, I'm sure. It's just going to be a matter of finding them."

"Chanel?"

He hesitated. "She's good."

"You haven't asked her?"

"It hasn't seemed like a good time."

"You're probably right. Anyway, I'm on a ferry, heading up the Amazon."

"Lucky you."

"Santos is putting restrictions on using the sat phone, but I'll check for messages."

"I know anything, I'll call," Claudio promised. "Be safe."

"Always," Monarch said, and hung up.

He found Santos at the forward rail on the third deck. The light from the setting sun threw her in a copper glow that made her even more beautiful, and turned the river burnt red and the jungle a burnished bronze.

Gazing all around with enchanted eyes, she beamed with happiness.

"You like the jungle," Monarch said.

"I love it."

"Why?"

"It's just so old and so impossible to comprehend. It makes me feel small."

Monarch watched her in profile, and had a hard time trying not to feel infatuated. But then he caught movement out of the corner of his eye and saw Todd Carson weaving through the crowd toward them, looking displeased to see Monarch with the scientist.

"I got you your Coke, Stella," Carson said. "It's actually cold."

Monarch turned from them when he noticed another ferry, smaller and faster, swing out wide from behind the ferry he was on, looking to pass. It too was packed with people and animals and cargo, but it was steadily overtaking the bigger vessel.

He saw several young kids waving from behind the rail on

the foredeck of the faster boat, and their mothers and fathers and older siblings standing behind them. Monarch smiled, and then happened to glance beyond them into the shadows under a canvas awning stretched above the foredeck. At first he saw only the silhouette of a very large, very muscular man. If he'd blinked, that's all he would have seen.

But for a split second a thin beam from the setting sun shot through the shadows beneath the stretched canvas, lit the man up from his waist to the top of his head, and then died. Monarch felt confusion and anxiety pulse through him when he realized he wasn't going to get a better look at the man as the faster ferry went by.

He stared after it, wondering if what he'd seen was possible.

"You all right, Robin?" Santos asked. "You look like you've seen a ghost."

"No," he said. "Just the light playing tricks on me."

Was that true? Had that brief slashing light just triggered an old and terrible memory, or had that really been Jason Dokken standing there?

The thief's mind went in reverse twelve years. Monarch saw Dokken, a Special Forces operator, cursing him for betrayal, and vowing revenge. The big black guy walking away from the private jet earlier had reminded him of someone. Dokken. The man had always had a distinctive posture and way of moving, easy, and with a lot of hip action, like a horse.

Was that Dokken on the boat and back at the airport? If so, why was he here of all places? Who were the guys he was with? And what were they doing here?

Monarch hadn't thought about Dokken in years. Wouldn't he still be serving out his sentence in Leavenworth? What did he get? Fifteen years? But it's only been twelve years since the court-martial.

Monarch had been released from Leavenworth after serving

less than eight months of his sentence by agreeing to try to steal the Iraqi war plan in advance of Operation Iraqi Freedom. In return, he received a total commutation of his sentence.

But Dokken had been left to rot away the prime years of his manhood. He'd be, what? Late thirties now? Forty?

The thief got his satellite phone out again, leaned over the rail, and called Gloria. But John Tatupu picked up.

"You missing some Samoan?" Tatupu asked by way of greeting.

"Every day," Monarch said, grinning. "Cold there?"

"Don't start with that," Tatupu said. "Guys like me aren't meant for places like Switzerland. What's it there, a hundred in the shade?"

"Ninety at night," Monarch said.

Tatupu groaned, but then said, "We're going to wait a few days before we try to take Hormel in for a little questioning. After Gloria's adventure in the woods, his security will be on full alert."

Monarch would have much preferred Hormel being squeezed as soon as possible, and certainly before he got too deep in the jungle to react quickly to any news of Sister Rachel's location. But he knew Tatupu's strategy was sound.

"So I had something strange happen just a few minutes ago," Monarch said. "I thought I saw Dokken go by me on a faster ferry."

"Heat's getting to you," Tatupu said. "Dokken's in Leavenworth."

"You know that for sure?"

"That why you're calling Gloria?"

"Can't hurt to double-check."

"I'll let her know soon as she wakes up," Tatupu said.

"I appreciate it, Tats, and everything you all are doing for Sister."

"You're welcome, but it's the least we can do."

"Have Gloria message me when she finds out about Dokken."

"Will do," he said, and hung up.

Monarch was consumed in thought for much of the evening, wondering about Dokken, wondering about the odds of both Dokken and Vargas coming back into his life at the same time. That couldn't be a coincidence. They had to be acting on behalf of the same third party represented by Hormel and Pynchon.

Who was it? Who was the son of a bitch manipulating him? Whoever it was, the swine was going to pay, and pay big time.

When he and Rousseau returned to the hold for a second shift, it was still hot, but no longer a furnace. Monarch slept for much of his time on post. As soon as he got back on deck he booted up the satellite phone and saw an e-mail message from Barnett.

It read: "Dokken paroled for good behavior and was released from Leavenworth six months ago. Current whereabouts unknown."

Monarch closed his eyes a moment, before muttering, "I know where he is. Probably ten miles upriver of me right now."

Indeed, when the ferry docked at the small town of Coari, a good seven hours into the voyage, the smaller ferry had already stopped and sailed on.

Monarch couldn't sleep even after the two graduate students said the hold had cooled enough that they would stay down there the rest of the night. He stood at the rail and smelled the jungle and the river and grappled with the sense that events from long ago were coming back around to him.

Still troubled, he decided to take a walk. There were people sleeping everywhere on the decks, but they'd left paths between them that Monarch padded, lost in thought as the ferry trolled ever onward upriver.

The thief was down on the A deck around 3:00 A.M. when he saw a great big slab of a man come up out of the gangway that led to the ladder down into the cargo hold. Monarch didn't recognize him. Or did he?

The man glanced at Monarch as if unconcerned, and brushed by him, heading the other way. The thief paused to look after him, but saw nothing familiar. Was he so tired he was imagining enemies everywhere now, all part of a vast conspiracy?

The area immediately around the gangway and over to the rail looked clear of bodies, and Monarch naturally gravitated to the space. But when he got on the other side of the bulwark, he bumped into cages holding chickens and other fowl.

Some of the birds began to softly squawk and cluck, making just enough noise to cover the sounds of footsteps. He didn't hear them until they were very close. The pace triggered a warning in his head, and he spun away from the birdcages.

The big dude who'd just come out of the hold was less than three feet away and closing fast. He held a knife with a wicked-looking black blade.

He had a reverse grip on the handle, and swung the blade as if he meant to bury it in Monarch's chest. The thief's reflexes took over. His left hand shot up and slapped the knife wielder's elbow before he could extend and slash down with his forearm, hand, and the point of blade. The slap deflected the line of the attack by inches. The tip of the blade barely touched Monarch's shirt and shoulder.

Monarch pivoted to his left, trying to close space, intent on grabbing the man's wrist and breaking his hold on the knife. His attacker was too quick. He spun with Monarch and elbowed him, striking him high on the right cheekbone.

The blow staggered Monarch, and he reeled backward, knocking over the cages. Chickens, ducks, and other fowl began to squawk loudly. People woke and shouted, adding to the din and alarm, but it didn't slow the guy with the knife in the least.

Sensing Monarch was shaken, he attacked again. In a

backhand strike, he slashed at Monarch's torso.

The blade of Monarch's right hand chopped back, almost along the same line. The strike connected with a nerve bundle on the underside of the big guy's wrist. It stopped the arc of the blade, and almost caused him to drop the knife.

Monarch's attacker was clever though, and tossed the knife to his other hand, catching it by the handle in a more conventional grip, as if he were about to cut steak. The thief stepped around his back, trying to grab him by the hair and get hold of his left arm and the knife.

He tore a hunk of hair out of the man's scalp, but couldn't control his head. The big guy mule-kicked at Monarch, and missed before twisting low to face the thief.

Monarch saw he meant to drive the blade up under his rib cage. As he sprang, the thief lunged a full step backward toward the rail, seeing the blade miss his sternum and flash by his nose.

He snagged the man by his left wrist and belt then. He pivoted hard and to the inside, feeling the man's balance dissolve before hurling him off the side of the ferry.

34

MONARCH HEARD HIM CURSE as he plunged headfirst fifteen feet into the murky water. The thief stood at the rail, panting, ignoring the squabbling of the chickens and the owners of the chickens who were now bitching at him in Portuguese, looking for the knife guy to appear in the glow of the ferry's running lights. But he saw nothing but the swirling Amazon and darkness.

When he finally left the rail, he glared at the chicken owners and they stepped aside. Then he glared at all the people who'd woken and witnessed the knife fight, and they got out of his way as well.

Monarch went to the ladder that led down into the hold. There were only two bare bulbs burning on the second level below deck, leaving the space dim and shadowed. When he reached the bottom of the ladder, he waited for his eyes to adjust, and then looked around, seeing many of the same people from earlier in the evening.

He found the two graduate assistants asleep in each other's arms, and nudged the boot of Edouard Les Cailles, Rousseau's aide. He didn't budge. Monarch kicked his foot. Les Cailles startled awake and shrank at Monarch's silhouette, waking Graciella Scuippa.

"What's going on, Edouard?" she mumbled, and then saw the thief.

"Did you see a guy climb out of here ten minutes ago?" Monarch asked.

"What?" Les Cailles asked. "*Non,* we were sleeping, why?"

"He just tried to stick a knife in me."

They both sat up. "Where is he?"

"Swimming."

They said nothing for several beats, confusion on their faces, until Carson's assistant asked in a wavering voice, "Do you think it was the same guy who killed Lourdes?"

"Why would you think that?"

Graciella shrugged uncomfortably and he thought he saw her eyes welling with tears before she said, "I have never known anyone murdered before Lourdes. And now a man tries to stab you, and you're with us, and I'm getting scared about this trip."

Monarch couldn't argue with her logic. Someone was targeting members of the research team. But who? And why? And what had made the guy come after him like that, almost as an afterthought?

"Go on up on deck," he said. "I'll stay here until we dock in Tefé."

The graduate assistants appeared uncertain at first, but when they saw Monarch wasn't budging, they gathered their things, stuffed them into knapsacks, and left the hold.

No one else below deck had moved since the thief came down the ladder. He lay back on the cargo netting, thinking that he'd sleep better if he dug down into the gear and retrieved the dry bag that held the guns he'd bought in Rio.

They hadn't been difficult to find. He'd paid six thousand U.S. dollars for a Brazilian-made IMBEL paratrooper-style automatic rifle, two Taurus twelve-gauge, pistol-grip, pump-action combat shotguns, and a Beretta 9mm pistol with one hundred rounds of ammunition for each weapon. He hadn't told Santos about his weapons stash, and wouldn't unless he decided they were all at risk.

Despite the earlier attack, that hadn't happened yet.

He closed his eyes, and drifted toward unconsciousness. The last thing he heard was the ferry hitting something in the river, a small rock or a tree limb that struck the hull and made a noise like a distant bell pealing.

The thief shut his eyes and his thoughts swung back to the bell at the front gate to the Hogar, and flashed on images from the days after most of the brothers had abandoned *la fraternidad,* and set out on a new path.

He relived how wonderful it had felt when Sister Rachel lifted the pack of rocks off his back and dumped them on the ground, and how grateful he'd been to her at that moment.

He was still grateful to her. Sister Rachel had given him, Claudio, and the others, a shot at a new life. The missionary doctor had shown him the road to redemption, or at least a way of balancing out his life by dedicating part of it to a cause beyond his own gain.

The thief opened his eyes in the dim hold. The image of Sister Rachel opening her arms to hug him the day he set off for America was so clear that he choked at the thought of her being held against her will.

Since Pynchon, the scumbag banker, had showed up at his hotel to show him the video of Sister Rachel being taken, Monarch had not once considered the consequences of failure. They were unfathomable, and yet his mind tried to conjure them. In two, maybe three seconds he saw all sorts of ways Sister Rachel might suffer at the hands of Hector Vargas, and at the hands of whoever was behind him.

Monarch sickened physically and mentally before feeling the ferry engines thrown in reverse, and the ship's momentum shift to port. They were docking at Tefé.

Taking several deep breaths, the thief willed all thoughts of failure and its consequences aside. When the ferry sidled into the dock, he bowed his head and vowed not to think about the future, or the past anymore. He would live for the moment, and he would use every moment to rescue her.

Monarch waited until Rousseau and Carson came to oversee the unloading of the gear, and went against the flow of a stampede on deck as passengers fought to get off, heading forward where he found Santos and the graduate assistants preparing to move the research equipment, their personal items, and the food.

The scientist took one look at the knot below the thief's eye, and said stiffly, "Did you get that in the knife fight?"

"Lucky elbow," Monarch said.

"Why didn't you wake me?" Santos demanded.

"I didn't see the need. The danger had been averted. And someone had to get a good night's sleep. It might as well have been you and your colleagues."

"I know you gave us the money, and I know you're protecting us, but this is my project, my expedition."

"You've got no argument from me there."

"Then I need to know what you know, when you know it. Am I clear?"

"As a bell," Monarch said. "How long are we staying here?"

"As long as it takes to inflate the rafts, and pack the gear," the scientist replied. "I want to be well upriver before darkness falls."

"How much farther?" he asked.

"We've still got a ways to go," she replied vaguely. "How fast we get there depends on the rains upstream."

Sensing he wasn't going to get much more out of her, Monarch said, "Let's start hauling stuff out of here then."

A helicopter came roaring upriver and passed overhead.

225

Monarch saw a logo on the side that read SJB Mining Company before the bird disappeared.

He stacked several large plastic bins holding food, picked them up and carried them toward the exit. Most of the passengers had fled the ship, and were moving en masse toward shore and Tefé, a town of seventy thousand people. Many of them looked more indigenous than African or European.

The hold was opened. A small deck crane lifted out the pallets that held the Zodiac rafts and outboard engines, and set them on the wharf, where Rousseau and Carson oversaw a crew of locals transferring the gear into the bed of an old pickup truck.

Monarch scanned the scene, looking up and down the wharf and the two piers beyond, looking for Dokken, but not finding him. This was a much smaller place than Manaus, and a crew of big guys would stand out.

It took several back-and-forth trips to get everything off the ferry, and into the bed of the pickup, before he noticed there were several loose bands of boys working the wharf, hustling people.

"Can you do some translating for me?" Monarch asked Santos.

"Sure," she said, and followed him as he walked to three kids eyeing him warily.

"Ask them if they saw a group of big guys get off the ferry that came earlier this morning," Monarch said.

Santos said, "What big guys?"

"The ones who got off that private jet back in Manaus," Monarch said. "I thought I saw them on the other ferry. So could you please ask?"

She chewed the inside of her cheek, and did. The boys nodded, replied. Santos said, "They think there were six of them."

"Big, big black guy with them?"

The boys nodded.

"Where'd they go?"

One of them gestured east across the river and spoke. Santos said, "They left here about an hour ago in fishing rafts. Peacock bass is a big business here."

"They had rods and gear?"

The boys nodded.

"Whose rafts were they?"

Two of the boys shrugged, but the smallest of them replied. Santos said, "They belong to a father of a friend of his."

"Ask him if he knows where I can find his friend's father."

"He wants money to tell you."

Monarch smiled. "Of course he does."

35

AFTER NEGOTIATING A PRICE and giving the kid half up front, Monarch and Santos followed him off the dock and toward the center of the small town.

"He says it's not far," Santos said, her face hardening. "Who do you think those guys are?"

"They may be just a bunch of adventure tourists for all I know," Monarch said. "But one of them looked like a guy I used to know."

"A dangerous guy?"

The thief glanced at her, saw her concern, said, "That too."

The kid took a left into a bar, and gestured at a short, squat man in his early thirties, who was happily three sheets to the wind at eight in the morning.

The intoxicated fisherman saw the kid, smiled, saw Santos, and smiled even more.

"Ask him—" Monarch began.

"I'll handle this," the scientist said, and walked up and sat on a stool next to the fisherman, who openly leered at her chest.

Santos crooked her finger, put it under his chin, and lifted it before smiling and talking to him in a low, but animated voice. He glanced over at Monarch once, but kept talking and taking sidelong looks at her chest.

She leaned over after about five minutes, kissed him on the

cheek, and laughed when he playfully spanked at her bottom as she moved toward Monarch.

"He got a call last night from a friend in Manaus," she said. "His friend said a group of fishermen from the States wanted to rent his rafts to explore and fish. He told them they had to hire guides, too, until they offered him twenty times the going rate for two weeks' use of the rafts. They handed him the money, loaded their gear, and left. They seemed to know where they were going."

"He see fishing rods?"

"And tackle boxes," she replied. "Satisfied?"

"For the moment," Monarch said. He still wasn't convinced.

He gave the kid the rest of the money, and he and Santos headed back toward the waterfront through the bustling town.

"So this is the last big outpost?" Monarch asked. "Tefé?"

"There are a few villages ahead, but this is the last of civilization," she said. "Beyond here, the real jungle begins. Beyond here, you better be prepared for anything."

"The people look different here," he said. "More Indian influence?"

"Very observant of you," she said. "It's why I started looking in Tefé first. This is the kind of place where indigenous people really do walk in from the jungle."

"Is this where your great-grandmother came out?"

"That's miles upstream yet, but this is where I began my original search."

Santos explained that after college, she was accepted into a dual doctorate program at Stanford in anthropology and biogenetics. Because of her great-grandmother, she wanted to study longevity, and began to do fieldwork in the so-called blue zones where there are high concentrations of centenarians, people who live more than one hundred years.

Santos was trying to find out what, exactly, made them live

so long. Her early findings pointed to things that had been suggested in other studies, including diet, exercise, friendship, a positive outlook, and, most important, a purpose, a reason for being. Some of the century-plus crowd said they drank antitoxin teas from certain plants, and ate diets rich in omega-3s, fish, avocado, and olive oil. Some were vegetarians. Some were out-and-out carnivores. A few were abstinent and chaste their entire lives. Others drank alcohol every day and enjoyed an active sex life well into their nineties.

But none of these links and contradictions, and none of these examples explained the people Vovo described, the ones she said lived to one hundred and thirty or more.

"I knew finding someone that age was like chasing a fantasy," Santos said. "But I figured that maybe the longevity had somehow spread out from Vovo's people. I decided to come here first, to Tefé, trying to determine if it qualified as a blue zone."

"Did it?"

"One of the bluest," she replied. "There are seventy thousand people in and around Tefé, and by my original count—four years ago—there were three hundred and fifty-six people who had lived a century or more within ten or twelve miles of where we are walking right now."

"That seems high."

"Astronomically high," Santos said. "In the rest of Brazil there are roughly twelve centenarians for every ten thousand people. By those numbers, Tefé should have roughly eighty-two centenarians in total.

"Instead, there are more than fifty centenarians per ten thousand here," she went on. "That eclipses the rate in Japan, which is thirty-four per ten thousand. In the United States, seventeen people per ten thousand live past the age of one hundred."

Monarch looked around as they approached the public boat launch, and had to admit he was seeing an inordinate number of spry old people about. When they reached the others, they found the Zodiacs already inflated, though the big outboards had yet to be mounted on the sterns. Most of the dry bags were aboard, and the food was being loaded and lashed down.

"Nice of you to join us," Carson said, wiping sweat from his brow.

"Just checking a few things regarding your security, Dr. Carson," Monarch said. "Now what can I do to help?"

Rousseau gestured at a big black dry bag with a padlock lying on the ground, said, "You can tell us what's in there. It's the heaviest single bag here."

"Cooking utensils," Monarch said.

"They're guns," Carson said.

"Like I said, cooking utensils," Monarch replied.

"You said nothing about guns," Santos said. "Where did you get them?"

"A friend of a friend."

"You mean they're illegal?" she hissed.

"No, just unregistered."

"That is illegal in Brazil."

He shrugged. "One way or another, they're coming. I like to have the odds stacked in my favor, especially when I'm far from legal authority. The guns will stay in the bag until they're needed. If they're not needed, they stay in the bag."

Santos looked at odds, but finally said, "Okay."

"Stella," Carson protested.

"Todd, are you an expert on security?" she asked.

"I don't like having the guns along," Carson repeated.

"I don't either," Santos replied, and left it at that.

Monarch picked up the gun sack and stowed it forward, tight to the gunnels alongside a smaller dry bag containing his satellite phone. Then he helped move and lash the fifty-five-gallon gas tanks into position aboard the follow raft, and led the effort to mount the outboard engines.

"You've done this before," Edouard Les Cailles said. "When we did this last time, it took us an hour."

"I've had practice," Monarch agreed. "It's a matter of knowing protocols."

"Well," Santos said, glancing at her watch. "That helps us a lot. We might make it all the way to the mouth."

"The mouth?" Monarch asked.

"Where we leave the last big channel," the scientist said.

"We running GPS?" Monarch asked.

The look that Santos shot him could have cut steel. "No GPS," she said. "Under any condition. No GPS coordinates are to be taken."

"Why?"

"Because the coordinates would get out, and then it would be over," she said hotly. "And that will not happen, not on my watch."

"Okay, so how do we find this place?"

"The same way we did the first time," Santos replied cryptically. "Are you okay with that, Mr. Monarch? Or do you wish to remain here until our return?"

"Last time I looked, you're going upriver on my dime, Dr. Santos."

"Be that as it may, those are my terms. Do you have a GPS?"

"He has a satellite phone," said Graciella. "I saw it."

"No GPS on it," he replied.

"Someone could get a fix off the satellite records," Rousseau said.

"The sat phone's nonnegotiable," Monarch growled. "I've got a sick mother down in Argentina. I need to and will talk to my sister every other day to check on her. And those are *my* terms. Accept them, or go off defenseless."

There was a long moment of tension between Monarch and Santos, but then she softened, and said, "I'm sorry about your mother. What's she sick with?"

"A cancer that came back to life last week," he said. "They're doing tests."

A flicker of skepticism flashed at the corners of Santos's eyes.

Monarch caught it, said, "You want to call my sister? Her name's Gloria. She can fill you in on the sad details if you feel you have to hear them."

There was another moment of indecision before the scientist said, "I have your word that you will not use the phone to figure out our exact location?"

"I promise," Monarch said. "I'll even give you the chip after we're done. You can do with it what you want."

"Okay, then," she replied. "We're off."

36

HOURS LATER, MONARCH STRADDLED the rubber gunnel of the lead Zodiac and watched for logs and debris in the river. Carson was at the tiller, with Santos sitting at the center of the raft. They were traveling at a fair clip, but the breeze did little to cut the heat and humidity, which was beyond oppressive.

Monarch took off his ball cap and neckerchief, leaned over the side and plunged them into the water and held them there.

"I wouldn't keep your hand in there long, Mr. Monarch," Santos said.

He glanced at her puzzled.

She said, "Piranha."

Monarch jerked his hand, hat, and neckerchief out as if he'd touched a live wire. The scientist smiled and looked away.

The river had narrowed considerably, and traffic had dropped off as well. Since leaving Tefé, they'd seen only fishermen and a few small ferries coming downstream from one of the lesser villages ahead. Moored along the bank were three speedboats Santos said belonged to a mining company.

"SJB," she said as if she were spitting. "They're criminals."

"Meaning?" Monarch said.

"It's a vast wilderness where we are headed," she said. "A forbidden zone, eighty-six million square miles set aside for the uncontacted Indian tribes, and by Brazilian law those lands are off-limits to logging and mining exploration. But SJB ignores the boundaries and sends in small crews to do tests. They have several mines right up against the boundaries."

"But then again, we're going into that forbidden zone, right?"

"In the interest of science, not money," she said in a huff.

"Is what we're doing illegal?"

She hesitated, and then said, "Technically, I suppose, but I'll deal with that if I have to. Again, it's all in the interest of science."

Pink and white wading birds flushed before them. The air at times smelled perfumed, and at others foul. Woodsmoke hung in the air as they passed small logging operations, and tiny settlements with long, thin, shallow draft boats pulled up on the banks. In the increasingly longer stretches of uninhabited jungle and river they saw caimans, South American crocodiles, dozens of them sunning along the banks, and floating in reedy backwater channels.

An old woman crouched in the water upstream of six or seven of the huge reptiles. She was washing clothes in the silted water. Seeing her, Monarch remembered all that Santos had said about the number of centenarians in Tefé.

He looked over at the scientist, and said, "So what did you find in common among the three hundred and fifty-six people older than one hundred years old in Tefé?"

"Most had indigenous blood in them," she said, seeming relieved to change the subject. "Which is odd because so many of the Indians who leave the jungle end up adopting the absolute worst habits of the Western world once they're exposed. They smoke too much. They drink too much. Their diet is horrible."

"So it's genetic?" Monarch asked.

"This trip is an attempt to figure that out," she replied. "But it could easily be the diet involved, or the things they smoke."

"Smoke?" he asked.

"Part of their spiritual life," she said.

"Okay," the thief said, not knowing what to make of that. "But back up. How did you get from Tefé to where we're going?"

"That took me nearly five years," she said. "Whenever I could come to Tefé for my fieldwork, I kept thinking about the village Vovo walked to after she was abandoned, and I finally decided to search for it."

"How?"

"I talked to as many of the centenarians as I could," she said. "Asked them if they or any of their ancestors walked out of the jungle to join society. I was shocked at the number of them who had left the rain forest on a long walk similar to Vovo's, or were born to Indians who'd walked out a generation before them."

Santos began to gather these stories of exodus. In almost all of them, the wanderer remembered coming to the banks of the big river for the first time. The scientist set out to find some of these places, traveling alone or with local guides, searching up one braided channel of the Solimões or another. She found several locations that matched the descriptions she was given, but discovered nothing there of note, no obvious beaten-down trail, no logic to any of it.

But then again, why would there be an underlying logic to how people left one life for another? One universe for another?

"I supposed their great walk was like any migration, forced upon them by environmental or societal factors, at different times and in different places," Santos said. "So trying to pattern the migrations in and of themselves didn't help much. And my search was hampered by the language barriers. The dialects up here change every ten or fifteen miles."

"How many languages in Brazil?"

"Thousands," she replied. "Most people speak multiple dialects up here, and there are trading languages, river languages, like Bororro."

"What about the dialect Vovo spoke to you?"

"That was the discouraging part. I tried to speak it to nearly everyone I encountered in Tefé and during my further explorations. Some of them almost seemed to understand me, but it wasn't solid, you know?"

Monarch nodded. "Did you ever find where Vovo came out?"

"I've narrowed it down to a few places, but not exactly," she said. "Somewhere upriver of where Vovo eventually met my great-grandfather."

Monarch looked beyond her and Carson. Rousseau was driving the second Zodiac with the two graduate assistants up front. The follow raft swung lazily behind them. They were traveling a long straight in the river, and he was able to look well over a mile back to the last bend.

It was late afternoon by then, almost evening, and the light had turned slanted. He caught a flash back there, the sun reflecting off metal. Another boat most likely. Two of those shallow-draft canoes came by from the opposite direction.

Monarch kept looking downriver as the sun sank lower, but saw no more flashes.

Twenty minutes later, Santos pointed inland toward a small lake and village, said, "That's Uarini where I had the biggest break. I had been interviewing centenarians there, and was getting ready to leave to go back to Tefé, when a friend of mine, a nurse who roams the river offering medical care, found me.

"She said she'd heard from one of her patients that an indigenous girl had walked out of the jungle three days before," Santos went on. "She was paralyzed with fear, and no one could understand a thing she was— Oh, look there: see those two huge rubber trees growing near the bank, how their branches join, and that little stream beyond?"

Monarch saw what she was talking about. It almost looked like a gateway. "I do."

"That's where I think Vovo came out," she said. "At least I like to think so."

"Kind of gives you chills," he said.

"Doesn't it?"

Before Santos could continue with her story, Rousseau slowed to ask her which way to go. The river was severely braided in this stretch, and she had to get up in the bow to navigate. Twice she got lost and they had to double back and find the right channel.

Finally, as dusk fell, Santos said, "That's it up ahead, the mouth, that tiny village there on the left, just beyond the confluence."

Monarch peered through the low light past a side channel to glowing kerosene lanterns hung on poles before a ring of shacks. Several of those long, thin skiffs were pulled up on shore, and men were mending nets.

Santos said, "So anyway, to continue what I was saying before, I first came to this little settlement late in the day after hearing about the girl who'd walked out of the forest from my friend the nurse."

Carson cut the engines and they drifted up beside the beached skiffs. Shack doors started opening and people in ragged clothes began piling out, shouting out cries of welcome and hello. Men, women, and children crowded forward around the scientist, kissing her, hugging her, and shaking her hand.

"The conquering hero returns," Monarch said when the hubbub had died down a bit, and the people had gone to greet the others.

Santos laughed, said, "That was not the way I was treated the first time I came here, I can assure you. They were very protective of her, and didn't want me seeing her at first. But eventually they let me, though they warned me I wouldn't understand a thing she said."

"Where was she?"

"In that shack there on the right," Santos said, looking like she was reliving the moment as she stared at the crude dwelling. "I went inside with a lantern. She was afraid of it. She was afraid of anything that was new, which was pretty much everything. So when I walked in, she cringed and hid from me."

The scientist spoke to her soothingly in the other two Indian dialects she'd learned, and got no response. Then she tried the language her great-grandmother taught to her, and the girl's head lifted in astonishment.

"She looked at me like I had come down from the sky to rescue her," Santos recalled in awe. "She came and threw her arms around me and started to sob out words to me, and my God, Monarch, I understood all of it."

Tears streamed down the scientist's cheeks when she said, "It was the greatest moment of my life."

"Stella!" a woman cried.

"Kiki?"

Kiki rushed out of the darkness, a young Indian woman in a khaki cotton skirt, sleeveless black shirt, and sandals. She threw her arms around Santos, and began chattering at her in a language that only the two of them understood.

Monarch was moved and fascinated by the entire experience. Obviously Kiki was the girl from Vovo's tribe.

At last, the scientist stood and gestured to the thief, calling him by name.

"This is my dearest friend Kiki," Santos said.

Smiling shyly, Kiki held out her hand. He shook it and found her skin like fine glove leather and her grip strong. Indeed, everything about her looked strong and powerful, until a fourth person came out of the darkness from upriver. A hard-looking man in a cut-off T-shirt, black shorts, and sandals, he was smoking a cigarette and eyeing the rafts, the people, and Kiki suspiciously.

He barked several words at Kiki and Monarch saw her diminish somehow.

"It's her boyfriend Nolomé," Santos said out of the side of her mouth. "He doesn't like me, but he likes the money I'm going to pay her to guide us."

The scientist said something that Monarch didn't catch and Kiki's boyfriend looked like he wanted to spit, but then nodded with disdain.

"Okay then," Santos said. "It's official. We'll start in toward the boundary first thing in the morning."

"How long will it take us to get in there?" Monarch asked.

The scientist shrugged. "It depends on the river and the jungle and what's happened since we went in last time. On the whole, though, I advise you to stop thinking so much about time because the place we're going is timeless."

37

"THAT HIM?" CHANEL CHAVEZ asked, gesturing through the windshield.

She was pointing across the street to a Latino in his early forties whose well-tailored clothes made him look out of place as he did the pimp roll along a row of grimy auto mechanic and body repair shops ten miles east of the Villa Miserie.

Claudio Fortunato threw up the binoculars, took a quick look at the man and his inner right forearm, said, "I haven't seen him in almost twenty years, but that is Alonzo Miguel. And he's still flying the colors of *la fraternidad*."

"What I tell you, Claudio?" said a heavyset man in the backseat of the rented Toyota van. "Did the brother steer you wrong?"

"Rico, you've never steered me wrong," Claudio replied.

Rico smiled, revealing an upper-right gold incisor.

The man beside Rico was whippet-thin, sharply dressed, and puffing on an electronic cigarette. Looking disgusted, he whined, "Shit, Claudio. What about that time at Las Cavernas, that nightclub on—?"

"Hey, Nelly," Claudio barked, looking in the rearview mirror. "Ladies present. Ladies present."

241

Chavez looked over her shoulder at Nelly and winked. Nelly scowled, and ran his palm over his slicked-back hair. "Didn't know it was a sensitive subject."

"So what now?" Rico asked.

"You and Nelly drive around the corner and down a couple of blocks and wait," Fortunato said. "Channel and I are going to pay old Alonzo a visit."

"You carrying?" Nelly asked.

Both Chavez and Claudio shook their heads.

"You should," Nelly said, clamping the electronic cigarette between his teeth. He slid up his right pant leg, and came up with a small-frame .25-caliber Beretta, which he handed to Chavez. Then he reached around his back, under his shirt and came up with a stouter gun, a .45-caliber Ballester-Molina that he gave to Claudio.

"Why're you packing so much heat?" Rico asked. "You're a hair dresser for Christ's sake."

"Better safe than sorry," Nelly sniffed.

Claudio stuck the .45 in his waistband, but he didn't like it. He'd been shot once, and the idea of a gunfight frankly made him queasy. He got out of the rental car, and angled across traffic toward a low, mustard-colored building with two open garage bays, and "El Camino Auto" painted in green below the flat roofline.

Chavez slipped up beside him, said, "How did Rico steer you wrong?"

Claudio licked his lips sourly, said, "I'm not avoiding this?"

"Nope."

The painter looked miserable, but said, "Years ago, Rico tells me that he's noticed a beautiful woman interested in me at a nightclub, so I go over. We talk, we dance, we go home, and things get interesting, and . . ."

"Out with it."

242

"She was a he."

Chavez snorted with laughter. "No."

"Oh, yes," Claudio replied, and chuckled. "A real eye-opener."

They were close enough to the engine repair shop that they could hear the whir of air wrenches and the banging of hammer on steel. Two cars were up on hydraulic jacks. Mechanics worked beneath them, and it smelled of decades of motor oil and gasoline.

One of the mechanics, a younger man with a grimy face, looked over at them suspiciously, said, "I help you?"

"Looking for Alonzo," Claudio said.

"Who're you?"

"An old friend. We grew up together. I'm just paying him a visit."

The mechanic ogled Chavez, and then gestured with a socket wrench toward a door in the rear of the shop. "You're lucky. He's back there."

Chavez thanked him, and they went to the door, knocked, and went in.

"Yeah?" said Alonzo Miguel, who sat turned at a desk, studying a ledger.

"Long time, brother," Claudio said.

Miguel cocked his head, and then pivoted quickly in the chair, his left hand reaching around his back. Before he could get a gun out, he saw Chavez aiming the Beretta at him from six feet away.

"Don't do it, senor," she said.

Miguel froze, smiled, and let his left hand drift to his lap. His eyes narrowed, and his chin retreated several degrees. "Claudio?"

"Like I said, a long time."

"Who is she?"

"A good friend."

243

"She knows how to use that gun?"

"Better than the both of us put together."

"Huh," Miguel said before sighing. "What's it been, twenty years?"

"At least," Claudio said. "You look like you're doing pretty well for yourself."

Miguel shrugged. "You know, maybe I did learn something from you and Robin. Six years after the split, I took my money and went legit. I own five of these places."

"Good for you."

He raised and lowered his eyebrows, said, "Heard you're a real painter."

"It's a reasonable life," Claudio said. "I've been blessed."

"You here to ask me to paint my portrait?"

"As remarkable a subject as your ugly mug might be in oil or watercolor, no. I'm looking for Hector Vargas."

That seemed to take Miguel aback. "Hector? Didn't you hear, man? Hector's dead. Shot during a bank robbery in Bariloché. They found his body in a burned-out building a few hours later."

"Yeah, I'd heard that, too," the painter replied, watching his old comrade's eyes. "But then about a week ago, Hector rose from the dead, tried to kill me, and Robin. Put a bunch of bullet holes in my car."

Miguel shook his head. "Got to be someone else."

"Same fucked-up ear."

"I went to Hector's funeral, man. Tito said his sister identified the body."

"I didn't know Hector had a sister."

"Galena, I think," he said. "She's younger."

"Know where I can find Galena?"

Miguel shrugged. "Tito might know, but who knows where that *pendejo* is now. I haven't seen him since the funeral."

"What was Tito into? Gone straight?"

Miguel snorted. "That'll be the day. He was into the same old shit."

"Territory?"

"No idea, man. I try not to live in the past."

Claudio said, "Thanks. Sorry to have bothered you."

"An old brother is never a bother," Miguel said with great bonhomie. "We should get together some time."

"Sure," the painter said. "We'll talk cars and art."

"Don't bring your friend though. She makes me nervous."

Chavez smiled at Miguel, slipped the small pistol into her pocket, and they backed out, shut the door. They kept a close watch until they were across the street, around the corner, and out of sight.

"You believe him?"

"About Hector having a sister, anyway. We need to find her, which means we're going to have to track down Tito Gonzalez, and that is going to be difficult."

"Why's that?"

"Tito was always good at staying below the radar," Claudio replied. "Back in the day, we used to call him *hombre de la sombre*. The shadow man."

38

MONARCH AND THE SCIENTISTS left the main river before dawn, and followed the route Kiki had taken out of the jungle two years before. But where she had walked the riverbanks for mile upon twisting mile, they roared up the tributary.

The channel was less than a quarter the width of the big river, and curled and double-backed, a serpentine waterway with a shifting floor: deep pools that gave way within feet to shallow muddy bottoms and then to light rapids that looked like simmering cocoa. In the first three miles, they passed two skiffs and one of those SJB Mining speedboats. Both were headed downstream.

Three miles on, they reached an obstacle that had not been there the last time the scientists went up this tributary. A microburst—a brief, intense windstorm similar to a tornado—had blown tangles of trees across the river, forcing them to get out, unload the rafts, and portage.

It was tedious, backbreaking work in ungodly heat. Noon had come and gone by the time they were repacked and moving again. Two miles farther on, they encountered more debris and portaged a second time. When they made camp a half hour before sunset, they had only gone thirteen miles from the confluence with the main river. While the others were putting up a screen-room tent, and organizing a meal, Monarch returned to the banks of the tributary to check the rafts, the supplies they'd left aboard, and their fuel tanks.

A breeze was blowing, sending up sighs and vibrations in the forest canopy, which looked different on the opposite bank: between thirty and forty feet up there were dense matrixes of thick vines lacing the trees. Monarch was thinking that they almost looked woven when he thought he heard an engine in the distance, a mile or more downstream. Turning his head to hear better, he caught movement in that tangle of vine.

In an instant the distant motor growl and all other sounds were silenced by a primitive noise that paralyzed him.

It came from up in those vine-entangled trees across the river, an incredibly loud, and long, bellowing that grew and turned hollow. It amplified yet again, and then turned into grunts and wavering hoots that echoed and pulsed through his chest and head. He'd never heard anything close to it.

Rousseau, Carson, and their assistants came down from the camp, gaping at the sound in wonder. Santos and Kiki smiled even as they covered their ears.

"What the hell is that?" Monarch yelled.

"Howler monkeys," Santos yelled back. "Loudest animal on Earth. They're telling their friends in other troops miles away that it's time to go to sleep."

"Oh, I'm sure it will be easy to sleep after this sweet serenade," Monarch said, and even Graciella and Edouard laughed.

At dark, the monkeys stopped their howling, and the insects came in furious clouds. Inside the screen room, Rousseau produced a box of Thermacel personal mosquito repellent devices that clipped to their hips. Monarch was impressed. The things actually worked.

247

After a freeze-dried dinner, and two fingers of Irish whiskey Carson had brought along, Monarch sat outside under a mosquito net while everyone else slept. He listened to the jungle, trying to learn its rhythm so he might notice any change.

There was a steady thrum of insect life, the shuffling of rodents in the underbrush, and night birds calling in the canopies. Late, after midnight, he swore he heard from far out in the forest the sawing cough of a big male jaguar. The thought of being in the home territory of a big cat like that thrilled him and he fell asleep contented.

The second day was tougher. One long portage, one shorter portage, and they managed to put only twelve more miles of river behind them. All day long, Monarch kept his attention downstream. The thief was dwelling on the engine he'd heard before the monkeys opened up. Not once during the entire day, however, did Monarch see or hear another person or boat.

Again, Monarch stayed up late after everyone else had retired, listening keenly to the forest cacophony. In many ways, the thief was a creature of the night. He was perfectly competent in the daylight, of course, but at night he thrived. Sitting in the jungle, listening to the symphony of his fellow creatures, he felt dwarfed by the complexity of it all. After finally drifting off toward sleep, his mind dwelled yet again on the sound of that distant motor.

On the third day, Monarch awoke with a start in the dawn light, and from deep in his subconscious, a suspicion budded and bloomed. He got up, put on his river sandals, and went down by the rafts with a headlamp and a flashlight.

He ignored the locked cases and the dry bags. Though they would provide easy hiding places, what Monarch was looking for required a clear line of sight to the sky. He examined the frame that gave the rafts lateral strength, and the steel lashing rings, the buckles and the straps and ropes. He inspected the outboard engines and even removed their housings. He studied the heavy-duty bracket that tied the motors into the tubular raft frames. On the raft he'd ridden in there was nothing amiss.

But on Rousseau's Zodiac, stuck down deeply between the engine bracket and the stern, he spotted a tube about the diameter and length of a golf pencil. He got out a Leatherman tool, reached into the tight gap, and fished it out.

There was no blinking light, no pulse in his hand, but Monarch recognized it as a tracking device. He stood there, popping the thing up in the air and catching it, letting past evidence shift and settle in his mind: the guys who tried to take Santos the night of the Carnival ball; the guy who'd tried to stab him coming up out of the ferry hold; and those peacock bass fishermen.

Monarch decided to check for redundant devices. He found one attached with clear strapping tape to one of the welded corners of the frame in the follow raft. It was unlike the first bug, wafer thin, circular, about an inch and half long.

Why two different kinds? Were there two different parties tracking them? Or was it one, but using two different frequencies?

He came up with an argument for one entity: the big slab of a guy who came up out of the hold, and tried to stab him. He'd been down there planting the bugs. But how had he done it while the graduate assistant lovebirds were sleeping on top of the gear?

Then Monarch thought back over the past few days, to instances where the rafts had been out of their immediate control, and came up with two.

He went back to the camp, and found Santos and the others, dressed, and drinking coffee in the screen room.

"We've got a problem," he said.

"What's that?" Santos asked, setting the coffee down.

Monarch showed her the electronic bugs, said, "Tracking transmitters. There's someone, maybe two different someone's following us."

"What?" Santos cried.

"Who?" Rousseau asked agitated.

"I'd bet whoever killed Lourdes, and tried to kidnap Dr. Santos," Graciella said.

"Those men back in Manaus?" Santos asked.

Monarch nodded. "The peacock bass fishermen. The question in my mind is whether those men were also involved in that attempt to grab you back in Rio."

"How did they get the transmitters into our gear?" asked Les Cailles.

"Good point," Monarch said. "Are you and Graciella light sleepers?"

Rousseau's assistant shook his head. "Me? No, I sleep like a log."

Graciella said, "Me too. If I'm asleep, you could have a whole troop of those monkeys around and I'd snooze right through the howls. Why?"

"Because I think it's possible that the guy who tried to stab me on the ferry put at least one of these bugs on the raft while you were sleeping," the thief replied. "It either happened then or when the rafts were on that flatbed between the airport in Manaus and the ferry, or in Tefé when that crew of locals was helping us load."

"I don't think this happened when we were with the rafts," Les Cailles said in mild protest. "I mean, I sleep deep, but I think I would have awoken if someone was moving around right next to us."

His girlfriend looked less convinced.

Carson said, "So what do we do? Throw those things in the river?"

"That's it," Rousseau said. "Leave the bastards high and dry."

Monarch thought about that, and then looked at Santos, and said, "Ask Kiki when we leave the water for good."

Santos spoke to Kiki in their language, and said, "About the same length of river we've come each of the past two days."

"So what, ten to thirteen miles?"

She and Kiki spoke again. "More like thirteen," Santos said.

The thief played with that information until he saw an angle that worked to every advantage, and said, "We'll keep the bugs with us a little bit longer."

They broke camp, and were back on the river by eight. The sky was clear and the sun beat down relentlessly. But for almost two hours they made excellent time, having only to clear a few trees floating in the river. By noon, they were nine miles beyond their second camp and the waterway had turned braided again.

On the sandbars, the slender islands, and the steaming banks above still pools, they saw the thickest concentration of crocodiles yet, fifteen or twenty in a quarter mile. Santos said they were roughly on the boundary of the forbidden zone right now, and four miles from where they would leave the rafts and walk.

"This will work," Monarch said looking around, appraising the terrain. He told Carson to pull up to a thin, reedy island to their left and cut the motor. Rousseau and the assistants drifted in behind them.

"Why are we stopping?" Rousseau demanded. "What are we doing?"

Monarch held a finger to his lips, whispered, "We're being quiet. And you are listening downstream, and Dr. Carson and I are going to do a little heavy lifting."

"What's this all about?" Santos asked.

"Trust me," Monarch said.

The river bottom was firmer than the thief expected when he gingerly stepped out into the ankle-deep water. The bank was relatively solid as well, and he got up onto it, pulling the head of the raft in tight to the bank. Then he and Carson brought the follow raft around, and rolled the half-full fifty-five-gallon barrel out of it onto the island.

They rolled the barrel where Monarch wanted it, and stood it on end, pushed back into reeds. The thief cut down other reeds, laid them loosely across the front of the steel barrel, and then reached over and set the two location transmitters on the top of the barrel.

"Why are you leaving them there?" Santos muttered.

"Doctor, I will never question your decisions regarding research, if you don't question my decisions regarding your safety."

Santos looked frustrated, but nodded.

Climbing back into the raft, Monarch murmured in Carson's ear, "I want you to take us at troll speed back across the river and beach us."

They crossed the channel with the engine making a low purr, giving wide berth to the crocodiles sunning on the banks, and floating in the pools. The rafts slid up onto a low area covered in ferns and grasses.

Monarch told them to get whatever they needed out of the follow raft. It was staying until they picked it up on the way back. Then he dug in his dry bag, found the two Rhino handheld radios, and handed one to Santos.

"What do I need this for?" she asked.

Monarch motioned her to lower her voice, and then replied, "You're going on upriver without me."

He held up his hand before she could reply. "I need to see who these people are, get a visual on them, so I know who we're dealing with, and then I'll come join you. In the meantime, you're going upriver to where Kiki says you pick up the path. You're going to strip down to essentials, carry only what you need, and hide everything else, including the rafts and the motors. I expect you to go immediately into the jungle once that's done, and get as far off the river as you can before making camp.

"The entire time you're walking, I want this Rhino on and in your hand," Monarch went on, and then shook the radio he had. "Your position will show up on my radio, and my position on yours. When I reach you, we put the radios away. No GPS."

Santos looked as if she was going to start arguing with him, but then held up her hands, said, "We'll do it your way."

"Smart move," the thief replied, and then retrieved the dry bag carrying the guns and ammunition.

He got out the IMBEL paratrooper rifle, and two twenty-five-shot clips, and then sealed the bag again.

"This is just a precaution," he told them. "We're a long way from anyone helping us and I feel like being prepared for anything."

"What do we do with the other guns?" Santos asked. "Hide them with the rafts?"

"No, you divide them up and you carry them," he said. "You can always drop them later if I find out there's no threat behind us. But if there is a threat, you won't be able to go back."

Carson and Rousseau appeared uncomfortable with that, but before either of them protested, Santos said, "You'll call me once you know?"

"When I'm on my way," Monarch promised.

A few minutes later, they pushed the rafts back into the water, and trolled upstream. Monarch pulled the follow raft almost entirely up on the flat, so it couldn't be missed from the river. He put the dry bag carry straps over his shoulders and snapped them in place with sternum and belt clips.

Climbing down off the bank into eight inches of murky water, the thief walked upstream. He'd gone sixty-five yards and was swinging his left foot forward, when he felt something sharp cut into his leg.

Monarch winced and cursed. The spiny fins of several fish bumped and glided along his bare lower legs.

Something sharp again. Cutting again.

He freaked.

Piranha!

39

MONARCH EXPLODED INTO A dance in the shallows, knowing that he was splashing enough to attract crocodiles, but driven forward by that one thought—*Piranha!*

The thief leaped out and up onto the bank, and lay there, panting like a spooked dog, and staring back at the swirling murky water. Few things frightened him, but the idea of being chewed up one bite at a time by razor-teeth little fish sent him into panic.

Monarch jerked around and inspected the bites. Blood oozed from small and ragged chunks of skin that were gone from the back of his left calf. A bigger one on his right shin was dripping.

There was a redundant first-aid kit back there a hundred yards in the follow raft. But he couldn't afford to walk there. There was a chance he would leave a trail of some sort, a drop of blood here, a broken branch there, enough that a talented man, or a group of talented men could read it and follow. Instead, he cut off the sleeves of his shirt and tore them into strips that he used to bind the wounds.

Monarch got himself in position one hundred and fifteen yards upriver of the follow raft, and one hundred and thirty-four yards from the drum of gasoline sitting out in the reeds and baking in the equatorial sun. From the base of a rubber tree growing on the bank, he used a machete to hack a path away into the jungle heading west-southwest for nearly a hundred

255

yards. He dropped the dry bag there, and returned to the river.

At the base of the rubber tree, he built himself a low blind of branches and vegetation and a rest for the rifle, and then sat in the shade among the roots, his back to the trunk, looking downstream. The thief settled in to wait. Knowing he had several hours at least before he'd have visitors, he closed his eyes and slept dreamlessly.

Three and a half hours later, he awoke with a start, shocked he had slept so long. He heard Santos's voice. "Monarch? Are you there?"

Monarch scanned the scene downriver, and saw nothing, listened, and heard nothing before triggering the radio transmit button.

"I'm here, Dr. Santos."

"Have you seen anything?"

"Not yet."

"We're going into the forest now."

"Keep your radio on, but don't call me again until at least two hours after dark."

"Oh," she said. "Okay."

He turned off his radio, clipped it to his waist belt, and waited.

They came, as predators do, in the waning light.

Monarch heard the outboard engine first from downriver. Ten minutes after sundown, a smaller Zodiac raft than the ones they were using rounded the bend, and trolled across the larger of the crocodile pools.

Monarch had binoculars on the men in the raft, three hard guys, ex-military, wearing jungle camouflage, combat harnesses, and floppy hats. And there was Kiki's boyfriend, Nolomé. Nice guy.

The thief saw no weapons, but knew they were there. He took

his attention off the men in the raft, and again looked downstream. Twenty seconds later, the second raft appeared. Even in the lowlight there was no mistaking that these guys were not bass fishermen and that the big, black dude riding up front was without a doubt Jason Dokken.

"Okay," Monarch said, exhaling deeply. "Game on."

The thief had expected whoever was following to come looking five or six hours after the tracking devices stopped moving. He had also expected that the predators would come by water.

What he didn't foresee was that they would also come by air.

As the first raft came cruising into the upper pool, almost between the follow raft and the gasoline drum, he heard the chug of an approaching helicopter, which swung in just off the treetops, circling the pool overhead.

Monarch reached forward, pulled the branches of his blind right onto him, and ducked his head. The chopper flew on in a lazy arc. He pushed the brush away slightly, and got the binoculars on the bird.

It was a small construction helicopter with a bay door wide open. The logo on the side said SJB MINING. He saw a man hanging out the side. He carried an AK-47 and the thief thought he recognized him.

Then he spotted the black, swollen eye, and knew for certain that he was one of the three men who'd tried to grab Santos back in Rio.

Swinging the binoculars back to the river, Monarch saw Dokken and his troop of five aiming rifles at the helicopter.

More armed men appeared in the helicopter hold as it swung about. One was the same big slab who'd tried to knife him on the ferry. The bird hovered forty-five feet above the pool facing Dokken's rafts, the tail rotor almost directly above the gasoline drum out on the island.

The thief dropped the binoculars, got in behind the gun, and took steady aim. He fired a full metal jacket round through the drum about three quarters of the way up. Sparks thrown from the bullet's penetration ignited vapors that had filled the upper barrel. The gas drum erupted in a thunderclap and a fireball that threw shrapnel. It billowed around the helicopter's tail and rotor.

Monarch touched off a short burst, strafing the water forward of Dokken's lead raft, and then sending a second short burst at the helicopter. He didn't fire another shot after that. He didn't need to.

Shocked by the explosion, Dokken's men thought the guys in the mining helicopter had shot at them and returned fire. The guys in the chopper thought the opposite and started shooting at the rafts.

Three guys in the forward raft were hit, including Nolomé, who slumped on the gunnel. The other two fell in the water. Dokken and his men in the rear raft were hammering the helicopter. Bullets smacked the fuselage, rotors, and blades. Two men tumbled out of the chopper hold, including the one with the black eye.

Then the thief heard the screech of steel sheering and knew one or more of the rounds fired from Dokken's raft had blown through the rear rotor housing and into the gears and bearings. The nose of the helicopter swung wildly left and right as the pilot fought for control, and then rose and dipped fast, like a horse throwing its head down before it starts to buck.

There was another harsh metallic noise and the stench of alloys braising before the helicopter veered off sharply, spun into the gathering darkness, and crashed into the jungle four or five hundred yards away.

Monarch became aware of men yelling and crying, and swung the binoculars back at the pool, seeing a strong flashlight beam playing across the water, finding two of Dokken's men and one of the guys who'd fallen from the helicopter, all of them screaming for help in a blind panic as the piranhas and the crocodiles came to the scent of blood. Dokken got one of his men out and into the rear raft. He was missing part of his leg. The others were pulled under.

The light went out. Monarch could no longer see the second raft, but there was no mistaking its location by the hysterical voice of the dying man. The thief gently pushed the branches of his blind forward and away from him.

He quietly got to his feet. The cries of the dying man cut off in a choke, and then there was no noise except the scorched reeds popping and cracking out there on the island. Monarch eased onto that path he'd cut, and started to creep down it, rolling the soles of his canvas jungle boots from the outer edges of the soles inward.

He got thirty yards before he heard Dokken scream, and then rant: "Fucking Monarch! I will find you and rip your throat out with my bare fucking hands!"

"Good luck with that," Monarch muttered, and went on.

He could still hear Dokken roaring insanely when he reached the dry bag and hoisted it onto his back. He turned his headlamp on to the red light, and then powered up the Rhino radio.

Monarch waited until he got a fix on Santos's radio, which was roughly four-point-eight miles away on a west-northwest bearing. He fought his way through vines and tight growing saplings for the next half hour, analyzing what he'd seen amid the chaos.

The way they'd all fired on each other confirmed that there were two parties after Santos's secrets: whoever was controlling Dokken and Vargas, and the guys in the SJB helicopter. Who were they? Either miners or an unknown third party that got use of the chopper. He thought the latter choice was unlikely, which left the mining company.

But why? There was no mention of valuable ore in Santos's research paper, no mention of minerals at all.

Monarch stopped clawing through the jungle. The thief stood there a long moment, listening for noise on his back trail, and heard none. He'd come at least a mile from the river.

In an open space, he'd have waited another two miles before using the machete.

But here, deep in the jungle, with tons upon tons of vegetation to absorb the sound, he pulled the machete from his waist belt, turned the headlamp beam on high, and started to chop his way forward toward Santos and her camp.

He could already tell it was going to be a long, long sweltering night.

40

SIXTEEN BELOW CELSIUS OUTSIDE, three-point-two degrees Fahrenheit, and Tristan Hormel could not have been happier.

For the past several weeks the Swiss banker had felt like he was being squeezed from so many directions he thought he might pop. Conditions had been horrible for his normal outlet in times of great stress, but then yesterday afternoon the wind had turned blustery out of the northeast, pushing a bank of cold air down from Russia and across the central Alps. A bitter wind had scoured the lake all night, blown onto land whatever snow had been left on the ice. Hormel's personal weather station was showing that the wind had stopped gusting, and was now blowing at a steady twenty-two knots. Humidity? Seventy-four percent.

"You sure you want to go out there?" asked Pieter Brooks, a security specialist Hormel had brought in. "Wind chill has to be twenty-five below."

"In other words, ideal conditions," Hormel said cheerily as he pulled an oiled wool fisherman's sweater over his merino wool long underwear top. "Want to come?"

"Uh, I'll pass," Brooks said.

"Your loss," the banker said, getting into black insulated bibs. "As skiers say, this is going to be epic."

A foam collar to protect his neck came next followed by snow mobile boots fitted with cleats, and a thermal hood, a long, heavy parka, and insulated leather gloves with wrist straps. A motorcycle helmet with a clear visor completed an outfit that made him largely impervious to the cold.

"You need help pushing off?" Brooks said.

Hormel shook his head. "I'm good. See you in an hour or so?"

"Sounds right. Cell phone with you, sir?"

The banker patted his chest before tugging on the helmet, leaving the visor up. Hormel left the house through a back door, and, not wanting to sweat up, walked slowly toward the boathouse. Hormel lived for mornings like these, and he quickly shoved aside all the worries and anxieties that had plagued him the past few months.

Even through the helmet he could hear the clanking of the ropes and hardware against the mast of the A-class Skeeter and it made him grin. The Skeeter looked like a cherry-red water bug, with a long, narrow, aerodynamic body that whittled down to a sharp nose. A four-foot titanium strut ran straight out from beneath the nose to a shock absorber and a skate bladelike stainless-steel "runner" about eighteen inches long. The rear of the hull sat on a perpendicular ten-foot strut called the plank, with shock absorbers and runners at either end.

The banker hurried the nose into the wind so he could raise the sail without flipping the boat. When he'd done so, he unclasped the chains from the cinder blocks, let the sail luff, and then pushed the Skeeter out from behind the boathouse. There was enough light now for him to dig in with his cleats and get the iceboat gliding before he climbed into the cockpit.

He buckled himself into a safety harness that connected him with an inner protective cage, and then settled his hands on the wheel that controlled the forward runner. He tightened up on the sail, and turned the craft north-northwest toward the point of land at Risch on the opposite shore, some two miles away.

The sail caught the wind. The iceboat accelerated.

Within seconds, Hormel was moving twice the speed of the wind, and then three times, clipping along at better than sixty miles an hour in a single, long rattling slice across the lake ice that thrilled him to his core.

"I got a need for speed."

The banker smiled as he altered course ever so slightly until the wind lifted the rear right runner completely off the ice, heeling a good six feet in the air.

He was pushing seventy now, the boat precariously balanced on the nose and left rear runners, using the opposite strut as a counterbalance and wind foil, cutting across the smooth ice, and loving every magnificent second of it.

After he'd passed the point, Hormel gave the sail some slack, turned the wheel, and prepared to come about into the wind. When he did, he noticed about a mile away another iceboat coming from the direction of Zug. The banker could tell at a glance that it was an older and larger boat than his Skeeter, a so-called stern-steerer with a single, maneuverable runner in the back, two runners amidship, and a main and foresail. He could also tell that the pilot knew what he was doing. Though stern-steerers were capable of higher top-end speeds than an A-Skeeter, Hormel's craft was nimbler, and far easier to control. And yet, the other pilot had his boat heeled and running hard and true across the ice.

As he came fully about, Hormel strained to see if he recognized the other boat and its pilot, but at that distance he couldn't make out the color of the hull. The pilot and a single crewman were mere dots.

Losing sight of them as he sped off, the banker wondered if this was a new boat or a new pilot on the lake. It would be nice to have stronger competition, he thought as he ripped by his estate, seeing lights blazing in the windows. Karen was getting the children ready for school. He raised a hand as he shot past in case they were watching, and then tacked south-southeast heading for a narrowing in the lake between the steep western shore and a large, forested thumb of land.

The wind was stronger in the gap and Hormel blew through it, traveling as fast as he'd ever gone in the Skeeter. Pushing eighty miles per hour, he thought, his skills taken right to their limits.

The banker screamed with joy as he gave the sail slack and prepared to come about again for another run through that gap. If he was lucky, he'd get two or three passes before he had to call it a day.

Hormel made two quick tacks to bring the iceboat closer to the western shore, and then set out north-northeast again, cutting diagonally through the gap, navigating toward the far shore of that thumb of timber. He knew the wind would be perfect for that course, and once again the Skeeter accelerated up near eighty miles an hour.

The banker was no more than two hundred and fifty yards off the northeast corner of the thumb, when he spotted the stern-steerer coming hard on nearly the exact opposite bearing. Hormel figured they'd pass within twenty-five or thirty yards of each other.

Good, he thought. Gives me a solid look at these guys.

He could tell the hull of the older boat was dark green now,

264

but still little about the pilot or crewman other than the fact that they were wearing white helmets. Hormel took his eyes off them to true his course and trim his sail. When he looked right again, they were virtually upon him, less than sixty yards away and closing. He almost panicked when he realized the boats would pass at under twenty yards. Too close!

He nudged the wheel to port a degree, and glanced up again only to see that the crewman was aiming a gun at him! The banker didn't hear a shot as they blew past him, but he felt a sharp stick of pain in his chest, looked down and saw a stubby, steel hypodermic needle with dart fins sticking out of his parka. He took his left hand off the wheel to yank it, and then realized that he was already passing out. He let out the sail, and turned with the wind.

Hormel knew in an instant that he'd overcorrected. The boat heeled wildly, and just before he passed out he saw trees and the thumb's frozen shore coming right at him.

Even with the sail swinging impotently, the Skeeter was still traveling at better than forty miles an hour when the front-runner hit a low shelf of rock. The iceboat flipped forward and smashed into several large trees.

"Fuck, we've killed him," moaned Gloria Barnett, who began to run along the shoreline about three hundred yards south of the crash site.

"No way," groaned John Tatupu through the bud she had in her ear.

"There were pieces of the boat flying all over the place."

"Coming about," Abbott Fowler said.

Shit, Barnett thought as she ran. He was supposed to crash, but nothing like that.

As Monarch taught them, they'd looked for patterns in the

behavior of Hormel and his family. After identifying the patterns, they'd looked for choke points, places where the banker was vulnerable. At first the banker's security team seemed to have covered all the bases. He went nowhere outside the house or his office without a bodyguard, and he had dogs, and armed men roaming the estate.

Unless they made a risky attack on the compound, there appeared to be no way to get at Hormel until Tatupu mentioned that if they could find a vice, like a mistress, or booze, or gambling, they could exploit it.

The banker's sole weak spot had come to Barnett almost instantly. The lake and his passion for sailing was where he was vulnerable.

Assuming that Hormel would go out in his custom boat as soon as the conditions were good, they'd come up with the strategy of renting an iceboat, and then getting close to the banker as he sailed through the narrow, darting him, and then letting him run aground. The plan didn't involve the banker's boat basically disintegrating.

When she reached the crash site, there was debris up in the trees, on the bank, and out on the ice. To her surprise the roll cage was intact, and the banker was still strapped inside it.

She got her finger on his neck. Slow heart rate, but that was the sedative, right?

"Tats?" she called. "I need you here, pronto. He's alive."

The stern-steerer came gliding to a stop, thirty yards offshore. Tatupu wrenched himself up out of the cockpit, and hurried to her looking monolithic in the insulated gear and helmet.

"I'm out of here then," Fowler said. "See you in an hour, maybe two."

Barnett did not reply. She was watching the big Samoan cut Hormel free of the harness and then pull him from the cage.

"What if his neck's broken?" Barnett said.

"He dies," Tatupu said. "But I think he's good."

With that, he hoisted the man up over one shoulder, and said, "How far?"

"Quarter of a mile at the most."

41

THREE DAYS AFTER CATCHING up with Santos and the other scientists, Monarch was limping under the weight of the dry bag lashed to a pack frame. He shrugged and drove himself deeper into that dispassionate place where he dwelled in times of hardship, disassociating himself from the pain of having walked nearly fifty miles beyond the boundary of the forbidden zone while suffering from piranha bites.

When he'd rendezvoused with Santos, he'd immediately cleaned the bites and applied antibiotic cream and bandages from the primary first-aid kit. He'd done the same twice since then, but the bites remained open and oozing.

There was something about the heat and high humidity that wouldn't let the wounds close. He'd heard about this happening in the tropics, and had tried to be careful and keep the wounds clean.

Every hour, however, the pain from the sores seemed to be getting worse, though there was no sign of infection. Making matters worse, he'd been unable to use the satellite phone, and had no idea what his teammates had discovered about Sister Rachel. The jungle canopy had blocked his signal every time.

Vines and underbrush snagged at Monarch's bandages as he followed the others deeper into the rain forest. For mile upon mile they'd walked like this, often navigating by dead reckoning, sometimes traveling on the barest of game paths.

Kiki was confident, however, and on the first day led them to a spring and a pool of water Santos and the others remembered from their earlier trip. They camped, filtered the water, and moved on. On the second day they reached a grove of trees the scientists also recognized. The trees soared high above the jungle floor, with no branches until the dense upper canopy, which blocked out all growth and satellite signals below, leaving a shadowed cavernous space that reminded Monarch of the interior of the cathedral in Buenos Aires.

Sister Rachel brought him to that cathedral the day before he left Argentina to return to America. There in the deepest Amazon the thief swore he could hear his eighteen-year-old voice whispering.

"I'll never forget what you've done for me," Robin told Sister Rachel. "I'll repay you someday. I promise you that."

The missionary smiled, said, "I can't tell you how much that means to me, but you're not done yet. I want you to go forward and on your knees up there, and I want you to ask God for his forgiveness and to bless your travels."

"Out loud?"

"However you wish."

Monarch remembered going down on the cold hard floor and surrendering his defenses and honestly asking God to consider the circumstances of his life, and his right to survive when judging him for the things he'd done as a member of the Brotherhood of Thieves.

Then he went back to Sister Rachel, said, "I don't know if the army is the right thing for me."

"Sometimes you have to take a leap of faith, Robin," she said.

*

269

Trudging through the jungle more than twenty years later, Monarch knew that the missionary had been gone more than nine days now. Based on his own experience, she was probably beginning to despair.

That idea pried Monarch out of that disassociated place in his brain, and he felt the ache in his feet, hips, and knees, and the fire in the bite wounds, followed by an instantaneous fury that wiped all personal pain away, made it inconsequential. He would hike another hundred miles in the dark, covered in leeches if that was what it would take to get Sister Rachel Diego del Mar back safe to the Hogar.

Fueled once again by that conviction, the thief went on until they passed on the third day through a section of the forest that was strewn with massive boulders and chunks of black rock clad in vine, lichen, moss. The big slick rocks were everywhere and navigating through them threatened to snap their ankles.

Beyond the densest concentration of the rocks, the way got easier and they were able to weave in and around of the stones and low-growing trees with riotous purple flowers, and waxy, lime-colored leaves shaped like elephant ears. Then the trees grew taller again and choked with crazy matrixes of vines. They spooked a troop of howler monkeys sleeping high above them in the vines. The monkeys' alarm roars hurt Monarch's eardrums so much he had to stick his fingers in his ears. Two hundred yards beyond the howlers, but still suffering their deafening verbal wrath, the group broke free of the jungle and emerged on the black-sand bank of a clear-flowing stream where a stiff warm breeze was blowing.

The jungle canopy opened up in many places, and it was the first time in nearly a week that Monarch had not felt closed in and claustrophobic. Now the thief could see a mile or more across the lower stage vegetation to a sheer-sided ridge that rose a good four hundred feet above the jungle floor. It ran north to south as far as he could see.

There were trees growing on top of the ridge, but only vines, ferns, and mosses clung to the flanks, which became cliffs, devoid of vegetation all together. The exposed rock was white in some places, and almost coal black in others with variations in between. From a V-like notch at the top of the highest cliff, water gushed and fell in a plume that disappeared into the low jungle, the source of the stream at their feet.

The howler monkeys behind them were still bellowing. Another troop across the river somewhere toward that waterfall joined in until it sounded like continuous, rolling thunder that forced them all to clap their hands across their ears and shout to be heard.

"This is it!" Santos yelled.

"This is what?" Monarch yelled back.

"Where Kiki woke up the afternoon of her sixteenth birthday," she shouted. "Just like Vovo. This is exactly as she described it, too."

The monkeys finally started to calm down a few minutes later, enough for them all to stop covering their ears and drop their dry bags. Rousseau got down on his knees and bent his head to the water, drank right from the stream.

"You might regret that drink in a couple of days, professor," Monarch said.

"Nonsense," Carson said. "This is some of the cleanest water we've ever tested, Monarch. Try it."

The thief hesitated. He had suffered through dysentery once and giardia twice. But seeing Santos and the assistants all cupping water and slurping it, he decided to take the risk.

To his surprise he found the water cool and refreshing, with a pleasant mineral aftertaste that left him thirsty for more.

"You think SJB is after whatever is in this water?" he asked.

"I have no idea," Santos said. "How would they know about it?"

"One of us would have had to tell them, and that's ridiculous," Rousseau said. "SJB would be the worst thing that could happen here. On that, we all agree."

Monarch watched as the others nodded with conviction.

"They're bastards," Les Cailles sniffed. "Care nothing for the environment."

Graciella spit out her words. "There are people in Tefé who have been brain-damaged by the stuff that leaches out of their mines, and the government does nothing."

"They must be paying a fortune in bribes," Carson said, "because there are more SJB rigs here every time we come north."

But what was the mining company after? Why try to kidnap Santos?

The thief drank until his belly was full, and then stepped into the shallow stream and walked around, feeling the water soothe his bite wounds. Even though they'd been walking for hours, he felt wide-awake, ready for another long hike if necessary.

Monarch climbed up on the bank, stripped the soggy bandages, let his legs dry, and then applied more antibiotic ointment to the bites, and wrapped them with clean bandages again. Light was fading. Carson and Rousseau built a fire, which drove away the surprisingly few mosquitos strong enough to fight the near-constant warm breeze out of the southwest.

"So we just wait?" Monarch asked.

Santos nodded. "We don't go to them. They come to us."

Monarch ate dried meat and several power bars as night fell. He drank more of the excellent water, and rested on the ground with his back supported by the dry bag.

"Someone should bottle that water."

Santos laughed. "That's what I said the first time I drank it."

"See there?" Monarch said. "We think alike on some things."

The scientist sobered and looked away. There had been friction between them since the morning after he'd left a smoking helicopter and a homicidal ex–Special Forces operator back on the river. When Monarch finally caught up to the scientists, he realized in a single glance that they had not brought the weapons.

When he'd asked why, they said they didn't feel comfortable exposing the primitive people to guns, or even the concept of guns. The thief had reacted angrily, telling them that he didn't feel very comfortable having to defend them with a single weapon.

Santos had gotten in his face after he described what happened. "People died?"

"Bad guys shot each other," Monarch said. "I was really just an observer."

"You provoked it."

"No, they provoked it by planting tracking devices on us," the thief replied. "Why would that mining company want to track us?"

"I have no idea," Santos shot back.

The animosity had lingered between them for nearly three full days.

But after Monarch had said they thought alike, Santos smiled, and said, "Maybe there *are* some ways we think alike."

"Breakthrough," Monarch said, grinned, and looked away from her to study the fire. Lost in the flames, he decided he'd wait until the others were sleeping before calling on the sat phone.

Santos coughed. Seconds later, he looked over to see the scientist rocked back across her dry bag, mouth wide open, and glazed eyes staring at the sky.

Monarch felt the sting at the side of his neck as if a particularly nasty mosquito was at work. But before he could reach up to swat it, he lost all control over his arms, legs, and head, and felt seasick. His muscles turned to taffy; he slumped over, jaw sagging, eyes wide open.

The thief drifted off into a nebulous haze wondering if the painted men coming into the firelight with primitive spears extended before them were real or just featured players in a particularly vivid hallucination.

42

"GLAD TO SEE YOU'RE finally awake," John Tatupu said. "You've been out nearly three days."

Tristan Hormel looked at him, and then the pitcher on the table by the bed. The Swiss banker said, "Water."

Tatupu poured him some, put a straw in the cup, and fed the straw into his mouth. Hormel sucked on it, coughed, and sputtered.

"Easy there," the big Samoan said. "Slow."

Hormel took two more sips, wincing in pain before flopping back on the pillow.

"I need a doctor."

"Other than the conk to the head, a few fractured ribs, and a right knee that's going to need some work, you're all right," Tatupu said. "Miracle actually, given how fast you were going when you hit."

"I hit . . . ? Who are you?"

"See, that's the thing, Tristan. Depending on you, I can be your best friend, or your worst nightmare."

The banker moaned, but said nothing.

"Tell me, why do you have armed men all around you and the attack dogs?"

Hormel's chin began to tremble before he said, "A very dangerous man, an assassin and a thief, has threatened to kill my wife and my family."

"Yeah," Tatupu said. "The thief's a friend of ours."

"Oh, God," the banker moaned. "Oh, God."

"He can't help you, I'm afraid," the big Samoan said. "Neither can your guards. And the GPS in your cell phone? It's on a train heading into Italy at the moment."

"Are you going to kill me?"

"Depends on what you tell us."

"What do you want?"

"Who hired you to hire the thief?"

Hormel looked nauseated and he shook his head ever so slightly.

"C'mon, now, Tristan," the Samoan said. "You're doing what bankers always do: thinking about money, or in this case the shitload of money some third party paid you to hire the thief."

The banker said nothing.

Tatupu sighed. When he had the choice he stayed away from violence and threats during interrogations, but he was getting nowhere being reasonable.

"You got a mom?" the Samoan asked.

"What?"

"Your mom. She alive?"

"Yes. But please, don't get her involved in—"

"Let me tell you about my mom," Tatupu interrupted. "Greatest woman I've ever known. Raised six kids after my daddy died. Put five of my brothers and sisters through college, and saw me become a highly decorated member of the U.S. Special Forces."

He paused to let that sink in, before continuing, "Great, great lady, going through a terrible thing, my mom. She's got early onset dementia. I went to see her a few weeks back in a nursing home. I'm her first born and she didn't even know my name."

It was true, and the Samoan had to work to keep his emotions in check.

After several moments of silence, Hormel said, "I'm sorry. I really am. But what does this have to—"

"Do with you?" Tatupu said. "See, here's the thing. You love your mother and your family. I get it. I love my mother and my family, too. And the thief? He most definitely loves his mother and his family.

"Now the thief is a very dear friend of mine, and so is his mother, who does a great deal of good in this world," he went on, pausing for effect before finally allowing his voice to betray anger. "We brought you here because we wanted you to know what a terrible mistake you've made having her kidnapped."

"I had nothing to do with—" Hormel began, before screaming in pain when Tatupu whacked a soupspoon against his kneecap.

When the screaming died, Tatupu said, "I figure your patella's broken there. What do you think? Should we try again? Make sure?"

"No, please," the banker begged, tears rolling. "Are you savages?"

"Hey, now," Tatupu said, going back to that agreeable voice. "You're involved in the kidnapping of a woman who's given her life to the poor, and the abandoned, and now you're calling *me* a savage?"

He snapped the spoon against the busted patella again. Hormel screeched and writhed.

"No more," he pleaded. "No more."

Tatupu dropped the spoon on a dresser to his left, and then said, "Give me a simple answer. Who hired you to hire the thief?"

Hormel began to sob. "You don't know these people. They're more dangerous than any thief, and—"

"Sorry to interrupt, but for your information, we have the badass factor in our favor," the Samoan said. "We could have just as easily attacked your home with machine guns and rocket grenades. But we were trying to keep your family out of it. If you don't answer me right now, however, I'm sending men to take your mother. Your wife will be next. Talk to us or we'll leave your kids orphans."

"No!" Hormel cried. "Please, I'll tell you. I'll tell you! His name is Esteban Reynard. He's an attorney in Buenos Aires. He works for the drug cartels."

43

MONARCH ROUSED TO THE cooing of doves. His head pounded, and his stomach was sour. He had no idea where he was when he first came to, only that he was lying on his right side on something hard and flat and that the air seemed a perfect temperature, and that he was as hungover as he'd been in his entire life.

The thief cringed at the sound of an ax striking wood at some distance, and then relaxed at the laughter of children. He felt beneath him. He was lying on woven mats.

Confused, he started to roll over, only to set off a new round of clanging in his head. It was several minutes before he could force his eyes open, and see that he was in a long, triangular-shaped structure. Rough-thatch walls rose steeply, supported by lengths of bamboo lashed to a thicker bamboo center beam to form an A-frame.

Monarch's memory started to return. He remembered being in Brazil, in the jungle, with Santos and the scientists, but had no sense of where he was now and how he'd gotten here. The thief tried to sit up, but a round of pounding and dizziness pushed him back to the floor with his eyes tightly shut.

The second time Monarch opened his eyes, he kept his head resting on the mats, and tilted it left and right, looking to see if he was alone. To his sides and beyond his feet, there were nothing but those reed mats covering the floor a good thirty feet or more to a triangular opening, and sunlight and trees beyond.

The thief heard a creak somewhere behind him and felt the floor shift. He rolled over slowly onto his stomach, and lifted his head, startled, and then gazed in disbelief at the apparition a few feet away.

Stone-faced and unblinking, the young man sat on his haunches, elbows and arms between his knees, hands clutching a primitive spear. A short skirt of coarse brown fabric clung to his narrow waist. His flesh was dark copper and loosely splotched with green and tan paint. About his eyes, like a mask, his skin had been dyed a deep red. His glistening ebony hair was pulled back into a ponytail, and two purple bird feathers had been tucked in near his temples. White teardrops were stenciled down his cheeks. Monarch guessed he was roughly eighteen.

Monarch's head started to throb horribly again, and he hung it, and groaned.

To his surprise, the Indian started laughing.

Despite the clanging in his skull, Monarch looked up to see the young man grinning now. He pointed at the thief, and then back to his own head before he started hitting the heel of his palm against his skull, laughing, and then jabbering in a language that sounded very much like the one Santos and Kiki shared.

"I get the feeling you've been in my state before," Monarch said back to him in English, before remembering the sting in his neck at the fire.

Obviously a dart of some kind, probably from a blowgun, but what the hell had the dart been dipped in? Monarch knew a thing or two about the drugs that could incapacitate a man. He'd used several of them over the years. Most took a minute or two to fully take effect. But he remembered going down less than five seconds after the sting. What the hell was that stuff?

The Indian handed him a carved bowl filled with water. Monarch accepted it gratefully. He took a sip, realized it had the same excellent taste as the water in the stream, and drank down the entire bowl, and two more. Then the young man held up fresh green leaves and gestured to Monarch to take and eat them.

When in Rome, the thief thought, and put them in his mouth, noticing a slight stinging on his tongue, and then as he chewed it, a clear taste, almost like fresh celery.

To his surprise, the nausea almost immediately began to subside, as did the general misery in his head. Soon after drinking the water, and swallowing the leaves, he could sit up. Soon after that, the Indian pointed at his chest, said what sounded like "Getok" and then pointed to Monarch with his red eyebrow arched.

"Robin," Monarch said. "Getok?"

The young man smiled, made an *ayy* noise and patted his chest. "Getok. Rawwbin?"

"Robin," Monarch said, and smiled back.

Outside, a rhythmic thumping noise began. Getok gestured with his spear toward the triangular opening at the far end of what Monarch had taken to calling the long house. The thief nodded, and started to get unsteadily to his feet before realizing there was some kind of paste smeared over his bites, and they no longer hurt.

He grabbed one of the bamboo roof supports for stability. The ceiling was low, and he had to bend over to walk. When he reached the triangular entrance, he beheld a scene that he would remember in detail the rest of his life.

Monarch looked out into a sun-flooded box canyon, with tiger-striped and black cliff walls that rose hundreds of feet to dense groves of towering trees roped in vines. Similar to the one he'd seen the day before, a waterfall plunged from a V-shaped notch in the top of the far cliff, a shimmering ribbon of water that disappeared into low trees.

Nearer to the thief, the rain forest had been cut down in strips twenty feet wide. The lanes radiated like spokes from a clearing and a settlement of seven long houses arrayed in a loose semi-circle around a large fire pit. Above the pit some fifty feet, the cliff turned under and protected the settlement from the sun and the rain. The ceiling of it was scorched from what looked like centuries of fire.

Santos sat on one of the logs around the pit and beneath the overhang speaking with Kiki, and two older, but very fit-looking Indian men painted like Getok. An older woman with a striking face and long, braided, steel-gray hair listened.

There were perhaps ten other people in the clearing, some of whom looked unmistakably indigenous, and others who looked almost Mediterranean. All of them except the children wore woven brown skirts similar to Getok's. Two women were using a carved log as a giant pestle to pound manioc root in a wooden mortar about two feet tall, the source of the thumping noise that had awoken him.

Three middle-aged men were using bunches of thatch to sweep leaves out from around the logs. The ground beneath the logs and indeed everywhere under the overhang was pale white crushed limestone. Beyond the protection of the cliff, however, the soil was fertile and dark. Children were playing some kind of game in those cleared lanes that ran out into the rain forest.

Santos caught sight of Monarch and called, "You're the third one up. How's your head?"

"Fine now," he called back, and he realized that life had stopped in the settlement. All eyes were on him as he climbed down the bamboo ladder with Getok following.

The children had stopped their play, and now ran toward him, gaping in wonder. Down on the ground, the thief realized why they were all so interested in him. He was by far the tallest person there. Getok couldn't have been more than five-five. Both of the fit men talking with Santos stood up, and they were even shorter. One of them stared at Monarch in awe.

But the other, who had his hair shaved up the sides like a Mohawk, turned cold. With his spear held before him, and the sharp stone head aimed at the thief, he shouted, "*Ketunga!*"

Then he took a step back and shook the spear, and said it again, louder and more insistent: "*Ketunga!*"

The older woman, meanwhile, stood her ground, her eyes flashing angrily, as she began to mumble in a low, frantic voice that seemed to disturb the other Indians, especially the three men who dropped their brooms and picked up their spears.

Kiki and Santos immediately started making calming gestures and speaking to them soothingly in their language. The other fit guy was yelling at the men with the spears, telling them to back off. The trio did, but Mohawk and the old woman still looked spitting mad. They began to argue and point accusingly at Kiki and Santos.

"You mind telling me what's going on?" Monarch yelled, rendering the Indians mute and wide-eyed.

Santos looked at him with some relief, bowed toward the fit man, and said, "This is Naspec. He's Kiki's father and as close as the Ayafal come to having a chief. The other one with the shaved sidewalls is Augus, a tribal leader. The old woman is Fal-até. She is the Ayafal's most powerful shaman."

"Back up, what's Ayafal mean?"

"The Children of the Moon," she said. "It's what they call themselves. And this whole place they call Tasen-Fal, the Canyon of the Moon."

"I gather the shaman and old Gus are not happy campers?"

"They hate that we are here at all," the scientist confirmed. "Fal-até says that we, and especially you, will mean the destruction of the Children and the Canyon of the Moon."

"Me?"

"That's what she said."

"And Old Gus?"

"He's intimidated, I think. Augus and the chief told us *we* could return, but to bring no one else, and now they're pissed at me and at Kiki for bringing you."

"Did you tell them I was along to keep you all safe?"

"Sort of," she said. "At least in their terms."

"Translation?"

"I told them there were demons that meant to harm us out in the jungle, and that you are a famous demon slayer," she said. "Which is what Augus was yelling at you. *Ketunga* means demon-killer in Ayafal."

"Great," Monarch said. "So the shaman sees me as some kind of Shiva, destroyer of worlds, and Old Gus thinks I am Ketunga, spirit warrior in a fantasy novel."

Santos fought against a smile, said, "That about sums it up."

"Where's my gun? My pack?"

"As far as I can tell, and for reasons I can't explain, they left the gun where we were camped. The packs are all over there."

"How did we get in here?"

"I don't know exactly," she said. "They keep the way in and out a tight secret. I imagine, however, that we were carried here."

"Tell Fal-até and old Gus I'm not going to destroy anything," he said. "And tell Naspec that I sense no demons here to slay, and give him my real name."

Santos hesitated and then spoke to them in their language, which had clicking noises deep in their throats similar to native tongues in southern Africa. When she was done, the chief almost smiled, nodded, and said, "Rawwbin."

"Robin," Getok corrected, and Monarch looked over his shoulder to find the young man standing there with that amused expression on his face.

"Robin," Naspec said, then touched his forehead, nose, lips, and chest.

"He welcomes you to his mind, his senses, and his heart," Santos said.

Monarch noticed that the shaman and the other tribal leader did not extend the gestures, but he bowed, and then repeated the movements to the chief.

Naspec grinned and then laughed, and all the other Ayafalians began to laugh with him. Except for old Gus and the shaman woman. Fal-até's lips squirmed like worms after a heavy rain, and she glared at Monarch as if she alone had a clear view of the dark side of his soul.

44

OVER THE COURSE OF the next hour, the other members of the scientific expeditions roused from their stupor. Tribal members brought them water and boiled yams and manioc mixed in with a fruit like papaya. It was delicious and Monarch found the meal as satisfying and refreshing as the water.

All the while, Santos tried explaining to the chief and the skeptical shaman about the research she wanted to conduct. She said she believed the Ayafalians when they claimed to be very old, but wanted to verify their ages, and take some samples of their blood and tissue.

Fal-até got incensed at one point, and, as Santos translated it, said, "We know exactly how old everyone is here. I've told you that."

"Many times. But you won't tell me how you know."

The shaman looked at the scientist as if she were an idiot, hesitated, and replied testily, "The Moon God tells us of course."

"You said that the last time I was here, too," the scientist countered. "But is there a way you can *prove* everyone's ages?"

That had set off an argument between the chief, Augus, and the shaman woman that even Santos couldn't follow. But when they settled down, Fal-até crossed her arms, raised her chin, and said, "We'll show you how we know."

The scientist looked shocked, but quickly agreed. Then she

looked to Rousseau, Carson, and their assistants, said, "Get cameras. Bring sample kits."

They all scrambled for their backpacks, and within minutes set off on a march away from the settlement, with the shaman woman leading and the chief right behind her. A sullen Augus followed. Monarch and Getok brought up the rear, which allowed the thief to see how the green and tan paint on the men's bodies seemed to make them almost invisible whenever they crossed through areas of sun-dappled vegetation. Even in the wide open, with plants at chest height or below, they seemed to blend right in.

They walked down one of the lanes cut through the jungle. Monarch noticed that they had been cleared by fire, and that not all trees had been taken. Every tree still standing in the lanes bore some kind of fruit or nut. Somehow the Ayafal knew that freeing up the trees would increase their yield.

Twice they passed gardens in the lane. The first two indigenous-looking women working the garden with Stone Age hoes took one look at Monarch and the scientists, shrieked and went down on their knees, trembling in terror. Kiki and her father went forward and calmed them, but even so, as they passed, the women looked at them like they were from another planet.

The second two women, however, had more Mediterranean features, and they shyly stopped their work when approached, giggling, gazing up at the outsiders with fierce interest, as if they were figments of their memories come to life. Santos showed Monarch how the Ayafal used a network of split bamboo logs to bring water to their gardens from the stream. It was primitive, and yet remarkably sophisticated.

They left the cleared lane and walked a well-worn path into dense foliage. The wall of plants on either side of the path went up twenty feet or more. It was the home of turquoise parrots that squawked and swirled overhead, and emerald green hummingbirds that flitted about scarlet flowers that bloomed on vines up and down the walls.

"Anyone know what that flower is?" the thief asked.

"No," said Rousseau, the botanist. "It's just one of the undiscovered plants here."

"And birds," Carson said. "We took a picture of one of these parrots last time, compared them when we got back to Rio and found no known match."

"It's true," Santos said, nodding over her shoulder to Monarch.

The thief's attention, however, was already beyond Santos to where the jungle opened up into a large rectangular area cleared of vegetation, except short, soft grass that felt spongy underfoot. Entering the clearing, his eye was drawn to the frothy waterfall, which cast wispy rainbows as it poured off the cliff. It was much bigger than he'd thought, a solid twenty feet across and shaped like a skirt where it cascaded into a large, deep pool of crystal clear water.

"They call it Fal-ané," Santos said. "It means moon water."

"Fal-ané," Naspec said, and smiled "Ayy." He smiled.

Monarch noticed the other scientists had a kind of contented expression on their faces as they nodded and said, "Ayy."

Santos must have seen the thief's puzzlement, because she said, "The Ayafalians have a big celebration here every full moon. We were part of it."

"It's beautifully crazy," said Graciella.

"I think the plants they use during the celebration are the cause of their longevity," her boyfriend said.

"Ridiculous," said Carson. "It's the water."

Monarch put a hand to his brow, looked up the face of the waterfall, said, "Where's the source of the water?"

Carson gestured up toward the cliff rim and the trees, said,

"We assume it's up there somewhere in that notch. At least that's where I'm going to look if I ever get the chance."

"Haven't the Ayafal been up there?"

"They say there's no way up," Santos said. "And believe me, they've looked. They think the forest on top is haunted by the spirits of their ancestors."

The thief trailed his hand in the pool and found the water that perfect temperature. Then he realized the air there felt cooler than it should have been.

He asked Santos about it.

She said, "It's the caves. There are dozens of them at the backs of the overhangs. The walls of the cliffs are riddled with passages. Cold air comes up out of them, regulates the temperature. At least that's our theory."

Monarch made to move away from the pool when he noticed something flash out of the waterfall and settle out deep in the pool, glinting as it sank. The chief, the shaman, and the tribal elder were leaving, crossing to the other side of the clearing with Santos and her associates close behind. Only Les Cailles and Graciella lingered, watching him.

"Did you see that?" the thief asked.

Rousseau's assistant hesitated. "See what?"

"Something brilliant, like a rock or something came down the waterfall, and it sank in there," Monarch said.

"Then there it stays," Graciella said. "You can drink from the pool, but you can't bathe or even wade. The Ayafal forbid it."

Les Cailles nodded, said, "They somehow know that swimming in the water could pollute it, make them sick. So they don't."

Monarch took one last look at the pool, and followed them and the shaman woman back into the forest. Within four hundred yards they again reached the overhang, which seemed to run the entire perimeter of the canyon. Fal-até led them deep beneath the overhang to where the back wall curved into the floor and appeared much lighter in color going left than it did right.

It wasn't until Monarch was close that he realized the lighter color on one side of the wall wasn't the result of mineral seepage, but hundreds upon thousands of two-inch by two-inch white cave paintings, all exact replicas of each other, showing the four quarter phases of the moon, repeated over, and over, and over again.

Going left, the cave paintings were stacked ten feet up the curve of the wall and onto the ceiling, and stretched as far as Monarch could see.

The shaman woman pointed to the only three paintings that weren't a replication of a lunar phase. In faded colors one painting showed what appeared to be a comet. Beside it was a depiction of an explosion with red, orange, and yellow flames. The third cave painting showed the sun and the full moon over a waterfall. At the bottom, stick figures gathered around a bonfire, which was depicted in a henna color.

The shaman woman said something in her language that seemed to take Santos aback. The scientist replied rapidly, looking confused. But Fal-até seemed confident in her reply, and the chief and the tribal elder nodded.

"What'd she say?" Rousseau asked.

Santos was staring at the cave paintings. "She says this is a picture of the beginning of time and life as they know it."

"You mean like their creation myth?" Monarch asked.

The lead scientist took her eyes off the painting, reappraising the thief, said, "That would be the smart thought, except she says it's when actual time, the canyon, the people, and everything here came into being."

"All at once?" Carson said.

"She says the moon god sent fire to create the canyon, and

with it time began," Santos replied, before speaking to Fal-até again.

The shaman replied, gesturing all around her for several minutes while the scientist listened intently, taking her eyes off the old woman only to look at the wall of moon symbols. When Fal-até stopped speaking, Santos appeared slightly dumbfounded.

"What is it?" Monarch asked. "What did she say?"

"The wall is a recording of every moon phase since the beginning of time."

"Which was when?" Rousseau asked.

Santos started talking. The old woman looked at the botanist like Rousseau was an idiot before replying and pointing at the creation paintings again.

"Okay," Carson said, reaching into his knapsack and pulling out a small digital camera. "Ask her how long the cave paintings go on like this."

"Yes," Rousseau said. "And ask her where time is right now."

Santos did, and Fal-até started to reply. But then Carson snapped a picture. The flash went off and things quickly degenerated.

Naspec, Fal-até, and Augus acted as if they'd been shot, and hurled themselves away from Carson. The shaman woman began shouting at him in a weird, wavering, voice that reminded Monarch of a short-wave radio being tuned. The effort required to make the sound had the old woman trembling from head to toe.

Santos put up her hands in surrender, and babbled at them. But Fal-até kept up her infernal screeching while Naspec and Augus flanked her with their spears extended at Carson.

"That the first time you've tried a flash photo?" Monarch asked Carson, who looked chagrined.

"I didn't even think about it," the chemist said, shaking his head.

"What are they going to think when we start testing them and using the computers?" Rousseau said. "You see? The pollution of their culture has begun, and we are the pollution. You see? Just by being here, despite our best intentions, we are already destroying them."

By then the old woman had stopped her wailing, and Naspec and Augus were listening to Santos. But the lead scientist must have heard some of what the French-Canadian was saying, because she whipped around, and said, "So what do you want to do, Philippe? Leave? Or try to do our job?"

"And what job is that?" the botanist shot back.

"We do our research," she said. "We document everything we can and use it as an argument that this place and these people should be left alone."

"After we learn their secrets so we can capitalize on them," Les Cailles said with a tinge of disgust.

"This is true," Rousseau agreed. "I mean, what do we do if we find some plant, or even the water is responsible for them living so long?"

"We don't know *if* they are living longer than most people," Santos shot back. "That's what we're trying to determine first. Remember?"

"We must think of these issues before we face them," the Canadian insisted.

"You face them," she said. "I've got work to do. And for the time being, let's keep the high-tech gadgetry to a minimum."

Santos and Kiki returned to the shaman, the chief, and Augus, who remained openly hostile.

Santos spoke with them a few minutes before turning. "Fal-até says the current moon phase is a long walk from here, but she will show us if we want."

"I want," Monarch said.

"Me too," said Carson, and his assistant nodded.

"Coming Professor Rousseau?" Santos asked.

The botanist looked at his assistant, and then said, "Of course."

By Monarch's wristwatch they walked for nearly two hours beneath the overhang, passing several settlements like the one where he'd awoken. The people were all uniformly frightened, and several children screamed and cried until Naspec spoke to them, calling them "*nee-fal*" or "friends of the moon." But then, in each case, Augus told his people not to trust them. Fal-até didn't help things, again referring to Monarch as a "demon who threatens us all."

Santos, however, saved the day when she spoke with the Ayafalians, which provoked gasps of wonder every time. Who was this alien who spoke their language?

The scientist told them about her great-grandmother, and used Vovo's name: "Ulé. Two very old women claimed to remember Vovo. They started to cry and hug Santos, saying that they'd grown up with her great-grandmother, and always wondered what had happened to her.

"You don't believe them, do you?" Monarch asked after they'd walked on. "That would make those women almost one hundred and, what?"

"Thirty," Santos said. "And yes, I think I do believe them. They told me they remembered the way Vovo laughed, how she'd hold her belly like she couldn't breathe. That's exactly what she used to do. I mean exactly."

Monarch reckoned they walked six miles from the beginning of time to the southern wall of the box canyon where the drawings abruptly ended about three feet above the ground with the moon in three-quarter phase. A charred stick lay on the limestone gravel below the last recording.

"We're past the three-quarter phase now, aren't we?" Monarch asked.

Santos nodded. "Heading into the full moon."

In the last mile or so, the thief had noticed other symbols interspersed with the lunar iconography. He gestured to several in the last few feet of the pattern, and asked Santos to ask the shaman about them. The old woman actually smiled at him as she gave Santos a long response, and then rotated her left foot to show a faded tattoo on her ankle.

Santos said, "She says every Ayafal is tattooed at birth. Each tattoo is different, and corresponds to one of those symbols you saw painted among the lunar phases."

Monarch saw that both the chief and Augus had small tattoos on their left ankles. So did Kiki.

"Where are *their* symbols on the wall?" Rousseau demanded.

Santos posed the question, and Kiki immediately went over about six inches to the right of the last symbol, and showed them hers. Monarch started counting, but then Kiki said something and the scientist translated, "She says there are two hundred and twelve full moons after her birth."

Monarch had always been fast with numbers but Carson was faster, said, "She's roughly seventeen and a half years old."

Augus showed them his symbol about two and a half feet to the right of the last moon, and said something to Santos, who translated, "He says he was born nine hundred and seven moons ago."

Carson whistled and said, "He's like seventy-seven years old."

"That's impossible," Les Cailles said. "Look at him. He looks fifteen or twenty years younger. In his fifties at best."

Monarch nodded. "And the chief?"

They went through the same ritual, and figured Naspec was roughly ninety-one, with the build and vigor of a man thirty years his junior anywhere outside of the canyon. Fal-até's symbol on the wall was over another five inches.

"She's one hundred and twenty-two," Carson said, in awe.

"Look at her. She looks about my grandmother's age when she died in her early eighties. This is crazy!"

"We can't simply believe this you know," Rousseau said. "If we confirm their age based on their own calendar, we'll be laughed at."

"Once they see the miles of lunar cycles recorded here?" Santos said. "No, I think people will absolutely believe us."

"We need more," Rousseau insisted. "Some scientific way we can measure this accurately."

"Hate to say it, Stella," Carson said, "but he's right. This is strong evidence, but if we can figure out a way to validate what's on the wall, we'll have absolute proof."

They all fell into silence for several moments before Santos said, "I might have a way. I mean, in theory, it *should* work."

45

CLAUDIO FORTUNATO LOOKED OUT the window of his art studio, saw darkness falling once more over the Argentine capital, and felt like putting his fist through a wall.

Almost a week had passed, and he still hadn't asked Chanel Chavez to marry him because they'd made no headway in the hunt for Sister Rachel. Making matters more frustrating was the fact that Gloria Barnett, John Tatupu, and Abbott Fowler had turned his studio into a command center, and he hadn't painted in nearly ten long days.

"Claudio?" Barnett called. "You with us?"

The artist turned from the window, seeing Barnett standing impatiently in front of a large whiteboard they'd hung on one of his walls. Tatupu and Fowler sat in front of laptop computers on a long folding table they'd brought in and set up where his easels used to stand. Chavez had gone to the courthouse and hadn't returned yet.

"Right here," Claudio said, with little enthusiasm.

"I know it seems like a pain," Barnett said. "But we need to have these intel-meetings every twelve hours so everyone knows where we stand. It makes a difference."

The artist nodded. It made sense.

Barnett pointed to the first of four names written across the top of the board.

"Alonzo Miguel?"

Claudio said, "I've got people watching him day and night. So far he seems to be what he says he is—a thief gone straight."

Barnett put a horizontal line under Miguel's name and said, "Tito Gonzalez?"

"Very hard man to find," Claudio admitted bitterly. "The word on the street is he left the thieving business four years ago, and deals drugs. But no one we've talked to has seen Tito in weeks if not months. Chanel is at the courthouse, looking at his files."

Barnett put a question mark under Gonzalez's name, said, "Galena Vargas."

"She's driving us crazy, too," Claudio said. "There is no birth record of a Galena Vargas born in Buenos Aires in the past twenty years. And nothing in the records in Bariloche that indicate a sister identified Hector's remains. Whoever really was cremated out there, his ashes were never claimed. We backtracked Vargas's mother and searched under her name, Maria Lopes Vargas, but the records say she had one child, Hector, before dying when he was six."

"Hector have a father?" Tatupu asked.

"None listed on Hector's birth certificate."

Barnett wrote, "Father?" under Galena Vargas's name, and moved on, saying, "Esteban Reynard."

Abbott Fowler, who used to work with Barnett on Monarch's CIA team, said, "Piece of work, that one. He's done criminal law here for nearly twenty-five years and represented some serious scum balls, including members of two Colombian cartels."

"But he's gone to ground," Tatupu said. "You call his office and they tell you he is away indefinitely because of a death in the family. Except, he's got no family. No wife. No kids. And he was an orphan like Robin."

"I think Hormel got word to him and he's in hiding," Fowler said. "He's certainly not at his house or his getaway up the coast. We checked both places."

Barnett nodded. "I've got Zullo digging into Reynard's financials. He's going for credit and debit cards first. With luck we'll be able to—"

The door to the apartment opened, and Chavez came in looking smug.

"You found something?" Claudio asked.

"A few things," she admitted. "I took that cabbage sample to an agricultural extension place last week. They said it's a strain called a Bonnie-Mega O-S that was developed in the United States, but is sold here in Argentina."

"Rare?" Barnett asked.

She shrugged. "It's a big cabbage. The head's like a basketball."

"I meant rarely grown around here?"

"He couldn't answer that," Chavez said, sobering.

"What else did you find?" Tatupu asked.

She brightened, waved some papers at them, said,. "Tito Gonzalez did jail time two years ago, busted with small amounts of cocaine and heroin, and Esteban Reynard defended him. I bought the court clerk lunch, and she told me that Reynard is a notorious bagman around the court. Bribery is one of his prime tools."

Claudio thought about that, said, "I'll bet Reynard was the one who got Vargas sprung from jail after he tried to kill me and Robin."

"Now we're getting somewhere," Barnett said, drawing a circle around the attorney's name. "He's our common denominator. We find Mr. Reynard, we find . . ."

She drew a line from the circle and scribbled, "Mastermind?"

46

GASPING, SWEATING, BEAU ARSENAULT rolled off Lynette Chambers.

"My God, Lynnette," he groaned. "I didn't think that was possible."

A big Cuban-American, Lynette had a laugh that was hearty, a smile that was easy to join, and skin that was a glorious mix of coffee and white milk chocolate. Her breasts were works of art, and she had dark berry nipples that were a gourmet confectioner's dream.

She put her head on his chest, propped her chin with her folded hands, said, "You like that, Beau?"

"Hard to believe a woman can be a genius on stage and in bed."

That pleased Lynette. She slid her thigh over him, rubbed him ever so sexily.

"Oh, God, sugar," he said. "The spirit is willing. But this old boy's done."

She pouted.

Arsenault turned his expression pitiful. "I won't be able to walk right as it is."

Lynette laughed then, deep and genuine. "I gotta be getting to the club anyway. You come watch the first set?"

"You know I would," Arsenault said. "But my daughter and grandson are coming into town this evening."

"That's nice," Lynette said. "My son was down with his baby girl last week."

"Hard to see you as a grandmother," he said.

She sobered, shrugged, said, "I started young. Too young. That's what makes this so important to me."

"You'll get your break," he said. "It's coming. I can feel it."

He got up and started toward her tiny bathroom. She sat up in bed, said, "Did you get a chance to talk to that producer you know?"

Arsenault stopped, tilted his head, grinned, and said, "I haven't. But only because he's off in Europe on vacation. He'll be back next week, and once he's gotten a chance to settle, I surely will call and tell him about the undiscovered nightingale singing every night down in the quarter."

"You think he'll come?" she asked, the hope in her voice ringing like a bell.

"How could he not?" the mogul said. "He trusts my taste, and I've delivered for him several times before."

Arsenault turned on the shower and got in feeling content and even-keeled. He loved this part of the cycle, when his dusky protégée was finally starting to believe in his power to deliver her dreams. Their sexual ardor was fueled by gratitude, and by the fear that something could always go wrong, that their long, longed-for vision could just slip by, like a feather floating just out of their grasp.

God, they liked to fuck when they were like this.

He loved Louisa. He really did. But when it came right down to it, there was nothing like the passion of a woman of color when she gets in heat and starts dreaming.

There was a trick to keeping them in this state. String them along, inch by frustrating inch, keeping that feather just out of reach. The truth was his producer friend wasn't in Europe. He could have called him ten times in the past week.

But as Arsenault turned off the shower, he knew he wasn't ready for this stage to be over yet. He wanted to enjoy it as long and as frequently as possible.

He dressed and went out into Lynette's bedroom. She was up, naked, arms folded. She gazed at him expectantly. "I'll hear from you after you talk to that producer?"

"You know you will," he said. "Right?"

Lynette nodded, her eyes watering. "I can't tell you how much I—"

"Shhh," he said. "Hush now. It's the least I can do for an artist like you."

As the mogul exited the shabby building, his car pulled up to the curb. Five steps and he was to the car, opening the door, and sliding inside.

"Twelve Oaks, Owen," he said, shutting and locking the door.

"Yes, sir," Owen said.

As they pulled away, Arsenault saw Lynette standing at her window, no doubt twisted with doubt and anxiety. He smiled. He enjoyed the tawdriness and desperation of this stage. He rested his head back, and began to close his eyes. His cell phone buzzed with an incoming text.

It was from Saunder's most recent burn phone, asking if he was available.

The mogul texted back that he was, and got a message in return that said, "Secure location. Skype."

That was good. He hadn't heard from Saunders in days.

"Got some work to do, Owen," Arsenault said, pushing the button that raised the soundproof wall.

Arsenault fished his iPad out of his briefcase, and called up Skype. He found a bogus account Saunders had created, and dialed an equally sham number. In moments, the face of his director of security filled the screen.

"Where have you been?" he asked.

"I'm still in Rio," Saunders replied. "I wanted to give you an update."

"I'm listening."

Even thought they believed the connection was secure, Saunders spoke in euphemisms, nothing concrete, but Arsenault got the gist of it because they'd decided to refer to Monarch as "the butterfly."

Saunders began by saying that the "butterfly's sister was fine and safe." Then his face fell, and he said, "But there have been setbacks and complications."

"Name them."

"The butterfly sensed his old friends," Saunders said. "He went to war, and lost them in the forest three days ago."

"Where are the butterfly's old friends now?"

"Sitting on his back trail."

"Okay," Arsenault said.

"And the old friends have allies."

"How's that?"

"There is a second party in the forest, an unfortunately familiar party."

That pissed the mogul off. Somebody else was after Santos's secrets, too? Somebody he competed in business with?

But then Saunders said, "They're after a place to dig."

The mogul squinted. "For what?"

"They're not saying."

"Party name?"

Saunders thought about that, and said, "Saucy Jello Buns."

Arsenault had no idea what he was talking about until his security chief repeated the phrase, emphasizing the first letter of each word: "S-J-B."

He tightened up inside, and leaned to the screen. "You got to be kidding."

"No."

The mogul restrained himself from making a snap analysis or judgment. This was too big a development. He set it aside for the moment, said, "That it?"

"No," Saunders said. "The butterfly's comrades have been to Switzerland, and are now hunting in the town of Saucy Jello Buns. But we're good. Everyone of consequence has been well paid to flee for the caves."

"Suggestions?"

Saunders nodded. "We give the butterfly's old friends more weapons. We show him that his sister's wings can be damaged or worse."

Arsenault thought about that. Something about it made his stomach sour. But there was no denying the effect it would have.

"Use restraint."

"Always."

"And the second party?"

"I know you don't want to hear this, but you need to rethink your alliances."

The mogul took the advice, and set it aside. "More?"

"No."

"Stay reachable."

Saunders nodded, and broke the connection.

Arsenault rode in silence, his brain ticking through the developments one by one, evaluating the potential repercussions of each until he reached the final one: Saunders's advice that he rethink his alliances.

That stuck in his craw and it took until they were ten miles from home for the mogul to finally swallow it. Then he went through his regular phone contacts, found Silvio Juan Barbosa's number, and hit send.

There was a good chance Barbosa would not answer, but to his surprise, he did on the third ring, saying coldly, "I thought we were done for good."

"I'm as heartbroken as you are," Arsenault said. "But past issues aside, I've come to learn that we have parallel interests in Brazil."

There was a long pause before Barbosa said, "Where in Brazil?"

"Amazon basin," Arsenault said. "Where else?"

47

TWO DAYS LATER, MONARCH watched Dr. Santos balance on a bamboo ladder up against the overhung wall as she carefully scrapped tiny samples from the cave painting of the full moon next to the shaman's personal tattoo symbol. The old wise woman watched with interest. She had given up trying to call down hexes on them.

Indeed, Fal-até had formed a bond with Santos upon hearing that she believed the Ayafal did know the age of everyone in the tribe. The lead scientist told the shaman and the chief that the tribe was important to all mankind, and that she needed help to figure out what made members of the tribe live to such an old age.

When she was asked how, Santos intertwined her fingers and told them that she thought she could perform a different kind of time measurement using small samples from the tattoo ink under her skin, and small samples from the cave paint. She believed that their equipment could perform basic carbon-14 and gas spectrographic analysis on both the paint, which was made from ash, and from the tattoo ink, which came from a succulent plant that oozed a bruised purple liquid when its stem was snapped.

Augus and his small clan had refused to cooperate. But Naspec agreed to let her take the samples, especially from the oldest Ayafalians. To their surprise, Fal-até had also agreed to taking samples from the moon phase cave paintings.

It turned out that the shaman was also a midwife, herbal healer, and vast repository of knowledge that the tribe had passed down generation to generation. The Ayafal, for example, knew that there was an outside world. Fal-até said generations of men, including both Naspec and Augus, had left the canyon and gone on long, perilous journeys that brought them to the edge of contact with the modern world, but they'd always turned back.

"Why?" Santos asked the first night as they sat around the fire on those logs arranged out in front of what members of the expedition had taken to calling the northern settlement. Sitting by the fire was a nightly occasion in the Ayafal culture. Every person in the tribe went for at least an hour to talk openly and about everything, men, women, and children.

The chief had shrugged at Santos's question, and said, "We'd already found what we were looking for, and it was time to return here with it."

"What were you looking for?" Carson asked.

"Girls," the shaman said matter-of-factly.

When Santos had pressed her on the meaning of her reply, Fal-até revealed that the Ayafal understood the dangers of inbreeding, which she said had been taught to them by the moon god at the beginning of time. This fear of inbreeding explained why Santos's great-grandmother and Kiki had woken up the day after their sixteenth birthday to find themselves abandoned in the jungle.

"For every girl who leaves," the shaman said. "Another must be brought in. This way, the blood of Ayafal babies remains strong."

Monarch had flashed on the tribal members who looked more Mediterranean than indigenous, said, "Is she saying they kidnap girls and bring them here against their will?"

Santos posed the question. Fal-até shrugged, and said, "It has always been so."

This news had distressed the lead scientist, who said, "Is it right to steal girls and bring them here when they don't want to come?"

Naspec had reacted angrily, saying, "They want to be here."

The chief called over a woman about the age of twenty, who balanced a baby on her hip. She looked more Latin than Indian. Her name was Petté, and she was brought to the canyon when she was a young girl, so young she barely remembered her other life, which she said was full of demons.

"So you want to be here?" Santos had asked in Ayafal after Portuguese had failed.

"This is my life," Petté said. "My husband, my children, the canyon. I am very happy. Ever since I came here I've been happy."

Santos, the other scientists and their assistants, and Monarch cringed at the idea that the Ayafal regularly abandoned girls born in the canyon, and snatched others to replace them. It destroyed the idea that the canyon was an Eden, and the tribe the perfect society. It was also soon apparent that the females who'd been kidnapped into the society were tattoo-less, and because of it they seemed to be held in somewhat lower esteem than the tribal members who'd been born in synch with the moon.

And what of the banished girls, the ones drugged and abandoned? The shaman said they were given up to the gods, though their sudden absence always caused a collective grieving, almost like a funeral or a wake. The banished girls themselves were always watched from afar as they awoke from the paralytic drug, and then wandered off into the jungle. Until Kiki, not once in any living tribe member's memory had a banished girl managed to return.

But then, about a year after Kiki was abandoned, the men in the village heard the howler monkeys going nuts. The monkeys, so curious and concerned about strangers in their midst, were like an alarm system. Several men, including Naspec, went out to investigate, and spotted Kiki sitting on the stream bank where the girls were traditionally left. The chief was secretly overjoyed. But it wasn't until Santos had started speaking in Ayafal that he decided to bring Kiki and the others inside the canyon the first time.

Though Augus and his clan argued that that decision had already damaged the tribe, the other members seemed, after getting over the initial shock of outsiders, very welcoming. Especially Getok, who followed Monarch everywhere, smiling, and watching from behind his red mask.

He was smiling even now as Monarch watched Santos climb down off the ladder with the samples from the cave calendar in plastic sleeves.

"That everything you need?" the thief asked.

"Everything we need from here," Santos said. "And Graciella and Edouard should be done taking the physical samples by the time we reach the settlement where those women who knew Vovo live."

"What samples are they taking?" Monarch asked, noticing that Fal-até was staring up at the moon and the symbol that coincided with her own birth.

"Mouth swab for DNA," Santos replied, writing on the plastic sleeves, identifying the samples. "And we make a slight stick of a very thin sterilized needle to get the dye."

"No blood samples?" Monarch said.

"I figured that might cause a revolt," she said. "Too much too soon."

"You're probably right," the thief said.

"We should get going," the scientist replied. "We've got a long walk before dark."

Fal-até came over to them and spoke. Naspec, the chief, listened, looked at Monarch with new eyes, and nodded.

"She says she's had a vision," Santos said.

"Out of the blue?" Monarch said. "Just like that?"

"Evidently. And evidently you were in the vision."

"Okay?"

"She misinterpreted you the first time."

"So I'm no longer the destroyer?"

"No," Santos said. "You are the demon slayer I told her you were."

"What's that supposed to mean?"

"You're going to save the Ayafal from demons."

"I'll be on the lookout," he replied with a wry smile.

But Monarch's thoughts were not on demons as they set off on the march north for the third time in as many days. He was trying to figure out how long Sister Rachel had been in captivity, and it took him awhile. As Santos had said, despite the Ayafal's obsession with the phases of the moon, there was a timeless quality to the canyon and its people that was seductive and impossible to ignore. After a day there, he'd stopped wearing his watch. For reasons he couldn't quite describe, it just felt like the right thing to do.

Increasingly, however, the idea of stealing the secrets to the Ayafal's longevity seemed the wrong thing to do. But what would happen if he didn't? Hector might kill Sister Rachel out of spite alone. That firmed his resolve. Stealing the secrets of the canyon *was* the wrong thing to do, but he was absolutely going to do it.

And even though it now felt wrong to him to use a satellite phone in the canyon of the moon, he was going to do that as well.

An hour later, when they'd made it to the clearing, he told Santos to go on ahead. He wanted to sit awhile and admire the falls. When he was sure he was alone, he got out the satellite phone and called Gloria.

"Where the hell are you?" Barnett demanded.

"In the enlightened Stone Age," he replied. "You?"

"Buenos Aires," she said, and then got him up-to-date.

"Which drug cartel does Reynard work for?" Monarch asked.

"Colombians, and Mexicans. Zullo got us Reynard's credit card and debit card numbers, and we're monitoring them. So far nothing."

"Tell Claudio to find Jesus Rincon. He'll know how to contact Tito."

"Jesus Rincon. Got it."

Monarch told her about Dokken and the mining company putting GPS bugs on the rafts, and how he'd lost them.

"Dokken and Vargas coming back into my life at the same time says coordination to me," the thief said.

"Agreed," Barnett said. "I'll make some calls, see if anyone in the FBI or CIA kept tabs on Dokken after he was released."

"And find out more about the mining company."

She promised she would, and Monarch almost signed off. But then he said, "They've had her almost two weeks, Gloria."

"She's a very tough woman," Barnett said. "You've got to believe that."

"Oh, I do," he said, choking up. "But still. Two goddamned weeks."

"I understand completely. Any closer to finding the fountain of youth?"

Monarch looked at the waterfall and the pool, said, "Maybe."

"Really?"

He told her about the lunar calendar and the DNA and environmental samples the scientists were taking.

"So what are you going to do?"

"Once I've got the age-defying source confirmed, I'm going to steal what I need and get the hell out of here."

"Well done."

"Once I've got it confirmed," he emphasized. "I'll let you know."

"And I'll leave a message if we find Tito or Reynard."

"Watch yourselves. Tito's slippery and the cartel guys are vicious."

"But we're professional and unpredictable."

They said their good-byes. Monarch hung up and was lowering the satellite phone's antenna when he heard a branch snap close by in the forest. He peered in through the branches, trying to spot the source of the sound. But he saw nothing, and heard nothing more.

Another day passed. The moon overhead was in its last waxing toward full. While Santos processed the cave painting and tattoo ink samples, Carson and Rousseau and their assistants were out in the field gathering water and plant samples for their research.

Monarch helped and watched the tribal members go about their daily lives. Men chopped wood, foraged for food in the jungle, carried water to the settlement, and built things. Women were in charge of the collective kitchen. Others spun that crude fabric they all wore with fibers harvested from the stalk of what Rousseau said was yet another unnamed jungle plant. Other women wove mats from rushes and reeds that grew downstream of the waterfall pool.

The Ayafal were hardworking, but not obsessive. After a few hours work, they lay around and talked. They loved to laugh. All of them. And they did a great deal of it.

Monarch never saw any of the children misbehave or get reprimanded. They appeared free to roam about seemingly without restriction, but spent long periods of time in their parents' arms, even the adolescents.

The tribe also understood that filth led to disease, and they took great care to dig latrines in the limestone areas where their organic waste would be filtered and purified. The thief found all of it fascinating, but he was just biding time.

Midafternoon, Santos came to Monarch. She was beaming. "We're in a special, special place, Robin. A miraculous place."

"You've got proof of the ages?"

"I think so," she said. "My first round of tests show a strong correlation between the age of the paint on the cave wall, and the tattoo ink, and the age they claim to be based on the moon charts."

"How strong?"

"Plus or minus two years," she said. "But with the right equipment, we might get even more precise."

"So now what? Repeat the tests?"

"I'll do that back in the lab. I'm going to switch to the DNA samples."

Before they could talk more, Carson and Rousseau and their assistants returned with their own samples, and began their own testing. Santos returned to hers as well. By evening, they knew that the water in the pool at the base of the waterfall had an alkaline pH of 7.4, putting it somewhere between salt water and distilled water, which Carson said would be expected from a limestone-based source.

"There's a lot of science out there to support the importance of keeping the body slightly alkaline in nature and longevity," Carson said. "There are also vital minerals in the water in almost optimal dilutions for human performance, and several trace minerals I haven't identified. If someone could bottle this stuff, they'd make a fortune."

"No one's bottling water here, ever," Santos said, looking horrified.

"Well, I most certainly am taking the plant samples and seeds back and growing them in my greenhouse," the botanist said. "From what Fal-até says, there are four very powerful ones here that she claims can cure all sorts of illnesses. And the more I study that *K-nay-afal* plant they use on full moons, the more I'm convinced it's in the cannabis family, except that it's got an unbelievably high concentration of cannabinoids in it."

His assistant Les Cailles nodded. "Off the charts."

"Translation?" Monarch said.

Rousseau said, "Cannabinoids inhibit certain neurotransmitters in the brain, especially in people with seizure disorders, and has shown promise as a cancer treatment. The plants could be part of why the Ayafal seem to rarely get sick, and their minds remain so agile into old age."

The botanist also said he thought the drug on the dart was a mutation of the curare plant. That was remarkable because in its raw form curare usually kills a human.

"There's almost too much to catalogue here," Rousseau said. "A lifetime of work could be done in this canyon."

Later, after the others had gone off to sleep, Monarch and Santos sat on a log a few feet apart, looking at the fire.

"You guys will get the Nobel for something like this, won't you?" he asked.

The lead scientist laughed, shook her head. "Not for simply finding people and testing them."

"No?"

"No," she said. "I'd have to figure out why they live longer and then scientifically prove it, which could take years. Decades."

"You up to the task?"

Santos smiled, "Yes. I think I am." She hesitated. "You've never made a pass at me."

"That right?"

"I think I would know."

"You would," he said. "But sadly that's not going to happen."

"No?"

314

"Conflict of interest," Monarch said.

"So you have a woman in your life?"

"I do."

"What's her name?"

"Rachel."

"I think, for the record, that Rachel is a lucky woman to have you."

"I'll tell her that," Monarch said.

"You introduce me someday?"

"Nothing would make me happier."

48

MONARCH AWOKE AFTER DAWN in that same long hut thinking that the dart drug might come in handy someday. But how would he get some? Steal Rousseau's samples?

He went to the bamboo ladder, looked out into the weak light, and saw Santos pretty much where he'd left her. She sat on a log in front of the fire, head down, staring at her computer, seemingly oblivious to the four or five Ayafala children who were gathered around the back of her, staring in awe and excitement at the glowing screen.

"You sleep at all?" he asked.

The lead scientist seemed not to hear him for several seconds, and then came out of whatever place her brain had taken her, and looked up at him.

"Not a wink," she said.

"You all right?" he asked.

"Just a bit in shock," Santos replied.

"Why's that?" he asked.

She blinked twice, shook her head once, and said, "It shouldn't happen this way. I mean you hear about these things happening, but . . ."

The scientist's eyes went far away again.

"Earth to Santos," Monarch said. "What's happened?"

"I think I've got it," she said. "I went on a hunch, and ran a few tests on the samples we gathered yesterday, and, my God,

316

I think I'm right. I'll have to test them all, of course, and the kidnapped girls to know for sure."

"Know what for sure?"

"Why the Ayafal live so long," she replied. "At least a major contributing factor."

"Wait, didn't you say figuring that out would take years?"

"If not decades," Santos said, nodding in bewilderment.

"So what do you think it is?"

Her expression turned dazed at that point. Monarch thought she might faint and keel over right there. "I don't feel right," she said.

"Because you haven't slept or eaten or probably had a thing to drink," the thief said, propping her up.

"I *could* use some sleep," she said, popping a flash drive from the USB port, and hanging it around her neck before closing the laptop and hugging it to her chest. "When I wake up I'll be able to tell if I'm right about this, or delusional."

As Monarch helped get her standing and walked her over to the long hut where she'd been sleeping, he kept a close eye on her computer. If Santos *was* right, the key to freeing Sister Rachel had to be on that computer and that flash drive. All he had to do was grab one and go.

Santos yawned, said, "Thank you, Robin. Can you hold this while I climb up?"

She handed him the computer, climbed up the short ladder onto the platform, and then turned and held her hand out expectantly. Monarch gave it over without hesitation.

"You're a good person, Robin Monarch," she said as she turned to go inside. "Your Rachel is a lucky, lucky girl."

Monarch walked away, sat on the log, looking at her long hut. The secret, or part of it anyway, was within his grasp. But how would he escape? How had the Ayafal gotten them in here?

Before he could begin to figure that out, the other scientists awoke, ate, and went back out into the field. He never mentioned what Santos had told him. The thief stayed within range, hoping Santos might give him an opportunity to steal the flash drive, or even better, her computer. But through the morning and well into the afternoon, there was no sign of her.

Monarch noticed, however, that there was more activity and more people than he'd seen there before. Indeed, there seemed to be a stream of Ayafal men and women coming in from other settlements in the canyon. Twice the ordinary number of women were cooking and preparing in the communal kitchen area. Some men were carrying loads of dried firewood. Others toted large gourds that seemed heavier than they looked.

Everyone was happy, excited, except the younger children, who glumly watched the frantic preparations. Monarch could not communicate other than through rudimentary sign language, so he had no idea what was happening.

The other scientists returned midafternoon.

"Are you ready for it?" asked Carson.

He had come up behind Monarch, and was watching the now frantic preparations with happy eyes.

"It?"

"The full moon celebration," Carson said. "The highlight of Ayafal culture as far as I'm concerned."

"What happens?"

He laughed. "Honestly, I don't want to spoil it for you. It's something you just have to experience the first time."

"But you had a good time?"

He laughed again. "Hell, yes. It's impossible not to."

"Then why are the kids all so sad."

"You've got to be fifteen or older to participate," Carson said. "If I were you, I'd take a nap. You're going to need the energy."

Monarch had other plans, but knew they were impossible to

execute at the moment. He considered faking an illness, letting everyone else leave the village for the celebration, and then steal the computer drive.

"I'll take your advice," he said, returned to his hut, not figuring to sleep at all.

He was surprised when someone shook his foot, and he awoke groggily to see Santos grinning at him.

"C'mon," she said. "You don't want to miss your first full moon among the Ayafal."

Monarch glanced at the flash drive dangling around her neck, but then nodded and sat up, seeing that it was late afternoon. The canyon was already falling into shadows, and the voices of the tribe were fading into the jungle. He followed Santos down the ladder and found the settlement empty except for fifteen or twenty children who all looked like they'd lost their puppies.

"No kids at the party?"

She laughed. "It would be, uh, inappropriate."

"Okay," the thief said. "Now you've intrigued me."

Santos made a zipping motion across her mouth.

"Right, Carson told me I have to experience it myself."

The lead scientist's eyes looked like they were laughing as she nodded.

"Lead on."

They took the now familiar route through the jungle to the clearing. He tried to get Santos to talk about her discovery, but she seemed amused to stay mute and study his apprehension.

They emerged into the clearing near the waterfall where the party was clearly under way. The moment Naspec saw Monarch, he rushed toward him carrying one of the gourds. The chief beamed, smiled, and said something.

"He's offering you the wine of the moon god," Santos whispered. "It's a drink they make from jungle berries. I highly recommend it."

Monarch nodded. Someone produced a carved wooden ladle of sorts. Naspec lifted the lid on the gourd and plunged it in, coming up with a deep, dark, red liquid that carried an aroma similar to brandy. The thief sipped a bit and felt it explode with differing tastes, all pleasant, a little nutty, a little fruity, and a major zing at the end. He drank the ladleful, and another without argument.

When the chief offered him a third, the thief looked at Santos, said, "They trying to get me hammered?"

"They're getting you in the mood."

"You're not getting in the mood?" he asked.

"After the show, thank you," Santos said with a smile.

The canyon was taking on shadows as the sun dropped in the west. Within minutes, Monarch was hyperaware of how the light in the clearing was changing, and he had a warm sense of well-being growing at the back of his head. He smiled at Santos.

"Feeling it?" the scientist asked.

"Uh, yeah," he replied, watching with fascination as the Ayafal started to segregate, with the men moving closer to the waterfall behind a pile of tree limbs arranged for a bonfire.

The Ayafal women were gathering in front of the pile. They and the other scientists seem to be entertained as they watched Monarch. The thief didn't care. He was focused on the Ayafal men, at least forty of them, who started pounding the ground with the butts of their spears and chanting in deep, sonorous, and harmonized tones that put Monarch in mind of recordings he'd heard of whales singing.

"They're bidding farewell to the sun," Santos whispered as the clearing was cast in darker and darker shadows.

When the chanting was done, the clearing and the jungle

320

around it fell into a deep, almost funereal silence. Down in the canyon it was near pitch-black now, but high overhead the sky had gone from the softest orange to stars that showed through a glimmer of dull aluminum light.

Then Monarch saw a glowing ember moving toward him in the darkness. The ember brightened as if blown by a bellows, and he smelled a pungent smoke different from marijuana's, lighter he thought, and sweeter. The ember came right up to him and he saw in its glow that it burned in the bowl of a pipe exactly like the ones he'd seen back in Rio in the offices of Santos, Rousseau, and Carson.

"If you want the full effect, you need to smoke it," Santos said. "Then that pipe will be yours forever."

"I'm not going to flip out, am I?"

"I thought it was one of the most tremendous experiences of my life, but if you want it you need to hurry up."

Against his better judgment, Monarch took the pipe from the chief and did as Santos instructed, taking three deep draws, tasting the smoke and finding it fungal on the way in, and vinegary on the way out.

At first the thief felt nothing more than very, very relaxed, his mind slowing, his thoughts not racing at all. Then the quiet seemed to filter out into his veins and through his body and he swore he might drift away on the sensation.

Clapping in unison, the Ayafal women began to sing their own chant at a slightly higher tempo than the men's.

"They're welcoming the moon god," Santos whispered. "That's her gathering strength in the sky above the waterfall. She's come to talk to you, Robin."

The thief found the sound of the waterfall in the darkness, looked toward it and up, seeing that the dull aluminum light was building and sharpening with every breath he took. His heart seemed to beat with the tempo of the women's chanting, which gathered pace and built speed, getting louder and more raucous by the moment.

Monarch felt mesmerized when the top of the moon appeared above the trees on the cliff. The men started chanting again, but in a higher octave and steadier beat. The thief could see the tribe now in the strengthening moonlight, and how the men had divided into two groups that retreated to opposite sides of the pool.

More of the moon showed above the notch. Its light found the uppermost part of the waterfall, turned it as shimmering as mercury. As the moon rose higher, in and then over the cliff notch, the waterfall continued to transform, inching down the cliff, glistening like molten silver and pewter.

The thief had no sense of how long it took. He felt untethered in time, and totally entranced by the waterfall appearing out of the darkness in those stunning colors until finally the moon had risen high enough to light the entire cascade top to bottom and to fill the pool side to side.

Monarch gasped and felt his eyes well. He had never seen anything quite that beautiful in his entire life.

The men and women stopped singing. For a beat the thief knew only the waterfall, the pool, and the beating of his own heart.

Then a lone, rich, and wavering female voice began to sing, and Monarch saw the shape of a woman appear inside the waterfall, right where it met the pool. She stepped out from within the falling water with her hands outstretched and her face tilted up to the moon. In his stupor the thief realized it was Fal-até, the old shaman woman, who was singing so wonderfully.

"She's the moon god's sister," Santos whispered. "It's what her name means in Ayafal."

The other women and the men picked up her song, and the collective, harmonic sound seemed to penetrate the thief's flesh, pulse inside him, and, echo and beat until spots appeared before his eyes, transforming the shaman woman into Sister Rachel.

Seeing the missionary bent back like that, her arms supplicated, pleading with the sky for mercy, an uncontrollable ball of emotion welled in Monarch's stomach and pushed up his throat. He began to weep and to sob, and felt himself go to the ground.

"Monarch?" Santos said, sounding far, far away. "It's okay. Just talk to her. Tell her the truth when she asks."

Monarch tried to close his eyes to erase the image of Sister Rachel suffering, but then a flame appeared in front of the pool and the waterfall. It built, threw light, and revealed one of the men on his knees coaxing an ember to ignite more dry grass, and the twigs, and cut branches. As the bonfire gathered fury, Monarch hallucinated Sister Rachel in the pool, consumed now in water and fire.

A silhouette appeared, blocking the flames and the waterfall. The silhouette started to speak. But the voice was distorted, the frequency of it rising and falling so he had no idea whether the person before him was male or female, friend or foe.

He felt himself rolled on his back. He gaped up at the full moon.

Monarch tried to talk to the moon god, pleading. He knew his jaw and tongue were moving, but heard no sound.

The drugs hit him like a crashing wave then, beat on him, stripped his mind of all thought, and bore him off into a cascade of color that rapidly accelerated toward darkness.

49

GLORIA BARNETT LOOKED UP from her laptop, her face grave.

"What is it?" Claudio asked.

The painter and Monarch's team were in a passenger van Barnett had rented, and Abbott Fowler had parked in a seedy neighborhood on the outskirts of the city.

"SJB," Barnett said. "The mining company that put the GPS trackers on the rafts. According to an analyst I know at the CIA, they're bad, bad news. The owner, Silvio Juan Barbosa, has half the Brazilian government in his pocket and seems to act with impunity up in the Amazon basin. People who complain about his mines or practices have a habit of turning up dead, or not turning up at all."

"Robin took their helicopter down," Tatupu said. "They're not in the picture."

"Barbosa doesn't give up easily. Robin should know his men remain a threat."

"Message him," Chavez said, and then gestured to Claudio. "Ready?"

Claudio glanced at his watch. It was past ten. He nodded.

"Break a leg," Barnett said.

324

"See you soon," Tatupu said, and pumped fists with Claudio.

He and Chavez climbed out, rounded the corner, and crossed the street toward the gaudy neon lights of Club Boom-Boom. A sign out front proclaimed that porn star Leonora Bunda was making a special appearance.

Looking at the packed parking lot and the small groups of men streaming toward the entrance, Chavez shook her head, said, "I never get the attraction of places like this and women like Leonora Bunda."

Claudio shrugged. "It's a guy thing. We're hardwired to want to look."

"You're not looking in there," she said. "Right?"

The artist crossed arms, palms on his shoulders, and crooned in heavily accented English: "I only have eyes for you . . . and your bunda—"

Chavez chortled, said, "You better, you know what's good for you."

"Alonzo Miguel was right, you are scary at times."

That seemed to make her happy as they went through the doors into a dimly lit lobby where they brought up the rear of a line. Dance music pulsated beyond a set of heavy black drapes. When they reached the front, the cashier gave Chavez the once over.

The sniper hugged Claudio, said sweetly, "We like the same things."

The cashier shrugged, took their money, and nodded toward the drapes. As they went through, Claudio said, "That was creative."

"I have my moments," Chavez said.

"Kind of turned me on, too."

"Down boy. Focus on what we're here for."

Claudio scanned the interior, which featured two stages: one long, narrow, and surrounded by men drinking in chairs, and a square one with a pole surrounded by VIP boxes set back against the wall. It took him less than a minute to spot the man he'd hoped he'd find.

"Got to hand it to Robin," he said. "He was dead on about Jesus Rincon. And Rincon was dead on about Tito."

"You mean he's in here?"

"He is."

Claudio reached up and flipped the switch on the tiny radio transceiver in his ear. Chavez did the same, said, "We've got a target."

"Position?" Barnett said.

"Back of the main stage, middle VIP booth," Claudio said. "He's at the rear of the booth and has company. Three women. And there are two goons out front."

"Give me a visual?"

The artist reached into his pocket, took out a pair of Google glasses modified to look like black, thick hipster frames with oversized silver hinges to conceal the camera. He touched a small button, said, "How's that?"

"Light's low, but it will do," Barnett said.

"Good," Chavez said. "Let's get this party started."

Claudio led the way across the room, around the back of the main stage where a blonde with fake boobs was warming up the crowd and the DJ was rambling on about "the legendary exploits of Leonora Bunda."

Claudio went straight to the goons with his hands up, said, "I'm an old friend, and unarmed."

"Fuck off," one said. "He's busy."

"Hey, Tito," Claudio said, showing him the tattoo. "It's me."

Inside the VIP area, three women in bikinis were mauling Tito Gonzalez, and for a second he didn't even look Claudio's way. But then the gangster came up for air. He stared quizzically at him, then at Chavez.

Tito had gained weight, gotten puffy, but he was still the rat-face Claudio remembered from twenty years before, with a long nose and narrow chin, and a gap between his yellow upper two teeth. But the eyes, which he recalled as almost black and cunning in their youth, were different now. They were glassy and bloodshot courtesy of the Peruvian pink flake cocaine laid out in thin horseshoe lines on the mirror table.

"Claudio Fortunato," Tito said as if every syllable were rancid. "Long time."

"Too short," Tito said acidly. "So fuck off. I don't hang with traitors, even two decades after the fact."

"We're not looking to hang," said Chavez. "We just want to ask some questions."

Tito shoved one of the girls off his lap, gave the sniper the psycho stare, and said, "Who the fuck are you, bitch?"

Claudio said, "Have some fucking respect, Tito. That's the woman I love."

"Yeah? Or what?" Tito asked. "Artist and his bitch gonna go gangster?"

"We can do better than that," Chavez said, taking a step to the side.

Claudio said, "The big Samoan sitting with his back to the stage looking at you? He's a CIA assassin. Any of you makes a move on us, he kills you all."

The goons shifted uneasily, as if they wanted to go for their guns, but stopped when they saw Tatupu show them the pistol already trained their way.

"You won't have a chance," Chavez warned. "He never misses at this range. Even if he does, the guy to his right two stools? Used to be a Navy SEAL. Small-arms expert."

Tito's street smarts climbed up out of the cocaine haze. His nose twitched before he said to the girls, "Get lost."

They started to protest, but he glared at them as if they were breakable. They grabbed their purses and threw hateful glances at Chavez as they exited. Tito nodded to the bench seats to either side of the mirrored table.

Claudio sat on the left and Chavez on the right. Tito looked past them to Tatupu, sighed, and gestured at the cocaine. "Tootskie?"

"Pass," Claudio said.

Chavez shook her head.

"You seen Hector Vargas lately?" Claudio asked.

Tito hesitated, and then his brows did a dance and he laughed. "You're six years behind the curve, brother. Hector went up in flames out in Patagonia somewhere."

"He faked that," Claudio said.

Tito sat back. "News to me. I saw his ashes put in the ground."

"At his funeral?" Chavez asked.

"That's usually how it works."

"It was staged, too," Claudio said. "The ashes of whoever burned in Hector's place were never claimed. We checked."

Tito was either a strong actor or he seemed genuinely surprised by this news. "I don't know what to tell you. I thought he was dead. Alonzo thought he was dead."

"How about his sister?" Chavez asked.

He squinted, said, "She was crying her guts out."

"Know where we can find her?" Claudio asked. "Hector's sister?"

"Fuck should I know?" Tito said. "I met the bitch once. She was sorry Hector was dead. End of story."

"Were they close?"

"Fuck no," Tito said. "She was like twenty years younger than him. I didn't even know he had a sister until the funeral. I think she just liked to cry."

"So she was Hector's father's daughter?" Chavez asked. "His half sister?"

"Something like that," he said. He sat forward, picked up a rolled bill, and snorted some cocaine.

When Tito was done shivering, Claudio asked, "Who's Hector's father?"

"What do you think I am?" Tito said, exasperated. "Genealogy dot fucking com?"

"Hector never mentioned his father?" Chavez said.

"Other than to say he was a prick who never gave a shit about anyone but himself, no, he didn't."

"So how did you know this woman was Hector's half sister?"

"It was how she introduced herself. You know, like 'Hi, I'm Galena, Hector's little sister. Thank you for coming?'"

"No last name?"

"Not that I remember," he said. "But she paid for the funeral, the party after. Why the fuck else would she do that if she wasn't his little sister?"

Claudio said, "Where was the funeral?"

"A chapel at some cemetery south of Villa Miserie?"

"Which cemetery?"

"Fuck, I don't remember. I was kind of wasted, you know?"

Claudio glanced at Chavez, who looked disappointed.

"That it?" Tito asked.

"You know an attorney named Esteban Reynard?" Claudio asked.

Tito seemed to take that question with surprise, and then wariness. "Yeah, sure, I know him. What about him?"

"We'd like to talk to him," Chavez said.

"So call him up. Go to his office."

"He's away on a family emergency."

Tito threw up his hands. "Can't help you. I haven't seen him for three years anyway. Knock on wood, I won't see him ever again."

Out in the club, the DJ was revving up the crowd, letting them know Leonora Bunda was about to make her entrance.

"We good?" Tito asked. "I wanna watch the show. I'm a big fanny fan."

"Bet you are," Chavez said, standing.

"You know it," Tito said. "I'll be watching yours when you go."

"Respect," Claudio said.

"Just telling it like it is," Tito said, amused.

Claudio felt like slugging him for old times' sake, but he let it slide. He wasn't into violence for the sake of violence.

He and Chavez left the VIP box, making sure Tatupu and Fowler still had a clear shot at Tito and his goons. The place burst into cheers as Leonora Bunda came out from their right, waving in the spotlight, an Amazon of a woman with a great big—

Chavez slapped Claudio on the behind, said, "You better get your ass and your eyes moving in another direction if you want to be in my bed tonight."

The artist did as he was told, never took another look to verify the legend, and went outside.

As they were moving back through the parking lot toward the van, Chavez said, "So that's how you refer to me now? The woman you love?"

"That a problem?"

"No," she said, fighting a smile. "Just new. Nice new."

Claudio wanted to take her someplace nice right then, and ask her to marry him. But then Tatupu and Fowler exited the club, and Barnett said in their ear, "Hello? You're on camera and microphone love birds."

"Buzzkill," Claudio said, removed the glasses, and shut off the radio transceiver.

They all got into the van, with Fowler behind the wheel.

"Waste of time?" Tatupu asked as they pulled away.

"From my perspective," Chavez said, nodding. "He either didn't know, or he was lying."

"Wrong perspective, love-of-life," Claudio said. "The best liars always bend the truth or give you only half the story. I think Tito was doing both, but he let slip enough facts to helps us."

50

WHEN MONARCH CAME TO, even before he opened his eyes, he felt at peace, as if he'd lifted burdens from his shoulders and set the weight aside. Then he smelled something brewing, weaker than coffee, almost like chicory.

He opened his eyes lazily, understanding that he was lying on his side in the fetal position on a woven mat in the jungle clearing by the waterfall. It was early morning and mist hung in the trees. Santos appeared, crouching to look at him in concern.

"You good?" she asked.

"Fine," he said, realizing his tongue was swollen.

"Better than good?"

"Now that you mention it," he said, and moved his shoulders as if he were shrugging blankets.

"It lasts a long time, that feeling," the scientist said. "As if you've dealt with old demons and survived."

The thief nodded. It did feel that way. "What happened to me?"

"You went on the same psychotropic trip I went on the first time I celebrated the full moon," she replied. "You've been lying there a good six hours, babbling, talking to invisible beings, and generally getting things off your chest."

Still lying there on his side in the fetal position, Monarch blinked, processing that, and then said, "What did I say?"

"Most of it was incomprehensible to us," she replied. "You speak quite a few languages."

"Nine," he said.

"Well, we got enough to understand a *few things* about *you,* Mr. Monarch."

"Such as?"

Her face went stony then, and her eyes harder. "You're desperate to have sex with me in as many positions as possible."

Monarch arched an eyebrow and fought a smile. After a moment of silence, the thief snorted, and made to get up on his elbow and sit up. Only then did he realize his wrists and ankles were bound.

"Hey, what the hell," he said. "You can't do this for saying I wanted to—"

"Course not," she said. "You're tied up because you're a thief and a liar."

"What? I said that?"

"Oh, definitely. You told the moon god numerous times in numerous languages. Funny thing was we got the feeling you like being a thief, no shame, no remorse. And you're here to steal something."

"What am I supposedly here to steal?"

"What everyone wants," Santos sneered. "The fountain of youth."

Monarch laughed. "Those were the drugs speaking. You can't judge me on something I might or might not say when my mind has been altered like that."

She sighed. "Rousseau's assistant, Edouard, overheard you speaking on your satellite phone yesterday. He clearly heard you were here to steal the secrets of the Ayafal, and that you planned to leave as soon as you did. It's a small miracle that I never told you what I figured out."

Monarch hesitated for several moments, made a decision.

"Look, I was forced into this," he began. "I must have told you in another language or something, but—"

She cut him off forcefully. "I don't care *what* your excuse is. I want you gone, Monarch. Now. You're a resourceful man. I'm sure you'll find your way back to one of the rafts."

The scientist said something sharp in Ayafal.

"Dr. Santos, I did it for a missionary woman," he tried. "A doctor."

"Oh, please," Santos said, turning from him. "You did it for money. It's always about money and greed and exploitation with guys like you."

"No, really. Listen. Her name is—"

Monarch heard a hollow, puffing sound, and felt a paralyzing sting as the blowgun dart found the back of his neck.

The howling of monkeys and a familiar and terrible pounding in his skull woke Monarch from his stupor. He was lying on the ground, soaking wet near the stream where he'd been darted the first time. The sun rode high. The air was suffocating and hot after the relative coolness of the Canyon of the Moon. Though his head felt ready to split in two, he forced himself to the brook and drank until his belly was full. It helped, but he couldn't imagine doing a thing until the infernal throbbing stopped.

The thief rolled back from the stream and looked off through the trees toward the waterfall that was almost the mirror image of the one inside the box canyon, feeling mightily irritated, but with no deep malice toward Santos or Rousseau, or Carson, and their assistants. He'd have done the same thing if he'd found a traitor in his midst.

Mostly, he felt like an asshole for having deceived Estella Santos, and crushed that he'd failed to help Sister Rachel. He sat there, looking around, feeling shitty. He hung his head and wallowed in it, accepting the pounding in his head as his due until another perspective wormed into his brain.

Stealing the fountain of youth wasn't going to save Sister Rachel. That much was clear. So he'd have to find another way. Job one? Get out of the jungle.

Ingrained survival skills took over. He needed to take inventory.

Monarch patted the pockets of his cargo shorts, and to his relief found his passport, his wallet with credit cards and cash, and that folding pocketknife with the small compass in the handle. He saw his odds of surviving go up. Even with just a knife and compass, the thief felt confident he could find his way back to the river.

But when he scanned around him, he had no knapsack, no satellite phone, and definitely no gun, though it had to be somewhere nearby, thrown into the bushes no doubt. He was about to go look for it, when he spotted the carved and painted pipe he'd smoked the night before next to Getok's gourd canteen and a substantial pile of those lime-green serrated leaves the young Ayafal man had given him the first time he'd woken up in the Canyon of the Moon. As before, after eating the leaves, Monarch almost instantly felt better. The pounding eased, he felt less nauseated, and his brain sharpened considerably.

Find the gun. The thief moved in a grid pattern, working a square forty yards in all directions, and then sixty yards, and eighty, but came up empty-handed.

Screw it, he thought. He was going to get the hell out of the jungle, make his way to one of the rafts. It would take days to reach Tefé, but once he was there, he'd contact Barnett. By then she'd have made headway figuring out who was behind the squeeze. And maybe Claudio had located Sister Rachel already.

Monarch used Getok's gourd to drink from the stream until he could drink no more. They'd had to rely on water filters on the trek into the jungle, and he had none to make the trek out. He knew he risked contracting god-knew-what disease or amoeba, and decided he'd have to do the journey with one gourd full of water. It would be difficult, but not impossible.

He put the pipe in the pocket with his passport, and began stuffing those serrated leaves in around the pipe, and then around his wallet in the other pocket, and completely filling both of his cargo pockets with them as well.

He stuffed the few leaves left into the side of his mouth. Juice from the leaves trickled down his throat, Monarch soon felt stronger, ready for anything. And his mind and perceptions seemed finely honed.

"Hang on, Sister," he said. "The cavalry's coming."

Checking the compass, Monarch set off directly against the bearing they'd walked in on. It was unbearably hot, but he got himself into a pace between a stiff walk and a slow jog, one eye on the compass, and one on the terrain ahead, his nimble feet bouncing through the roots and vines. To his surprise he remembered certain places in the forest, the way the canopy looked, the kind of roots that were exposed, and then that infernal rock and boulder field that he had to negotiate.

Without the weight of the pack, he covered ground much quicker than he'd anticipated and reached that cathedral-like opening in the rain forest just before dark. Somewhere above the canopy, he knew the full moon was rising, but for some reason he was glad he couldn't see it. Curling up into a ball in the exposed roots of a gigantic tree, he drank a mouthful of the water, and prayed to all who might hear him.

"She's an innocent person," he muttered as he fell into sleep. "She does more good than fifty people I know put together. You've got to get her through this. You've got to help me get her through this."

51

BY THE FOLLOWING MORNING, Sister Rachel knew she'd contracted some kind of intestinal parasite. She was lying on her side. Her stomach was cramping, and she was drained from repeated bouts of diarrhea. Given the squalid nature of her captivity, she was hoping it was giardia and not dysentery or cholera, which were both capable of killing her sooner than later.

To make matters worse, she had no idea whether the water from the pump was clean or not. And then there were the sores on her body. Several were definitely infected, and she was trying to keep a sharp eye out for signs of abscess or redness traveling away from the wounds.

One of the best ways to deal with difficult situations beyond your control was to establish a routine however threadbare that routine might be. To that end, despite her circumstances, the missionary was trying to keep to her old habits of praying and thanking God for another day of life upon awaking, and then cleaning herself as best she could.

When she was done, she passed the time until Vargas brought her food by keeping her mind engaged in her work. She made incessant mental lists of everything that had to be done at the clinic and the orphanage. She dissected the needs of every child under her care, contemplating how best to lovingly handle them when she returned home.

She imagined conversations with the other missionaries who

worked with her. She daydreamed about expanding her work to other cities in Argentina and the rest of South America. And she thought often of Robin Monarch.

Vargas had said he was the reason she was being held captive. At first, she'd been angry at Robin. But now he'd become a source of hope for her. She believed in her heart that he was doing everything in his power to get her released. That's just the way he was. That's just the way he'd always been.

He'll come. He will.

But how much longer could she last as sick as she was? And how many more of Vargas's cruel whims could she endure before her nervous system fried and gave out? There had to be a limit to what a body could take, and she wondered whether she was fast approaching it when the keys slid into the lock.

Wracked by abdominal cramps, she tried to be stoic when Vargas came in with the duct tape, the GoPro camera, and his little toy.

"Fucking stinks in here," Vargas said.

"I'm sick," the missionary said. "I need medication."

"Oh, right," he sneered. "I'm going to just take you out to see a doctor."

"I am a doctor, you idiot," she said. "I can tell you what to get."

Vargas flicked the toy in his hand. "You calling me an idiot?"

For a second she thought she'd blown it, and that he was about to inflict his cruel revenge on her with twice the ardor.

But she stopped him, saying, "Go ahead, idiot. Do what you want, idiot. But either I get those meds, or you'll find me dead in here one morning, and you'll no longer have leverage over Robin Monarch."

Vargas glared with laser intensity at her, but then relaxed and rubbed the tape against his chin.

"I'll get your meds," he said. "But you have to help me and the people I work for, bitch."

"How?"

He gestured up at the GoPro camera on his head. "They want you to record a little message to your buddy. You can do that, right? Scratch our back if we can scratch yours?"

"And if I do, you'll get me medicine, better food, and clean clothes?"

Vargas ran his tongue along his upper lip before saying, "You'll get the medicine, but you'll have to do a damned good job to get the food and clean clothes."

"Agreed," she said.

"Get up then," he said. "Can't film you in a shithole like this."

The thief awoke before dawn, hearing the jungle come alive. He ate a handful of Getok's leaves and drank half the water in the gourd. The second he had enough light to see the compass, he took off on a trail he recognized. He jogged until the heat turned unbearable, and then slowed to drink half the water that remained in the gourd and to roll another plug of leaves into his mouth.

He took off his shirt, rung it out, and tied it around his head. The bugs swarmed him as he skirted a swamp. They bit everywhere and he felt like he was being tortured. He stopped then, and lay in mud on both sides of his body, then smeared it to protect his skin, and moved on.

Monarch crossed through an area he recognized with downed trees and thorny vines. By four that afternoon, he reached the pool of water that they'd filtered on the way in.

He ignored it, not daring to take a drink, and pushed on, driven by the idea he could get to the riverbank before dark, find the provisions and eat and drink before rigging one of the motors to the raft. Could he do that alone?

If he couldn't, he didn't care. There were oars and he'd be heading downstream. He'd be at the mouth of the river in three days' time, maybe to Tefé in four if he could catch a ride in another motorized boat.

But then around five, Monarch got turned around taking the trail he'd followed from the river to intercept Santos and the expedition on the way in. It took him almost an hour to get back on track, and darkness quickly overtook him.

It began to rain. He opened the top of the gourd and let it fill. For the second night in a row, he slept fitfully at the base of a giant tree. When dawn came, the thief found the gourd almost full and he drank the rainwater greedily before wolfing down more leaves and setting off once more.

An hour later, he found a muddy trail that still showed the boot prints from the expedition passing the week before. He followed it. He smelled the river before he heard it, and quickened his pace, head down, watching the tracks, and then suddenly emerging onto a slip of land devoid of brush and trees.

He'd told Santos explicitly to hide the rafts and engines and the other gear. But there it all was, pulled almost completely out of the water. They'd fucked up, but after everything he'd been through in the last few days, he was glad of it.

Monarch went and found a chest, opened it and found four warm Cokes. He cracked one, drank it down, belched, and then opened another. That was about as good as anything had ever tasted. He burped again, and began rummaging in a carry box that held freeze-dried foods, when over the sound of the river he thought he heard something behind him.

Monarch turned and found three men aiming automatic weapons at him. They were gaunt, bearded, swollen from insect bites, and beyond filthy. But the thief instantly recognized the one in the middle, the one with the crazed leer on his face, the one who said, "You didn't think we'd give up so easily, now did you?"

"Hello to you, too, Jason," Monarch said, extending his hand. "Long time no see. What brings you to this little neck of nowhere?"

Dokken sneered at Monarch's extended hand, stayed locked down on the rifle stock, said, "You must think I'm a moron."

"Not at all," Monarch said, acting offended.

"Get down on your knees or I put a round through one," Dokken snapped.

Monarch could tell he wasn't bluffing, and went to his knees.

"Face down now, hands laced behind your head," Dokken said. "Zip him, Timbo. Panic, help him."

Monarch did as he was told, aware of the one they called Timbo looping around him, and then pressing a rifle muzzle to his head, and stepping on his back between his shoulder blades before Panic cinched his wrists with a zip tie. They hauled him back up onto his knees.

"Robin Monarch suppliant before me," Dokken gloated. "Do you know how many years I've been waiting on this day?"

"I won't suck your cock if that's what you're asking," Monarch said. "I heard after ten years in the stir you get a taste for that kind of thing."

Dokken's kick came instantly, driven right into the thief's stomach, and blowing all the air from him. "I should cut your liver out, piece by piece, you piece of shit," he seethed, and then just as Monarch got his breath back, kicked him again, this time targeting the kidneys.

The pain was excruciating, and the thief puked up the Coke, inhaled some, and choked and coughed until his eyes filmed over with tears and he lay there panting.

"Okay now," Dokken said, walking around him. "That's a

start. We can work with that. Yes, sir. That's some punishment, right there. Some revenge, right there."

"You come all the way to the Amazon to kill me?" Monarch said. "You a masochist now, too?"

Dokken smiled again. "Hell no. Boy, what you're seeing here is a goddamned two-fer for yours truly. I make a fortune three months out of Leavenworth, and I get to kill you in the process. Ain't it grand?"

Timbo and Panic started snickering.

"What do you want from me?" Monarch demanded.

"The fountain of youth," Dokken said, sobering.

"Don't know what you're talking about," Monarch replied.

"Sure you do. Those scientists wrote a paper saying the Indians in there are living to one hundred and thirty. That's why they went back. To figure out for sure and why."

"Yeah?" Monarch asked. "Who told you that?"

"A little birdie in a tree, who offered millions to me," Dokken said.

"To find the fountain of youth?"

"Whatever it is makes them live so long. The scientist with the amazing tits and ass, she's figuring it out, right?"

"There's nothing to figure out," Monarch said. "The Indians were full of it. They aren't that old."

Dokken squinted at him. "How's that?"

"Her carbon-14 and DNA tests didn't jibe with their age claims," Monarch said. "She's still in there testing people, but I've seen the data. It's a hopeless case, a loser. No evidence to back the claim up. That's why that paper of hers was never published. Her peers sensed that she didn't have the goods, and won't. I figured that out, and split. I've got better things to do, and so do you."

The other two men appeared uncertain, and looked to Dokken, whose face revealed nothing for several seconds. Then he grinned, and laughed at Monarch before saying, "Boys he's lying through his teeth. I'll bet she not only proved the little jungle bunnies live that long, she knows why, and so does he."

The thief shook his head wearily. "This is a lost cause. You want to kill me, get to it. But men have been looking for the fountain of youth since time began, and guess what? They'll need to keep on looking, because it isn't back there."

"Sure it is," Dokken said. "You know I learned the hard way that you always have an angle, Monarch, and that angle is usually a hundred and eighty degrees off what you're talking. It's that traitorous mind-set of yours that put me in a prison for more than ten years."

"You got ten years for shooting women and children," Monarch said, seeing the reaction among Dokken's men almost immediately. "Oh, he didn't tell you that?"

Before they could answer, and before Monarch could tell them what really happened to get them both thrown in Leavenworth, Dokken swung his rifle by the barrel in an uppercut. The butt stock struck the thief under the chin, and turned his lights out.

52

CLAUDIO FORTUNATO PERCHED IN the shadows on a secluded ledge near the top of a wooded hillside high above an early autumn landscape of farms, vineyards, and orchards.

Wearing faded camouflage and a floppy green hat Claudio had his eyes pressed to two Leica spotting scopes mounted side by side on a bracket attached to a tripod. He peered down through the powerful glasses, monitoring a farm roughly eight hundred vertical feet below and six hundred yards to the west.

Beside him on the ledge and resting on a bipod was a U.S. Repeating Arms Model 70 in .338 Win-Mag. Equipped with a Swarovski tactical scope, it was one of Chanel Chavez's guns. She was up the hill behind him, talking by sat phone to her brother-in-law.

Since they had moved into position shortly before dawn, they'd seen little to say they were justified being there. The road that passed the farm was fairly busy with traffic going to, and from, Córdoba. But the hundred-and-forty-acre farm, while cultivated, appeared uninhabited. There were no livestock or animals on the property. And so far the only humans they'd seen set foot on the land were two *campesinos* who arrived in the back of a battered pickup truck driven by a man in a straw gaucho hat.

The workers entered the farm through a gate in an adobe wall that surrounded the boarded-up ranch house and yard. They went to a barn of sorts, came out with hoes, shovels, and wheelbarrows, which they pushed through a second gate to a lush vegetable garden that covered several acres on the near side of the compound. The two men had been at it for nearly three hours without a break, and were still going hard, weeding, pruning, and moving irrigation lines and sprinkler heads.

Claudio pulled his head off the glasses, picked up a walkie-talkie with a seven-mile radius, and said, "Anything?"

After a pause, John Tatupu came back. "Negative. Quite a bit of activity at this end of town, but we haven't seen either of them yet."

"Ditto," Abbott Fowler said.

"Patience," Gloria Barnett said. "If we're right, this is a target-rich environment."

Claudio had his doubts. Were they right? Or was this a goose chase?

Before he could dwell on the facts, he heard Chavez behind him, and up the hill.

"Okay," she was saying, pressure and anxiety threaded through her voice. "Tell her I love her, and call if there's any change. Thanks, Denny."

A moment later, Chavez eased down beside him. Claudio glanced at her face, found it hard and distant. He could tell rural Argentina was not where she wanted to be.

"How's Regina doing?"

Chavez looked in her lap, said, "She'd had almost two good weeks, you know? Numbers were looking great. Everyone was thinking . . ."

"What happened?"

346

Chavez shrugged. "Denny said she had a really tough day and night after the latest chemo round. She was too weak to talk to me."

"You said cancers ebb and flow toward remission," he said.

"I know. It's just that . . ."

"Do you want to go back to Texas?"

"No," she said. "It's not that. It's . . ."

"What?"

Tears began to pool and spill from Chavez's eyes. She turned her head to him with a piteous expression. "Denny thinks she may be starting to give up. She's been fighting so long, it's just taken its . . ."

She couldn't go on, broke into soft sobs, and buried her face in his chest. The Brotherhood of Thieves had taught Claudio to rarely show his emotions, but as he wrapped his arms around her, it was like Chavez was part of him, so connected that he suffered as she suffered, feared as she feared, and grieved as she grieved. Soul mates. Wasn't that what they called this?

Claudio had the urge to ask her right there, up in the woods, hoping that he could replace the pain with the joy he felt whenever he thought about having her as his wife.

She said, "I don't know what I'll do if she dies, how I'll ever be happy again."

That almost broke Claudio's heart.

"I know it's not exactly the place for it," he began. "But . . ."

Out of the corner of his eye, he caught movement down on the flat. The two field-workers were moving back toward the ranch house.

"Something's happening," he said.

"K," Chavez said, pulling free of his grasp.

Claudio fought off the urge to hold her again, and looked into the parallel eighty-power scopes. The field-workers had stopped in the garden rows closest to the adobe wall, and left their tools in the lane. They were crouched now, and working together to pick— Was that a giant head of lettuce? He fiddled with the power and the focus knobs, got a better look. His heart beat faster.

"All right," he said. "Maybe we do have something here."

"What?"

"Those guys are picking cabbages," he said. "Huge cabbages."

"Let me see," Chavez said, and he let her get behind the scopes.

"Bonnie-Mega?" he asked.

Chavez looked, said nothing for several beats, and then pulled away from the glasses, saying, "It's some kind of O-S cross, that's for sure."

She took the radio from him, said, "They're picking mega cabbages over here."

There was silence for several moments before Barnett came back. "I don't know if that's enough."

"It's more than we had ten seconds ago," Chavez snapped.

"And I appreciate it," Barnett said. "But—"

"Hold on," Claudio said. "We've got someone new pulling up to the gate."

The artist got back in behind the spotting scopes, ignoring the friction in the banter between Chavez and Barnett. He swung the scopes off the farmworkers, who were looking toward the road, and found the gray Toyota pickup.

Through the tinted-glass windows, Claudio couldn't make out the driver, or whoever was in the backseat, but the front passenger window was down. The woman had dark hair pulled back in a ponytail and was turned from him. Her head pivoted slightly into quarter profile as the driver, a big, broad-shouldered guy, got out and went to the gate. Then she looked off toward the fields and the guys harvesting giant cabbages.

348

"Hello, Galena Real Montez," he said.

Chavez stopped arguing with Barnett, said, "Really?"

"Right there, with the hubby," Claudio said, watching as the truck carrying Hector Vargas's half sister entered the old ranch yard.

Chavez moved over beside him, looked through a pair of binoculars.

Feeling vindicated, Claudio's mind ripped back through all that had gotten them to this little piece of nowhere, hundreds of miles from Buenos Aires. When they left the Boom-Boom Club, he'd been convinced that Tito Gonzalez had let slip enough of the truth to help them. He'd probably lied about seeing Vargas. He'd probably lied about not knowing Galena's surname. He probably even lied about having the fake funeral south of the Village of Misery, the location anyway. But he would have no need to lie about it taking place in a chapel on cemetery grounds. It only made sense.

Though it took two days, a lot of phone calls, and a visit to the director of the municipal cemetery in Zarate, a small town sixty miles northwest of Buenos Aires. The director, after a little money had passed under the table, had agreed to check his records. The ashes of Hector Vargas had indeed been placed in a crypt there six years before. Galena Real of Zarate paid for the simple service and the crypt space.

It had not taken them long after that to find that Galena Real had subsequently married Luis Montez, a farmer who lived southwest of Córdoba. When Barnett had checked property records in Córdoba, she'd discovered that Montez owned two pieces of property: the one where he lived, and another the truck farm Claudio was watching.

Galena Montez stepped from the car wearing jeans, a canvas coat, and boots. If she seemed nervous, she wasn't showing it.

349

Neither was her husband, who was starting in the direction of the garden.

"C'mon," Claudio said. "Show us he's there. Show us where he's got her."

Then the back door of the truck opened.

"Son of a bitch," Claudio said, and pulled off the scopes to reach for the radio.

Chavez had beaten him to it. She triggered the mike, said, "Gloria, you need to call in some favors, pronto. We need a drone and backup over here."

53

MONARCH HEARD A CHUGGING noise that was becoming louder. His jaw hurt deep in the joint, and one of his molars felt loose. The pulsing came louder now and he opened his eyes to see two helicopters coming upriver. One was a large open bay Northrup construction chopper bearing the SJB Mining logo. The other was a much smaller Cicaré that was unmarked.

They arced overhead, and landed, the Northrup and then the lighter bird, forcing the thief to duck his face to his chest until the rotors stopped turning and the engines died.

When he looked up, Dokken was speaking with three armed men who'd come out of the bigger bird. The Cicaré's passenger door opened and a great big slab of a man with bandages on his face and a cast on his left hand got out. He glared at Monarch, but went to Dokken, argued with him a minute, and then handed him a digital tablet. The thief recognized him as the man he'd thrown off the ferry, and been aboard the SJB helicopter that crashed downriver the week before.

Dokken and the big guy came over to Monarch.

"He wants to kill you right now," Dokken said. "His jaw's broken. Wrist was spiral fractured. And one of his best men died in that crash."

"Kill him," the thief said, pointing at Dokken. "He shot you down."

Dokken kicked Monarch, and then crouched down, holding the tablet.

"We went to the crash site, found him," Dokken said. "Explained what you'd done. He appreciated our help in calling for help. And it's like that old saying: the enemy of my enemy is now my friend?"

The thief said nothing.

"Turns out, for their own reasons they want to find that lost tribe, too," Dokken went on. "So when I called them, and told them I had you, and that you knew how to get us in there, they offered us a ride. Wasn't that nice?"

"Can't help you," Monarch said. "We're talking dense, dense jungle. No place to land. You want in, you walk, but without me."

Dokken shook his head. "You didn't read Santos's paper closely, did you? If you did, you'd have seen reference to several clearings in the forest where the tribe lives."

"Just the same," Monarch said. "I'm not guiding you."

"No?" Dokken said, smiling. "Maybe this'll help persuade you."

He thumbed the tablet, and turned it to face the thief.

In the video clip Sister Rachel looked worse than Monarch ever expected. They had her bound to a wooden chair with wide nylon straps across her chest and others around her wrists and ankles. Her eyes were drawn down in their sockets, her skin gray, and she was hollow through her cheeks. You could see the terrible strain of the experience everywhere about her.

It all hit the thief like a sledgehammer, but he told himself to stay strong, keep the Ayafal and Santos out of it, figure out a way to escape and get downstream.

Then the missionary began to speak, and destroyed his resolve.

"They want me to talk to you, Robin," she began in a weak

and trembling voice. "They have said that I will be released if you do what they say."

Sister Rachel closed her eyes a moment, seemed to gather strength before she looked right into the camera, and said, "Whatever you do, act for the greater good, not mine, Robin. If what they are asking you to do involves a greater wrong, you must sacrifice me. You must . . ."

Sheer horror crossed her face as she looked off camera. "No. No, please!"

The torso and legs of a man in black entered left of frame, moved to her as she struggled, and then stuck a Taser against her neck. The missionary arched against her bonds, and for the briefest of moments looked just as she had in his hallucination back in the Canyon of the Moon: her back bent, her head tilted to the sky, and her hands splayed out in agony.

Then the torturer pulled back the stun gun, and she collapsed unconscious, head lolling before the screen went black.

Dokken said softly, as if in pity: "Next time, it'll be longer, and then longer, until you show us the way in there, Monarch. So what's it gonna be?"

The thief hung his head, said, "Get me on board. Up front by the pilot with a pair of binoculars."

Fifteen minutes later, Monarch sat up front beside the pilot in the construction helicopter with Dokken over his right shoulder, pressing a Glock to the back of his head. They rose in a spiral above the river.

"Bearing?" Dokken demanded.

"West-southwest," the thief replied. "Deviation plus or minus two degrees."

"That's a lot of slack, Ranger," Dokken said.

"Got me in and out, didn't it?" Monarch said.

The pilot was called Pearl. He said, "How far we flying?"

"Fifty? Sixty miles?" Monarch said.

"That do it?" Dokken asked the pilot.

Pearl said, "I've got a hundred and thirty air miles beyond a round trip in there, but the Cicaré will need all our spare fuel to make it back to Tefé."

The leaden clouds began to weep mist that shrouded the jungle canopy below, making it look even more impenetrable. On a clear day, the thief would have used binoculars to search for the ridge. But in the fog, the jungle unfolded like puzzle pieces.

"Coming up on restricted zone," Pearl said into his microphone.

He listened, and then reached over and turned off a switch, said, "There better be a good lawyer waiting when I get back, Correa."

Looking out the windshield with the gun against the back of his head, Monarch recalled Sister Rachel telling him to act for the greater good. He knew what she'd say in this situation. If Santos had discovered the key to the Ayafal's longevity, she could affect the future of mankind. The good and the right lay with Santos and the tribe. There was no doubt about it.

And yet, in his mind all he could see was Sister Rachel when the Taser hit her.

It occurred to the thief then that there might be another course of action he could take. With the mist swirling like this, he might be able to lead them around until they ran out of gas and crashed. Correa had lived through one crash. He'd take his chances.

But what good would that do Sister Rachel? Being shipwrecked in the darkest reaches of the Amazon was of zero benefit to her. Every way the thief looked at his predicament some people were going to lose, with him a guaranteed loser in all of them. No matter what course of action he took, he was committing both good and evil.

Rather than wrestle with that, Monarch did what he always did when faced with moral conflict: he looked away, and searched for ways to turn the tide in his direction.

After several moments of reflection, he said, "There are several different theories active among the scientists."

"Yeah?" Dokken grunted. "Name them."

"Carson believes it's the water," Monarch replied. "Rousseau thinks it's the plants they eat and smoke, and to be honest, I'm with him."

"I don't care what the fuck it is, long as I get it and deliver it," Dokken said.

"Deliver it to who?" Monarch asked.

"An interested party."

"The interested party have a name?"

"I'm sure it does, but since a name doesn't matter to me, I don't care just as long as I get paid."

"Who pays you?" Monarch asked.

"None of your business," Dokken said. "Why do you think it's the plants?"

Monarch said, "Reach in my right pants pocket. There are some leaves you need to check out."

Dokken eyed him suspiciously, but then dug in Monarch's pocket and came up with six or seven of the crumpled leaves Getok had given him.

"What is it?"

"I have no idea and neither does Rousseau," Monarch said. "It's an as-yet-undocumented plant."

"What's it do?"

"Eat a couple. Or better yet, put some in your cheek like chew."

Dokken looked at the leaves, said, "You first."

Monarch held up his bound hands, took three of the leaves, and put them in his mouth, tongued them into the pouch of his cheek, feeling that healing, euphoric sense almost immediately.

Dokken paused, but then put the leaves in his mouth. A few moments later, he cocked an eyebrow, said, "Who needs coffee?"

"Right?" Monarch said. "The leaves in my pocket are what you're after, Jason, or a good part of it in my opinion. So why don't you turn this helicopter around and get us the hell out of the jungle and go get your money? I figure what I'm offering has gotta be worth twelve years in jail. We call it good, turn around, and go home."

"I'm with you," the pilot said.

"Not happening," Dokken said. "We're going in and making sure these leaves are the real deal."

They flew on in silence, weaving back and forth across the deviation of four degrees once they were fifty miles beyond the border of the forbidden zone. But with the mist, they were seeing little if any relief in the jungle canopy.

Then Monarch spotted big black boulders through openings in the canopy, and realized they were close. Behind him in the hold, several of the mining guys saw the boulders and began jabbering to one another in Portuguese. He didn't know exactly what they were saying, but he understood the rocks made them excited.

A few minutes later, out of the mist Monarch saw the stream and the bank where they'd been darted, and where he'd awoken a few days before. He even spotted what looked like the paratrooper's rifle lying in some high grass well downstream.

"In this mist, you'll want to land down there, cover the rest on foot," Monarch said. If he could get to that gun, he had a chance.

"I've got the ridge on radar," the pilot said, swinging them away.

The visibility dropped and the helicopter slowed.

"I'd get some altitude if I were you," Monarch said a second before the cliff work appeared out of the fog, no more than forty yards off the nose of the chopper. Up close like this, he could see an intricate matrix of vines that covered much of that section of the tiger-striped wall. But then they gained altitude, and reached the sheerest section of the palisades where the rock was fully exposed. The mining men exploded into cries and shouts of astonishment

"What's got their dick all twisted?" Dokken asked Pearl.

The pilot spoke in Portuguese, and the men replied.

Pearl said, "The rock formation makes no geological sense."

"Explain that," Dokken said.

The pilot and the two men in the back, geologists, spoke rapidly.

"This was once all under water, a great sea," Pearl said. "Millions of years of shellfish dying created a limestone crust at the bottom. When the sea dried, the limestone almost immediately began to erode, except here."

"Okay?" Dokken said.

"They'll have to test the dark material, but . . ."

The helicopter bucked a few times and through the windshield, the waterfall appeared out of the mist. Monarch got a good look down into a jagged V cut in the rock ten feet deep. At the bottom, there was a slot perhaps twenty-four inches long and ten wide out of which pressurized water fountained six feet and fell in two directions before spilling off the near and far cliffs. As they passed over the top of it, the thief saw something else, something that surprised him.

Then the geologists began jabbering again, and Pearl said something that surprised Monarch even more. "See those ribbons of black ore in the limestone there, how it becomes all black?"

"Yeah," Dokken said.

"It doesn't make sense unless you think . . ." the pilot said, and then stopped, looking dumbstruck.

"Unless you think what?" Dokken demanded.

"Asteroid," Pearl said in awe. "An asteroid hit this ridge a millennia ago or more, gouged out the canyon."

Monarch flashed on that cave painting that depicted the beginning of Ayafal time, thought of that boulder field back there in the jungle, and looked at the canyon from the air as if seeing it for the first time. Of course that was how this place was formed. It just made sense.

"That good for mining?" Dokken asked.

"Depends on what the asteroid was made of," Pearl said. "But based on a previous sample they've seen, this could be a very, very good thing."

Previous sample? Monarch thought.

He was no longer looking at the miraculous geology of the canyon, he was staring down into its bottom, the jungle and the clearing by the waterfall, and the lanes cut in the vegetation. But try as he might, he couldn't make out any of the settlements, at least not from that height, and he understood how this place could have been overlooked for so long. The canyon was under hung. The dwellings were back under the cliff. Everything else was brilliant camouflage.

"This doesn't look like where I was taken," the thief said.

The words were no sooner out of his mouth than a group of Ayafal warriors, led by Augus and Naspec, came out of the jungle into the waterfall clearing to brandish their Stone Age spears. Fal-até, the old shaman woman, followed them, arms raised at the helicopter as if she meant to curse it out of the sky.

Laughter seized the interior of the hold.

"Like taking candy from a caveman," Pearl said, provoking more chuckles.

"Do me a favor?" Dokken said. "Before you land, take us out over the trees on the rim. I want to give the Flintstones a show."

Pearl veered off toward the rim. Dokken grabbed Monarch by the collar of his shirt and put the gun to his head again. "Easy now, I want you back in the hold, partner."

"Why?" Monarch said, turning in his seat.

"I want you to be the first thing Santos and the other scientists see," Dokken said. "I want them to know it was you who betrayed them."

Monarch scowled, but got up out of the seat, spotting the Ka-Bar knife Dokken had strapped to his thigh. He moved with his captor as Dokken hauled him toward the open bay door. The thief faked a stumble, causing Dokken to grab him by his shoulder. Monarch had been a fine pickpocket as a teen, and he unsnapped the sheath, and got hold of the knife as his old comrade stood him up.

Dokken smiled. "Now that we've found this place, Monarch, you have no value other than as a source of pleasure to me. And you know what? As brief as this is gonna be, it will please me very, very much."

Then he shoved Monarch away from him just as the thief sliced upward with the Ka-Bar, missing Dokken's belly by centimeters.

The mercenary kicked, caught Monarch in the chest, and blew him backward out the side of the helicopter.

Five minutes earlier, Dr. Estella Santos had been down in the clearing by the waterfall, taking the last of her DNA samples from Augus and his clan, the last of the Ayafal to submit to her study. She'd cleverly enticed the tribal elder by noting that his family boasted some of the oldest living people in the Canyon of the Moon, and adding that it would be a shame not to have them singled out for high praise in her research.

With what we've got, Santos thought, we could be ready to leave in the morning. She was saddened by the idea, yet also looked forward to returning to her lab in Rio. She wondered whether Monarch would ever come back into her life. She hoped not, but knew all too well that she'd given him the first rights to her research.

But that could be easily fought in court. At least, Santos thought so. It would largely be, like all difficulties, a function of money. If the samples substantiated her theory, there would be no shortage of people willing to back her continuing research—

Up on the cliffs, high in those vine-choked trees, howler monkeys began to bellow and roar. How the hell had they gotten up—?

Santos heard the helicopters then over the howling. She was instantly pulsing with fear and regret because the Ayafal were about to see something truly modern, a flying machine, something that might shake them to their core.

"Run into the trees!" she yelled at the dozens of people in the clearing and the members of her expedition. "Demons are coming in the sky!"

Naspec and Augus had hesitated, but then looked up, awe-struck at the sight of the two mechanical birds. Several tribesmen fell on their bellies, screaming that the Moon God had returned.

The rest sprinted into the jungle with their family members and the shaman right behind them. Rousseau, Carson, and their assistants hurried into the vegetation after Santos. She dug out the binoculars she'd taken from Monarch's things. She peered up through the branches and leaves at the helicopters, seeing the SJB logo on the big one. Its bay door was open. Hard men with guns were looking out the side.

Then Augus, Naspec, and six or seven other warriors, broke

out into the clearing, screaming at the helicopter with Fal-até chanting some kind of spell to strike the demon dead. Santos could see the men in the bigger helicopter laughing at the Ayafal before the bird veered over trees growing on the rim and hovered.

The chopper was now more than four hundred feet above the scientist and back three hundred more, but she saw a struggle inside the hold before a man pitched out backward, twisted as he fell, and disappeared into the trees.

54

I'M SCREWED, MONARCH THOUGHT after he'd turned over in space and saw the jungle canopy rushing at him from thirty feet below. The thief instinctually curled up into a ball just before he smashed into the upper branches of several intertwined trees. He crashed down through leaves and smaller branches before he hit bigger limbs that blew the breath out of him and slowed his fall before snapping and breaking. He fell again.

He bounced off a bigger branch, felt a crunch high in his left arm before hanging up in a tangle of branches. Then the tangle gave way and he dropped a third time, ten or twelve feet, before slamming sideways into what felt like a cargo net.

Monarch lay shaking, trying to get his breath back, eyes closed, sure that whatever held him was going to unravel and he was going to plunge yet again, this time all the way to the ground. Then the howling began, louder than speeding locomotives blaring their horns. He opened his eyes, and saw that he was caught up in one of those high matrixes of vines the howler monkeys seemed to like.

The lesser apes were all around him, screaming at him from the edge of their nests twenty feet away, and from the branches of the trees that supported the vine system. The noise was overwhelming, as if hammers were striking his eardrums and he raised his bound hands to try to cover his ears.

It was only then Monarch realized that he'd managed to hold

on to Dokken's Ka-Bar as he fell through three stages of jungle canopy. He tried to get the knife turned, but his left arm was numb and useless, and the sheer volume of the howling kept destroying his ability to think. Finally, in utter desperation, the thief screamed back at the monkeys with every bit of energy he had left.

Down in the bottom of the canyon, the howling of the monkeys and Monarch's scream of rage and desperation were swallowed whole by the throbbing of the helicopters' engines and rotors as they came in for a landing.

Naspec, Augus, Fal-até, and the other Ayafal who'd been brandishing their spears and spells finally broke ranks, and disappeared into the jungle opposite a shocked and sickened Estella Santos.

She'd realized it was Monarch who'd been thrown from the helicopter. She had no love for the thief, but she had not wished him dead.

"They threw him out!" Carson shouted. "Did you see that?"

"And they've got guns," Rousseau said. "Lots of them."

Santos looked at the members of her expedition, and almost told them she was sorry that she'd ever started them all on the long path that had led them to this moment. But then the scientist felt her fear turn to rage.

Santos broke from the jungle as the helicopter set down. She stomped forward, stood there, hands gathered to fists as the rotors died and Dokken and Pearl came out the side of the big chopper with two heavily armed men in tow.

"You are breaking Brazilian federal law!" the scientist shouted. "This is a restricted zone! Landing is prohibited!"

"So is coming in on foot, Dr. Santos," Dokken said.

Meanwhile, a huge white guy with bandages on his face and a

cast on his arm climbed out of the smaller helicopter carrying a pump-action shotgun. He headed toward the waterfall with two other men who had gear bags and sidearms in holsters.

"Who are you?" Santos demanded. "How do you know my name?"

"That's irrelevant," he said. "You saw what happened to the thief?"

Her head retreated several degrees.

"I hope you all saw it," Dokken shouted. "Because if I don't get what I want, I will start throwing cavemen, women, and children out of that bird."

Santos started to say, "You wouldn't . . ."

"Oh, but I would," Dokken promised. "So the way it's going to work, Doc, you help me out, I leave, simple as that. You don't help me, they take a . . ."

Augus and Naspec charged from the jungle, spears up, shouting in Ayafal, "Go back to the sky, bird demon. Or we kill you!"

Before Santos could intervene, Dokken pulled a Sig-Sauer and put a nine-millimeter round through the Ayafal chief's forehead, and another through the throat of the tribal elder. Both men collapsed like puppets sheared of string. Blood poured from Naspec's wound, streamed across the red mask around his eyes. Augus's blood ran down his chest.

Screams of shock and grief went up back in the jungle, followed by the sounds of crashing as many in the tribe began to flee. Kiki, followed by Fal-até, however, burst from the rain forest and went to the dead men's side, keening and weeping.

"Tell them they can run, but they can't hide," Dokken said.

The scientist barely heard him.

"They've never seen guns," Santos sobbed. "They didn't know what—"

"I don't give a shit," Dokken said. "But I will start hunting the others if you don't start cooperating and answer my questions."

Kiki was trembling head to toe before she lunged up off her knees away from her father's body toward Dokken, scratching at his face with her nails, and screeching at him in Ayafal. She ripped his cheeks open before he could backhand her to the ground with such force that she lay there stunned as he aimed at her head.

"No!" Santos screamed. "What questions? What questions? I'll answer, but don't hurt her. Don't hurt any more of them!"

Dokken didn't pull the trigger, but glared over at her, with the scratches on his face already oozing blood. "How old are they? No bullshit. How old?"

Up on the cliffs, the monkeys began to howl again.

Monarch's shout back at the monkeys had momentarily shocked them mute. A dozen bolted immediately, and he saw them retreating, some dropping through the branches, and others using loose vines like rappelling ropes. The rest of the troop clung to their positions, no longer howling, but chattering and snapping their teeth at the thief.

Monarch's attention was still on those retreating monkeys as the first of them reached the rim some forty feet below. Then he felt his left hand start to tingle and come back to life. If could get even thirty percent of use from it, he thought he could get down as well.

Using his mouth, he got hold of the butt of the Ka-Bar and began sawing at the plastic cuffs. Dokken's blade was razor sharp and quickly severed Monarch's restraints. He could feel his left arm on fire up near the shoulder, and he realized it was dislocated. But nothing felt broken.

Slowly, Monarch rolled over on his back, heard vines grind

and pop against the tree trunks and each other. The tangle shuddered, and he thought for sure it was going to give way. Instead, the knots of it seemed to tighten as he rolled to his belly, biting his lip against the pain in his shoulder.

The thief rolled to his back and then belly a second time, and felt cracking beneath him. He got his fingers wrapped into the vines a split second before a section of the tangle broke free, and he swung down into space. His left side slammed so hard against the tree trunk his shoulder relocated.

Monarch cried out in agony at the same time two gunshots went off down in the canyon, and the monkeys remaining in the canopy went ballistic.

"Fuck is that?" Dokken demanded, stepping away from Kiki, who lay dazed.

"Howler monkeys," Santos said.

Dokken grimaced, shouted, "How old are the cavemen?"

"Old," the scientist said. "Insanely old."

"You know what makes them live so long?"

Santos did not reply. She couldn't. Not now.

Dokken pointed his pistol at Kiki, and then over at Fal-até, who still held Augus, rocking the dead tribal elder and sobbing in grief. "Tell me or both these bitches get it."

The scientist believed if she did tell him she was going to die, that all of them were going to die, so again she said nothing.

Rousseau came out of the forest, hands up, crying, "Don't shoot! I think it's the plants they eat that lets them live so long!"

"I think it's the water," Carson said, following his colleague.

"I think it's the smoke they use on the full moons," Les Cailles said.

Graciella emerged last, and said, "Or that liquor they drink."

"Which one is true, Dr. Santos?" Dokken demanded.

The other expedition members stared at her, and Santos hesitated, believing even more deeply that if she told the truth, she was dead, that they were all dead.

The scientist stammered, "I don't—"

Fal-até began to screech, not in grief, but in anger. The old shaman woman set Augus's body on the ground, snatched up his spear, and rushed toward the waterfall.

It was only then that Santos saw that the huge white guy was standing by the cliff wall at the back edge of the sacred pool, the shotgun at his side. The second guy was chipping at the wall with a hammer and chisel. The third was in the pool up to his thighs. He wore a snorkeling mask and had his face pressed to the surface of the water.

Dokken raised his pistol, swung it after the old woman, meaning to shoot her in the back. Santos sprang out, knocked his arm, sending his shot wild. The big white guy spun around. Before the Moon God's wife could throw the spear, he pulled the trigger on the shotgun. Fal-até was fifteen yards from him. But the shot threw her backward. She went down, dropping the spear. On the ground, she writhed in agony.

Monarch jumped the last few feet off the tree and landed in a squat. His left shoulder still felt like there were coals smoldering inside it, but the joint was fairly functional and would probably stay fairly functional as long as he kept it moving.

A third shot echoed up out of the canyon.

Why are they shooting? Monarch thought anxiously as he scrambled toward the canyon rim, about thirty-five yards away. He slipped up to a tree, looked over and saw Rousseau, Carson, and their assistants standing in a tight, shaken bunch with two of Dokken's boys holding guns on them.

A few yards away, he could see two bodies and knew that

Naspec and Augus were dead. Kiki was close by, injured, but moving. Monarch was completely appalled. Dokken had opened up on essentially unarmed people. Then again, Dokken had done it before.

The thief heard Santos sobbing, and got closer to the edge, seeing the scientist on her knees by the fallen form of the shaman woman. Unwilling to process the grief and guilt that flooded through him, he hardened into combat mode, and his whole world narrowed and got purposeful.

Dokken was behind Santos. With the odd acoustics in the canyon, Monarch heard his every word.

"Didn't have to be like this, Doc," Dokken said. "All I'm looking for is the truth. So do I shoot another Fred and Wilma, or do you tell me what makes them live so long?"

The scientist slumped, "I swear to God, I don't know why they live so long."

"Wrong answer!"

"No, wait! I don't know why, but I think I know how they live so long."

The mercenary squinted at her. "How?"

"It's in their genes. It's like they were programmed for longevity."

"What about their genes?" Dokken pressed.

Sniffling, hiccupping, wiping away her tears, the scientist got unsteadily to her feet and faced him. In a trembling voice, she said, "Do you know what a telomere is?"

"No."

"They're specialized proteins that form caps at the ends of chromosomes, which contain our DNA," she said. "Every time a cell divides via mitosis, the telomeres lose some of their thickness and length, ever so slightly. Many scientists, myself included, believe that aging is a result of the slow decay of telomeres. So when I got their DNA samples, I decided to look at the caps first. And it was just right there, so obvious.

"Their genetic caps are thicker and harder than any I have seen before," Santos went on. "The Ayafal children exhibit the thickest caps, of course, but even the oldest person here has stronger genetic protection than their counterparts twenty years younger in the outer world."

"Why?"

"I told you I don't—"

"But you gotta have a theory," he said. "You scientists all have theories. Does the water make the caps stronger? The plants?"

Santos hesitated, said, "It's just my working hypothesis."

"Spit it out."

"There have been studies done where scientists have added an enzyme/protein called telomerase to chromosomes and they've seen some reversal in telomere degeneration," she said. "I can only speculate that, well, maybe there's something like telomerase in the water or soil and therefore the plants here."

"Why here?" Dokken pressed.

"I don't know, maybe from the asteroid. But like I said, the evidence of their genetic hardiness is explicit. The rest is just mystery and conjecture."

Dokken didn't seem to like her answer, but he seemed to accept it because he turned away and yelled at his men, "Watch them. I got a call to—"

There was a cry of joy from the man in the sacred pool. He was holding up a piece of something bright and shiny. "Correa! I've got palladium!

The big slab of a man pivoted. "For sure?"

"Definitely."

"It's here, too, in the wall," the other geologist said. "Huge veins of it. I'll bet if you chip away all the charred limestone,

369

we'll have platinum, too. Asteroid had to have been rich with both."

Correa gazed all around in greed and wonder, and then pulled out a satellite phone from his pocket. "I've got to make a call."

"Me too," Dokken said. "Timbo, anyone moves. Kill them."

Timbo grunted.

Dokken walked into the jungle near the base of the cliff where Monarch could not see him. But he could hear Dokken breaking branches as he struggled to get out of earshot of the clearing. The thief paralleled him along the cliff rim, listening for his movement and then quietly matching them until they were both about seventy-five yards from their prior positions.

Again, because of the odd acoustics, Monarch heard beeping and then Dokken clearly say, "Your thief problem is a thing of the past, and I have the goddamned fountain of youth in hand, and a lot more. It's your call what I do now."

55

IN BEAU ARSENAULT'S UPSTAIRS office at Twelve Oaks, his security chief listened to a burn phone, and gave the tycoon the thumbs-up.

"Hold on," Billy Saunders said, hit mute. "My plan B has eliminated Monarch and gotten hold of whatever it is making those cavemen live so long."

The billionaire walked quickly to his office door, closed it, and locked it, understanding that his initial reaction to this news was mixed. He was pleased that Saunders's plan B had found the secret to the primitive people's longevity, but Arsenault was also pissed that the thief was dead. In his fantasies, he'd been on hand for Monarch's ultimate demise.

"He's sure he's dead?" Arsenault asked.

Saunders posed the question, hit mute again, and said, "He says he's sure."

"How much did you promise him?" Arsenault said.

"Just what you authorized," Saunders said. "Six million."

"I damn well need solid proof before I make that kind of payout."

"Of course," his security chief said. "That goes without saying."

"He has no idea who I am?"

"He has no idea who I really am, so yes."

"Put him on speaker. I want to hear this."

Saunders did, said, "Are you still there, Mr. D?"

371

Though his voice sounded as if it were echoing in from outer space, Dokken said, "That's affirmative."

"Can you send us a photo of the thief, dead?"

"A photo of the thief, dead? I dunno I—"

"We need a photo or we don't pay out."

"That's bullshit. You've got my word."

Arsenault shook his head.

Saunders said, "Send a photo."

Dokken cleared his throat, said, "It's a pain in the ass, but I'll find the corpse and take a picture. Anything else?"

"What makes them live so long?"

"Their genetics, and this place," Dokken said, and then explained Santos's theory that the asteroid may have infused the canyon with telomerase. He finished, saying, "And you should know there's another party interested in this place for a whole other reason."

"We know," Saunders said. "We formed an alliance with them days ago."

"Nice of you to tell me you'd agreed to cooperate."

"It was a last-minute development. What's their interest in that canyon?"

"Palladium. Shitload of it. Maybe platinum, too."

So that's what Barbosa was after, Arsenault thought. The mining scum had been evasive about his exact reasons for wanting to find the Canyon of the Moon.

Platinum and palladium.

Arsenault had investments in mines around the world. He knew both precious metals were rare, and in high demand these days. But the really substantial platinum and palladium finds had all been in Africa, Asia, and North America. Up to now, there had never been a mineable discovery of either metal in Central or South America.

He scribbled, "Was it found in copper ore?"

Saunders relayed the question.

"Not that I know of," Dokken said. "They think it came in on a huge asteroid that hit a limestone ridge here a couple of million years ago. The whole interior of the canyon is black, but you scratch away the charred surface and you see bright shiny metals."

The billionaire chewed the inside of his lip. Both palladium and platinum were hard to tarnish. It took incredible heat to blacken them, two, three thousand degrees or more. He supposed an asteroid coming into the atmosphere and then crashing into a ridge would generate enough heat to scorch even such lustrous metals.

But how big was the deposit?

He couldn't know that now, and neither could Barbosa. Setting the mining opportunities aside for the moment, he turned his strategic mind to the allegedly long years lived by the savages, and thought: Maybe it's the water. Maybe it's the exotic plant life. Hell, maybe it is the asteroid. The only thing for sure is the genetic proof Santos claims to have.

Several questions popped into his head. He scribbled again and handed the note to Saunders. His security chief said, "How many people are in the tribe?"

"I dunno," Dokken said. "Fifty? A hundred?"

Arsenault wrote a third time and handed the note over.

"Does the presence of the tribe help or hinder future mining activities?"

After a pause, Dokken said, "Gotta hinder them. This is a restricted zone. No one's supposed to be in here."

Arsenault hesitated, but then his brain went into overdrive and he saw his best long-term move, which was both plain and ruthless. When it came right down to it, bringing the secrets of a Stone Age tribe's longevity to the masses was like marketing a shirt or dress with more durable fabric. Both were money losers. Mining palladium and platinum with Barbosa, however, looked like a massive winner.

Plain. Ruthless.

With a set jaw, the billionaire made a decision, scribbled the note and gave it to Saunders. His security chief read the words, stared up at Arsenault as if he'd never imagined his boss having this kind of dimension, and mouthed: "Are you sure?"

Arsenault nodded.

Saunders seemed to struggle, but then said, "I am authorized to offer you another ten million dollars for some additional work."

"So sixteen million altogether?" Dokken said, sounding surprised before falling into silence. "What do I need to do for that kind of money?"

"Kill everyone in that tribe, and the scientists," Saunders said. "Dump the bodies where they'll never be found. Shouldn't be too hard in a restricted zone."

After another long silence, Dokken said, "Make it an even twenty million total, and I'll make sure the only living things left in this canyon are birds, spiders, and snakes. And it'll take archaeologists a thousand years to find the bones."

Arsenault nodded. His security chief said, "Deal. But again we need proof."

"I'll send pictures when it's done. That work?"

"It does," Saunders said.

The tycoon nodded once more, and thinking that he needed to call Barbosa, get a formal agreement going.

"It will probably be tomorrow by the time I'm done," Dokken said.

Saunders signed off, looked at his boss, and said, "I need a raise. A big one."

"I'm doubling your salary," Arsenault said without hesitation.

His security chief thought about that, nodded, said, "What about Sister Rachel? She's the last thread."

Arsenault had his phone in his hand and punched in Barbosa's number, saying, "Once we have proof that Monarch is indeed dead, cut it."

Monarch had heard enough to put it together. Whoever was behind all of this had gone to a whole other level. It was one thing to kidnap a missionary, and squeeze a thief to commit robbery. But wanting a picture of the thief dead? That was personal. And ordering genocide? And wanting pictures of that? What kind of twisted fucker was he dealing with?

For a moment, Monarch looked to the sky, begging God for the strength to stop Dokken. First job? Get off the rim of the canyon. But how?

As far as he knew the cliffs were sheer on both sides of the rim. But the howler monkeys were likely the same troop that the expedition encountered shortly before it reached the riverbank. If it was the same troop, they had a way to get up here.

Remembering that all of the monkeys had gone north once they'd dropped from the trees and vines, the thief hurried in that direction, his eyes scanning the leaves and soil, and soon found tracks and spoor of several dozen primates moving north along a beaten trail that soon led him to that V notch in the canyon wall.

Monarch peered over the lip, and saw the jagged walls of the notch. He focused on the source of the waterfalls, which plumed up under pressure from that jagged slit he'd seen from the air. He thought of something else he'd seen from the air, and belly crawled to where he could better examine the crest of the exterior cataract, right where it left the notch and fell away four hundred feet to the outer stream.

There, under the sparkling clear water, the bottom of the

notch was a jumble of rock slabs about ten feet long by five feet wide and maybe six or seven inches thick. From the scars on the notch wall above them, it looked like they'd sheared off eons ago. Two of the slabs stuck out of the jumble and off the side of the notch perhaps four feet. It was from there that the waterfall began.

Monarch moved again, and the new vantage gave him what he was looking for. A dark gap in the rubble, an opening perhaps thirty inches wide.

On the canyon floor, Santos crouched by Fal-até, who was moaning. She'd been shot through her right thigh. The round had broken the femur, but spared the artery. The scientist had torn off her shirt and wrapped it around the wound, but she needed modern help. Without a medical doctor, the wound was a death sentence.

I did this, the scientist thought. *I brought guns and death and—*

Dokken came out of the jungle. He glanced at her the way a man might a trifling thing, and went to Pearl and Correa. He drew them aside and began talking.

Santos felt like she was in a trance as she got up, and started walking toward the three men, seeing the pilot of the smaller chopper getting back into his seat. Pearl, the other pilot, retreated two steps at something Dokken said. She heard the one they called Correa say, "The savages will hinder us, of course."

"Call your boss, then. Tell him my fee to fix the situation and—?"

Dokken saw the scientist approaching, said, "What the fuck do you want?"

She'd meant to ask for first-aid supplies, but now, sensing a deeper threat, said, "What are you going to do?"

Correa turned away, punching in a number on his cell phone.

376

Pearl followed him, saying, "I never signed up for anything like this."

"You want to tell the boss that?"

Dokken ignored them both, said to Santos in a reasonable voice, "We're gonna take care of things, then leave you, this place, and these people be. That work for you?"

The scientist eyed him in disbelief. He'd killed four people already. But she grasped at hope. "You'll leave them be?"

"Once we've taken samples of our own," Dokken said. "Yes."

"What kind of samples?" the scientist asked.

"Same as yours," he said. "DNA from every man, woman, and child in this canyon, and I'll be on my way. You speak the lingo, right? Call them all in, get them all here, we'll take samples, and we'll fly out of your life forever and a day."

Santos didn't know his exact angle, but she felt in her gut that it was a brutal one.

"You can take my samples," she offered. "I got every one of them."

"C'mon, Doc," Dokken said, showing his palms. "You know we've got to have independent verification in our own labs to make this all work."

Santos knew nothing of the sort. She said, "I can't help you then."

Dokken cocked his head at her. "That right?"

"Yes," she said, standing her ground.

"You know," he said, coming at her. "I've found that life's all about competing interests and trade-offs. There's always an interest more compelling than another and there you have the root of a tradeoff."

"I don't know what you're talking about," Santos said, fighting against the tremor in her voice brought on by how close he was to her now.

"Panic," Dokken said to his other comrade. "If this bitch

doesn't get her head on straight, and start cooperating I want you to put a round between that French kid's eyes."

"With pleasure," Panic said, and shifted his gun at Edouard Les Cailles.

Correa had finished his second call, and turned as Rousseau's research assistant cowered in fear. Graciella stepped in front of Les Cailles, shouted at Correa and Pearl, "You two stop this! We had a deal with Senor Barbosa! Stop this right now!"

Dokken frowned, looked at Correa, who shrugged, said, "Where do you think we got the palladium samples in the first place?"

The news penetrated Santos's brain like a railroad spike. She, Carson, and Rousseau looked at their assistants in shock. Les Cailles and Graciella had brought out metal samples during the first expedition. They'd gone to Barbosa, and—

"We have a deal?" Dokken said.

Correa nodded.

"These two critical?" Dokken asked, gesturing at the assistants.

"Well, when it comes down to it, no," Correa said.

"What the fuck!" Les Cailles screamed at the miner. "We fucking took care of Lourdes for you, man, and this is how you treat us?"

Took care of Lourdes? Santos felt ill.

The scientist didn't know the particulars, but she could guess the gist of the story. Her late research assistant Lourdes Martinez must have figured out that her comrades had negotiated a rich reward should they lead miners to the mother lode. The other research assistants had killed Lourdes, made it look like the aftermath of a crazed sex act.

It was all so depressing, Santos wanted to cry.

"So what's it going to be, Dr. Santos?" Dokken asked.

"I'm not helping you," she said. "And certainly not for them."

"You heard her, Panic," Dokken said.

His man flipped off the safety on his rifle.

"Dr. Santos, please!" Graciella shouted in terror. "My God, we were just trying to put some security in our lives. You can understand that, can't you? Think of the research we could have done! Think of what we can still do!"

"Think of the blood on your hands!" Santos shouted. "Think of what you've done to the Ayafal! To Kiki! To Lourdes!"

"Help us, for God's sake!" Les Cailles bellowed.

"Panic," Dokken said.

Panic reacted like a dog unleashed. He flipped the butt of the rifle underhand, and used the stock to slap Graciella aside before reshouldering the weapon.

"*Mais non!*" Les Cailles whimpered, holding up his hands. "Please, no!"

"Nothing personal, man," Panic said, and shot Rousseau's assistant on the bridge of his nose, shattering his glasses, and sprawling him in a halo of his own blood.

56

MONARCH HEARD A THUD, but could not decide whether it had been a rock falling or a distant clap of thunder or yet another gunshot. *Would I even hear something like that in here?*

The thief was behind the exterior waterfall, ninety feet down inside a chimneylike recess in the cliff face, his feet and hands splayed and pressed to the slick, ragged walls of the chimney, which was no wider than a yard in any place so far. And there was enough monkey hair and sign on the rocks to suggest that it wouldn't get any wider the rest of the way down.

His shoulder ached from the punishment, but he forced his mind away from the pain, and kept up his descent, finding handholds, and cramming his jungle boot soles against outcroppings in the wet wall. Fifteen minutes later, he reached the limits of his abilities: narrow ledge that formed the bottom of the chimney a solid thirty feet above the base of the waterfall.

Below him there was water on his side of the cataract and what looked like crushed, glimmering stone. He had no idea how deep the water was directly below him, but he sensed it wasn't deep enough to absorb a thirty-foot jump.

So how did the monkeys get down from here?

He gazed down between his feet and saw where the chimney became a crack in the face of the cliff, no more than one or two inches wide as it splintered into other cracks in the rock surface. He supposed a monkey, or a skilled rock climber with the right equipment could make child's play of the last thirty feet of the cliff. But the thief was not a monkey, his shoulder was hurt, and he didn't have the necessary equipment.

Monarch quickly realized he had one chance of getting off the cliff intact. An instructor in Ranger School had taught him never to leap into an unknown body of water if he could avoid it. You just never knew how deep the water was, or what might be floating below the surface. If the interior waterfall was a mirror image of the exterior cataract, the water might be four, maybe five feet deep. But maybe not even that.

Sometimes you have to take a leap of faith, Robin.

Before he could talk himself out of it, he coiled, and sprang off the ledge.

The thief closed his eyes, burst through the two-foot-thick waterfall, and kicked his feet forward. He fell as if positioned in a reclining chair. He tucked his chin, snapped his eyes open. He caught flashes of the jungle outside the ridge, tried to see what was below him, and then splashed into a pool of water six feet deep.

Monarch quickly surfaced, gasping for air, and gauged what to do next. His soldiering years had taught him to always seek the most firepower possible. That part of him wanted to head back to their encampment, and try to find the assault rifle.

But a much bigger part of the thief said Santos, her expedition, and the Ayafal did not have the luxury of time. So he turned to the waterfall and dove under it. He came up thirty feet below the ledge he'd jumped from, facing a cave passage.

Monarch had suspected that such a passage existed given how quickly the Ayafal had been able to get him in and out of the canyon while under the short-term effects of that paralytic drug. The cave passage was only five feet high. The thief had to crouch and duckwalk, feeling his way into the dark tunnel that he believed connected the canyon to the outer world.

Three hundred yards in he was proved right when he started seeing dim light far ahead of him. Another hundred yards and he could hear the rumble of the interior waterfall and see pale daylight shining through it.

"My God, no more!" Rousseau cried at Dokken after his research assistant collapsed dead; and Graciella threw herself hysterical on her fiancé's corpse, choking out incomprehensible screams of grief and pain.

"Tell her," Dokken said, gesturing at Santos.

Santos felt like she was having a nervous breakdown. Her research had started with such good intent. But now it was all wrong, so terribly wrong.

"Estella?" Carson said. "Just do what he says or he'll kill us all."

"Yes?" Rousseau said.

Santos started laughing bitterly. "For such smart men, you're sure stupid sometimes. He's going to kill us whether I help or not."

"No," Rousseau said. "He said—"

"They're going to kill off the tribe, and us, no matter what we do."

"Now what makes you say that?" Dokken said, eyeing her warily.

She pointed at Correa. "He said the savages would hinder him. And you said you could fix the situation."

She gestured at Pearl, who was walking back toward the construction helicopter. "And the pilot said he wouldn't be a part of it."

Dokken looked at his hand as if it were a recent transplant. "Can't get a damn thing by you, can I, Doc? Timbo? Panic? Why don't you see that Dr. Santos's deepest fears are confirmed?"

"One by one?" Timbo asked.

"With her last," Dokken said. "I want her to witness the tangible consequences of her actions. I want her to fully understand that while it's an inconvenience for us to hunt down these Neanderthals, for the money we will do it, and we will do it well."

Through the waterfall, Monarch could hear muffled voices, and see the blurred outline of people in the clearing where the Ayafal held their full moon ritual. The closest person was the geologist still in the water. He was standing sideways and close to where the cascade met the surface of the pool. The thief saw him turn his back to the waterfall just before he heard people screaming, and then a gunshot and more screams.

No time for subtleties. No time for thoughts. Just action and reaction.

Monarch rejected swimming under the waterfall. Instead he bowed his head, and walked into it. Stopping when barely an inch of water ran like film down his face and body, the thief threw out his good right arm, hooked it around the man's neck, and dragged him back and down into the raging water before he could yell out in alarm.

The second they were both submerged behind the waterfall, the thief's left hand slashed the Ka-Bar's blade across the man's throat. As the frothy water all around him turned pink, the geologist struggled, and then surrendered.

Monarch dragged him to the surface, yanked off the mask, put it on, and then relieved the man of a Glock 21 in a nylon holster on his hip. Monarch went to check the magazine, but then heard a woman scream, followed by another gunshot.

No time. He ducked back into the waterfall. This time he came all the way out, and stood there as the dead guy had stood, facing the clearing, taking it all in.

Timbo and Panic were standing about forty yards in front of him, looking down on the corpses of the two research assistants. Rousseau, Carson, and Kiki were no more than ten yards from Dokken's men. About forty yards to the thief's left at two o'clock, Correa and the other geologist watched without expression. Behind them, the smaller chopper was starting up and Pearl was almost to the construction helicopter.

Santos was on her knees to Monarch's right at eleven o'clock, weeping again. Dokken had the muzzle of his pistol pressed to the back of her head.

"Who's next?" Panic asked, sounding amused by his gruesome task as he moved his gun back and forth between Carson and Rousseau. "Eenie, meenie, miney, Frenchy."

"I'm Canadian," Rousseau sobbed.

"Who gives a flying fuck?" Panic said, and made to shoot the botanist.

He never got the chance.

Monarch had ducked into the water, slithered forward, and was now crouched behind the rock ledge that defined the pool with the Glock aimed over the top. He opened up rapid fire.

The first shot took off a chunk of Panic's head. The second shattered Timbo's wrist, and blew his rifle from his hand. He swung for Dokken, trying to get a bullet into him before he could execute Santos.

But instincts and reflexes almost as sharp as Monarch's had taken over. Dokken was rolling away from the scientist. The thief tried to track him, but then another gun went off. A shot from Correa's scattergun pinged off the ledge at the front of the pool.

Monarch threw himself sideways, twisted and fired at Correa and the other geologist who were now sprinting toward the helicopters. He hit the geologist square in the spine and dropped him. Correa fired the shotgun again. The thief almost got turned

384

before the birdshot stung his face, head, and right flank like scores of angry hornets.

He felt the blood spraying and dripping before catching sight of the second helicopter pilot trying to aim a rifle at him. Monarch shot him in the throat, and then tried to shoot Correa again. But the huge white guy was already in the smaller chopper, and it was lifting off.

Where the fuck was Dokken?

Monarch's attention swung again, trying to find him, seeing Rousseau, Carson, and Kiki running for the jungle. Timbo tried to get his gun up with one hand. Santos was still there on her knees, bewildered by the whirl of violence around her.

Ignoring the blood dripping in his right eye and the flaming pain everywhere the birdshot had penetrated his skin, Monarch aimed and fired. Dokken's last remaining ally acted like someone had tickled him. He hunched up, looked down at his stomach, and then keeled over.

The action of Monarch's Glock locked open. He was out of ammunition. Overhead the smaller chopper was arcing away when Monarch leaped from the pool, ran toward the dead geologist, spotted his pistol lying beside—

"Drop the gun, you fucking cat!" Dokken bellowed behind and to his left. "I'll blow every life out of you! Nine of them. Ten, I don't give a shit."

Monarch glanced over his shoulder, saw his old nemesis had gone into the jungle, flanked, and was now kneeling at the edge of the vegetation, his rifle shouldered, his enraged face welded to the stock. They were no more than fifty yards apart. Dokken wouldn't miss at that range. Monarch dropped the Glock, and looked at Santos who was gaping at him as if he'd risen from the dead.

Dokken got up, and marched to within ten feet of Monarch, gun still up, finger quivering on the trigger as he screamed, "You turn now. Look right at *me,* Robin! I want you to be looking right in my eyes. Last thing you ever see."

The thief nodded to Santos, and then turned to face his destiny, seeing Dokken's glassy, bloodshot, and vengeful eyes staring down the sights of his rifle.

"That's nice," Dokken chuckled. "Smile for me now. Kiss the bullet that's coming down your—"

Dokken jerked upright before he dropped his weapon, and looked down dumbly at a bulge beneath his T-shirt, off center right and slightly high.

"Fuck is that?" Dokken croaked.

Blood sprayed from his lips before he stumbled and tumbled forward, his body slamming the ground less than two feet from the thief. The long shaft of an Ayafal spear stuck up out of Dokken's back.

Monarch gazed in shock past the man who had been about to kill him, finding Gotek creeping from the jungle with a terrible smile on his face.

The thief grabbed Dokken's head, turned it, and found him barely alive.

"Where is she?" Monarch demanded. "Where have they got Sister Rachel?"

"Piss off, Monarch," Dokken said, half laughed, choked on the blood pouring from his mouth, and died.

57

"I HAD NO IDEA this was what they had in mind," Pearl complained. "Seriously, she heard me. I was against it all."

"I don't give a shit," Monarch said, training a gun on him from the copilot's seat in the construction helicopter. "Just fly us to Manaus."

"We don't have enough gas."

"Then fly us to Tefé, refuel, and then fly us to Manaus."

"What are you going to do to me?"

"Depends on your level of cooperation," Monarch said, glancing behind him into the hold. Rousseau and Carson were loading the last of their equipment and samples. Santos crouched by Fal-até's side. The shaman woman's leg was in a tourniquet, and she was gazing around in sleepy wonder courtesy of several narcotic painkillers from a first-aid kit Monarch had found aboard the helicopter.

"We good?" he said.

"I think so," Santos said, looking at her fellow scientists.

Carson nodded. "I took the pictures with Dokken's phone, just like you said."

"Fly," Monarch said, and nudged Pearl in the ribs.

The pilot flipped a switch. The rotors spun. The chopper shuddered when he gave power and they lifted off. Hundreds of feet below, Gotek and his people were gathering wood for the biers that would consume the bodies of the dead.

As they flew over the top, Monarch glanced down, hoping to see some of the howler monkeys that had, in effect, saved his life. But the notch and the trees were already cast in deep shadow.

"How far to Tefé?" Monarch demanded.

"Hundred and twenty air miles," Pearl said.

"Tell me about Barbosa."

The pilot's face constricted. "That is not a man you want to fuck with."

"Actually, I do," Monarch said. "Very much."

Pearl said he'd seen Barbosa, but never met the man formally, only his underlings and thugs like Correa.

"I'm just a pilot," he said. "I pick people up. I drop them off."

"Where's Barbosa live?"

"Rio."

"What's his weakness?"

He shrugged. "I don't know much about him other than he owns the company, and he's a big guy, likes his gourmet food."

Night fell. The moon rose over the rain forest. Back in the hold Monarch heard the old shaman woman start to babble, and then to sob. Santos was talking to her in their language. The thief didn't understand a word, but felt her soothing tone. It wasn't working. Fal-até seemed to be growing more agitated and then began to cry out in pain.

"Give her another painkiller," Monarch called back. "But keep a close watch on her heart rate and have adrenaline ready."

Within minutes the shaman woman's agitation had lessened, and she was softly singing what sounded like a children's song that Santos sang along with her. Fal-até's voice gradually faded, and so did the scientist's.

Santos came up to the cockpit.

"She okay?" Monarch asked.

The scientist looked drawn down. "She got worked up when she saw the moon out the hold door. She thought she'd been swallowed by the flying demon, who was taking her away from the moon."

"About sums it up," Monarch said.

"I know," Santos said, and she began to cry. "Fal-até said you would be the end of the Ayafal, but she saw it wrong. *It was me.* I was the end of the Ayafal. I went looking to prove Vovo's story at any cost, and that contact destroyed their way of life. Rousseau was right. We never should have gone in. Finding Kiki should have been enough."

She hung her head, crushed.

"It doesn't have to be that way," Monarch said. "You can be the person who fights to protect them, or to protect their interests because people like Barbosa *will* go into the forbidden zone unless you stop them."

"What about Augus and Naspec? They died because of me."

"They died because of Dokken," he said. "You couldn't control him. I couldn't control him. I know that doesn't help right now, but with time you'll come around to that perspective and see I'm right."

She sniffled, blew her nose, and then looked over at him.

"Who are you? Really?"

"Robin Monarch," he said.

"Are you a thief?"

"Among other things."

"Is there a missionary? A Rachel? Is your mom sick? Or was it all just made up."

"It's all true, and Sister Rachel, the missionary doctor, and my mother are one in the same," Monarch replied, and then explained how she'd been kidnapped in order to leverage him into stealing the secret of the Ayafal's longevity.

Santos thought about that. "So who was Dokken working for?"

"I don't know yet," he replied. "But I'm going to find out."

The scientist fell into another silence, before saying, "I've got something that belongs to you."

Monarch looked over and saw his satellite phone in her hand.

"Thanks," the thief said. "That will help."

"We have to go straight to the authorities," Santos said, sounding morose.

"Why's that?"

"Why's that?" she shot back indignantly. "Maybe because eight people died, including two research assistants on my expedition!"

"So what are you going to do, have the Brazilian national police go into the Canyon of the Moon? That *will* end the Ayafal culture. For good."

Santos struggled, said, "So what do we do? What do we say at the hospital? I mean, Fal-até is suffering from a shotgun wound."

Monarch thought a few moments, said, "You came in contact with her along the river, and were interviewing her as part of your research. Somehow she found the shotgun and there was an accident. Pearl happened to be flying back from dropping a team of geologists, and you shot a flare. He landed and offered to fly us Manaus."

"That'll work," Pearl said.

The scientist chewed on that. "The dead miners? And Edouard and Graciella?"

"They're still back there in the jungle," Monarch replied. "Waiting for you and Pearl to return. When you do go back, they're gone. No trace of them. But lots of jaguar tracks in the area, which there are. End of story. An unsolved mystery. The other deaths, at least as far as you're concerned, are something that happened in a very bad dream."

"Do you ever tell the truth?"

"Sometimes," Monarch said. "But I've found that twisting the facts to suit my purposes is more useful."

Before she could reply, he turned on his phone, and punched in Barnett's number.

She answered, "My God, Robin, haven't you been getting our messages?"

The thief's heart beat faster. "You found her?"

"We think so," she said. "I pulled some strings at the agency and we've got a drone with a thermal imaging system on our way to make sure."

Barnett explained how they'd tracked Vargas's half sister to a leased farm south of Córdoba. Earlier in the day Chavez and Claudio had seen the sister and her husband drive into the farmyard in a four-door pickup. When the backdoors opened, Tito Gonzalez and Alonzo Miguel climbed out.

"No shit."

"No shit."

"Hector?"

"We still haven't put eyes on him or Sister Rachel, but Galena, Tito, and Alonzo went into the farmhouse with supplies," she said. "An hour later, four pros with AKs arrived. They've been patrolling ever since."

"She's got to be there," Monarch said.

"We think so," Barnett agreed. "But we don't want to go busting in there until we know for certain."

"What's the ETA on the drone?"

"Ten, twelve hours," she said. "But I think we're good. Hector's not going to do a thing to her until whoever hired him hears if you stole the fountain of youth or not."

"Not," Monarch said.

"No?" she said, sounding disappointed.

"They think I'm dead. They also think Dokken has the secret, and ordered him to destroy it and the Ayafal tribe."

There was a pause as she digested the information. "But Dokken doesn't have it?"

"He did, but he's dead, and his handlers don't know it."

Barnett paused again. "Then Sister Rachel has become dispensable. She's no longer leverage."

"Dokken's handler is waiting for proof that we're all dead: me, the scientists, and the entire Ayafal tribe. He wants pictures before he makes a payout, which I'm hoping means he'll keep Sister alive until he sees a picture of me dead."

"Pictures? That's ghoulish."

"In the extreme," the thief said.

"Where are you?"

"In a helicopter on my way to Manaus," he said. "Can you send a jet for me?"

Barnett paused. "What's your ETA there?"

"Two, maybe three hours."

"I'll get one on the way."

"If I give Zullo Dokken's satellite number, can he hack into it? Trace future calls?"

"I'll ask. What's the make, model, and number?"

Monarch got Dokken's satellite phone from Carson, and gave her the information.

"That it?" she asked.

Monarch thought a moment, and then said, "Give Zullo the second Cayman account number. We could have a substantial amount of cash moving into it sometime tomorrow. I want him to backtrack the transfers."

"Got it," she said. "I'll text you flight information when I get it."

"Anyone ever tell you you're the best?"

"Nearly everyone I know." She laughed, and cut the connection.

"Sister Rachel?" Santos asked, yawning.

"We may have a lead," Monarch said, and left it at that.

They reached Tefé shortly after 10:00 P.M. Pearl landed them on the SJB pad near the smaller helicopter Correa had used to escape the Canyon of the Moon. Monarch stood guard with Dokken's rifle as Pearl refueled using a company card. They were lifting off when an open-top SJB jeep came flying onto the brightly lit tarmac.

Out the window, he could see Correa was in the front seat. Correa spotted him in the open hold. Fear registered on his face and he ducked a moment before Monarch put two rounds through the windshield.

"Get us out of here," the thief commanded.

Pearl swung the chopper away, heading east, and almost immediately the radio lit up with the sound of Correa cursing in Portuguese.

"What's he saying?" Monarch asked.

"To turn back, or I'm a dead man."

"Tell him you're not turning back. You're on a mission of mercy."

They were soon out over the river again. The thief felt exhausted, but knew he couldn't sleep. He dug into his shirt pocket and came up with another bunch of those leaves Gotek had given him. He stuck them in the pouch of his cheek and almost immediately felt more alert.

Monarch considered his situation. Correa had seen him. He had to assume Correa would call Barbosa. Based on what the thief overheard when Dokken was talking to his handler about wiping out the Ayafal, there was a decent chance Barbosa would, in turn, call the handler, give his ally the information. Or would he? The thief supposed it depended on their level of trust.

In any case, he felt compelled to create doubt now, a smoke-screen of sorts to keep Barbosa and his ally off-balance. The thief retrieved Jason Dokken's phone from Rousseau, and hit redial.

Monarch listened to it ring four times before a man with a Midwestern accent said, "Is it done?"

"Yup," the thief said, imitating Dokken's deep voice.

"All of them?"

"Affirmative."

"Disposal?"

"In a location it will take an archaeologist a hundred years to find," Monarch said, riffing on the way Dokken had spoken on the phone earlier in the day.

"Proof?"

"I have pictures. Except Monarch. We're still looking for his body."

There was a long pause, before the man replied, "Send the other pictures now. Reynard will make immediate payment on that part of our deal. The rest will be cut when you get us the picture of the thief."

"That works," Monarch said, and then gave him the Cayman account number, and the routing codes.

"Nice doing business with you."

"You as well," the man said.

The connection died, and Monarch started to send pictures.

Pearl landed the helicopter on a pad at the Manaus Hospital around midnight. Monarch feared a crew of SJB men, but only medical workers came to the helicopter. They were shocked when they saw Fal-até was the patient. The thief guessed that while indigenous peoples were known to wander out of the rain forest upriver, they rarely arrived in a helicopter with a shotgun wound.

When they wheeled the comatose Ayafal woman away, Santos said, "I should go in with her. She's going to be frightened when she wakes up in the land of the demons."

"We'll go with you," Carson said, and Rousseau nodded.

Though they weren't happy about it, the two scientists had agreed to go along with the story of how Fal-até was wounded and that their assistants had stayed behind in the jungle.

"I'd get all your stuff out of the helicopter and secure it first," Pearl said. "I'd think someone from SJB will be along soon, probably with police, and you don't want your stuff impounded."

Rousseau and Carson started grabbing their gear. Pearl helped them.

"I need to find a taxi," Monarch told Santos. "Get to the airport."

"I haven't thanked you for saving our lives, and the tribe."

"It was the least I could do."

"Is there any way I can repay you?"

"The money that funded the expedition wasn't mine. So you owe me nothing."

"And our agreement?"

Monarch thought about that. "If anything ever comes of your research, donate part of the proceeds to the Sisters of Hope."

"Agreed, but nothing for you?"

The thief squinted. "Well, seeing as how I'll never see you again, I'd take a kiss."

The scientist smiled shyly. "That's all you want?"

Monarch laughed. "Oh, I want so much more, Estella, but a kiss from the most beautiful woman I've ever seen will have to do."

Santos blushed, smiled again, and walked into his arms.

Monarch gazed into her eyes and then leaned in to—

Two men started yelling in Portuguese. They were running toward them, moving very fast, and wearing SJB shirts and carrying guns.

Monarch stepped back from the scientist. "What're they saying?"

"No one move. The police are coming."

"Pearl," Monarch said.

The pilot jabbered at the two guards. One of them listened, but the other ignored him, walked up to within three feet of Monarch, and pointed his gun at him, shouting.

Santos started speaking, and gestured to the thief. He yelled back at her, and looked at Monarch furiously.

"He says you're an assassin," the scientist said. "He wants you down on the ground, hands behind your head."

"Tell him I'm a thief, not an assassin," Monarch said, took a step closer to the man, hands out to the sides, palms exposed.

Santos translated, and the guy got confused.

Reading the name embroidered on his shirt, the thief softly said, "Ramon?"

Knowing that the sweetest sound in any language is a person's name, Monarch believed the man would lean slightly toward him. When he did, the thief twitched his injured left shoulder. The instant he saw the man's attention dart there, Monarch chopped his left hand toward the gun.

The revolver fired.

Monarch staggered and fell.

And Santos began to scream.

58

BEAU ARSENAULT WAS ALREADY awake, drinking café creole in his office. On his computer screen there were photographs of dead Amazon savages, and the corpses of men and women he assumed were part of the scientific team. The mogul felt not a lick of pity as he closed the pictures and deleted them. Great politicians had no compunction about going to war and killing innocents to get what they wanted. Why should a great capitalist be any other way?

Arsenault turned to the rough memorandum of understanding he and Silvio Barbosa had worked out the evening before. It was a good deal. For a thirty-three percent stake in the future mine, he would fund all development, hire the attorneys to get around this forbidden zone bullshit, and—

His cell phone rang. The mogul looked at the screen, saw a familiar number, and hardened. Silvio Barbosa was calling. This was typical of Barbosa, agreeing to something, and then, after some thought, trying to take it back.

"A deal's a deal, Silvio," Arsenault growled.

"Forget the deal. We have a problem," Barbosa said. "Your thief? Monarch? He survived being thrown out of a helicopter.

397

He killed three of my men, and it looks like he killed the entire team you sent in, and saved the tribe and the scientists."

"What? No, I've seen—"

"I don't care what you've seen!" Barbosa shouted. "One of my men saw him alive late last night in Manaus. Monarch shot at him from one of my helicopters. He used my helicopter and my pilot to bring an Indian woman to a hospital in Manaus, and then disappeared along with the scientists."

Arsenault felt like flinging the phone. "Your man's positive it was him?"

"No doubt."

The mogul said, "I'll call you back."

Arsenault immediately phoned his chief of security, told him about the call.

"Jesus," Saunders said.

"Jesus?" the tycoon thundered. "Jesus isn't helping us here!"

"Calm down, Beau. There's still nothing that links you to any of this."

"Really?" Arsenault shot back. "I'm looking at a deal sheet with Barbosa. It's right here on my desk."

"But Monarch doesn't know that," Saunders said.

"Barbosa does, and the thief sure as shit knows *his* men were in there."

There was a long silence before his security chief said, "Give me a few hours."

"What are you going to do?"

"Clean house," Saunders said. "Get rid of anything that ties us to the situation."

Arsenault said, "Be quick about it."

When Sister Rachel awoke on the sixteenth day of her captivity, she felt better than she had in a week, and that made her anxious and increasingly fearful. Vargas had backed off after he'd jolted her with the Taser in front of the camera. That shock had knocked her out for hours. When she awoke she suffered mild seizures.

Vargas realized he'd gone too far. At least that's what she'd theorized. Ever since then, he had not touched her, fed her well, and even got her clean clothes and antibiotics.

Still, the missionary suspected that the stronger she got, the more likely Hector was to bring out his particular choice in torture devices again. But maybe not. Maybe circumstances had changed. Maybe Robin—

Footsteps.

The key slid into the lock. The door opened. Vargas entered carrying the tray he usually used to bring her food. She perked up, but then saw the duct tape on the tray along with the Taser.

"Want to hear something sad?" he asked, looking downcast.

Sister Rachel raised her chin, said, "What's that?"

"I got word last night about your boy, Robin?"

"Yes?" she said, feeling a knot in her stomach.

Vargas snorted, shook his head, said, "They're saying he's dead. Can you believe that? I was supposed to get a guaranteed crack at the motherfucker. But no, even in death, Robin Monarch steals from me."

The missionary heard little beyond "he's dead."

Scores of memories of Robin over the last twenty years caromed in her head. The night she'd found him bleeding out in the garbage heaps. The day he'd failed to turn his brothers toward a better life. The look in his eyes when most of his brothers came to the orphanage after all. The genuine happiness woven through his face when the children had come to sing carols to him this past Christmas.

That last one broke through the shock, and unleashed a grief that had teeth and claws that began ripping her insides out.

She gasped, hunched up against the pain, and vomited on the mattress.

"No," she groaned. "You're just trying to torment me in some new way."

"What I was told," Vargas said. "Hurts me as much as it hurts you."

He began to tear strips of duct tape off and hang them from the edge of the tray. She didn't care. For the first time since she'd joined the Sisters of Hope nearly thirty years before, Sister Rachel Diego del Mar felt despair, true despair, and then a flash of anger at God. No parent wants to outlive a child, even one that is adopted.

She could sense the horrible weight of that curse pressing against her chest and wondered if it was possible to suffocate from loss.

Raising her trembling head, the tears boiling down her cheeks, she said, "How?"

Vargas sneered in mild disgust. "Way I understand it, he got thrown out of a helicopter somewhere over the Amazon."

Sister Rachel dropped her chin, and wept until she heard a phone ring. Wiping her eyes with her sleeve, she saw Vargas check the number before holding up a finger to her.

"This I gotta take."

Gloria Barnett shook her head violently. "You can't do that."

"We attack and Hector *will* kill her out of spite," Monarch said. "We do it my way, and I'm positive she lives and goes on with her work."

They were all gathered in thick pinions high on that hill a half mile from the farm. The drone's thermal imaging had clearly shown a small-statured person, likely female, in the basement of the farmhouse. A male was living upstairs.

"But Robin—" John Tatupu said.

"But nothing," Monarch said before looking to Chavez. "You okay?"

Chavez said, "Following your lead, Rogue."

"I was saved for a reason, brother," Monarch told Claudio.

Claudio looked torn, but nodded. "I'm with you."

Monarch was lucky to be alive.

Back in Brazil, not ten hours before, the thief had hit the guard's wrist hard enough that the muzzle had been pointing almost straight down when the gun fired. The .38 caliber bullet blew off more than half of Monarch's right third toe. The pain had been so intense and burning, he'd staggered and gone down.

The guard stepped up, gun shaking, angry enough to kill, and pointed it at his head. Monarch believed his luck had run out. But he caught a flash in his peripheral vision just before a rock the size of a goose egg struck the guard in the temple and dropped him in his tracks.

Carson had come out of the shadows, pointed at Monarch, and said, "Louisiana State. Third base. Second team all American."

Standing there in pines in Argentina, his foot throbbing despite three Novocain shots, Monarch thought that the guard could easily have blown his head off. Carson's throw could easily have gone wide.

Barnett's cell phone vibrated. She looked at the number, answered, "Zullo?"

She listened, and looked up in panic. "He says Vargas just got a call from an unidentified American male who told him to clean house."

Monarch didn't pause to question it. He exploded into a limping sprint toward the road. Claudio and the big Samoan were right behind him.

*

Upstairs in the farmhouse, El Cazador returned the phone to his pocket. So Monarch *was* dead. That was unfair. But he'd take second-best revenge, especially when it paid well. He'd clean up, collect his money, pay his sister something, and call it good, disappear. The hunter roaming once more.

As he headed for the stairs, his mind flickered with the possible ways he could inflict pain and humiliation upon the missionary doctor. He decided on no particular course of action. He'd just unleash decades of hatred and see where it led him.

El Cazador unlocked the door and went in. Sister Rachel sat with her back against the wall, watching him.

"All good things must come to an end," he said, putting on gloves.

He picked up the Taser, looked at it like an old friend, and said, "But let's have one more little go at it."

The hunter triggered the Taser as he moved toward her. The electricity jumped between the two metal nodes in a ragged blue volt that made Sister Rachel whimper.

El Cazador smiled, coiled, and got ready to lunge at her, give her a lick of old sparky, just enough to terrorize her.

Shouting upstairs stopped him.

Claudio rolled down the window and put his hands up in surrender as Tatupu pulled the gray panel van up to the gate. Through the bars, Claudio could see that beyond the two guards with the AKs, Tito Gonzalez and Alonzo Miguel were in the courtyard not thirty yards away talking with Hector Vargas's sister, Galena. Both carried hunting rifles.

"I'm unarmed," Claudio yelled out the window. "Tito? Alonzo? Hector?"

The men turned in shock, and for a moment it looked like they were going to order the gunmen at the gate to shoot.

402

Claudio kept yelling, "There's a way out, a way you all aren't dying today!"

Galena bolted for the house and began banging on the door.

Inside, El Cazador ignored his sister's cries to let her in. Gun drawn, he peered through cracks in the boards that covered the windows. That was Claudio Fortunato leaning out of that car. And that had to be the big Samoan assassin dude that Tito had described in the driver's seat.

They'd found him. He didn't know how, but it didn't matter. Life was like that in the hunter's experience. A snap of a finger and everything flipped. He'd survived for decades by accepting that fact and not being surprised or upset when it happened.

He shouted at Galena to shut up, before calling out, "What's the trade?"

"Sister Rachel for Robin Monarch," Claudio shouted.

Monarch?

"No deal," he shouted. "Monarch's dead!"

The back door of the van opened. The thief stepped out with his hands up.

El Cazador saw all the lines and angles of his situation in the blink of an eye, and understood that every one of his options led eventually to his death. It was a certainty in his mind. But it didn't make him shrink. It actually felt good.

The second he got the chance he was going to kill Monarch. He was going to watch the thief die first. The rest of it really didn't matter much to El Cazador anymore.

Monarch ignored the armed men at the gate and Gonzales and Miguel and Vargas's sister. He was focused laserlike on the farmhouse.

"Deal!" Vargas shouted.

"Bring her to the door," Claudio shouted back.

There was no answer.

Monarch yelled to Gonzales and Miguel, "Come to the gate. You'll bring me in and make sure she gets out unharmed. You hurt her, you're dead men."

The men glanced at each other. Gonzales said, "Police?"

"Not unless we have to," Monarch said.

Miguel nodded first and lowered his gun. Gonzales followed his lead.

"Galena?" Claudio shouted. "You bring her to me, or you die. Understand?"

Vargas's sister was still on the porch, and trembling with fear. She nodded feebly.

Hands still raised, Monarch went to the gate. Gonzales and Miguel came to him.

"I'm unarmed," the thief said, raising his shirt and the legs of his pants.

"We still got to frisk you," Miguel said.

"Frisk away," he said.

The gate opened. He stepped inside the yard and didn't move a muscle while they patted him down.

"What are you up to, Robin?" Gonzales asked.

"I'm saving someone who matters more than I do, Tito," Monarch said.

"You're up to something."

"Not this time."

A few moments later, the thief heard a latch thrown. The front door opened. Galena put out her arm. Sister Rachel shuffled out onto the porch without her glasses. She was blinking and looking around in confusion. Monarch felt like crying, but swallowed at his emotions, and turned soldier.

"Let's go," he said, and started walking.

They were almost abreast of each other before she recognized him. "Robin?"

"You're safe now, Sister," Monarch said. "Go home, go back to the kids, and live a long, long time."

She burst into tears. "No. You can't do this."

"It's for the greater good, Sister," Monarch said, and looked away and walked on toward the farmhouse and the door.

Behind him, Sister Rachel choked and called out to him, "I love you, Robin."

He fought back tears, and said, "I love you, too, Sister."

When they reached the small veranda, Monarch heard something heavy being dragged inside. He paid it little attention, and looked behind him. Claudio was helping Sister Rachel into the van. The second they were both inside, Tatupu threw the transmission in reverse and peeled out of there.

At peace now, the thief turned to Tito and Alonzo, said, "I'll take it from here, brothers."

Inside El Cazador was taking no chances. He crouched behind a heavy oak table turned on its side, aiming a twelve-gauge, double-barreled, sawed-off shotgun. Close quarters like this, there was no way fucking Monarch wasn't getting hit with double-ought buck.

When he heard the thief tell Tito and Alonzo that he'd take it from here, the hunter reached up and turned on the GoPro camera. Killing Monarch once would not be enough. In whatever remaining time he had left, he wanted to relive the moment, savor it, and study every twitch and groan the thief might make dying.

The door opened. Monarch's foot became his leg, torso, and head. He had his hands up and looked calm for a man in his

405

position. That pissed El Cazador off. He wanted to see fear. He wanted to see regret. He wanted—

"Been a long time, Hector," Monarch said.

Vargas knew better than to engage with the thief. He should just shoot him. But he felt an overwhelming need to see his victory register on Monarch's face.

"Seems like yesterday," he said.

The thief said nothing for a moment, and then asked, "Who bailed you out of jail after you tried to kill me the last time?"

"Some fucking American," he snarled. "I don't know his name, and I don't care. Like I told Sister Bitch a long time ago, *la fraternidad* does not forget. And now you will die for what you did."

"I gave my brothers a shot at another kind of life," the thief said. "Every one of them is the better for it."

A rage nurtured for two decades ignited inside El Cazador. The heat of it pulsed through every vein and artery. It took everything not to just pound the triggers and blow the fucker off his feet.

The hunter stood up, pointed the sawed-off at the thief, and roared, "You ruined it! You ruined it all. *La fraternidad!* My life! I was *jefe!* I was gonna take the brotherhood to *Scarface* times ten! But, no. 'Cause of you, I spent fucking nine years in prisons in Chile, Bolivia, and Uruguay. 'Cause of you I had to kill myself to stop from running."

He was shaking now, sweating and laughing. "Know how I got through it all? Every day—every stinking day!—I thought of this moment right here. Every day I thought of killing you, and now here we are."

"Can't say I've given you much thought at all, Hector," Monarch said. "But here we are. I'm unarmed. You've got a shotgun. Hardly seems fair. Don't you think after twenty years of waiting, you should be man enough to kill me with your bare hands?"

El Cazador almost threw down the shotgun, jumped the table, and went after the thief's throat. He'd bite it. He'd tear out Monarch's windpipe with his teeth.

"You'd like that, wouldn't you?" he sneered, putting pressure on the trigger.

"Even Julio gave me a fair fight," Monarch said.

The hunter kicked aside the table, took two steps toward the thief, and let go of the shotgun's forestock with his left hand. He thrust the sawed-off at Monarch. The barrels were less than three feet from the thief's face. Monarch dropped his hands.

"Ain't you heard?" El Cazador said, squeezing the first trigger. "Life ain't fucking fair."

The shot caught him under the armpit, two hundred grains of mushroomed copper that blew through the farmhouse's flimsy wood siding a nanosecond before it smashed through Vargas's rib cage, ruptured his lungs, and blew up his heart.

Vargas's body rocked sideways, his head and neck whipsawing. The shotgun tumbled from his fingers. He'd already hit the floor, glaze-eyed, and tongue limp in frothy bright blood when from eight hundred yards away the report of Chavez's sniper rifle finally reached the thief.

Monarch closed his eyes, and let out a long, slow breath of gratitude. Chavez had said she thought she could shoot through the wall with the .338, taking her aim based on the real-time thermal images the drone was sending to Barnett's computer.

But you never knew.

59

SISTER RACHEL'S FINGERS WENT to the bandages around her neck as she peered out the windshield of the van taking her up the last of the steep winding road to the Hogar d'Espera. Feeling blessed to be given a second chance, she bowed her head and vowed that the rest of her days would be spent in even greater service to abandoned children and to the sick and to the poor.

"Here we are," Abbott Fowler said, turning into the open gates of the orphanage.

The missionary doctor took one look at the cheering children and staff gathered on the lawn, and broke down crying.

When Monarch reached over the seat to pat her on the shoulder, she grabbed his hand and squeezed it tight.

A weeping Sister Evangeline rushed the van and opened the door to help her out. Sister Rachel climbed out slowly so as not to wince. She did not want to show the children any pain, or anger, nothing but love and rejoicing. Greeting and hugging the children and staff one by one, the missionary doctor felt humbled and honored to have been given another chance.

At last, Sister Rachel turned to Monarch and the team. "I can never thank you enough," she said, tearing up again. "To see them again. To hold them. It's almost too good to be true."

The thief's eyes welled. He rubbed at them with his sleeve and saw Fowler's lower lip was trembling. Tears were rolling down Barnett and Chavez's cheeks. And Tatupu, always the softie, was openly crying.

"You not doing what you do?" the Samoan choked. "That wasn't happening."

The missionary nodded, grinning through her tears. "Bless you. Bless every one of you, and especially you, Robin Monarch. You've been . . . you are . . ."

She couldn't go on, and threw her arms around him.

Monarch felt her love and returned it, saying, "Always. Always."

"Well," Sister Rachel said when she broke their embrace. "I need to go see what's become of things while I've been gone."

"Can that hold for a couple of seconds, Sister?" Claudio asked from the back of the group. "I think it would probably be a good thing."

The missionary, Monarch, and the others looked at Claudio in puzzlement. He went up to Chavez, who'd been quiet and reflective since taking the shot.

Claudio dropped to one knee. Chavez's hand went to her mouth, but her eyes never left his.

"I've been trying to . . . since the day you got here," the painter choked as he revealed the diamond ring. "But there was just no place or right time to . . . to say, Chanel Chavez, will you marry me?"

The sniper couldn't talk. She just nodded, burst into tears, and threw her arms around him.

"Awww," Barnett and Sister Rachel said.

Fowler whistled. Monarch grinned at the knowledge that he'd brought them together. And Tatupu lost it again.

"All this crying's going to destroy my reputation," he sniffled.

"Already has," Monarch said.

After Claudio had put the ring on Chavez's finger, they

all clapped. And there were hugs, and back poundings, and delighted words of heartfelt congratulations.

"Stand up for me?" Claudio said to the thief. "Be my best man?"

"I'd be honored, brother," Monarch said. "Honored."

When Sister Rachel at last broke from them and started up the hill to the children and her life, a small, red, four-door sedan pulled up the drive and parked by the van. A long, whippet-thin black man wearing round wire-rimmed glasses got out.

"Robin?" Barnett said, gesturing at the man with both hands. "Meet Zullo."

"Mr. Zullo," Monarch said, walking to him with his hand outstretched. "At long last we meet."

Zullo seemed to be uncomfortable, but nodded, and shook the thief's hand. "Nice to meet you. Can we talk about something?"

Monarch glanced at Barnett, who nodded. "Sure," the thief said.

"Robin?" Claudio called when they began to walk off.

"Two minutes," Monarch said.

They walked over near Zullo's car. The thief's toe and his shoulder were aching, and he wondered if he should see a doctor. But then Zullo told him what was on his mind, and he forgot all about the pain.

"You're a good man," Monarch said, shaking Zullo's hand again. "I hope we'll see more of you."

Zullo nodded uncertainly, and then got back in the car and drove off.

"What'd he want?" Barnett said.

"Want?" Monarch said thoughtfully. "Nothing. He didn't want anything."

Before Barnett could reply, Claudio, with his arm around a beaming Chavez, cried, "We must go to the finest restaurant in

Buenos Aires and order bottle after bottle of the finest Malbec, and celebrate this momentous occasion!"

The others cheered this idea, but Monarch said, "I'm all for celebrating when the time is right, but I think you two need to be alone."

"Buzzkill," Claudio said indignantly. "You got somewhere else to be?"

"Rio," Monarch said. "And sooner than later."

60

RIDING IN THE BACKSEAT of his bulletproof Mercedes-Benz, Silvio Barbosa realized he had not heard a word from Beau Arsenault in more than twelve hours, and it made him nervous. He'd doubled his bodyguard detail and destroyed anything on paper, disk, or computer that talked about mining in the forbidden zone. He'd also thought about leaving Rio, heading to his beach house in Bahia, lying low, and riding this thing out.

But who would run the company? It just wasn't—

He felt a pang of hunger. He knew he should go straight home. He had a panic room there. But a man had to eat, didn't he?

"Take me by Quadrifiglia," he said, referring to his favorite restaurant of the moment.

Correa turned around in the front seat, said, "You sure?"

"It's a small place," he said. "Easily controlled. We'll be in and out in an hour."

The bodyguard nodded, but Barbosa could see he didn't like it. Tough. The mining magnate didn't like other men getting in the way of a great meal.

412

Ten minutes later, they pulled over in front of the restaurant. Barbosa waited until Correa had gone in and scanned the interior. Then the driver, who was also armed, came around and opened the door.

Barbosa moved fast across the sidewalk with the driver and Correa flanking him.

Inside, he ordered his favorites on the menu and for the first time that day allowed himself to relax and savor the food and wine. During dessert, he decided to put the palladium mine on the back burner. It wasn't over. Not in the long haul. Just on a ten-year versus a five-year horizon now.

Barbosa nodded to Correa when he was done. The huge slab of a man got out his cell phone, and called the car back.

It pulled up in front of the restaurant and idled in the street when Correa motioned to Barbosa that it was safe to move. The mining executive got to the door. His bodyguard gestured to him to stop when an old man in an orange jumper appeared, pushing a trash cart and carrying a broom. He looked like his day had begun long before dawn.

"C'mon, let's go," Barbosa said.

Correa waited until the old man passed, and then walked out onto the sidewalk, where the driver waited. Barbosa stepped out and was flanked by his bodyguard and the armed driver. They were a step from the curb, and a bus was passing, when Barbosa thought he heard a thud.

Correa wobbled and fell, blood streaming from a wound to his head. Barbosa lunged toward the car, hearing a second thud and a moan as his driver was hit. The door was unlocked. He wrenched it open, dove inside, and tried to pull the door shut.

A hand grabbed the door, pried it open. The old man with the trashcart lifted a sound-suppressed pistol and aimed it with cold precision.

"No!" Barbosa cried, throwing up his hands. "Mercy!"

The assassin jerked and fell dead, half in, half out of the Mercedes.

Barbosa was in total shock when an enormous man with a sheer white stocking over his face appeared and used one hand to hurl the dead killer out of the car and into the gutter. The front doors of the car opened. Two more men wearing sheer stockings jumped in. The driver threw the car in gear and screeched away.

"Who? Who are you?" Barbosa stammered.

The one beside him said nothing. The one in the front passenger seat said, "We're not with the guy who just killed two of your men, and tried to put a bullet in you."

Barbosa was confused. "Who are you then?"

The one in the front pulled off his mask, looked over his shoulder at Barbosa and said, "My name's Monarch. I'm a thief."

"No," Barbosa groaned.

"Odd thing," Monarch said. "We were waiting to snatch you and here someone tries to end your life. Lucky for you we were around."

Barbosa thought about that, but said nothing.

"You have enemies, Silvio?" Monarch asked. "People who want you dead?"

"I . . . I don't know, I . . ."

"Obviously there's someone other than me. Who?"

"I don't know," Barbosa said. "Seriously."

"My gut sense?" Monarch said. "The guy who hired that assassin? Same guy who sent in mercenaries to kill me in the jungle. Same guy you partnered with to wipe out the Ayafal and the scientists, and get that palladium."

Barbosa knew the thief was right. Who else would want him dead now? And Arsenault had not returned his calls. Wait, he thought. Monarch doesn't know that Arsenault is involved.

Sitting up straighter, Barbosa said, "If I give you his name?"

The thief pondered that, said, "By all rights I should be killing you, or turning you over to the national police."

"But if I give you his name, you won't?"

"That's right. But here's the deal. You're going to cease and desist in ever trying to get at that palladium. And you're going to clean up your act, change the way you do business—the pollution, the human rights violations. And you're going to give Estella Santos five million dollars so she can—"

"Five million! That's too much. I—"

Tatupu grabbed Barbosa by his throat, said, "Shut up, and hear the man out."

"Make it six million dollars," Monarch said. "So she has a war chest to fight any effort to open up the restricted zone from development by assholes like you. I will have people keeping tabs on you for the rest of your sorry-ass life, Silvio. Make one move toward that mine, and you will die. Don't clean up the way you do business and you will die. Tell your partner that I'm coming for him, and you will die. And don't go thinking that hiring new and improved bodyguards will help you in any way, shape, or form."

Tatupu drew his hand back. Barbosa choked and sputtered.

"Silvio," Monarch said. "You have exactly fifteen seconds to accept this deal, or suffer the dire consequences."

"Deal," Barbosa said hoarsely. "His name is Arsenault. Beauregard Arsenault. Do you know him?"

If the thief was surprised, he didn't show it, said, "Transfer the money to Santos."

"Now?" he said. "I can't."

"Sure you can," Monarch said. "I'm sure a guy like you can do it from your phone. I've got her account and routing number."

Barbosa started to protest, but Tatupu reached for his throat again, and he said, "Okay, okay."

Fifteen minutes later, he looked up and said, "It's done."

415

"Thank you, Silvio," the thief said. "And it would probably be smart for you to disappear for a few months."

The driver pulled over. Barbosa looked out the window, saw that they were on a muddy street in one of the favelas, the crime-ridden slums of Rio. Small mobs of young men were eyeing the Mercedes hungrily.

"Get out," Monarch said.

"Here?" Barbosa said, horrified at the idea. "Are you mad? I—"

Tatupu leaned across him, jerked the door handle, threw open the door, and heaved Barbosa out sideways. He stumbled and fell hard in the mud.

Fowler yelled something out the window in Portuguese, and they sped away.

"What'd you say there?" Tatupu asked, pulling off the stocking.

Fowler grinned. "I said, 'The fat one's stinking rich and he's all yours.'"

The thief smiled as he picked up the phone, hit send.

Barnett answered.

"Give Zullo the bonus," Monarch said. "His instincts were dead on."

"Beau Arsenault," Barnett said. "How did he get on to you?"

"Spreading a lot of money around, I imagine."

"Well, we finally have the real target," she said. "What next?"

The thief thought about that, and then said, "Arsenault's rich, ruthless, and without conscience, maybe the most dangerous and powerful man we've ever faced. We take our time. We quietly find his enemies. And then we make the son of a bitch squirm."

61

FLANKED BY TWO ARMED security guards as he left the Board of Trade around eleven in the morning on a warm, blustery June day, Big Beau Arsenault was thinking that life was good. Very good. Corn and soybean prices were strong. So were U.S. Treasury futures, and the tycoon was long on all of them. Hell, he was up nine percent overall from the beginning of the year, nearly three billion bucks in four months.

Could life get any better?

Arsenault flashed on his suite at the Drake, and allowed himself a grin because his life was about to get better in a big, big way. Janelle Ford, his newest protégée, would be waiting for a few hours of uninterrupted gourmet chocolate bingeing before he had to fly back to New Orleans.

A limousine pulled up in front of the Board of Trade, and the tycoon climbed in the back, surprised to find Billy Saunders inside.

"Thought you were in New York," Arsenault grunted.

"On my way," his security chief said. "And then I found out

417

you were here, and I figured we could take care of a few things in person."

"I'm on my way to an urgent meeting," Arsenault said, irritated that Saunders had forgotten his routine.

"I'm aware of that, Beau, and you won't be delayed a minute," Saunders said, before telling the driver to take them to the hotel and rolling up the divider.

"What's on your agenda, Billy?" the mogul asked impatiently.

Saunders got out an iPad and handed it to him. Arsenault put on reading glasses and saw he was looking at a satellite image of dense jungle interrupted by blackened cliffs and a river fed by two waterfalls. He knew where it was in an instant.

"That's the canyon?" he asked, fascinated.

Saunders nodded, said, "Took awhile, but I was able to backtrack the signal from Dokken's satellite phone. I typed in the GPS coordinates into Google, and up it came."

The mogul's attention was riveted on the image. He zoomed in on the interior where the savages supposedly lived. Other than the clearing by the waterfall, and some lanes slashed through the jungle, there was no evidence of them. No structures at all. Dokken had done his job well.

"Enticing, isn't it?" Saunders asked. "A mega-fortune in palladium right there for the taking? And no competition now whatsoever?"

It was beyond enticing. Every high-tech electrical device used palladium now. And Saunders was right: there was no competition. Barbosa's stripped and stabbed body had been found in a garbage dump near a Rio slum nearly three months ago. How had Saunders pulled that off? Arsenault didn't know, and didn't want to know.

"We'll face opposition," Arsenault said.

"That's what money's for," Saunders said.

"Greed helps in this sort of thing," the tycoon agreed. "What else?"

The security chief looked as if he was about to taste something bitter, but said, "Sister Rachel, the missionary doctor in Buenos Aires. She's not dead."

Arsenault's head swiveled. "What? I thought you said it was done, and we paid."

"We paid, but it evidently wasn't done," Saunders said.

"When did you find out?" the mogul demanded.

"Last night," he said. "An attorney I know in Buenos Aires sent me a video of Sister Rachel alive and well last week. And Vargas, the guy we paid to take her and . . . you know . . . he's long gone."

"How much we out?"

"Nine hundred and fifty grand," Saunders said.

"But there's nothing that links us to her, right?"

"When I clean, I clean."

Arsenault thought about that, said, "What about the thief?"

"Nothing," he said. "Santos and her people are back working in Rio, but Monarch hasn't been seen or heard from since that night in Manaus."

These were both unfortunate circumstances as far as Arsenault was concerned. He still believed that if Santos published her research, it was averse to his portfolio. And the thief's disappearance bothered him. He didn't like loose ends.

"Hormel and Pynchon?" he asked.

Saunders nodded. "I learned through intermediaries that they are still nervous Monarch might come after them, but as of yesterday they were alive and healthy."

The limo pulled into the turnaround at the Drake.

"That it?" Arsenault asked.

"The rest can wait, Beau," Saunders said. "Enjoy your treat."

The mogul raised an eyebrow, grinned, and climbed out.

Life *was* good, Arsenault decided once again, nodding to the doorman and entering the hotel. He'd have a little taste of cocoa. Hell, he'd have a chocoholic's feast, and then some quality time with Little Beau and Sophia, both of who would be waiting at the jet. Do the boy some good to be away from his spineless father. Dear Louisa would have a late dinner for them at the plantation. And he and his grandson would go bass fishing in the morning. It was all good.

The concierge sprang to his feet the moment Arsenault caught his eye. He rushed over, said, "Mr. Arsenault, how good to see you."

"The key?"

"Yes," he beamed. "The manager upgraded you to the presidential suite. And your visitor has already arrived."

All good. All very, very good.

Arsenault plucked the key from the concierge's hand, said, "No need to explain the suite's accommodations. I've stayed there before."

"Very good, sir," the concierge said to the tycoon's back.

In the elevator Arsenault used the key to unlock the penthouse floor. As it rose, he studied himself in the mirror with a sly smile. He had the world by the balls, beholden to no man or nation, a creator of his universe, a God of investment, a visionary with guts. And in a few minutes, at age fifty-three, no less, he would be a stud courtesy of the little blue pill he popped in his mouth as the elevator slowed and the doors opened into the oval anteroom of the suite.

There was a large flower arrangement in a massive vase on a pedestal at the center of the entry, but Arsenault paid it no mind as he hurried toward music playing deeper in the suite, piano music, a sad, tender melody beautifully played.

The tycoon quickened his pace and emerged into a dramatic living area with floor-to-ceiling glass windows facing Lake

Michigan, furniture arranged around a flat-screen television on the wall, and, in the far corner, a Steinway grand where a lovely figured cocoa-skinned woman sat with her back to him, her hands coaxing wistful notes from the keys. She wore hair extensions that hid her face, and a white cable-knit sweater with a loose neck that revealed tension when she stopped playing.

"Janelle?" Arsenault said. "I didn't know you were so good at the piano."

"She's not," said Cassie Knox, who turned to face him.

"Cassie?" the mogul said, coming up short and hardening. "Where's Janelle?"

Knox rubbed at the tears on her cheeks with the underside of her sleeve, laughed harshly and said, "I scared her. She's not coming."

"What the hell have you—?"

"You did it, just like you said you would."

"What?"

"Ruined me," the singer said. "Destroyed whatever reputation I had. For what?"

Arsenault hated scenes like this, and abhorred scorned women. He'd suffered a few of these hysterias before and—

"For what?" Knox shouted.

"Cassie, you destroyed yourself," the tycoon sniffed. "I read all about it in the papers."

"You read what you wanted written!" Knox shouted.

"I think you should leave now, Cassie," Arsenault said, growing tired of the drama. "Or I'll call security."

"No, you won't," she said. "Someone showed me how you did it, smeared me in the press, destroyed my distribution, pulled my contracts, all of it."

"Really," he said, sounding bored. "And who might that have been?"

"Me," said a male voice behind him.

Arsenault looked over his shoulder, and saw a man carrying a pistol loosely aimed in his direction. His eyes shot in panic to the gunman's face. He didn't recognize him at first. Then he did and felt rocked.

"We've spent the past few months taking a real hard look at you, Big Beau," Monarch said. "Picked apart your financial records, rooted around in your computers, talked to people you've wronged over the years. Identified your habits. Your patterns. It's not a pretty picture once you get beyond the billions."

"I don't know what you're talking about," Arsenault said, feeling nauseous.

"No?" the thief said. "How about gourmet chocolate?"

The tycoon licked his dry lips, and said nothing.

"That's a deranged habit, right there, the work of a true sociopath," Monarch said. "Acting the kind patron and mentor to women of color, all the while plotting to bed them, build them, and discard them. Does Louisa know of your serial sexual obsessions? Of just how low you'll go on a regular basis?"

Arsenault fought off the urge to puke. He'd always been more than discreet, yet he suspected that Louisa suspected. She seemed willing to tolerate his behavior as long as it was done at a distance and with discretion. What would she do if it were flung in her face like this? He flashed on that image of his wife up on the Mardis Gras float, high above the court jester whipping the aroused and deadly sin of lust.

"Your son-in-law Peter has been a great help to us," Monarch said.

The mogul blinked. "What?"

"Despite the fact you're his son's grandfather and wife's father, he hates your guts," Monarch said. "Saturday of Easter weekend? When you had too much Maker's Mark? Peter got your keys and rummaged around in your desk. He found that

422

secret little diary you keep about your chocolate escapades, and copied it for us."

The tycoon felt wobbly. Peter was a pussy. A coward. How had he—?

"I read all about myself, or at least what you saw as me," Cassie Knox hissed. " 'Hot cocoa and cayenne' and all that. What will Louisa say? With her lily-white ass and ice-cold skin? Especially when she finds out you started cheating three months after you were married, about the same time you impregnated her with Sophia."

Arsenault felt as if he had come out of woods he knew like the back of his hand, only to find himself on the rim of a vast, deep, and dark canyon.

"What do you want?" he asked bitterly. "How much?"

"It's not always about the money, Beau," Monarch said.

The tycoon laughed caustically, said, "It's always about the money."

Monarch shrugged, said, "Okay, how does four billion sound?"

"What?"

"Four billion dollars," Monarch said.

When he saw Monarch was serious, he snorted, "That's absurd. At that point, I might as well just let Louisa divorce me."

"Maybe this will change your mind," the thief said, and called out, "Doctor?"

Behind Cassie Knox, one of the bedroom doors opened, and a stunningly beautiful woman with deep bronze skin stepped out wearing a blue skirt and white blouse, and carrying an iPad. She stood there, gazing at Arsenault with big brown eyes.

The tycoon found her breathtaking. In another place and time . . .

He looked at Monarch, said, "Who is she?"

"Dr. Estella Santos," she said, "of the Vovo Institute in Rio de Janeiro."

Time seemed to slow for several breaths as Arsenault tried to grasp the ramifications of her presence.

"Do you recognize her now?" Cassie Knox asked.

"No," he said, trying to act puzzled. "I've never heard of her before in my life."

Monarch said, "You know that's not true. You know all about her and her work."

He fought the urge to scratch his neck, said, "Work?"

"On genealogy and longevity among the members of a primitive tribe called the Ayafal," Santos said. "They live in the upper Amazon. Does that ring any bells?"

"No. You must be mistaken," Arsenault said.

"You are deeply pathological," Monarch said. "Even Billy Saunders thinks so."

Santos turned the iPad and held it out for the mogul. There he was in the backseat of the limo coming across town, copping to all of it.

"Billy's been a great help," Monarch went on. "Once we confronted him with the fact that he was part of a conspiracy to commit genocide, he started acting quick to save his own ass, and threw you overboard big time."

Arsenault's jaw felt locked. Every joint in his body felt locked.

"Genocide?" he whispered. "Me? Never."

"Bullshit," Monarch said. "Saunders says you gave the order to Dokken to wipe out the tribe and Dr. Santos and her colleagues because having people live longer wasn't a good business proposition to you. That totally jibes with what I heard Dokken saying to you on the sat phone. I don't care who you are, that's genocide."

"I'll fight that charge in court until the day I die," Arsenault shot back. "And I'll see you destroyed along the way!"

The thief shook his head wearily. "You still think you're running your despicable life, don't you?"

Arsenault kept his chin high, glaring at him.

Monarch rubbed his right fist into the palm of his hand. "Taking Sister Rachel to leverage me was stupid. It was personal and it made me mad."

The mogul sneered at him, "You stole from me. That was personal, too."

Before Arsenault could move a muscle, the thief dropped the gun and flew at him, hit him with three quick blows to the face, breaking the mogul's nose and dropping him to his hands and knees.

Blood gushed from his nose as he groaned, "What the fuck? She's alive."

Monarch grabbed his suit-coat collar, and jerked him back, exposing his neck. He got right down in Arsenault's face, said, "If she wasn't alive, I'd be crushing your larynx right now, and watching you suffocate while I stomped your nuts into pulp."

"No, please," Arsenault whimpered.

"But she is alive," Monarch said, throwing him down. "And there are things you've done that are as bad or worse that ruining women's lives, or kidnapping, or genocide, things for which you must be punished in a very special way."

Even through the swelling and the blood, the thief could see his confusion.

"You were brilliant at hiding your participation in the abduction of Secretary of State Agnes Lawton last year," Monarch said. "But we found enough to reach out to her quietly and show her how you conspired against her and the United States of America."

"I did no such thing," Arsenault shouted, trying to get up.

"You did," Monarch said, and drove a boot to his stomach. The mogul fell on his side, retching, and gasping for air. "No."

"Yes," the thief said. "As we speak, the FBI is raiding both your homes, and your offices in New Orleans, New York, and around the world. They'll find what we didn't, and then, Big Beau? You're going down for treason. They'll drag your name through the mud, publicly and with no mercy. In the end, I personally hope they stick you in front of a firing squad."

Stricken, the mogul shrank from Monarch as if he were some angel of damnation.

"And you know the best part?" Monarch went on, almost taunting him. "The one that will really get to you? This morning Cassie and your son-in-law, Peter Solomon, as well as a group of all the women you've wronged put millions of dollars I lent them into the futures and options markets. We used every instrument at our disposal to benefit from the hammering your company's stock is going to take once you're led out of here in handcuffs. I figure we'll be taking four billion from you. Maybe more. And most of it is going to a charitable foundation that will be run by Sister Rachel for the benefit of the poor and indigenous people like the Ayafal."

"No!" Arsenault bellowed as if gored. "You can't do that! Give it to fucking cavemen and orphans?"

Monarch laughed harshly. "Of course I can. I'm a thief. I can do anything I want."

62

IN A LOUNGE AT a private jetport at Chicago O'Hare, Monarch watched a Bloomberg News report featuring clips of a defiant Beau Arsenault doing the perp walk into federal court on charges of treason.

"I have been beaten and framed," the mogul shouted into the cameras. "Not a word of what they're saying is true! A god-damned thief made this all up!"

Barnett sipped from a fruity cocktail, and then snapped at the screen, "Try 'the goddamned thief pithed you like a froggie.'"

Santos, Tatupu, and Fowler raised their drinks to Monarch, who bowed and said, "I couldn't have done any of this without the brilliant and fearless efforts of each and every one of you, and Chavez, and Claudio, and everyone else who played a part. This was a team victory if there ever was one."

Barnett gestured at the screen. "Five minutes until the closing bell."

Monarch looked back to the screen where the anchors were agog and flustered at the depth of the unfolding scandal and the bearish effect it was having on the markets. The stock of ABI, Arsenault's public holding company, had tumbled nearly forty percent in the last three hours. The major indexes had plunged as well. Both the New York Stock Exchange and NASDAQ were off four percent and dropping.

"It's a debacle," said one anchor.

The other replied, "It's what happens when someone as politically and economically powerful as Beau Arsenault gets hit with treasonous allegations. People doubt the integrity of the government, they lose faith in the markets, and they go to cash."

Barnett said, "Which is what we're about to do, right?"

Monarch nodded and hit send on his cell phone.

"Peter Solomon."

"Get us out."

"Orders went in two minutes ago," Arsenault's son-in-law said.

"Perfect," Monarch said, hesitated. "How's your wife and son taking it?"

"Sophia's shocked and humiliated, and Little Beau doesn't want to hear a word about it," Solomon said. "I can say a lot of things about Big Beau, but he was a decent and caring grandfather."

"Your mother-in-law?"

"Sedated and hiding from the media mob camped out in front of Twelve Oaks."

"You still prepared to testify?"

"If I have to—" Solomon began. "Hold on. The trades have all cleared. I . . . I . . . my god. Total take: four point one two billion dollars!"

Monarch pumped his fist, repeated the number, and everyone in the lounge exploded into cheers. The thief thanked Solomon, promised to be in touch, and hung up.

"Four point one two billion," Tatupu said, shaking head in wonder.

"Think of the work Sister Rachel can do with that kind of money," Barnett said.

"Think of the places and people who'll be protected now," Santos said, tearing up.

A perky blond steward came in to say that their jet was ready for boarding.

They grabbed their gear, and followed the steward down a hall, and through a door out onto the tarmac. Monarch trailed them all. The Gulfstream was already whining. They'd be in Buenos Aires early in the morning, enough time to get some sleep before—

Monarch's phone rang as he was climbing the stairs. He looked down and saw a number he recognized. He almost didn't answer, but then did.

"Dr. Hopkins?" Monarch said.

Willis Hopkins, the director of the Central Intelligence Agency, said, "Well done, today, Robin."

"Appreciate it, sir."

"In England, they'd give you a knighthood for this sort of thing," said Hopkins, a passionate Anglophile. "Defender of the realm and all that."

"If you say so, sir."

"Yes, well," Hopkins said, clearing his throat. "The president was wondering if you're available? We have something of a situation going on in Mumbai."

That interested the thief. He'd never been to India.

"When would I have to be there?" he asked.

"Tomorrow?"

Monarch ducked into the jet, saying firmly, "Sorry, sir, but that's not happening. I'm on my way to my brother's wedding."

ACKNOWLEDGMENTS

I AM INDEBTED TO many people who helped in the course of writing *Thief.* João Carlos Desales and Lais Tammela were my excellent guides in Brazil. My son, Connor, read and reread the drafts, and helped me with the science behind the story. Keith Kahla, my editor, pushed me to make the story bigger and better. Hannah Braaten, his assistant, kept everything moving and on schedule. My agent, Meg Ruley, was and is the book's champion. I thank you one and all.

OUTLAW

Mark Sullivan

AN ENEMY EMERGING FROM THE EAST

The US Secretary of State is abducted while conducting secret negotiations aboard a tanker in the South China Sea. 'Seven days' is her captors' warning. Seven days before she is beheaded, live on the internet. Seven days for Robin Monarch to save her.

A TREACHERY TRACING TO THE TOP

The CIA asset and master thief journeys into the underworld of Southeast Asia to locate and extract his target. But as he navigates this shady labyrinth, he unravels a worrying conspiracy: stretching from the red-lit underbelly of Asia to the White House itself.

Quercus

www.quercusbooks.co.uk